CHALLENGE

CHALLENGE

Bob Hoffman

Tom and Freda,
Thank you
Enjoy

Acorn Publishing
A Division of Development Initiatives

CHALLENGE

© 2006 Bob Hoffman

Published by Acorn Publishing
A Division of Development Initiatives
P.O. Box 84, Battle Creek, Michigan 49016-0084

All rights reserved. This book, or any parts thereof, may not be duplicated in any way without the expressed written consent of its author or publisher. The information contained herein is for the personal use of the reader and may not be incorporated in any commercial programs, other books, databases or any kind of software without the written consent of the publisher or the author. Making copies of this publication, or any portions, is a violation of United States copyright laws. The only exception is brief quotations in printed reviews.

Cover artwork: www.arttoday.com and Ken Richards © 2006

Printed in the United States of America
First Edition, 2006

Library of Congress Cataloging-in-Publication Data

Hoffman, Robert Lee, 1950-
    Challenge / Bob Hoffman. -- 1st ed.
       p. cm.
    ISBN 0-9774449-2-9 (pbk.)
    1. Conspiracies--Fiction. 2. Telecommunication systems--Fiction.
I. Title.
PS3608.O4784C47 2006
813'.6--dc22
                                                    2006009412

ISBN 0-9774449-2-9

For current information about all releases by Acorn Publishing, visit our web site: http://www.acornpublishing.com

*To Von, my wonderful partner of all these years,
and to my fine, strong sons, Lee and Chris.
They are truly wonderful.
In a world where the written word
is becoming an anachronism,
this is my defense of the wonder
of reading and writing.
This book is dedicated to all readers
who live and die with the words.*

Chapter 1

"Class, remember always that the perception of reality is as important as reality itself. This need for either reality, or a presumed reality, becomes self-perpetuating and self-fulfilling. It isn't that something is or is not real—for in the end that doesn't matter. As we go through our lives, we constantly create reality through our perceptions."

The old man brushed his white hair from his forehead, reseated his glasses, and studied the lecture hall. He noted the students were a passive audience bent over their laptop computers or writing in their notebooks. He continued, "Let me repeat that. I said our perceptions of our individual experiences are the important thing.

"We see these experiences through an interpretive lens that is ours alone. The truth is that there is no one reality; there are only interpretations of reality. Given that there are nearly 200 people in this room, I assume that what I just said has been interpreted at least 200 different ways. I say 'at least,' because I too have to couch what I perceive.

"Given another day, another lecture hall, and another group of students, I would probably not say the same thing. I don't know that I would not. In fact, it would be my task to address you in the same way. But I am not sure this is possible—or even desirable. At any given moment there is a nexus of our lives and experiences. Once that moment has passed, it is simply not possible to bring it back again.

"But, and this is important, just because we do not see things in exactly the same way, there is adequate commonality to allow us to function as a society. The problem comes when we're led to conclusions that are either in error or formulated by someone else choosing to manipulate information. In the end, less and less of our world is subject to our interpretation and instead is controlled. Who would do such a thing? If you ask yourself this question, you will know. The answer is obvious. This realization is the reality I speak of. The rest is bullshit." The expletive reverberated around the room absorbing whatever noise was present until there was complete silence.

The old man placed his glasses on the lectern and continued. "Who controls what we see? What we hear? And last of all what our reaction to that information should be? We venture each day into territory that is unexplored. We base our reactions to such ventures on a reality we presume to be our own. But is it? The truth is that this reality may be one chosen for us from the time we were children.

"Our parents contribute to the assumption that we have free will, as their parents did. Our teachers perpetuate the idea, because they know no other way. Finally, in our lives those people who employ us enforce the strictures of their acceptable version of reality until we become blinded to its nature. But is this correct?

"Now, we are damned with a media that constantly parrots the talking points of the current administration without regard to either the worthiness or the truthfulness of these points. In essence, they have muddied the waters of reality until we are left searching for truth without a framework for judging this same truth.

"For the past year I have been away from this fine institution examining this loss of our collective memories. It is a fascinating study as it appears that, with the help of our corporate, controlled media, we may have irrevocably lost our ability to discern truth. We seem to have lost our ability to place information into the equation that differentiates reality from wishful thinking.

"If we only believe what we want to believe, or what someone tells us to believe—whether it is truthful or not—we are doomed. I do not say such things casually. In fact, I am convinced that this particular moment in our collective history is the most dangerous we have faced. We are at supreme risk of losing not only our freedom, but the concept of individualism which is the basis for that freedom.

"Certainly an attack like the one on September 11th was a major blow to our collective psyches, but should this one incident result in a grievous wound to our national identity?

Not in my estimation. But apparently it has and we have no qualms about condemning and killing in the name of freedom with the methods of a tyrant.

"We have been cast into a world without memory and without values. It is as if we have fallen into the rabbit hole made famous by Alice and we keep searching for the exit, but there isn't one. The only thing we have to counter the lies is truth. But whose truth? At this point I am unsure of nearly everything I think I know.

"What I want you to take away from this brief introduction to this course in contemporary American thought is this: question everything. Don't take anything for granted. Challenge the premise that the argument is based upon. If you look beneath the surface, perhaps you will see the manipulators at work. I have seen them—and now my time at this fine university is finished.

"Remember, challenge the premise, not the argument. Arguments can be persuasive, reality is not in the argument, but rather in the bases of these same arguments. If you question the foundation of your beliefs, then perhaps your way will be cleared for a more perfect understanding. I have little hope that what I am telling you will have some lasting effect on your existence. But as I have little choice in the matter, I have offered these words of wisdom.

Now, I leave you with no bitter recriminations. Instead, I leave the simple message I have just stated. Maybe one of you will be strong enough to counteract them. I have tried and failed. Still, there is hope that one of you may someday examine the nature of your own existence deeply enough so that what I have stated will at least make a modicum of sense. Now, I choose to punctuate this message with a final statement."

The old man reached into his coat pocket, pulled out a shiny silver revolver, put the barrel to his temple, drew the hammer and let it rest momentarily in its ready position. With a look of sadness in his eyes, he gently squeezed the trigger. The engine of death spit once....

Dead silence filled the lecture hall. The electric clock ticking off the seconds suddenly sounded like a bass drum.

The students sat stunned in disbelief for a suspended moment. Suddenly doors from the rear and the front of the room burst open as startled staff and students rushed out into the early spring sunshine.

ଔ ଔ ଔ

The walnut-paneled office smelled of old leather and older books. Sitting in the rarefied air of this room was John Goslin, Chancellor of the University. He was reviewing the quarterly financial reports from each department. In the current political climate, with Washington passing demand after demand without the money to pay for them, the budgetary concerns of the university were becoming acute. Chancellor Goslin thought it incredibly unfair of them to do this, but he also understood that the aim of the radical politicians in charge at this moment had little interest in being fair. Instead they were more interested in punishing anyone who did not believe as they did or were not rich enough to merit their attention. In this atmosphere, it was essential that each portion of the overall budget was as austere as it could be. Where would these assaults on quality education end? As he read, he occasionally made notes on the documents.

Chapter

The phone buzzed intrusively. Ignoring it, he was secure in the knowledge that his assistant, Martha White, would handle it. Martha had been with him many years; he trusted her judgement. If she deemed the call important enough, he would be told.

Surprisingly, there was a quiet knock on the door. He carefully collected the papers and placed them on his desk. Looking up he saw Martha walking painfully across the room toward him. Her ashen face spoke volumes. "What is it, Martha? What's happened?"

"It's Professor Kline—he just shot himself in front of his freshman class." The words drained from her in disbelief.

"My God! No! Surely, it can't be?..." he added plaintively. Her tears began to fall.

He walked to his secretary and friend and offered his arms. She melted into them and clung tightly. John stroked her back lightly and hugged her. After a few tortured moments he said, "I'll go right over there. Can you call the police or coroner or whoever?"

"I'll take care of it." She sniffed and returned to her desk fumbling for the box of tissue she had secreted in one of the drawers.

VanderLaan Hall was just over the rise of a small hill in the middle of what was known as The Oak Grove. The early spring air was pleasantly refreshing compared to the musty air of the Chancellor's office. Trees were beginning their process of first budding, the precursor to unfolding leaves. The sun created spider webs of shadow on the smooth sidewalk. As he walked, his own shadow darkened the subtle silhouettes until they were obliterated, only to find new life with his passing.

Richard was dead. He knew that. Richard Kline possessed the most perceptive mind of anyone he knew. If he had decided to kill himself, he had no doubt he would succeed. "Oh, God, why?" he asked aloud. There was no answer.

As he closed his eyes, the memories flooded back. He could see Richard when he was just completing his doctorate and they were both junior professors. Richard was offered a position on the staff of the Philosophy Department, while he was selected as a staff member in the Sociology Department. They served as graduate assistants together. When they were both invited to stay on as professors, they gratefully accepted the offers.

Attaining their positions at the university had been a time for well-deserved celebration. That evening, they took their wives to the best restaurant in the small town of Mason. Diane, his wife, looked radiant that evening. The glow of her husband's success created a visage which reflected her inner happiness. Richard even had a small smile on his normally furrowed face. This was unusual, for Richard was always serious. Sometimes he wondered how Louise could live with him. As far as he could tell she was the absolute opposite.

Louise, with a constant smile gracing her lips and a light step, contrasted with Richard's sullenness and plodding gait. Richard was a fine man and a good friend, but he just didn't seem to have much of a sense of humor. To him the world was always something to be challenged.

John quickened his pace at the sound of a siren. After all, he should be present when the authorities arrived. He could see a few students, some with tears in their eyes streaming out of the building as if they were air escaping a pierced balloon.

He steeled himself for the inevitable and worked his way through the onrushing crowd. He removed his top coat, folded it carefully, placed it neatly under his arm, and continued toward the lecture hall.

VanderLaan Hall occupied the far side of the Grove for well over a hundred years. Just as the old building and the grove stood side-by-side like allies, Richard and he had occupied their places at the university. John took the road of administrator, better known as bean-counter, while Richard continued to be active in the academic world. The two good friends had lost touch over the last five years. Now, they would never have the chance to regain their companionship.

John's eyes scanned the walls of the old building. He knew it was destined to be replaced in the next few years. Yet, that was not public knowledge. In his position as chancellor, he had to let the plans for a building's replacement be announced at the proper moment. Removing one of the old buildings nearly always dried up alumni contributions, at least for a while. And with the minimal funding from the government and annual budget cuts, these contributions were becoming paramount.

He forced his mind back to the problem at hand. What should he do to control the situation? The campus police were already in the process of unrolling plastic tape with the legend, "Police Barrier" in black letters on bright yellow plastic. He nodded to Jim Davis as he passed. Big Jim was the head of the campus security forces and had been one of John's first recruits.

Jim's years of experience in Chicago, dealing with problems which were undreamed of on campus, helped. John moved toward his reassuring presence. Jim left a group of students he had been talking to and went to meet the chancellor. "Dr. Goslin, I'm sorry about this."

"I know. Have the city police arrived? I am assuming that they should be called, shouldn't they?"

"Yes on both counts. It is a capital crime so they must be called. The person in charge, Detective Tom Johnson, is in the lecture hall."

"I'll go and see what I can do. Can you handle everything here?"

"No problem. I'll talk to you later."

Those students who hadn't run from the building immediately were giving the campus officers their names. They stood silently in a line.

Chancellor Goslin stood awkwardly before the police barrier separating the hallway from the room. Hesitating, he wondered if it would be more dignified to stoop down or straddle the tape. He decided on the former and bent to the task. With a heaviness in his chest he'd honestly never felt, he entered the room and walked to the front.

First, he forced his averted eyes to examine his friend. In the surreal scene nothing seemed out of place—except the gaping wound on Richard's head. His socks matched, his shoes were well-worn, but still practicable. His tie was neatly knotted, and his shirt was clean. If he had been hoping for some outward sign of bizarre behavior, it was not apparent.

He looked on the lectern and found Richard's notes. Without thinking, he gathered them into a pile and took them. He looked around for a briefcase, but did not find one. He was still searching when he was interrupted. "Excuse me, Sir. Are you in charge here?"

"Yes, I am Chancellor John Goslin. And you are?"

"Detective Johnson," the man said extending his hand. John shook the man's hand coldly. The detective asked, "What happened here?"

John, whose emotions had reached the boiling point, exploded, "My God, man, he just killed himself in front of 200 young people."

Taking stock of the raw pain he saw in the Chancellor's face, the detective started again, "I understand that. What I mean is, why?"

"I have no idea. He only returned from sabbatical a week ago. I said hello to him, but that was all. We haven't talked in some time."

"Would you take me to his office? I'd like to look through his papers."

"Do you think there will be a note?"

"It varies. Sometimes there is, other times there isn't. It depends on the state of mind of the person. People who are despondent will sometimes not even want to burden their friends and families with their troubles. Let's go take a look."

"Certainly, come with me."

By the time they walked up the sloping aisle to the exit, the ambulance attendants were pulling a Gurney through the front door. Detective Johnson moved to the men and pointed toward the eerily still scene. "He's down there. Take him to General and from there someone will call."

The Emergency Medical Technician acknowledged this as

he wheeled the stretcher to the front of the hall. Chancellor Goslin and Detective Johnson walked out the back door and headed across the grove. They did not talk—there was nothing to say.

Detective Johnson's eyes roamed across the campus and noted the buildings and the benches placed strategically along the walk. He had lived in Mason all of his life, but he had never bothered visiting this particular area of Harmson University.

He had not been fortunate enough to attend school here. His education was completed at the State College in Lansing. And while he valued his educational experience, he did envy the quiet grace of the smaller college.

"Where is his office?"

"Guardian Hall. The old building with all of the ivy," he said, gesturing in the structure's general direction.

Already there were signs of increased activity around the staid structure. The detective noticed people looking out of the windows toward VanderLaan Hall. Others had gathered at the front of the building and were pointing in that direction as well. He quickened his pace and the older man matched it.

Detective Johnson wanted to arrive before those involved had much of a chance to talk. If they shared too much information, they would all coordinate the facts to fit the situation. That could be a serious obstacle to his investigation.

The arches of the entrance were ringed by ivy, now browned and dormant, with just the barest signs of life. "Guardian Hall - Humanities - Social Sciences," was etched in the glass. John Goslin opened the door and ushered the detective into the building.

Chancellor Goslin mounted the well-worn stairs. His shoes fit neatly in the footfalls which had been chiselled into the marble by decades of use. The ground floor was taken up by the Art Department. Nearly fifty years ago, they moved from another building and ensconced themselves on the main floor arguing that some of their art was too heavy and awkward for the upstairs. The Social Sciences were on the second floor, and the English and Philosophy departments on the third.

This building had, at one time, been used for classes. That had been too many years ago for anyone to remember. However, it still had the appearance of classrooms in places. The rooms were large and, if you looked carefully, you could see where they had added doors and walls to make offices.

John walked down the carpeted hall toward the end office on the corner. Anxious professors stared through their open doors. He silenced them with a glance. They walked on.

When they arrived, they entered a reception area. The departmental secretary was on the phone. John waited a moment out of politeness and then cleared his throat. Finally, the lady hung up and turned to greet them. There were tears in her eyes. Without speaking, she handed John the key to Richard's office.

The original locks had been replaced many times over the years and this latest incarnation was a dead-bolt type which required a key for either entering or exiting. John slipped the key in the lock and turned.

He reached mechanically for the light switch and flipped it. Richard's desk was against the wall. Above it was a bookcase filled with the remnants of thirty years of teaching. The wall along the hall also housed bookshelves. The only spot not covered with books was an alcove where Richard had placed a comfortable chair.

John went to the desk and found a neatly written note addressed to the police. He picked it up and handed it to Detective Johnson. As the officer examined the letter, John looked over the desk. Beneath where the presumed suicide note had been left, was a small brown envelope with his name on it. He picked it up and pocketed it.

The detective sat in the chair in the alcove and read the note quietly. When he was finished, he placed the note on the desk and said, "This seems to be it. It says that he was despondent about his life and had no wish to continue. He also states this place brought back too many memories. His last sentence is, "I have gone on alone, as I always have. Sorry to have caused any inconvenience."

Chapter 3

"Well, Chancellor, this seems pretty straight-forward. We have a suicide note and more than two hundred witnesses. I'll send a report to the coroner, though I'm sure he'll rule this a suicide. I guess about the only thing I need from you is a list of the students in the lecture hall."

"What for?"

"We'll contact some of them and get their statements on file, in case the insurance company needs the information." He looked at his watch and continued, "I think I'll be going now."

"Thank you very much for your help. I'll try to get that list today. If not today, at least by tomorrow morning. Can I have one of my people drop it off?"

"That would be fine. Nice meeting you, Chancellor. Sorry about the circumstances," he said as his voice trailed off.

John went to the chair in the alcove and sat. He looked at the campus through the sparse branches of an oak. In the early spring sunlight, some of the leaves were still tenaciously clinging to the branches in spite of the Michigan winter's best effort to strip them. These remnants of last summer's growth would soon be supplanted by new growth; buds were clearly visible.

Though it was not that early in the day, the level of activity was subdued. Occasionally, he noted a couple walking hand in hand. But given the time of the year, he would have expected the grove to be much more crowded. Knowing his friend would have overlooked this very scene thousands of times sent a chill down his spine.

Reaching into his pocket, he pulled out the small envelope. There was nothing extraordinary about it. It was about two by four inches with the flap sealed, the sort of envelope teachers keep in their desks to hold small items. From his other pocket he pulled his pipe tool, opened the knife, and sliced the small envelope neatly. He shook a small key into his hand. Examining it, he read, "Mason Bank and Trust." He turned it over and found a four-digit number.

Thinking that the key looked familiar, he absentmindedly pulled out his ring of keys and after searching for a moment found the one he was after. He placed his key next to the other and found them to be same size and shape. He turned over his safety deposit key and found that it also had four numbers. After carefully locking the office, he stopped by the departmental desk.

The secretary was still busying herself, but she turned to look at him. John said, "I'm keeping the key to the professor's office. I don't want anyone in there. If someone feels compelled to enter, please have them see me." He saw the tears in her eyes and said, "Listen, why don't you take the rest of the day and tomorrow off? I think the department can manage. Besides, it is in my mind to call off school for the remainder of the week."

The walk to his office took less than five minutes. He greeted Martha and closed the door behind him. Retrieving a piece of paper from the right-hand desk drawer, he began to make notes.

1. Call Diane and ask her to call Louise.
2. Call Professor Morgenstern and see what kind of counseling he can set-up.
3. Arrange a staff meeting to determine a plan for the rest of the week.

He dialed his wife. "Diane, I have some bad news."
"What?"
"Richard committed suicide this morning. He did it in front of his freshman class."
"Oh my God!" The silence dragged for long moments. The passing of each second increased the intensity of her reaction. Finally, John interrupted her silence and said, "I know. There's not a lot to say. Would it be possible for you to go to Louise and tell her? I could go over there, but I think it would be better if you went. Tell her that we only know the barest of details. Authorities will be investigating. This is so

counter to everything in Richard's life and career—find out what she needs to get through this, won't you, Dear?"

"You're right, John. I think I'll offer to stay with her tonight, if you don't mind. When do you think you'll be home?"

"I'm not sure. I know it'll be late because I have to schedule both a staff meeting and a board meeting. I should be there by 9:00. I think I'll pick up something for supper. Let me know what you are doing."

"I will."

"See you."

He could hear her crying softly as he hung up. He dialed again. After a few rings the phone was answered with a subdued, "Psychology department."

"This is Chancellor Goslin. I need to speak to Dr. Morgenstern."

"Just a moment, I don't believe he is in. Let me check his schedule." There was a rustling of papers and after a moment she said, "He had a class scheduled, but it should be over by now. Should I have him call you?"

"No, that's all right. Maybe I'll just go see him. Where was his class meeting?"

"According to the schedule, room 34 of Callister."

He thanked her for her help and headed for the door. "Martha, I am going over to Callister to see if I can meet up with Danton. If there are any calls, give them my cell number."

Leaving the administration building, he headed across the grove again, self-consciously fingering the phone on his belt. He could simply call Danton, but it seemed an effrontery. No, this would be better to do in person. The sun, so clear in the morning, had been swallowed by the overcast, as the wind keened from the north. Amplified, it easily pierced his woolen coat chilling him.

Although Richard had never been what he considered political, he understood the process very well. It was Richard who'd helped him achieve his present position, and he was thankful. All of the times he had gone to his friend for advice came back to him in a flood. He picked up his pace and headed for the Callister Cultural Center.

He took great pride in this building, because it was largely due to his efforts that it existed. He had raised the money and overseen its construction. He found the professor about two-thirds of the way along the paved path. He waved him to come over.

Dr. Danton Morgenstern was chairman of the Psychology Department and an eminent practicing psychologist. John took a seat on one of the benches and waited for a moment while Dr. Morgenstern walked to meet him.

"What is it, John?"

"Danton, Richard Kline committed suicide about an hour ago in front more than two hundred students, mostly freshmen."

"My God!...We're going to have to set up some counseling for those students. What do you want me to do?"

"I need a plan. Why don't you get some of your people together and draw up something? I'm calling the board in tonight, but I'd like to have a draft approach to give them. Do you think I should call off school?"

"I think that would be most prudent—under the circumstances. We may need to bring in some outside agencies to help with the counseling. Is that okay?"

"Do what you have to do."

"Richard was a good friend of yours, wasn't he?"

"The best."

"I'm sorry, John."

Though the emotion was heartfelt, John did not acknowledge this. It was still far too painful. He waved him off and headed to his office. The words reverberated in his head. "Richard was a good friend of yours..."

He sure as hell had been. Committing suicide was not an action he would have ever imagined Richard capable of. If he was depressed, why did he return? He still had sufficient release time. And if he were going to do this, why choose a gun? And even if a gun was the weapon of choice, why do it in front of the students? Questions for which he had no answer beckoned for attention. He only knew that this was incongruent with the man who had been a lifelong friend.

He entered his office. For the first time in many months he was forced into the real world, rather than the insulated world he had chosen. These brushes with reality did not suit him, and he felt more tired than he had for a long time.

Martha was on the phone, but she motioned for him to wait. He took his coat off and went to hang it up. He returned and saw her going through the standard gestures necessary to complete a phone call. She was nodding her head, and kept interrupting whoever was on the phone with the little phrases so typical of the situation, "Well, ...I guess so," "I have to go now," and several more like it. Finally, she said the ultimate, "Good bye!" Before he could speak she said, "That was Donna in personnel. Boy, does she like to talk. Well anyway, what time do you want the staff meeting?"

"4:00 would be fine. Anything else?"

"Do you want me to call the board?"

"Yes, try to schedule for 7:00 tonight."

ଔ ଔ ଔ

"Gentlemen and Ladies, I want to make this meeting as short as possible. As most of you are aware. Dr. Richard Kline committed suicide just after noon in front of his freshman class. I have talked with Dr. Morgenstern and we agree that school should be called off for rest of the week. I would like the students to spend their time discussing this in the dorms with group and individual counseling readily available, rather than in the classrooms. Reverend Taylor, could we schedule a memorial service for Friday morning?"

"Certainly, I think that would be wise. I agree with your canceling classes. If we take the three days and add in the weekend, perhaps we can begin again on Monday without too much of a pall. Young people are most resilient."

"Please, do whatever is necessary. Does anyone disagree about canceling classes?" He examined the faces and found no dissension. "Then it's decided. We'll get the news out as best we can. Wait a moment, Henry, can you ask one of your assistants to call the adjunct professors? We don't want them to show up for their night classes needlessly. Besides, we might have to pay them..." The words escaped his lips before he could stop them. It was one of the hazards of his job, always seeing things in terms of money.

After the department heads left, John checked his watch. It was nearly 4:30. Still time to make it to the bank. He left the conference room and checked with Martha. "I am going downtown. Is there anything else I need to take care of?"

"No. I have drawn up the school cancellation notices. Do you want me to get the campus police to post them?"

"Yes, good idea. Well, I'll be back within the hour."

He headed for his car in its parking place designated, "Chancellor of the University." With tears pushing behind his eyes, he drove to the bank.

He had visited the room where they kept the safety deposit boxes on many occasions and was very familiar with the procedure. He first went to speak with the bank president. After all, he was not entering his own box, but rather a friend's. He went to the office and told the receptionist he wished to see Mr. Daley.

He was immediately ushered in. After explaining the circumstances, he was led to the vault area. The box required two keys to open: one from the bank and one from the owner of the box. It was soon opened and the president carried it to one of the carrels.

In John's mind he had imagined the box would contain the same types of things he kept in his own. The deed to the house, bank books, insurance policies, certificates of marriage or birth, the usual paper trail humans build for themselves. What he found surprised him.

The long narrow box was completely empty except for a single CD-ROM in a plastic case. He looked at the handwritten label. It read simply: "For John Goslin." With nothing else to see, he closed the box and sat there in the quiet.

To the best of his knowledge, Richard had never been interested in computers. What could possibly be on this thing? If its contents were complex, he would have to recruit help. After all, his own knowledge of computers was limited to use of a word processor and a spread sheet program. These thoughts and others did little to help him deal with the contents of the mysterious disk—or the rising wake of emotions.

Chapter 4

" . . . And and now I choose to punctuate this with a final statement." The words hung in the room until they were drowned out by the report of the gun. When in the lecture hall, she had flipped the switch on the tape recorder to the off position. Janna Joseph repeated this action for the fourteenth time that afternoon. She repeatedly listened to the old man's words.

She kept listening to the words hoping for some light to shine into the darkness threatening to envelope her. But all she could come up with were more questions. What did he mean? At best his argument was obtuse. The whole concept of presumed reality and assumptions of purpose where none should be had confused her and shook her understanding of the world.

It seemed that in another lifetime, though it was only a few hours ago, she had been jolted from her sleep by the alarm. When she got up that morning, life had been simple and purposeful. Now, one old man on a Tuesday afternoon had managed to teach her more in five minutes than all of her previous teachers.

She remained on the bed and pushed the rewind button on the tape recorder. The fascination with the event that she felt was remarkable. It was like seeing it on TV. The main difference being that on the television the actor would get up, brush himself off, and go home to his family and friends. Richard Kline would be buried. It added gravity to the words.

"You gonna listen to that all day?" Sylvia, her roommate, asked.

"No, just a couple of more times. There is a certain finality to it that interests me."

"More like a morbid captivation with it, I'd say."

"No, I don't think so. I mean when he pulled the gun out, I turned my head and closed my eyes. I guess it was that he was famous for this class and he was well-respected on campus. It doesn't make any sense to just end his life."

"Well, he was old," Sylvia said with the certainty of someone who would not be nineteen for another three months.

"So what? There are millions of old people who do not kill themselves. Sure he was old, but he still seemed to be all right."

"I don't know. When I get to be that old, maybe that's what I'll do. Really, I mean, he was over sixty, wasn't he?"

"I think so. Still, I keep going back to the words. They seem to indicate that he felt there was some sort of conspiracy."

"Could be just the delusions of a crazy old man?"

"Yeah, you may be right. Well, anyway, they will probably call off school for a few days, and that will give me time to finish some stuff I've been meaning to do."

"You really think they will?" Sylvia said, hope shining in her eyes.

"It makes sense to me. When there is a problem, people usually believe the best cure is time."

"No way! I can't believe that. I mean it wasn't like he was anyone important or something. No, school will go on as before. I suppose you might get a new professor or something."

Within half an hour there was a knock at the door and Sylvia rushed to answer it. It was Karla, the resident manager of the dorm. "Girls, school has been canceled for the week because of the terrible incident this afternoon. Friday morning, there will be a memorial service for Dr. Kline at the chapel. If you know of anyone who was in the class, the Psych department has set up a counseling schedule. I have it at my office. If you were there, you should sign up." Sylvia looked at Janna and started to say something. Janna stopped her with a look, and the older lady left.

"Why didn't you tell her?"

"I don't know. I guess I don't feel the need for counseling. If you told her, she would bug me—I'm not in the mood."

"Suit yourself. Listen, I'm heading down for supper, you want to come?"

"No, I don't feel like eating."

"See you."

Checking her watch, she noted that it was nearly 6:00 PM. She walked over to the desk, picked up the remote, and turned on the TV. After the run of commercials promoting a series of undesirable products, the sartorially resplendent *I Witness News* team appeared, with every hair in place and plastic smiles gracing their lips.

ଓ ଓ ଓ

Chancellor Goslin stopped at a carry-out store and picked up a sandwich and cup of coffee. He felt the need to eat before the board meeting. It would have been possible to get the school's food service to bring something over, but he didn't want to bother them. More than anything, he wanted a few minutes alone to collect his thoughts. Richard had been his best friend.

His passing generated waves of mental turbulence he must try to control. It would be unseemly for a person in his position to show the stress he was feeling. He would be meeting the board in a few hours. They expected him to be reassuring and in absolute control. They would want some sort of explanation for Richard's actions, but he had none. No, he needed a few moments for reflection.

He carried the bag containing a sandwich and coffee from the car. While he was fumbling for his keys, the night watchman saw him and ran to open the locked door.

He acknowledged the man's help and headed toward his office. Seeing no messages at Martha's desk, he continued. Lifting some scrap paper from the trash can next to his desk, he set the now leaking bag down. After removing his coat, he ate in silence.

The tasteless bites were no distraction from the lurking questions about the contents of that solitary disk Richard had left him. He took it from his pocket and placed it on the desk. He swivelled in his chair to face the computer and turned it on. Taking the disk, he pressed the button to open the drawer

CHALLENGE

on the CD-ROM and inserted the disk. The light came on. After several moments the operating system displayed a series of programs that were capable of accessing the disk. He would have to choose one of them. Word Pad was associated with the text file and it was loaded. Words leapt onto the screen.

Dear John:

By the time you read this, I will be dead. This is a choice that I am making with remorse. The reasons for my action are contained in the other file on this disk. It was written with an encryption program, one that I am assured is not able to be broken easily. John, I am trusting you with this. Please don't try to read the file until you are certain that everyone associated with us is safe: Louise, Diane, everyone. There is a key for the program—you will have to discover that for yourself as I do not want this information that cost me my life wasted. If someone tries to read the file without the key, it will delete itself. And do not even try until you are certain that people are protected. Please!

I am sorry to leave this world in such a way, I feel I have no choice. I have always treasured our friendship, and I will miss you. Give my love to Diane. If I felt I had any other choice, I would have taken it.... I did not.

Farewell, Old Friend—

Rich

Richard had left a quandary for him. Really, what was all this encryption business anyway? He loaded in Windows Explorer. Doing a directory of the disk yielded this message:

Goslin.txt   2134   12/19/01

CX___3__E. 10,908,235KB   12/19/05

It wasn't like his old friend. Richard had always been the thoughtful, studious type, certainly not one given to hysterics or melodrama.

As he removed the disk from the drive he made a note to call the computer department to arrange a time to see Dr. Jones. He intended to know why his friend of so many years had chosen to end his existence in this manner. He carefully placed the disk back in his pocket.

He resumed eating his meager supper and thinking about the future, a future now forever altered by the actions of a friend, actions that were so out of character as to be ludicrous. He reached for the remote control in his desk drawer and turned on the television to see how the story was being reported.

> At Harmson University in Mason today, Professor Richard Kline committed suicide in front of his freshman class. Witnesses report he started his lecture in a rambling, disjointed way, and seemed incoherent. Professor Kline had recently been passed by for a promotion and it is believed that he was despondent over a woman becoming chairperson of the department. School has been canceled for the remainder of the week. We will have a report at eleven from the scene. There will be a memorial service on Friday at 10:00 in the Beckworth Memorial Chapel.

ಯ ಯ ಯ

Janna turned the TV off and went back to her bed. What was that woman talking about? He was not incoherent. He was perfectly lucid. Although his topic had been obscure, he was not rambling. She thought about these things, turned the tape recorder back on and listened.

ಯ ಯ ಯ

The news over, Kira Morris let her on-camera smile relax and unclipped the microphone from her fashionable silk blouse. Stacking the pages of copy neatly, she placed them in the designated folder. The pages with the times and handwritten camera angles were handed to the floor manager, and she then retreated to her dressing room.

There was so much about this news reporting she did not understand. Why was the press release from the University faxed from a number in the 703 Area Code? She reached for the phone book on her desk and after a few minutes found that 703 was the Area Code for the vicinity in Virginia just outside of Washington.

Don Franklin, her co-anchor and senior on the staff, was walking by as Kira went into the hall. "Don, I don't get it. Why was the press release on that professor guy sent from Virginia?"

"Oh, I don't know. I suppose the University has a public relations firm that handles such things, and they are probably located there. What difference does it make? I mean, it is accurate, isn't it?"

"As far as I know."

ଔ ଔ ଔ

As Janna drifted toward sleep, the image of the professor invaded her mind again. "Class, remember that the perception of reality is as important as reality itself..." Over and over the words reverberated; with each cycle through her mind they intensified. Even as she moved nearer to the respite of sleep, she realized that she was not only frightened by the finality of the professor's violence against himself. She was also becoming very frustrated by the trail of questions he left in his wake.

What did he mean? Why had he spoken in platitudes? Why couldn't he have just said what he meant? The questions kept bounding about in her mind. When sleep finally took her, it was not the restful sleep of the young; it was the elusive, tense un-rest of an adult. Changes were flooding her psyche much faster than she could accept them. The person who would rise in the morning would be significantly different from the person who had been startled from slumber that fateful day.

Chapter 5

After the completion of the story, John sat in stunned disbelief. "What in the Hell were they talking about?" This news report didn't make any sense and he knew it. Richard hadn't been denied a promotion. In fact, he asked to have his name withdrawn after he was nominated. John distinctly remembered Richard saying he didn't want to be distracted by administrative responsibilities in his last years on the faculty. In reality, it had been his recommendation that Evelyn Johnson be given the job. Early in her career, Evelyn had been Richard's protege. He was tremendously supportive of her career. Besides, he had explained the job should be taken by one of the younger staff members because they had more "passion for that sort of thing."

His reasoning was that younger people had new ideas and were not afraid to pursue them. They were young enough to both believe in the possibilities of ideas and to challenge the status quo in tangible ways. When a person gets to a certain age, they have seen trends in education come and go. Their depth of thinking may be very accomplished, but the energy of earlier stages of personal and professional development promise a higher level of action.

On the news report, there was no mention or even conjecture of a reason other than those stated erroneously. Richard was in fine health. Come to think of it, Richard had just had a physical before he came back to work. No, something was going on.

John sat in the chair, stretched his legs and hooked them on the edge of the desk. Clasping his hands together behind his neck, he closed his eyes. The news report both shocked and disturbed him. The station reported as fact things that simply were not the truth. He tried analyzing where they could have received such misleading information, but he had no explanation.

When the Federal Communications Commission began tearing down the wall between the dissemination of information and the corporate entities searching for new means of marketing, John knew there would be problems. Now, even though the station was local, he knew that they were owned by some nondescript news-media company that knew little and understood less about the happenings in the small town of Mason. Regardless, he thought he would at least contact the news director and try to determine the source of such drivel. Whoever was spreading lies about his school and his friend would be brought to task. At least that was his hope. The truth was that his agitated determination was more bravado than confidence.

Outside of his office, the first arrivals for the board meeting were making their presence known. He removed his feet from the desk and rose to go and meet his board.

Board meetings were usually fairly predictable. After all, being on the board of directors of a private university more or less entailed giving a healthy annual contribution and a certain amount of respect delivered by the Chancellor—and good tickets to all of the university's events. A more ominous cloud hovered over this unscheduled gathering. He succeeded in convincing them of the necessity of closing school for the week and informed them of the schedule of counseling that had been established. He also received permission to reimburse any private agencies that might be needed. They expressed dismay over the circumstances, concerns for the students and Professor Kline's family. They inquired about efforts to minimize the negative PR the school could receive. The meeting lasted less than an hour. Most of the men and women who gathered did not want to discuss the situation in detail. It was as if by failing to dissect it, the incident would be sooner put behind them and the university.

John ushered each of them out of the administrative offices and retreated to his desk. He absentmindedly fondled the disk in his pocket, collected his notebook and headed for home.

The drive along the tree-lined streets took about five minutes of which he remembered very little. When he finally turned the car off, he realized how glad he was to be home. Here, within the confines of his place, he could close off the world that had caused his friend to end his life. He sat in the garage and thought. Letting go of the silence, he opened the door and went into the house.

Diane met him at the door and melted in his arms. As her arms went around his waist, he returned the gesture, trying to offer comfort he wasn't sure he had to give. After a few moments, she stiffened, then withdrew from him and brushed a tear from her eye. By the puffiness around her eyes, it was obviously one of many she had shed for their friend. Her first word to him was a simple, "Why?"

"I don't know. It doesn't make sense. This was not something that I would expect from Richard. How is Louise taking it?"

"Hard, very hard. But she said she wanted to be alone, so I came home. She and Richard were still very much in love. I asked her if she knew of any reason for him to do this. Clearly, she did not. It was shocking and overwhelming."

"I was hoping that maybe she could give us an idea of where to start to look.... Did you happen to see the news?"

"No, lately there's something about the news I don't like. It bothers me, so I have started avoiding it. Why?"

"There was a report saying that Richard was despondent about not being named chair of the department."

"But that's crazy. You told me that the staff nominated him and he withdrew his name. Where would they get an idea like that?"

"I don't know, but in the morning I intend to find out. Diane, I would like to sit alone for a while—if it's all right with you?" he added tentatively.

"Certainly. Would you like a cup of coffee or something?" she asked, worry evident in her voice. He noticed this and added, "No, I'm fine. I just want to rest a little. I don't know how many days like this I could tolerate."

He removed his tie and slowly retreated to his study. Removing his jacket and tie, he stretched out on the recliner and closed his eyes. Sleep found him sooner than he would have believed possible. The gift of sleep is given to those who need its simple reaffirmation of living. He drifted into a better place and stayed in its comfort for the night.

Diane came in to check on him and saw him sleeping peacefully. She bent down, removed his shoes, covered him with a blanket, and after kissing him softly on the cheek turned off the light and closed the door.

ଔ ଔ ଔ

Harvey Kelly had been a night watchman at Harsmon University since he screwed up his back ten years ago chasing a suspect over rough terrain. While his back was not severely impaired, it did limit his physical activity. The good thing was that being a night watchman was not a very physically demanding job. And although he had other health problems, including emphysema, he found that he didn't mind the work. The good thing about working around academic types was they were not very demanding. It seemed to him that they did so little physical work that they couldn't comprehend anyone doing more. He liked it that way.

His work was amazingly easy. Mostly it consisted of sitting in a chair and watching the clock. Sometimes he would read, other times he would bring along a radio to keep him company. Tonight he did neither.

The stillness of the evening surprised him. It was as if someone had covered the campus with a cloak silencing the normal activity on the campus. Even the routine night sounds of campus life were absent. There was no noise of student's stereos booming across the commons, no sounds of cars passing—it struck him as odd.

Leaden clouds drifted overhead to either obscure the moon completely or carve it into constantly-shifting macabre designs. Although the spring would be here in earnest in a little over a month, it was still cold and the remnants of the winter's snow glistened in the cold light of the moon.

He checked the front door. Satisfied it was still locked, Harvey returned to stand by his desk for a minute before he resumed his nightly vigil.

He never saw the movement to his left. The first time he was aware of it was when a strong arm closed across his body pinning his arms. He tried to shout out, but a noxious smelling cloth was forced over his mouth and nose. He tried to hold his breath, but eventually he had to breathe. When he did, he passed out.

The man in the three-piece suit placed the guard down on the floor with hardly a sound and went about his business. He detached the keys from the man's belt and opened the door to the Chancellor's office. He performed a methodical search of his desk and filing cabinet. Finding nothing of interest, he sat in the chair and turned on the computer. He carefully searched through each directory.

After a few keystrokes he satisfied himself that what he was looking for was not there. But just to be certain, he removed several CDRs from his pocket and backed up each directory. The process took only a few moments. Since the Chancellor's computer had the latest technology, his task was simplified.

As the computer copied the directories and files to the CDR, he went out to search the outer office. When the computer was finished, he carefully closed the desk drawer and tried to arrange the items as they had been. He retreated from the office and repeated the actions on the secretary's desk and files. After finding only frustration, he left. He carefully locked the doors to both the inner office and the reception area and returned to the watchman. Returning the keys to man's belt, he slipped out of the building without being seen.

      ଔ ଔ ଔ

Janna was deep in sleep, when she was awakened by the room's light. Sylvia stumbled in, carefully navigated to the chair, and plopped down with a drunken thud. Janna opened her eyes and watched her roommate as she lifted her foot and attempted to untie her shoelaces. She fell flat on her face. Obviously finding the effort to get up from the floor to be too great she immediately passed out. Janna got up and helped her to her bed.

Sleep quickly took her again and instead of being jolted awake by the jarring of the alarm, she woke to the late winter sun playing through the curtains onto her pillow. She rolled over to her other side and attempted to find that place of peace she had just left. It was impossible. Knowing she'd slept enough, she sat up on the edge of the bed.

Outside, she could hear the drip of the last vestiges of snow melting off the roof. Its incessant drumming heralded the faithful march of the seasons from winter to spring.

During the night, she reached the conclusion that she might just as well be home for these five days. Here, there were too many distractions and temptations. At home, she would have the time she felt she needed to catch up on her work.

Janna looked at Sylvia, still sleeping deeply, and went to her desk. Turning on her computer, she checked first to see if her parents were online; they were not. She sent them an e-mail explaining what had happened. After pushing the *Enter* key to send the letter, she decided that she might want to call.

Retrieving her cell phone from her bulging purse, she dialed her parent's number. After a few rings, her father answered.

"Daddy?"

"Janna, why are you calling?"

"Would you and Mom mind if I came home for the weekend?"

"Of course not. When do you want us to pick you up?"

"I was thinking of coming home today."

"Today! It's only Wednesday."

"I know. We had a tragedy on campus yesterday and they've decided to call off school for the week. Didn't you hear about it?"

"No, haven't read a newspaper or watched a news report in a couple of days. What happened, Janna?" She heard a chord of alarm in his voice.

"One of my professors committed suicide." She paused before adding, "It happened in front of his class."

"Oh my!...I can come and get you after lunch if that would be all right?"

"That would be fine. I'm looking forward to it. See you."

She clicked *End*, severing the connection reluctantly. She felt that she wanted her father to control the world and explain it to her as he had when she was younger. She had not yet discovered that adults have almost as few answers as young people. This would be another milestone on her way to being an adult. But that was somewhere up the road.

Janna headed to the cafeteria for breakfast. Sylvia was still sleeping as the door closed softly behind her. Outside, the day was warming and the melting of the snow continued uninterrupted. By the end of the day there would be very little indication that the winter white had ever visited.

☙ ☙ ☙

"Mason Police Department."
"Hello, this is Harvey Kelly. I am a night watchman over at the college. I believe our administration building was broken into last night."
"Would you like an officer to call?"
"Yes."
"Can you state some particulars?"
"Last night, about 2:30, I made my rounds and was standing by my desk when someone grabbed me from behind and forced a cloth over my face. I smelled something foul and passed out. I just woke up a few minutes ago."
"Did you inform the campus police?"
"Yes, and they said to call you."
"A car will be there in a few minutes. Where exactly are you located?"
"The administration building. It's right off Third Street. I'll see you in a few minutes."

After Harvey was awakened by the morning sun warming his face, which was pressed to the ceramic floor, his first impression was that he had a terrible dream. But when he tried to stand, he became aware of something entirely different. He found that he could not breathe and went into a coughing jag for several minutes.

Gasping, he found his emergency oxygen container and after a few moments, caught his breath. Then he remembered. He moved from the front of the desk to the chair behind it. He did not check the building. That would be the responsibility of the police. His main responsibility was to inform the campus police of what had happened. He dialed the number and within a couple of rings a young man answered.

After Harvey explained the situation, he was directed to call the police.

ଔ ଔ ଔ

"Detective Johnson?"
"Yes."
"We just got a call from central dispatch concerning a breaking and entering at Harmson University."
"So?"
"I thought you'd like to know. I mean, you were there yesterday."
"Is it just one of those campus pranks?"
"I don't think so. Why?"
"I've investigated many of those. Essentially they all boil down to the University declining to press charges, and it turns out to be a monumental waste of my time."
"I don't think that applies in this case."
"Okay, give me the particulars."
"Last night the night watchman at the Administration Building says he was assaulted and knocked unconscious with some liquid on a handkerchief."

Something clicked in the detective's mind. Why would anyone break into the Administration Building? Detective work is essentially examining all of the premises and deciding what has value and what does not. He felt an urge to check this out personally. There were too many coincidences.

Chapter 6

Janus Joseph pressed the *End* button on the phone and went to the bedroom to wake his wife. He moved softly over the hardwood floor, knelt down by the bed and gently kissed her cheek. When her eyelids fluttered, he said, "Karen, Janna called. She would like us to pick her up today."

"In the middle of the week? Why?" she asked sleepily.

"I don't know for sure. She mentioned something about a disaster on campus." With a mother's studied alertness she snapped awake and asked, "What happened?"

"It seems some professor killed himself in front of his students yesterday." Almost as an after-thought he added, "I'm not sure, but I sensed that Janna was in the room. She didn't seem to want to go into it on the phone, so I thought it best we get her home and talk through it all in person."

"When do you want to go?" she asked as she sat up.

"I told her we would come for her right after lunch. I suppose we will have to go in a few minutes, since it takes almost two hours to get there."

Karen threw her legs over the side of the bed and scurried to the bathroom. Janus watched as she hurried by. He went back to the porch, turned on the computer and accessed the web page of *The Detroit Press*. Once he located the search box, he typed in "harmson university." In a moment the articles were listed from the most current to the oldest. He picked the current article and waited while the story was loaded.

The length of the article was hardly surprising; the paper was not local. And although Mason was two hours away, it certainly was more newsworthy around this area than it was in Detroit. Janus read the local papers and few managed to transcend cliche'. When they tried to cover the world, they used the wire services' first few paragraphs. Janus wanted more. When they covered local stories, their perspective was slanted toward a perception of what the current movers and shapers of the community wanted. It was not so much that they lied; they just selectively reported, which in the end, can be tantamount to the same thing.

This lack of reliable, comprehensive and readily available information was sufficient reason for his daily surfing through the newspaper sites on the Internet. But even more importantly, he read through his favorite web logs or blogs to see what the perspective from the bloggers was. When he first accessed these personal journalism sites, he was highly dubious of their content. Now, having been immersed in the community for years, he understood that if intelligence and perspective were the goal of reading the news, then the blogs were simply better. It helped him to start the day on a positive note. If the news media have faults, which they certainly do, Janus thought, the main one was their lack of perspective of the citizens of this country. They predicated their news and views on a sort of "cool kids" mentality that assumed everyone who was not a part of the "DC experience" was also a boob waiting to be led. The phenomenon, started in the late seventies, had driven people from watching or even reading the news without a jaundiced eye away. The problem was reaching its apex now. When one television network practiced right wing editorializing as a badge of honor, the world was heading toward disaster. Already mistakes were being made at the executive level of government that were not reconcilable with the facts, as Janus understood them. These mistakes led to a disastrous war, failures to protect the citizens, and a general curtailing of American freedoms. It sickened Janus.

In daily life after sixty, the only facts of consequence with which we can interface meaningfully are self-generated. However, that did not diminish his quest for perspective on the broader issues. In the end, it is not so much the facts that generate opinions; it is the understanding of these facts within the hierarchy of one's experiences. Here in rural Michigan, his perspective was much different than those of his cyber-friends. Whether it was the husband and wife team of English professors, who also sought and promoted somewhat obscure pop music, or the lady lawyer who lived in Texas and managed to spend the summers in rural Colorado with the splendor of nature contrasting with the dearth of natural beauty left in the concrete monstrosities we call cities. No, Janus knew and understood that there were many people whose opinions and perspectives were different than his own and that their positions had merits. He loved talking with the teachers from California and the writers from NYC and the rest of his friends who guarded their private lives voraciously, but whose intellectual acuity belied the silly names they chose for themselves, names often predicated on lines of poetry, classical mythology or just plain whimsy. Quilt Lady in New York was one of his personal favorites: amazing mind with a talent for stating her perspective clearly.

But in the end, Janus appreciated their presence as it—they—enhanced his life. He found their opinions so much more valuable than those actively promoted on the television and in the conventional press. It had kept him in a constant state of flux until he realized that the opinions of groomed intellectuals and other promoted benders of the truth had become increasingly empty. Ultimately, so many of these people were simply tools of the status quo, willing participants in the sham our culture has become. In that world the truly meaningful events, policies, movements and actions are masked or drained of both color and importance, while the meaningless is showcased and awarded importance. Bad guys get rich, poor guys suffer, malcontents are purchased, and everyone eventually compromises whatever it was they believed in at one time or another, usually for a much smaller price than anyone would have believed possible.

Former Senators regularly shilled for drugs on television ads. The society that Janus lived in was becoming increasingly preposterous. Each piece of evidence added credibility to his decision to simply withdraw. With the advent of the religious right, the situation was going from absurd to abysmal. It was not enough any more to simply disagree with such screeds; now if you did disagree, you were condemned as a heretic. This joining of radical religious thought and politics was an ill-conceived marriage that worked at cross-purposes to the charter of the United States. Janus simply was not enamored of the future of the United States as a beacon of freedom. In fact, it was possible that these people who had lied their way into power, controlling the executive, the legislative and judicial branches of the government, might actually manage to irreparably maim the very freedom they espoused so vociferously.

He read the article about the university carefully, trying to identify any meaning between what it said and what it did not. He knew from long experience, you can often garner more information by thinking about what is not in the piece.

The newspaper story reported the professor had been despondent over not being named chairman of the department. The writer of the piece made a point of saying that the professor had been sixty-two years old. The strong implication was that he was therefore too old to be taken seriously. Janus threw the paper back into the recycling bin.

He sat looking through the porch's windows and stared at the lake. He was thinking about the gap between what he expected to find in the article and what he actually found. It was profound.

On first blush, he was tempted to dismiss this incident as just one more crazy man in a world filled with crazy people of all ages and backgrounds. But something was wrong.

He went to check on his wife's progress. But he was still thinking. Just backing away from the problem for a few minutes enabled him to find the perspective necessary.

As he walked, he suddenly was aware of the thing about the brief article which disturbed him. Although the man may have been older, the reasons stated for his action were simply not the reasons older people are motivated by. The premise that old people killed themselves over trivial matters was, in his mind, spurious. On the surface, the premise seemed to be logical and beyond questioning. If a person of this age were going to kill himself, there had to be an overwhelming motivation. They certainly would not respond like this after being passed over for a promotion. Janus knew these minor affairs of the ego are more the province of younger people. Older people have generally accumulated enough bruises to not let one more minor blow derail them.

No, there had to be a deep emotional reason for doing so: the death of a spouse, pain of your children's troubles, loss of interest in living. These might be viable explanations. Not being passed over for a feather-in-the-occasional-cap, meaningless promotion, toward the end of a distinquished career.

The Josephs lived at what had once been their summer home. On the shores of the Orchard Lake, they kept the occasional goose or wayward duck company in the winter as they passed by the cottage on their way to points south. At the inlet of the river, the water never froze and some of the birds even wintered in this northern land.

Although most of the people in the surrounding cottages returned to the city before the snow began to fly, the Josephs did not. As time went on, they found that they enjoyed the serenity of the winter.

The contrast between the manic activity of the summer and the absolute pastoral purity of the winter offered them a constant topic of conversation. He often sat by the picture window and watched as the day passed. Nothing much happened to interrupt his solitary vigil. It seemed to him that just being an observer was the most important task he could accomplish in the brief cold days of winter. Someone who would see the beauty of the snow as it gracefully fell from the sky drifting gently toward the earth, only to be whipped into delightful shapes by the ever-present winds off the lake. One human who was not too busy to record the sunsets as the days began their march of being first shorter and then longer.

Janus discovered over the years he actually enjoyed the cottage on the lake in the winter more than he did in the summer. Summer brought activities that made the lake seem to be some sort of large playground. He knew it was more than that. By contrast, the winter was a time of quiet reflection. There were few people to disturb the solitude and peace which extended over the lake like a blanket. With the absence of peopled frenzy, the forest animals made their appearance. He remembered sitting in the front room and watching a herd of deer walk stealthily to the lake and drink at the edge of the water by the inlet. The memory was clear even though it had been many years ago, for it was at that moment that he began to forge plans to live in their cottage after his retirement from the schools.

He had been a teacher. After nearly five years out of the profession, he found that he enjoyed not being a teacher more as each day passed. Now, he could hardly envision going back to work. The prospect of dealing with so many parents' failures was hardly something he would choose to do again. He had noticed, even when he was still teaching, that there was an almost incredible growth of rudeness. Schools tend to reflect the society in general. This could account for the increasing tensions at the heart of the schools. For some reason he could not possibly understand, society has managed to stretch and amplify everyone's anxiety.

He felt that we constantly honor, even revere, those things which are ultimately disrespectful. By managing all activities with an eye to doing it as cheaply as possible, we seem to have set our boats on a course heading forcefully toward some distant shoal. Janus could hear the waves crashing and sat back to enjoy the view from a safe distance. And if this catastrophe seemed far away a few years ago, the current political climate of hatred and contempt seemed to hasten the coming demise. Janus felt that tension between private and public realities acutely.

Now, when there is a power failure, people riot and loot. There was a time, in his lifetime, when a natural calamity resulted in people pulling together. Janus thought we seemed to have lost something inherent and essential to strong human community. Not that there are not instances of this happening, for there certainly are. Rather, taken as a general trend, it seems to be out of style to help one another and much more popular to exploit others to personal advantage.

Janus felt we had chosen this course by selecting the wrong people to lead. And we have done it with a consistency that was simply remarkable. Instead of choosing someone schooled in the history of this country, we have installed an anti-intellectual man whose experiences and demeanor are an anathema to the founders of America. The president not only consistently mislead the people, he did so with a fervor that was so patently offensive that he no longer could go out in public for fear of the hatred he had engendered. When he did speak in public, it was to selected groups who signed a loyalty oath before they were permitted entry—something that would have made the Commissars in the old Soviet Union blush with shame. Consequently, the leader of the American people was ever more isolated in the White House while his minions used the mass media and corporate connections to lie and deceive the pitiful people who were not capable of understanding their lies. Janus called them the *sheeple*, people willing to give up their perspective in favor of some prejudice that made them feel more moral while enjoying the condemnation of the Sodomites and bleeding-heart moonbats of the left without ever considering that their positions were as defenders of freedom and as advocates for those the government sought to exploit.

He often wondered about such things as he sat near the window with the hearth to his right. A leather bookmark protruded from his current book, measuring his progress through another, delving into the sweet magic of the writer. Why were we constantly placing unstable and hurtful individuals in positions of power? He thought often and long on this issue and could reach no conclusion. There seemed to be no logical reason to do so. Yet, deep within, he felt as if there was some sort of controlling force behind this mess. But what could its purpose be? He had no idea. Perhaps, all of this was occurring because of happenstance. Maybe it really was a remarkable coincidence. But he doubted it.

While these considerations bothered him immensely, he needed to assign them a secondary place in his life. For here at the lake, there was so much to do: someone had to feed the ducks, someone had to read all of the books he had been putting off for years, someone had to think; there was music to listen to—all of these and a thousand other activities took his time. Still, the belief that the public, the people, were being manipulated for some end that may not be in their own interests was a niggling thought that would not go away.

Karen was through with her shower and the hair dryer was screaming noisily. He didn't say anything to her in hope of speeding her preparations, but walked to the garage to check the fluids in the car. Since they would be driving more than into town, he always felt a little better checking the oil and the coolant. The day was cold, but the unnatural coldness of the winter had passed and though the thermometer read in the twenties there was a certain lightness to the air. The sun seemed to shine a little brighter and the wind did not cut near so deeply as it had a month ago.

Everything checked out. He went into the house, poured another cup of coffee and took up his seat at the table. After forty years of marriage, he knew the best thing he could do to help her get going as quickly as possible was to not bother her. So he sat and waited patiently.

ଔ ଔ ଔ

Chancellor Goslin was surprised to see the police car parked in the visitor's lot as he drove in to work. Ordinarily, the police hardly ever visited the campus. Now, something had occasioned their second visit in two days. His curiosity piqued, he pulled into his parking space and killed the engine.

Detective Johnson greeted him from the front desk and waved him over. "Good morning, Mr. Goslin. This is about the damndest thing I've ever seen. Your watchman, Mr. Kelly, says that someone broke in last night and knocked him out."

"Was Mr. Kelly injured?" John asked, immediately alarmed at the thought of another violent incident.

"Yes, he says that someone put a rag with some chloroform or some such thing on it. Now he keeps coughing something awful. I think maybe he'd better go to the hospital to be sure. He says he is under treatment for emphysema."

"I think that would be best. Has anybody been able to determine what was taken?"

"Your assistant, Mrs. White, has been most helpful. As near as she can tell the answer is no. We don't know what they were after or if someone was here at all."

"What do you mean?"

"Maybe Mr. Kelly imagined the whole thing. I mean, being the night watchman in a tomb like this is bound to get to anybody eventually."

"I don't know about that. I've always enjoyed the peace and solitude of this old structure. I think I'll go to my office; you want to come?"

The detective didn't say a word but fell into line behind the Chancellor. Martha was on the phone trying to contact the other secretaries in the building to determine if they had "lost" anything. John stopped and asked her if she knew any more than had been reported. She shook her head and he continued into his office.

He looked around the room and tried to detect if anyone had been in there. The first place he looked was in his desk. Everything that had been there yesterday appeared to be there today. He certainly did not see anything out of place. He went to the bookshelf and examined it. There were some valuable books which could have been taken if it had been an ordinary theft. They were still in place. He moved back to the desk and addressed the detective. "It appears that everything is as it should be. I don't get it. If someone went to the trouble of breaking in here, why didn't they take anything?"

"Maybe they did, and you just don't know it."

"I guess so, but several of those books over there," he said as he waved his hand toward the bookshelf, "are worth thousands of dollars to a dealer, no questions asked."

"Beats me. The whole situation appears to be something out of a novel of intrigue. Well, if you notice anything missing, will you give me a call?"

"Certainly. I appreciate your time. I wish I could be of more help."

The detective started out the door and almost as an afterthought he said, "I think I'll have the lab boys take a look around, if you don't mind?"

"That would be all right, I guess. Do you want me to vacate the office for a while?"

"That might be a good idea."

John left the office and told Martha he was going over to see Dr. Jones. He walked through the outer office and into the hall. Harvey Kelly was in the corner, coughing madly. He went to him and said, "Mr. Kelly, do you want some help getting home?"

"I don't know. I think maybe I'd better go to the hospital. I can't seem to catch my breath."

"Come along, I'll give you a ride. Who's your doctor?"

The man told him and John stepped back into his office and asked Martha to place the call to the doctor's office.

While waiting for his secretary's response, he helped Mr. Kelly to a more comfortable chair and sat beside him. He thought of beginning a conversation but the older man's condition seemed to be deteriorating. He didn't want to tax him by asking a lot of distracting questions that could wait.

Mrs. Smith came out of the office and said that the doctor would meet them there. John helped the old man to his car and drove the three blocks to the hospital.

ୡ ୡ ୡ

Janna was amazed to see Sylvia walk into the cafeteria. She assumed Sylvia would sleep the day away. Considering how drunk she'd been last night, she didn't look bad. Her hair was disheveled, her clothes wrinkled and stained, but she walked without staggering; that was a definite improvement.

She saw Janna from across the cafeteria and walked over to the table. "Sylvia, I didn't expect to see you until afternoon. How are you feeling?"

"Like shit. I don't know, I woke up and just wanted to get out of the room. Do people eat like this every day?" she whined as she wrinkled her nose.

"The whole world is up and running by this time. You gonna have some breakfast?"

"Janna, you've got to be kidding. I think I might be able to get one bite down. Of course, it would probably come up again." She grimaced and turned her face away from the food.

Janna put down her fork and said, "I'm going home for the weekend."

"When did you decide that?"

"Last night. I have so much to get caught up, that I think I could work at home a lot better than here at school. There are simply too many distractions."

"Well, I'll miss you. I hear they are going to have another party tonight at the triple Omicron frat house with a band and everything. You sure you don't want to come?"

"Positive."

Chapter 7

After the hospital's admission procedures were followed to the letter, Mr. Kelly was granted help. The fact that he sat in the wheelchair wheezing horribly didn't seem important to the officious woman taking his information. Although she typed with remarkable speed, the process still seemed interminable. Shortly after she completed the forms and garnered the proper signatures, Mr. Kelly was taken by wheelchair to an examining room. His wife frantically rushed in and tried to explain to the same woman who she was and who she needed to see. After she was given the requisite visitor's pass, she joined him.

With his wife in attendance and the doctor on the way, John felt free to leave. He went through the electronically controlled sliding doors, retrieved his car from the parking spot designated for emergency use only, and drove quickly out of the lot.

He felt as though the air in the hospital had infected his lungs; a sudden depression overcame John. As he drove, he considered the role of hospitals in our lives. On an intellectual level he understood the need and the good performed in these institutions and saluted them mildly. However, on another level he hated them for their pasty white walls and antiseptic smell. He resolved the conflict by deciding that hospitals are fine, for other people, but not for him.

His mind was far from clear. There were so many things happening that he felt as if he were driving a car that was sliding out of control on a slick road. 'Why would anyone want to break into the Ad building?' He considered this problem over and over and could find no answer.

It couldn't possibly be cash. Anyone who was aware of university policy would know cash was not kept in the building. Every expenditure associated with the college came through the purchasing department and had to be approved by a department supervisor. When a requisition passed these tests, a check or payment order would be issued on the local bank. There simply was no money to be had on campus.

It was difficult to find an answer for a problem with no logical answer. So much of his life had been dictated by logic he almost forgot that the world did not recognize or understand his need for logic. This world seemed driven mainly by emotions which were constantly being stimulated, often artificially, to produce a desired reaction, as if the people were rats caught in a maze. He knew on some level the world could be made to be anything a person wanted it to be. This thought had not yet made its way out of his subconscious, so he was frustrated in his attempt to understand the apparent contradictions in his mind. Perhaps, these contradictions ultimately did not exist. Still, he had no way of knowing the simple answers to his questions. He drove on to the college.

At every turn his thoughts about the web of problems led back to the disk. 'What could that large file contain that was worth dying for?' He only knew for sure that he wanted to know what was on the disk. And the only way that he could possibly find out was by having Dr. Jones tackle its contents.

He parked his car in the faculty lot and walked toward the Com/Math Duplex. He entered the modern glass and concrete monument to technology taking pleasure in its light and airy passages and wide corridors. The building's construction had been initiated and completed on his watch as chancellor. He felt a great deal of pride as he made his way to the end of the hall. The largest office in the building was the professional kingdom of Dr. Ira Jones.

"Dow" Jones was a legend on campus. Years ago, when he was still an undergraduate, he had been recruited by the Dow Chemical Corporation to work in a relatively new area of study called computer science. Actually, when he was recruited, that science was in its infancy.

His experience, working so early in the information age, served him well as he gained intimate knowledge of the amazing technological breakthroughs in hardware, software and programming development. His incredibly sharp intellect and quiet, affable personality kept his place at the roundtable of innovators. He knew most of the people his students read about in textbooks. In fact, he was in touch with most of those who were still living. Although he worked for several years at the chemical giant easing their transitions through more than one generation of electronic digital computers, he continued to pursue his graduate studies. After completing his degree, he took a job at Harmson.

When he began teaching, he taught introductory courses. Now, they were the only classes he would teach. Many of his students looked forward to that hour more than any other. The administration—underscored by several visits from John—had been after him for years to take on some of the more advanced classes. He steadfastly refused, explaining that he, "...enjoyed, more than anything opening students' minds to the possibilities the computer represents." This was where he found his joy in living, and this was where he would stay.

John knocked. Dow would not tolerate a secretary because he felt they intimidated students. From behind the door John heard, "C'mon in, it's open."

John opened the door and left his world behind. Computers were placed on nearly every available space. Some were in pieces waiting for parts. A few were switched off, and the rest were tuned merrily into whatever tasks had been assigned to them. Dow sat at his desk behind an enormous personal computer. This was the legendary "Dora."

Dora was housed in an old style PC tower case. The dual motherboards were so large that they, even with all of the hardware Dow had installed, still had room for more. Students who used Dora were amazed at the features it contained. It had three different hard drives, CD-ROM and DVD-ROM drives, more than 10 gigabyte of main memory, the primary connection to the university's Internet server, and more original software than they had ever seen. From Dora, the world was Dow's.

One of the activities he pursued as a hobby was being a professional hacker. He was frequently employed to break into a corporation's computer systems and give them a report on the effectiveness of their security systems. His work was legendary. He had never been beat.

He looked around the edge of the flat screen monitor, spotted Chancellor Goslin and got up. "John, what is it?"

"How are you doing, Dow?"

"Pretty good, I guess. To what do I owe this honor? You know darn well I am not going to train any accountants or such."

"Of course not. I wish that was what was on my mind."

"Sure," he said with a grin. "Seriously, what can I do for you?"

"You know about Richard, don't you?"

"Terrible. What do you think happened to him?"

"I don't know. I guess that's what I'm here for. Ira, I need your help."

"You've got it. I always enjoyed arguing with Rich. Anything I can do, you know I will. What did you have in mind?"

"Among the effects in his office, I came across this disk." John took it from his pocket, held it up, and continued. "I read the letter, but there is another file, well over eleven million bytes, I dared not try to access. Do you think you can get at it?"

"I don't know, let me see it."

John handed the disk over and pulled up a chair. He didn't want to disturb the man while he worked. After punching a few keys, he sat back and read the letter. A moment later he got up, walked to the coffee maker and poured himself a cup. "You want one?"

"No. What do you think?"

"I don't know. It seems as if he didn't want to do it. It was as if someone were forcing him."

"That's the same feeling I had. What about the other file? Do you think you can figure it out?"

"Depends on the encryption he used. It could be done. By the way, I believe him when he says that if you try to tamper with the file, it will be destroyed." He brushed the hair from his eyes and continued with a twinkle in his eye, "However, there are other ways."

"What do you mean?"—a sudden burst of hope springing in John's mind.

"I think it might be possible to make copies of the file and play around a bit with those. I can't guarantee I will find anything, but I can give it a try."

"By trying to copy it, won't you set off the part of the program which will destroy the data?"

"Yes. But only if I use the normal methods. I have some other ways, some of which are certainly illegal, but they are of my own design. They should work. I believe I can guarantee that I will not destroy the original."

"Good, I'd like to know what is on this thing."

"A word of warning. I think we can look at the file, but it might not mean anything to us."

"What do you mean?"

"It is possible that the encryption program created code which is itself a cipher, or a collection of symbols or letters which needs a key to interpret. These types are probably the hardest to break."

"Well, do what you can. I need an explanation beyond what I have. It seems there must be a reason. Now, I think there is a reason, but I don't know."

"John, I'll do the best I can. I want to know why Richard did this too. Have you thought about telling the police about the disk?"

"I've thought about it, but I decided against it for now. Maybe after we have copies, I could tell them. Something about the situation tells me I shouldn't. It's nothing that I can put my finger on, just a feeling. I don't think this would qualify as a piece of evidence. Well, maybe it would, but I want to look into this. I feel I owe him."

Dow acknowledged his statement with a nod, reached for blank disks in a large file behind him, and bent to the task. John turned and left the room.

Dr. Jones scribbled a *Do Not Disturb* note on a piece of paper and placed it on the office door. He carefully closed the door and drove the lock home. He crossed the room to the coffee maker, refilled his cup and returned to the computer.

The first order of business was to make copies of the disk. The disk itself did not seem to be extraordinary. He checked and found that, though a CD-RW disk, it was formatted in a conventional way with no hidden files or subdirectories.

He went to his E drive where he kept his personal programs. He had built security into this part of the computer which was as sophisticated as that of any bank or governmental computer installation. The information kept on this particular drive could have made an unscrupulous person very wealthy. In the past, he had released some of the programs. Most he kept for his own use. He went to his utility directory and pulled out his bit mapping program. He loaded it and looked at the disk from the lower level.

Every diskette, CD-RW or hard disk has several levels of programming that people never see. When the drive is first formatted by the user, that format is an upper level format which could not be accomplished without the help of the low-level format. He wanted to examine this format to see if there was something which would prohibit him from making a copy. He waited for a minute while the program generated a report of the location of information. When the contents were displayed on the screen, he examined them carefully. He could tell the information which was saved was text. When he had written the original program, he eschewed the usual fancy displays for letters. T for text, D for data, S for systems, and P for programs.

His monitor showed nothing but Ts and Ds. He exited the program, went back into his directory and loaded a special copy program. This one could have made him richer, if he had chosen to do so. He did not. He specified he wanted an exact duplicate of the disk in drive F. The machine whirred for a few minutes and came back with the message "Copy completed." He used the utility's other option, a compare disk check, and found them to be exact. He repeated the steps six different times and labeled each disk with a felt tip marker. He removed the original disk and put it away in his notebook disk case.

He loaded copy one and tried to read the file. Specifying the text reading utility, he pressed the *Enter* key and waited. Usually this program worked very quickly; as the seconds dragged on, he knew something was wrong. He was about to switch off the computer in order to start over again, when the message flashed:

    Unauthorized Entry. Program Aborted

He saw by the light on the drive that the hard disk was being accessed again. He pressed the control and break key at the same time and watched while this command was completely ignored. After a minute of activity the screen went blank and he heard the computer start its boot routine. He smiled to himself, but that faded when the DOS message was printed on the screen:

No or unformatted disk. (A)bort (R)etry or (I)gnore

This was a concern. The computer should have booted normally. He pressed the A key which told the computer to Abort the action and reached into his disk file for a boot disk. He started the computer with the boot disk.

He asked the computer to do a directory listing; his drive had been completely erased. This was a momentary concern as he typed the letter D: and repeated the action. Everything was fine. He copied his root directory backup from D: to C: and shook his head. There was a twinkle in his eyes as he asked for a directory of the F:, the drive with the CD-ROM. The DOS message flashed on his screen:

No or Unformatted Disk. (A)bort (R)etry or (I)gnore

He removed the CD-ROM and threw it away. Whatever was there, was gone. He loaded in number two.

There was a small program in DOS which kept a history of the activity of the machine. He loaded it in and read the screen messages as they flashed one by one on the screen:

Unauthorized entry - del *.* /s

Frantically he typed in the TREE command which would delineate the directory structure. It came back completely blank, except for the root directory he had just loaded. A look of consternation flashed on his face as he reached for the DVD which contained his latest backup. He placed it into the drive, turned off the monitor and went for the phone.

Challenge

Chapter 8

Morning stillness on the country road was momentarily disturbed by the Joseph's car. As noise diminished, the late-winter forest resumed its sleep. In the distance a squirrel moved swiftly from tree to tree. Occasionally, a bird drifted silently from one bare branch to another. Deep inside the trees, signs of spring's rebirth were appearing, but it would be several weeks before the first buds would be visible. Overall, a sullen quiet permeated the northern forest.

Janus drove efficiently, engaging in little conversation. If he spoke, it was only the meaningless talk of one whose mind was occupied elsewhere. "The weather's warmer today....Do you think it will snow?...The car seems to be running well."

He actually liked driving long distances; it gave him time to consider the world beyond his cottage. He'd always found simple activities to be beneficial to his thought processes. Everyone who thinks does this occasionally. Sometimes it happens when we sit watching TV and fail to comprehend what is on. Some people play music to achieve the same effect. With countless ways for human beings to do this, one commonality is that it must be some familiar activity. It is as if the very act of engaging in some physical activity actually frees the mind and facilitates the thought processes.

The road was nearly deserted and Janus was glad. Although the weather was not what anyone would term bad, it was still near the end of February, and the potential for bad driving conditions existed. Sometimes, it could be as simple as an errant snow shower bringing a dusting of snow to the road, causing it to ice over. At other times, the warm winds aloft dropped the tiniest rain droplets that would freeze as they hit the ground. The most dangerous of all is the snow that melts and reforms into what the locals call *black ice*. It is treacherous, because you don't see it until it is upon you. When a person is driving as if the pavement were dry, and it is suddenly covered with ice, deadly accidents are common.

Janus drove carefully, vigilant for errant patches of ice. When he found one, he eased his foot off the accelerator and coasted. He did this without having to reason the proper response. He'd driven this area for well over forty years and knew if you crossed the ice under power there was a chance that the wheels could slip. And on this particular morning, he did not want to be delayed. There was an overriding feeling that his child needed him, and he wanted to help.

Karen concerned herself with worry while she stared vacantly at the road. Her thoughts were with her daughter. 'How is she doing? What must be going through her mind on this still and silent Wednesday morning?' The only thing in this world that could take this look of worry from her face would be the sight of her daughter, and the sure and certain knowledge she had not been harmed.

Janna was eighteen, but her personal well-being was still very much paramount to Karen. Janna had been a wonderful addition to their lives. Karen was older—thirty-nine—when Janna was born. She had learned enough of life to thoroughly embrace and enjoy the experience of child-rearing. As a mature couple, they both understood that when people have children too young, they often do not have the time or energy to spend with the child to make certain that they have done the best job possible. Karen knew that the young have too many other activities begging for their attention. Ultimately, secondary things like trying to gain a promotion, deciding which kind of house they wanted and other decisions that seem so important at the time, eventually pale in comparison. When people are in their late thirties and early forties these questions have by-and-large been answered or prioritized differently.

Doctors claimed Karen and Janus would never have children. When told this, they made a resolution to live their lives the best way they could. They had many long discussions about adopting, but by mutual agreement failed on a number of occasions to return the necessary papers to the agencies. Somehow, the information required seemed far too personal. Though they fully intended to complete the forms, they never did. Their lives increasingly reflected the lack of children.

Without children, Janus had devoted more time to school. He even agreed to be the coach of the debate team, without pay. Karen had been involved in community projects and spent her time trying to raise money and community awareness of the many problems of the poor. Their lives were filled and everything seemed to be falling into place. Although not a perfect substitute for children, it was acceptable.

Then one day her period was late. She wasn't too concerned other than the thought that crossed her mind about entering menopause. Still, she was only thirty-nine and this did not seem likely. She waited a few days before giving it much thought. Then one morning she was brushing her teeth when she felt nauseous. In that moment she realized that she did not feel sick: no aches, no fever; in fact, none of the outward signs of illness. She did not tell Janus, but made an appointment at the doctor's office for that afternoon.

While he was busy at school, she received the most wonderful news. She was pregnant. The tears tracked slowly down her flushed cheeks, and she felt a joy she had never known. She had convinced herself that having children was not that important. But when the doctor said she was pregnant, she knew that for the lie that it was.

She dressed quickly and headed out of the office, her feet barely touching the ground. Her joy was unexpected and because of this unmatched.

Her pregnancy had been wonderful—even when they wanted to do amniocentesis. She knew enough of the circumstances to understand the necessity of this intrusion. She had accepted it knowing that whatever the test showed, she would have the baby. Still, if there was something wrong, she wanted to be prepared for it. Janus accompanied her when they received the results of the test.

They sat in the office holding hands as if they were a couple of teenagers. The doctor looked at them and then at the paper. He smiled and announced, "Everything is normal. That is not to say there will not be problems later, but the baby is fine. Do you want to know the sex?"

They looked at each other for a few seconds and simultaneously nodded their heads affirmatively. Even at this date, over eighteen years after the fact, she remembered hearing, "You're going to have a girl."

Again, joy overwhelmed her. She smiled and squeezed her husband's hand. Janus was delirious with the good news that everything was fine. When he considered it later, he was just thankful for having a baby, more for his wife than himself. Still, he could be selfish in his consideration of the child and its addition to their lives. A lifetime of teaching had helped prepare him for dealing with children. They were both glad beyond measure.

As he drove, Janus considered the day in a way that most people would not. He saw each day as a new opportunity for reflection. Lately, the thought had crossed his mind that he should spend some time writing. It didn't seem to be fruitful to think without at least trying to record these thoughts. He had very little communication with other people and knew that he missed expressing himself. Even with this need to communicate, he was aware that a part of him did not want to disturb his solitude.

He felt he had something to say and after a lifetime of living, he knew he could do it. 'What would he write about?' He answered his own question with more questions. 'How does one actually write a book?' He knew how to write a letter, and he was pretty sure that he could write a term paper if, heaven forbid, he were forced to recall this skill. But a book! That was a different beast altogether. How does one ever find enough information to write four or five hundred pages? Even with his life's experience, he was unsure of his capability in this area.

The miles dragged on and he did not look forward to joining the highway for the remainder of the journey to Mason. There would be other cars on the highway, and he would have to end his reverie to concentrate on driving.

ෆ ෆ ෆ

Martha answered the phone. Speaking softly for a minute, she transferred the call into John Goslin's office. "Hello."

"John, this is Dow. This is a pretty tricky son-of-a-gun."

"Why do you say that?"

"I just tried working with one of the copies and it erased my hard drive."

"How did it do that?"

"I don't know for sure, but I am working on it. Just thought you would like to know that I have made little progress, but it has my full attention."

John knew that was the best he could hope for. "Thank you for trying; please keep me informed. And thanks, Dow."

John returned to the paper he'd been scanning, another in a long series of letters to a potential donor. He made a couple of swift notations and placed it in the outbox on his desk. Even though he had been doing this job for nearly seven years, he felt he was just beginning to understand the subtlety necessary to be successful.

When he had first taken the job, he was lucky. Now, luck has nothing to do with it. Years of experience helped him to understand how to deal with the alumni—and when.

He got up from his desk, walked to the window, and looked over the campus. Here and there small groups of students were walking, but overall, it had the appearance of being deserted. This desertion led to a momentary gloom that crossed his face as if a cloud had passed by the sun on a bright summer's day. He went back to reading again.

ଓ ଓ ଓ

Dow Jones watched the red light on the DVD/ROM flash on and off. Even though his drive was fast, it was still taking some time to download everything. He had never backed up everything in this way before. Certainly, all of the programs had hard copies stored away, but he had never felt the need to move them to another computer. Now he did. That last trick threw him. Though the letter said that there were elements of protection written into the file, he did not expect them to be anything other than rudimentary. The erasure of his hard drive was not some sophomoric game; that had been fancy programming, low-level stuff which enabled it to defeat the system software. Now, he was growing suspicious.

After reconstituting the system, he did a directory on the drive that contained Richard's letter. He found it had been erased, including the factory installed low-level formatting.

He whistled in admiration. He knew several ways to do this, but there were not many people who did. As the drive continued whirring, he sat quietly and watched.

When he completed his task, he would go to the stockroom and get a new machine, set it up and load in the programs from the DVD-ROM. Then, if the same problem happened again, he would be protected.

He did not want to risk "Dora" on this venture. She'd been his ally for more than four years now; he was used to everything about her. Though all the information was backed up and ready to reinstall, he didn't want to risk the next trick.

ଔ ଔ ଔ

Janna finished breakfast and placed the dishes on the counter at the cafeteria's window. She returned to her room and slid the suitcase from under the bed. Opening it on her bed, she started packing. The first item packed was the tape she made the day before. Next, she placed her portable computer, and finally some clothes. Janna was looking forward to being home. After all, she felt she had about the most wonderful parents a person could have.

While the other kids' parents were doing their best to ignore them, Janna's had worked a subtle magic, and she found them to be there just enough. They let her have her freedom, but were also there when she felt she needed them.

After packing her suitcase, she went to the bookshelf and took everything she thought she might need. She placed these in a backpack and with a last look around, closed the door and went to wait. She figured she had about an hour to kill, so she brought a book along to read.

Chapter 9

Dow slit the boxes with a small cutting tool and placed them on the floor. He looked around the room and determined which of the tables had a bit of room. The space on this table was a rarity, as most of the available surface was absorbed by computers in every imaginable stage of repair.

He did not mind taking care of the school's computers. In fact, that had been one of his concessions to the administration; he would supervise the repair and replacement of faulty equipment. He actually wanted to do this anyway, and if he pretended he did not, well, he still only taught his beginning classes.

After unpacking and setting up the computer, he flipped the switch. Everything was as it should be. It was a simple operation he had performed countless times before. He took another copy of Richard's disk and placed it in the drive. He loaded the letter to see if there was something indicating the nature of the encryption. He read it slowly and painstakingly—nothing there. He dumped the letter and changed his drive designation to the hard drive where he had loaded his text reader. It would read whatever was in the file. The difference in this particular text reader was that it would read system files as well as text files. He watched as the information flashed across the screen, one screen full after another.

He did his best to find familiar characters or groups of binary, octal, or hexadecimal numbers. He was not that lucky. Instead of the numbers he expected, he found control characters of every description: happy faces, sad faces, the signs from decks of cards, foreign phonetic characters, the whole panoply of seldom-used symbols available to computer programmers. The problem was that these characters could represent anything. Their use was designated by the designer of the program. He needed a key in order to decipher the message. Without a key, the process could be long and painful.

He shook his head and turned on the printer. It sprang to life. Watching the pages roll into the machine, he determined it would be some time before the procedure was finished. He checked the machine to be sure that there was enough paper and went about the task of shutting the other computers and lights off.

☙ ☙ ☙

Janna carefully bent the top right-hand corner of a page in the book and placed it on her purse. Checking her watch, she knew the time must be getting close for her parents to arrive. She looked around the lounge area and realized she was the only student sitting and waiting. Small groups came and went. Some made their way to the cafeteria for lunch. Others were obviously leaving campus to shop in the small downtown area located only three blocks from campus.

A few young men waited nervously by the desk after they called their date's room. Janna watched and saw several perform the same routine: check their shirt to see if it was tucked in, look at their shoes to be certain they were tied and presentable, and run their fingers casually through their hair. She smiled as the pantomime was repeated. For a moment she felt like an outsider.

Instinctively, her hand reached for her book with the folded page.

☙ ☙ ☙

The highway drive was as monotonous as Janus remembered. He was glad to spot the sign for the exit. It was as if he had turned his mind off. Maybe a better way to describe it was for his brain to go into overdrive, the same process as overdrive on a car. For those times when the full power of an engine isn't needed, engineers had designed a system whereby the engine could work less than it normally did. His brain was doing the same thing. When he saw the sign, a wave of relief swept over him.

"Karen, Karen, Honey, we're getting off the highway." He reached over and gently shook her arm. She came awake slowly. It was almost always her habit to fall asleep in the car, something Janus had never succeeded in doing. He often asked her how she did that. With an incredulous look her only reply was, "You just close your eyes."

She moved the lever on the side of the seat and returned to an upright position. Without asking, she grabbed the rear view mirror and twisted it so that she could tidy her hair after the journey's nap. Janus secretly disliked this intrusion on his territory. But as with all successful marriages, he tended to ignore the little idiosyncrasies of his mate and concentrated more on the positive aspects of their relationship. After a minute, she twisted the mirror back into position. With only a hint of irritation, Janus silently adjusted it so he could see again. They took the exit and entered the town of Mason.

ങ ങ ങ

"*I Witness News.*"

"Hello this is Chancellor John Goslin of Harmson University. May I please speak to the news director?"

"Please hold."

He allowed himself to be put on hold and was rewarded with a string quartet doing Beatles songs for a minute or two. The receiver clicked in his ear and a male voice said, "This is Don Franklin; may I help you?"

"This is John Goslin, I have some questions about how the story of Richard Kline's apparent suicide was handled."

Don's face dropped a little. He thought for a moment and said, "Why don't I patch you through to the reporter who did the story? I think she'll be able to answer your questions."

Before John could respond, the phone was answered by a soft feminine voice. "This is Kira Morris. How may I help you?"

"Ms. Morris, this is Chancellor Goslin of Harmson University. On your news show last night you reported that Professor Kline was disgruntled over not being named chairman of the department as an explanation for his actions. Who told you that?"

"Why?"

"Because it is not the truth. In fact, the job was offered to him, and he turned it down."

"What? That doesn't make sense. The public relations notice we got from your agency stated clearly that he had been turned down for the position."

"What public relations agency?"

"Yours. The one in Virginia."

"Sorry about that. We do not have a PR firm. In fact, we do it all ourselves out of our Community Relations Department. I should know; I approve their budget every year."

"Are you saying that you did not authorize the faxed announcement we received?"

"That is precisely what I am saying. Did you say you received a fax?"

"Yes, it had all of the particulars. A brief biography of the professor, as well as relevant details."

"Do you still have it?"

"I believe the station keeps them. I personally don't have it. Do you want me to check?"

"Yes, Ms. Morris. I would appreciate it if you would. There is something going on that I am not happy about. You know, when an event has impact on the University and deals with such a tragic loss of a member of our faculty, the troubling inaccuracies of your report are of deep concern. Could you get back to me today?"

"Yes, I'm pretty sure it will take only a few minutes to locate the news release. Did you want to come and see it?"

"I would like that. Why don't I meet you after lunch? Oh, say about 1:30?"

"That would be fine. Just ask for me in the reception area. Thank you for bringing this to our attention. Inaccurate reporting is not something I condone—for myself or anyone. Bye."

John placed the phone into the cradle and tried to channel the thoughts which were springing from his mind. It was as if an artesian well had been tapped and the waters of his mind were flowing in every direction. He reached for his desk calendar and noted that he would be with the *I Witness News* Team from 1:30 to 2:30. This done, he left the office for home.

Chapter 10

Kira charged down the corridor to Don Franklin's office. Initially, she was not upset; she just wanted the news release so she could show it to the Chancellor. It was her nature to be in a hurry. Even as a child she had always been in a rush to do everything. She ate fast. She ran fast. And she grew fast. Her mother often scolded her, but to no avail. No matter how others manuevered to slow her down, Kira's gears seemed programmed to hurry. Sometimes, if she forgot to consider the consequences of her actions, she found herself in trouble for her brashness. But a smile, her wit and seemingly innocent demeanor were usually enough to extricate herself. In the TV newsroom, she felt as though she had found her home. Everyone here was concerned primarily with getting the job done on time. They tried for accuracy, but the value driven into the ground was timeliness.

She noticed the difference in people when she was in college. Very few people in her television classes could react quickly to put the best face on everything. It was a way of looking at the world: seeing only the broad brush strokes instead of the fine lines which ultimately give meaning to the world. Looking too closely, you tend to see things which could cause you to re-examine your positions. In the TV news business, at least in her experience at this and other stations, this attention to detail was a luxury that would not take precedence. Time and resources were limited. Not every detail could be checked.

Everyone around her performed in much the same way. They shared a mutual unspoken belief that, ultimately, it was not so important if the story was 100 percent accurate, but that it was possible to visualize for the masses on the small screen, i.e. that the broad brush strokes represented a *marketable* story and that they were the early bird in the region to cover the story. News, after all, was a business. If they only highlighted the basics, if some of the content was subject to interpretation, it could hardly be counted as *most important*, for the news on television was a transient thing. If yesterday's newspapers are used to line the bird cages of the nation, yesterday's television reports are ephemeral, a ghost floating through the consciousness of the nation.

After the Chancellor left, Kira began to feel pangs of—what?—regret, conscience, honest consideration of where her career had taken her. Wasn't it really relevant, even important, if their reporting of the university suicide was misleading? That professor must have a family. He had a lifetime of accomplishments. He had colleagues who respected him. The university itself had a history of service to the community, the state, hundreds of thousands of students over the years. Things flashed in her mind about the role of responsible journalism.

In those hurried steps to Don's office, a shift happened in Kira's consciousness. Had truth on television become relative, even dispensable? Rarely did anyone successfully challenge the authority of the anchormen or anchorwomen. If the story was correct for that day and fit with the overall presentation scheme, it was enough. It was much more important that the news come in a package that could easily be explained. Even better if there were pictures to accompany the story. If the story would not lend itself to being explained in less than five minutes, it was likely not suitable for consideration by the people of this country. Had truth become expendable to convenience, secondary to sound-bite appeal?

In this fast-paced business, Kira always knew that her appearance had been an asset highly regarded in promotions. In quiet moments she sometimes resented the focus on slick appearance. For some, appearance was not the main thing; it was the only thing. Yes, she had an attractive figure, long blonde hair, and what one producer once called "finely chiselled Nordic cheekbones." But she prided herself on her intellect and work ethic, too. She wanted to think those were the qualities that had made her an anchor. But if the quality and content of her reporting had slipped over the years, was she just a symbol on the six o'clock screen of every man's fancy at the end of a day of work?

If they at *I Witness News*—she and her colleagues—weren't always capturing the truth in those two-, three-, or five-minute news segments, if the complexities of truth *couldn't* be fairly summarized in those marketable bites, what was she doing behind this attractive facade? Maybe the mind of that hopeful college sophomore, the one she was long-ago, had been arrested in its growth by the stifling functionality of the group-think mentality gripping her industry! Yes, it was her industry, her career, that Chancellor Goslin was questioning from his position of dealing with the painfully unthinkable events earlier that week in his world.

She had to admit it: a dangerous mentality was fostered every day in television journalism, not to mention the nearly mindless entertainment arena. That mentality did not require consideration of the broader ideas or thoughts, the bigger political, cultural, sociological, psychological or spiritual picture that should be of concern to us all. It constantly begs for a new slick star to thrust on the public's consciousness, often to be then dismissed as soon as the novelty wears off.

That TV mindset collided this week with a human tragedy. Kira's fear was that in the process, she and her rapid-moving crowd could have done a great disservice to both that tragedy and the truth. She felt more alone than she had in years as her feet carried her between offices. She had alligned herself with a worldview and a system, which at the moment felt as empty as the cistern on a deserted farm in Arizona.

She arrived at Don's door and charged in as if she were a fullback going for the goal line. Don looked up and asked, "Kira, what's up?"

"You know. After all you are the one who referred Chancellor Goslin to me just a minute ago. He's pretty upset about that story we did last night about the old professor who committed suicide in front of his students."

"What precisely is he upset about—that we didn't try to put a better face on it?" he said with contempt.

She dismissed his sarcasm and continued, "He said that Professor Kline was not disturbed at having been passed over for the department chairmanship. In fact, it had been offered to him and he turned it down. According to the Chancellor, nothing in our report matches reality. He wants to know where we got the information."

"So, what did you tell him?"

"I said we received the information from a news release put out by his Eastern public relations firm."

"That's good. What did he say about that?"

"He said they don't have an outside firm for public relations. In fact, they have their own staff handling media relations for the university. Listen, do you have the release? I told him he could look at it."

"Kira, I wish you hadn't said that. When we start answering to the public there never will be an end to it. Oh well, I suppose it won't hurt this time. It should be around here, just a minute." He rose from his cluttered desk and went to a huge filing cabinet. After a moment's diligent searching he came back with a manilla folder. Kira could see from the label that it was the news scripts and documents from the day in question. Don placed it carefully on his desk and started shuffling through the papers. Removing a video cartridge from the folder and setting it aside, he concentrated on searching the papers, particularly the wire services copy. The seconds turned to minutes as he rifled through the stack again and again. Finally, in frustration he said, "Apparently we do not have the press release. I don't know where it could have gone. It should be here."

"But that isn't possible, is it?"

"Kira, anything's possible. But I didn't authorize anyone to go into my files, and I certainly don't remember taking it out. Come to think of it, I am very concerned. Let me check with security. I'll get back to you in a while."

"Sure, Don. The thing is, he's coming here at 1:30. What do you want me to tell him?" Kira's frustration with the situation was mounting, and even her normally cool veneer couldn't mask it.

"I don't care. I guess you could say that we are having trouble locating the document. I don't see that it is any of his business, anyway."

༶ ༶ ༶

The phone buzzed softly until Martha White answered, "Chancellor Goslin's office. How may I help you?"

"Martha, this is Louise Kline. Is John available?"

"Yes, Louise, just a moment."

John shoveled the paper from his desk to the out tray as fast as he could. Most of these were just routine stroke papers, something to keep the donors happy. Making sure that their collective fur was being rubbed in the right way was what his job had evolved into. The only difference was that there were only a few people who deserved his personal attention. Most of his time was spent attending to the details which made it possible for him to do his job. In the end, his job was to solicit money from alumni, other groups and foundations, and he had developed a methodology for doing so. As the intercom buzzed, he reached absentmindedly for the button. "Yes, Martha, what is it?"

"Chancellor, it is Mrs. Kline on line 1."

His heart stopped for just a moment as he was yanked back to the sorrow that had nearly suffocated him this week. Extending his hand to the lit button, he considered for a moment how well she knew him. He had not mentioned he had a great desire to talk to Mrs. Kline. Yet, she had known instinctively. He placed the phone on his shoulder and said, "Louise, I am so sorry for your terrible loss. Are you making your way through it? Is there anything I can do?"

"No, John, I think things are pretty much in order. The funeral will be on Friday afternoon. Can I count on you to be one of the bearers?"

"Certainly. It would be an honor. Rich was the best friend I ever had. I still don't understand what happened." There was a pause in the conversation that felt like a masive canyon neither of them knew how to cross.

Trying to bridge it, John asked, "Just out of curiosity, was Rich working on anything before he came back?"

"Yes, he was. But I don't have any idea of what. He was smiling like a Cheshire cat for days at a time. He was as happy and excited as I had ever seen him. Of course, that was before he came back to work. After he reclaimed his position, his mood changed to solemn, somber. I could hardly get him to smile. A blanket of depression seemed to fall over him. I don't know. I asked if it was the university. He just shook his head sadly and said something like, 'If only it were that simple.' Then he gave me a hug."

"Louise, did he make any notes?"

"Oh, I am certain he must have. I haven't had the heart to go into his office since that day. Oh, John, I miss him so..." she said as her grief melted again into tears. John did not interrupt but waited for her voice to come back on the line. After a few moments, she cleared her throat and said, "I am sorry. Lately, I have taken to crying...."

"Louise, after those many years you spent together, you are more than entitled... If it would be possible, I would like to look at Rich's notes."

"He would want you to. When did you want to come?"

"I don't know. What is the best time for you?"

"How about later today, say around three? I would like you to go through them before the rest of the family gets here and we get involved with other matters."

"Later today will be fine. You do know that if there is anything I can do, I will...."

"I know. Goodbye, John."

He put down the phone and went back to inspecting another sheaf of papers. He read each one carefully and made notations where necessary. The questions that concerned him about Richard's death plagued him; he had trouble keeping his concentration.

ଔ ଔ ଔ

Dow stood before the darkened office for a moment and listened. Identifying the sounds of the printer through the heavy wooden door, he could hardly believe the file had been printing since he left. He opened the door and turned on the lights. Gravity worked in his place, leaving the papers accumulated on the floor in a neat pile. He went to the printer and stared. Whenever he watched the printer working, he found the process magical and the quiet, repetitive sound almost meditational.

He retrieved the student's programs from their notebook and began to go over them carefully. Every space not where it should be was circled in red. Every time he read a line of code that was incomplete, be marked it. He looked at the program's run to see if it had succeeded. This, in the final analysis, was the important thing. On Dow's grading scale, if the program worked without causing any major errors, it deserved a B. The rest was all window dressing. He had been working for three-quarters of an hour when he noticed the silence. He bent down, picked up the massive sheaf of papers and returned to his desk.

He placed the students' work back into his notebook and carefully set the printout down. He found the beginning of the pages and placed a 1 in the upper right corner. He followed the paper trail from one sheet to another placing the next digit carefully in the corner with a pencil.

This activity took him twenty minutes; when he was done he had numbered the pages up to 232. Two hundred and thirty-two pages of margin-less and essentially meaningless trash, from which he hoped to derive a code. He took a notebook with a compression clasp from his desk and methodically made an impromptu book of the mess.

When he was done it was early in the afternoon. Checking his pocket to be certain he still had one of the disks he copied from the original, he picked up the notebook he just created and headed for the door. Since classes had been canceled, he had time to devote to figuring out what it said.

03 03 03

Janna drove carefully and competently. They were nearing the turnoff for the rural highway that would take them to the lake. Her mother slept in the back seat and Janus stared out the window as the scenery seemed to mesmerize him. Janna thought that it felt so good to drive again. At the college, freshmen were not allowed to keep automobiles on campus. So, it was nearly two months since she had driven. 'My goodness,' she thought. 'That was at Christmas. It seemed like so long ago.'

Schools are always organized in a bizarre manner. The longest period of the year is that time between the beginning of the second semester and spring vacation. It seemed like the days went on forever. Nothing to look forward to, only more of the same. When she drove, she felt free. It was a feeling that planted itself firmly when she took driver's training two years ago. She went through a period when she would invent an errand just for the privilege of driving. Those days were mostly gone, but not completely. She still drove at every opportunity.

Her parents understood this and were more than willing to relinquish the chore to someone who obviously enjoyed this mundane responsibility of the adult world.

Chapter 11

John left the office at noon and headed across campus to have lunch. The Administration Building did have a cafeteria, but on this day John preferred to eat with his colleagues. As Chancellor of the University, he found that eating among his friends and associates was more enjoyable than eating with the secretaries and pencil pushers of the administration staff.

When he ate at the administration cafeteria, he had to put up with all of the sycophants. If there was one thing that gave him indigestion it was the unabashed butt-kissing that occurred. When he ate with the regular faculty, it gave everyone a feeling of having access to his office, an idea he wanted to support. The university was only as good as the professors and students would allow it to become. He wanted Harmson University to be the best in the country, if not the world.

As he carried the meager tray of chicken soup and an apple, he saw Danton Morgenstern sitting alone and moved to join him. While walking toward the psychologist, he tried to organize the questions he wanted to ask in a meaningful form. "Danton, do you mind if I sit?"

"Not at all, John. How have you been doing?"

"Are you asking professionally or personally?" At his small joke they both broke into smiles.

"I suppose if you start telling me your personal troubles, I'll have to start charging you."

"On my chancellor's salary, I don't think I can afford your rates."

"We have easy payment plans available and take most insurance."

"Not interested; besides if I confessed my limitations to you, you might want my job." They both laughed heartily at that one. Danton was by nature a loner, and both men knew of the difficulty he had in dealing with large groups of people, which John, by the nature of his job, did all of the time.

He continued, "By the way, how has your counseling been going with Professor Kline's students?"

"Pretty well. We've detected about five cases of severe trauma/depression over the incident. With individual and group sessions underway, I think we have implemented the necessary steps to address student needs for now. We'll follow up over the next several weeks, particularly with students who may have left campus. Those five students I mentioned are going to need some continuing therapy. I would hesitate to lay all of the blame for their depression on the incident. It is a fairly normal occurrence for freshman to be somewhat depressed about leaving their homes and such. I suppose the most worrisome aspect of the affair is that the ramifications of an action don't always become known until later."

"What do you mean, Danton?"

"Sometimes an action can set off an echo which reverberates through the mind, picking up strength. The full results of this echo can be felt years after the incident. We see this all the time. Childhood trauma does not necessarily manifest itself until the person reaches adulthood. Child abusers are a good example. It has been proven that child abusers, in many instances, were also abused as children. Post-traumatic stress syndrome is one way of looking at it. The person may not have any direct knowledge of this. Still, it is in his or her mind and eventually finds an outlet, usually in some form of deviant behavior or inability to cope with daily life."

"Danton, do you think it could happen in this case?"

"I don't know. I guess we won't know for years."

"Do you think that the school could be liable?"

"No, at least not now. We've put all the therapeutic mechanisms in place that could be reasonably expected. But who knows? Maybe in the future our understanding of the human thought processes will be more advanced than it is now. The arena of legal accountabilities is always up for grabs, and we could be."

"Well, that is a happy thought. Let's set that aside—I mean we can't do anything more, can we?"

"Not that I am aware of. We are following the guidelines of professional psychology in dealing with such incidents. We are doing the correct thing, the best the institution can offer on the heals of a tragic event."

"How are the majority of the students doing?"

"Amazingly well. Actually, they're doing much better than I anticipated. I don't know, I suppose it is the spring breezes that are beginning to blow. It tends to send young people's thoughts off in a completely different direction."

The two older men laughed. About midway through the meal John again stopped eating his soup and took a sip of coffee. "Danton, is there anything more you need to complete the job?"

"No, we've put positive gears in place. Whether it will be enough, only time will tell."

"I appreciate your efforts. I'm glad you are here."

The rest of the lunch was spent in idle chatter about the weather and such until the clock registered a little after one. John explained that he had to get going and admonished the psychologist to call him if there was anything he needed done from an administrative level. He left the dining room for the television station.

଼ ଼ ଼

Dow examined the sheaf of papers for a third time in the last hour. He looked over the meaningless figures and tried to plan a method of attacking the problem. Language is redundant. Linguists have known for years that the majority of our speech patterns and words are predictable, in fact, relatively few in number. Edward Dolch, an educational theorist and linguist, reduced these words to lists. They are known as Dolch words, recognized as the building blocks of our language.

Three hundred words comprise fully 80 percent of our language. These are the common words, the words we actually use to communicate. Certainly, people use more than simple words. Yet, their more complex words are surrounded by these common words. Identifying the common words can leave one well under way to deciphering the cryptogram.

The simple, understandable words include those like: this, that, the, when, who, what, but, if, as, begin, end, middle, and others.

Dolch words aside, the first task Dow had to accomplish was to identify the spaces between words. If the number of uncommon words is not that significant, the sum of letters used to create these words is. In addition to the twenty-six lower case letters, there are twenty-six capital letters, each of which could generate a different symbol on the encryption. There are also ten numbers and another twenty odd characters. Together there are nearly a hundred letters or symbols with which he had to be concerned. However, the most popular character would always be the space.

After every word there would be a space, or a character or characters representing it. If he could only identify the character they were using for this purpose the task would be greatly simplified. Then it was only a question of identifying the most common letters. As well as Dow could remember it, the most popular letter was N, followed by the T. Then the vowels E and A. It was something he would have to check on. He tried to remember the source of this information.

Once you've decided which letters are most common, it is a matter of casting the encryption within the terms of the commonality of the letters. He looked at the document again, placing circles around what he perceived as spaces.

He had no rational explanation for why he thought these were spaces. It was a process that philosophy calls induction. Making a specific recommendation on a partial glimpse of the information is called inductive reasoning. Computers are by nature deductive machines—humans occupy both spheres. Most of our actions, in fact, are not based on deductive reasoning but on induction. We have given names to this process, often called intuition, a hunch, or "guesstimating."

He tried to let his mind wander and drift as he looked at the code. There are subtle clues which might not be able to be identified by deduction. He wanted his mind free to find these.

Absent the kind of training he'd had, some would say that he was guessing at the answer. That would be correct, but only up to a certain point. When one bases a "guess" on information they may have gleaned over a lifetime, it is not a guess. It is a possible answer they have used inductive reasoning to formulate.

Dow continued, making notations with a pencil. He was assuming he was correct, but he prepared for the eventuality that he was not. He wrote lightly so that he could easily erase his pencil marks.

He was aware his chances for interpreting the data in this manner were not great. Already, his mind was designing a code-breaking algorithm which he could enter into the computer to recruit its help in solving the problem. He was afraid he would end up doing just that, and because he understood the need, he was already well into designing it.

Still, he read and occasionally entered a circle around a character. He did not believe in hunches in the traditional sense, yet he thought it might be worth the effort. And with these damnable three days off he had nothing better to do.

ଔ ଔ ଔ

"Janna, did you want to stop for lunch?" her father asked.

"Do we have anything at home to eat?"

"I suppose. Did you want to wait until then?"

"Yes, I had a big breakfast and I'm anxious to get home. It's important to me."

"By all means, go for it. I think your mother has fallen asleep again anyway. And I don't want to wake her up until we are home. You know how she is when we have to wake her."

"Crabby you mean." They both giggled. "I think it's funny the way she always falls asleep. She's like a baby. I never could sleep in a car. It seems she can't ride in a car without sleeping.

"Daddy, when we get home, I'd like you to listen to the final lecture given by Professor Kline."

"Why?"

"I don't know for sure. I think there's something there. But I can't see it very well. I'd like your opinion."

"Certainly." He placed his hand on her knee and said with

gravity in his voice, "Are you okay?"

"Yes, well—I guess. It just seems to be such a waste. I mean, he wasn't that old. I know what he said, but I don't know why he said it. The message seems unnecessarily cryptic." The cloud that appeared over her face dissipated in a moment, and she shifted the focus of the conversation with an intentional smile. "How's everything at the lake?"

"Good, really good. The geese are starting to return and the ice is away from the edges of the lake. The water is always so pure this time of the year. There isn't a lot of snow left, and it looks as if it will warm even further before the weekend."

"I'm glad. I don't think you know how much you miss a place until you don't go there anymore. Sometimes, when I drive by our old house in town, the pangs of wanting come to me. I mean, I did grow up there."

"Janna, you know my feelings. Things, all things are or should be transient. If you place too much stock in a thing, you are likely to be disappointed. Things can be lost or taken away. You still have trouble seeing that. The memories are the important things. The house is just a trigger for these remembrances. In the end, it is how we feel about something that is far more important than the actual thing."

"Yes, Daddy, I know. You keep telling me this. But I still have trouble understanding."

"It's like my sports car. My old Austin. I'm sure it is sitting somewhere rusting, or crushed and recast into something new. But the fact that it is gone has not removed it from my mind. I remember the day your mother and I went to pick it up. I remember how it felt to drive it, how at thirty miles an hour, you felt like you were flying. When I stepped on the accelerator, it revved so high it nearly screamed. And I remember the day I sold it. That was shortly after you were born. We needed a car with room for more people. I was not sad. I was melancholy. I knew it had to be done. And I did it willingly, but still it marked the end of an era.

"Now, Janna, I do not have to go and sit in the car to have those feelings again. Those feelings and the knowledge, the memories of it all are with me. They have become internalized. I know what it was like and therefore, in a strange way,

I still have the car. Even though physically it is gone, it is a part of me.

"The same with the house. The people living in our old house are accumulating memories at this moment that will live with them forever. Though the stairs may creak in the same way they did for us, their presence will be remembered in a different way. Their remembrances may or may not be the same as ours. But in the end that doesn't matter, for their memories have no less validity than our own."

"Geez, Dad. I was only making a simple observation. I didn't need the whole litany explained to me."

"I know, dear. I guess I miss you so much. I still think you are the only one who actually listens to my nonsense. Your mother has ignored it for years. She just listens and goes on. I appreciate the fact that you are a little like me, in that you are willing to weigh and measure the world. In the end that is our choice: to be active participants or be recluses. I have been both and can find parts of each to recommend them."

As the exit loomed before them, they left the superhighway and all it represented behind and headed down the country road which would take them to their world apart from this world.

Challenge

Chapter 12

Chancellor Goslin pulled his car into the circular drive and parked in one of the spots marked "Visitors." As he entered the modern building, he glanced about and saw tell-tale signs of opulence. A variety of quality paintings and sculpture were tastefully arranged for viewing. In front of each a couch had been placed. The luxurious carpeting served to dampen any sound. He felt as if he had just walked into a church or a library.

He walked to the receptionist's station. She appeared to be busy doing her nails. With a look of concentration on her face, she might have been gathering her thoughts for the next task. It was his experience that some people take longer to prepare than others. From the vacant look in her eyes, he assumed that she would have to take a good long time to prepare her thoughts.

He finally cleared his throat. She stopped her activity and said, "Can I help you, Sir?"

"Yes, I have an appointment with Ms. Morris."

"Yes, Ms. Morris works here. And your name?"

"Dr. John Goslin, Chancellor of Harmson University." He disliked using his Ph.D. as an appellation. Still, under the circumstances he felt it best. The receptionist pushed some buttons and spoke softly into a telephone headset. John busied himself glancing around the room again. After a moment the young lady said, "Please have a seat, she'll be right with you." She dismissed him with a glance and returned to her nails.

John did not have long to wait. About the time he sat on one of the couches, Kira Morris came charging through a large door marked PRIVATE. Her smile was infectious as she extended her hand. "Chancellor Goslin, I'm Kira Morris. Pleased to meet you and thank you for coming. I was sorry to hear about the incident at the college. It was a tragedy."

"Certainly, we all feel very badly about it. Do you have the press release?"

"The press release... well... ah..., something has come up. I went over our records and couldn't locate it. It is very strange."

"Strange? In what way?"

"I remember examining it when I wrote the story, and in fact, it was with my script when I did the news. It is our policy to hand the scripts, notes, and everything associated with the broadcast to the news director. That information is then filed. We keep a copy of every broadcast and all associated items. There is no question that the information was filed in the director's office. Normally, Don, the news director, holds onto them for six months. After that they are bundled and shipped to our warehouse as archives. When you called this morning, I went to him and he tried to find it. He did not succeed. He is still in the process of trying to locate it. I am sorry to have troubled you. I feel very badly that I said I had something which I cannot produce."

"What do you suppose happened to it?"

"We don't have a clue. It should have been in with the notes. It wasn't. There is no explanation."

"Well, I don't want to take any more of your time. If you run across it, I would like to see it. And before I go, let me add one word of admonishment. In the future, if it concerns the University, could you please call me?" As he handed her his card he emphasized, "This has my business phone, as well as my home phone. I am not carping about the coverage, except that it was wrong. But I can certainly see your position. If the situation were reversed, I believe I might have acted in a similar manner. It all comes down to examining your sources. If the source seems to be legitimate, then, I suppose, you don't have any choice. I do regret that you didn't call me."

"Thank you very much. I promise that I'll call if there is anything of an awkward nature to report. It is our job to report the facts. And Harmson University certainly deserves our attention. Again, I am sorry to have inconvenienced you."

John returned to his car and headed back to the University. Two questions were added to his growing list.

Where was the phony news release? And, of a darker nature, what if they had the news release and wouldn't show it to him? Again without answers, he pulled into his parking place. He managed to drive from the TV station to the school without ever once thinking about the activity. He shuddered when he thought of the implications of driving that absentmindedly. What if a child had run into the path of the car?

He remembered his appointment at Richard's house. Though it was early, there wasn't enough time to do anything meaningful in the office so he drove to the Kline home. It had always been his policy that arriving early causes far fewer problems than arriving late. And besides, he knew Louise would not be offended if he came early.

Richard and he had often talked about the lack of time he had to pursue things of a non-job related nature. It was one of the curses of his position. Every minute was spoken for. He reassured himself again that she would understand his arriving early.

ଔ ଔ ଔ

He did not notice the car as it pulled from the parking lot across the street from the television station. The occupant made notations on a computerized form and was doing a professional job of shadowing the car. John had no inkling at all that anyone was aware of his activities. In fact, at this moment he was still blissfully ignorant of the waters of change swirling around him. He did not know his activities on this day were of more than casual interest to a group of whose existence he was unaware.

There was a slight problem for the watcher, Mr. Smith, when John pulled into his parking spot at the university and immediately pulled out again. The driver managed to predict which way he would go. He had been following him for several days and knew the streets he traveled and his general routine. It was one of the things that made the job of surveillance possible.

People, all people, go about their tasks in a predictable

manner—except when they are aware their activities are being monitored. But that had not yet occurred with the Chancellor. Mr. Smith circled the block and had the chancellor in sight before he was a minute away from the college. He followed closely and when John Goslin parked his car in front of a house, he drove by. He noted the house number, parked his car where he could easily observe the chancellor's vehicle and reached for the computer on the seat next to him.

After plugging the cellular phone into the modem, he inquired who owned the house the chancellor was approaching. The answer came back in a matter of seconds. A thrill registered on his face when the house was identified as belonging to the late Richard Kline. He reached into his briefcase for a phone log and dialed a special number, which enabled him to listen to conversations within the residence.

Last night another operative had managed to search the house and place listening devices in every room. He switched the button on the phone, allowing him to listen without having the phone to his ear. Readying his notebook, he used one of the forms from the back of the book and entered his code and the code which had been established for the action. He listened as the doorbell rang....

ඥ ඥ ඥ

Janna had always found her mother's travel sleep amusing. But by far her favorite part of the experience was how quickly she would wake up after the car's engine stopped. It was as if she were a cordless appliance removed from the plug, fully charged and ready for action. It happened again when she pulled into the driveway of their house and turned the key to the off position. She thought there must be something in the melodic humming of the motor conducive to her sleeping. Janna often envied her the rest. She frequently wondered if her mother thought all trips were fifteen minutes long—about the time that it took her to fall asleep.

The lake was beautiful. Even with the trees stripped of their leaves, they were still remarkable. The grey of the branches was so thick that it created a delicate gauze shrouding the edge of the lake. This hazy grey mingled with the showy green of the pines and cedars and occasional patches of white snow to create a tableau whose beauty was not diminished by the transitional season.

As Janna exited the car, she heard the frantic activity of the ducks near the beach. The faithful creatures had obviously missed their mid-day meal and were excited about their return. She smiled.

She went to the back of the car with keys in hand and popped open the trunk. She picked up her suitcase in one hand and her backpack filled with books in the other. Her father rushed to join her. "Can I help you with these, Janna?"

"No, I can handle them."

Her father headed for the house with his key in hand. Her mother was already by the door waiting patiently for one of them to use their key. The thought of fumbling in her purse for her own keys never entered her mind.

Janna took her suitcase and backpack to her room and threw them on the bed. A wave of nostalgia overtook her, and she returned to the living room and sat on a recliner with a good view of the beach through the sliders. "Gee, it sure does feel good to be home."

Her mother sat on the couch and said, "We're glad you're here. You mentioned that you have a lot of work to do. When do you have to start?"

"Later. Right now I just want to sit here and rest awhile. It has been an amazing twenty-four hours. Some of the kids were glad for the time off; I wasn't. Sure, I have some work to finish, but I think I would rather have gone to class. I guess I can see the University's point. It's like they didn't have a choice, did they?"

"No, I don't think so, Janna. Look at your father feeding those ducks. In all of the years we've been married, I have never seen him so devoted to a non-work related activity. He is having a wonderful time."

"Mom, how is Daddy doing?" There was an uncommon gravity in her tone.

"Oh, he's fine. His last checkup was good. There are the usual aches and pains associated with being over sixty years old, but no major complaints. No, he is just fine and so am I for that matter. I guess we are lucky; many people who get to our age no longer have their health. Well, anyway, what do you want for lunch?"

"I don't know. Anything I guess. What do we have?"

"Let me go check the fridge. I'll let you know."

Her mother left her looking at the lake while she went and rattled around in the kitchen. Janna tried to put some distance between the school and herself. Her theory was that physical distance would help her gain the perspective she sought. She closed her eyes and considered the events of the last twenty-four hours. It wasn't long before she went to sleep.

೦ಶ ೦ಶ ೦ಶ

John rang the doorbell and waited. Louise Kline answered the door and ushered him in. "John, thank you for coming. Do you want a cup of coffee or anything?"

"That would be fine. I'm sorry, I'm a little early, but I had the time and I was anxious to see how you are."

"Oh, I guess I will get through this. It's hard though. Richard and I have been married for a long time and now, he is gone. It wasn't even like he was sick or in the hospital. It's the shock that bothers me. Most people, when they get to our age, have at least a perfunctory understanding of death and separation. I suppose it is a natural thing. As you get older and frequently go to funerals, you are made aware of it—whether you want to or not. Still, unexpected death is shocking."

"Yes, I know what you mean. I am going through the motions myself, tending to the necessary preparations and responses from the students and faculty, but, Louise, I am still numb with disbelief. I can only imagine how it must be for you.... Remember, if there is anything that I can do...."

"Of course, you will, John. Richard always considered you his best friend."

After a moment, a plate of cookies and coffee cups sprouted on the kitchen table. Since Louise had performed these activities while carrying on a conversation, they seemed to have appeared magically. John was somewhat apprehensive about being there. It brought home the finality of Richard's act. A gloom and depression were beginning to grow in his own mind."

"Where did Rich do his research?"

"Mostly at the Michigan State Library, although he did a lot of it using his computer. You know, he bought that thing against my wishes, I might add. But as the years unfolded, he seemed to get a tremendous amount of use from it. He was delighted with its information-gathering and said so often how he was constantly on the Internet talking with people all over the country. His original reason for taking the sabbatical was to research current government policies that he believes, or believed, contradicted personal freedom. I don't think I'll ever get used to a past tense with Richard."

"Really, that was what he was doing? He and I often talked about such matters. I just didn't think he had way to codify such a thing. It is so ephemeral. It is like trying to capture a cloud. You know it is there, you can see it; but when you try to grab it, it has no substance."

"Yes, I believe he did find a way to study it. The first couple of months he was frustrated, but he discovered what he considered to be the key. From that moment on he was hooked.

"You know how he felt about the changing of the world. He kept saying that the changes were too regular and pervasive to be happenstance. As the year went on, he became more excited...and oddly enough, more depressed. He felt as though there was some kind of conspiracy dictating the nature of the change."

"Did he talk about it?"

"When he first started his research, he did. As his research deepened, he began brooding more than talking about it. Then a few months ago, he got really excited and would positively gleam with joy when he came from his office upstairs. Periodically, I asked him what was going on. He always said, 'Not yet—But I am getting closer.'"

ଔ ଔ ଔ

The watcher scribbled the intonations of the conversation as quickly as he could. The longer the conversation continued, the more anxious he became. He tried to keep his mind clear, but thoughts of the ramifications of what he was hearing were starting to filter into his mind. He stopped writing for a moment to clear his head. He rubbed his temples, while listening to the conversation. He resumed his writing. Beads of sweat formed on his forehead as he worked. The temperature did not precipitate the sweating. It was nervousness, apprehension about the secrecy of the center being broached. If this continued, he would have to call for help from a higher-level trouble-shooting squad in the organization. He continued writing.

Chapter 13

"Well, I suppose I should show you to Richard's office. I haven't been in there since the school called. I don't know—It just seemed too private and far too difficult. You know how he was about his work. I always respected the space he needed to allocate for that. After nearly forty years of marriage, he still didn't want me messing about. He'd always accuse me of losing something. Though it usually turned out that he had lost it himself. Oh, I knew better than to argue with him or take it personally. It was just his way. He was a very private man by nature."

"I understand, Louise, take your time. Whenever you feel ready, we'll go. I am not in a hurry. If I can't devote a few hours of my time to my friend, what kind of man would I be?"

"John, don't ever think you are less than you are. Richard thought the world of you, though you stopped teaching.... Well, let's get on with it."

Richard's office was in the spare bedroom on the second floor. The third bedroom was devoted to an art studio. Louise was a noted watercolorist, and John could tell she had been working. A glance showed him the painting she was working on. A muted picture of grays and blacks, the sort of color scheme you would expect a person suffering a loss to use. Still, there was an accomplished dignity in the composition.

The door to Rich's office was closed. Leaning her head against its frame for a moment, Louise turned the handle and swung it open without a glance at the interior. Somewhere, deep in the recesses of her mind, she still harbored the totally irrational hope that when she opened the door, he would be there at his desk with a grin on his face saying, "My, that was a good one, wasn't it, Louise?" On a rational level she knew this couldn't be true. The room was empty.

John moved inside and sat at the desk. He did not know precisely what he was looking for. He just figured that he would search for something that didn't fit.

Years ago, desks were outfitted with pens, blotting pad and paper. In the late twentieth century these were replaced by the computer and all its paraphernalia. Richard's office was no different. The computer was most prominent on the desk. 'May as well start with the computer,' he thought as he switched on the machine. After a moment, it flashed:

> No operating system found: do you wish to boot from disk?

John wondered about this, but saw a plastic disk case next the computer. After searching through the program disks, he found one labeled BOOT DISK. He placed the disk into the drive and pressed the *Enter* key. Normally machines with a hard drive use the system files on the hard drive to load this software. The files on the hard drive had obviously been corrupted, so it was necessary to place the information into the computer from another source.

The machine hummed for a moment before displaying A:/>. He pressed the C with a colon after it and waited for the machine to respond. A message appeared on the screen:

> No or Unformatted disk: (A)bort, (R)etry or (F)ail

Pressing the F key, the A:/> appeared. He tried doing a DIRectory on C: and received the same message.

> No or Unformatted disk: (A)bort, (R)etry or (F)ail

Turning off the machine, he made a mental note to call Dow and see if he could do something.

Although a dedicated computer user, John was not an expert in their functioning. He could perform the perfunctory tasks necessary to operation, but that was the extent of his knowledge. Dow knew how they worked and understood them intimately. He might be able to do something with it.

He opened the desk drawers: nothing earth-shaking or even significant. He desperately wanted to find something which would give him a clue to the contents of the diskette. Unfortunately, there was nothing. He went to the filing cabinet and searched through the papers: mostly materials and assignments for his classes. In one drawer he found a manuscript neatly typed and tucked in a cardboard box.

He hadn't known that Richard was writing another book. His first, *Classical Considerations,* was now out of print. It had sold quite well at the time in academic circles, but now was a forgotten footnote to Richard's life. This manuscript was untitled. He picked up the box and set it aside. He planned to ask Louise if he could read it.

The rest of the filing cabinet was filled with papers accumulated over a lifetime of teaching. There was nothing either incriminating or remarkable here. He went back to the desk. Glancing at the manuscript, his mind wandered as he fingered the pages. 'Maybe it would be better to give Dow a call now and see if he could do anything with the computer.'

He stepped from the room and walked downstairs. While Louise was finishing the dishes he said, "Do you mind if I call Dr. Jones and ask him to come look at the computer?"

"Ira, why?"

"There's a problem with the computer; perhaps he can help."

"That would be fine. What kind of a problem?"

"I don't know for sure, but it appears that all of the information has been removed from the system. You don't know if Richard did this, do you?"

"Not that I am aware of. He loved that darn thing so much, I doubt if he would want to do something like that."

"Well, I would like to have Dow look at it. After all, he is the expert."

John took his cell phone from his pocket, called his office and asked Martha to please have Dow contact him at this number. He lifted a mug from the sink, helped himself to another cup of coffee and waited for the call to be returned. He had a feeling that Dow could unearth more from the computer. Although he was not an expert, he was aware that information removed from a computer can sometimes be found in its inner recesses. It was a slim hope in his mind, but at least it was a hope. He believed the computer was the crux of at least some critical aspect of the matter.

ଔ ଔ ଔ

Janna's father finished feeding the ducks and entered the door stomping his feet on the rug to remove the excess snow. He carefully latched the storm door and then the inner door. It is standard procedure in northern climates to have two doors. Janus had cursed the stupidity of Hollywood over and over when they tried to treat a story with snow. He felt like screaming every time a car careening around a curve on the snow let out a squealing noise. This was simply impossible. When the actors struggled to close a single door against the storm he hooted with laughter. You could find the meanest tar paper shack in the north and it would have a storm door. It just didn't make sense to him that people could be so ignorant about the world. Still, with what passed for entertainment in this day, he was not surprised.

He removed his boots, went in and sat. "Janna, did you want to play that tape for me?"

"Yes, do you have the time?"

"Certainly, go get it."

Janna left the room and returned a moment later with the tape in hand. She walked to the stereo and inserted the tape. "Dad, before we begin, remember, these are the last words of an intelligent man. I believe he was trying to say more, but was somehow afraid. It is quite shocking and eerie. Are you sure you want to listen to it?"

"Quite sure." Janus thought about how much she had grown. Here she was worried about his sensibilities, when, in fact, he was concerned with hers. Janus was aware this was the way it should be. We teach a child to care for themselves, and they end up trying to take care of us. He heard the stereo begin to hiss, sat back and closed his eyes.

The professor's voice droned on. Janus found himself lost in the words. They were the same words he had used to describe the world many times. He closed his eyes and waited for the inevitable shot. It came.

When the tape ended, he got up, rewound it and listened again. Four different times he repeated the procedure. Karen was fussing in the kitchen, but his thoughts were not with her. His thoughts were centered on two things the professor had said. He tried to listen again, so there could be no mistake.

"Who controls what we see? What we hear? And last of all, what our reaction to that information should be? We venture every day into territory which is unexplored: We base our reactions to such a venture on a reality we presume to be our own...." And, "If you look beneath the surface, perhaps you will see the manipulators at work. I have seen them, and my time at this fine university is now finished."

"Janna, I agree. There is more here than is readily apparent. It seems to me that he was frightened. I don't think he wanted to do it; it's like he is being forced. Who or what could force a man to do this?"

"I don't know. He sounded pretty scared. I know this sounds ridiculous, but he sounded a lot like you."

"Yeah, I noticed it. I probably have given you that same talk many times. Maybe, that's why it seems to fascinate you. That, and the fact that he talks about those who control our perceptions.

"I have felt for years that somewhere there may be some sort of super censor deciding what we should like and what we should despise. There doesn't seem to be a lot of room for the middle ground. Our society seems to be bent in two directions: abject failure and glorious victory. I have noticed more of this is the last ten years than before. I think it is the distance between myself and the world which has allowed me to perceive this. Either that, or I am a stark raving lunatic.

"Sometimes, I am not sure there is a difference between the sanity of living and insanity of existing without a sentient thought in our heads. Examples of this abound. Take the publishing industry. Sometimes a book is published with the assumed knowledge it will be a best seller. We are told of its arrival from a variety of sources and it is sold on nearly every book rack at every store. However, some books seemed destined for failure and their prospects ultimately rest in the 'Under $1.00 bin' at a discounter. How are such things determined? Some of the best books I have read, I bought for little money. And some of the worst seemed to have been foisted upon me without my consent. I mean, if they know which are going to be successful, why do they even bother publishing the others?

"Television and movies seem to follow the same pattern. Certain stories appear to be anointed as hits and others are doomed to failure. Once this decision has been made, the people who schedule these programs seem to fulfill their own prophesies. Those that are chosen are given the best time slots, and they succeed. The unlucky ones are given those slots opposite those shows that are already successful. Movies are more of the same. Sometimes a good movie is simply forgotten, because it could not find a theater to be shown in. Or a distributor will refuse to handle it. I don't know. It just seems that there is some logic behind it. I have a hard time believing the happenstance theories we accept as the truth."

"I know, Dad. Sometimes, I think it's easily seen. Then you have to pinch yourself to come back to reality. How could such a thing exist in our world? Did you hear what he had to say about seeing the manipulators at work? Is that just the ranting of a crazy old man?"

"No, Janna, he does not appear to be crazy. He seems to be a little overly-rational to me. In my experience people who contemplate too deeply are not particularly happy. The irony of this is once you begin this process of allowing your mind to perceive, you can't stop it. As far as seeing the 'manipulators at work,' I don' t know..."

"Hey, you two, come and get it." Karen stood in the doorway with her apron on and said, "Wash your hands and come and sit; you two will have time to hash this out later. Right now, lunch is served."

They left the living room and sat down at the kitchen table to eat. Janus led the prayer, "Lord, grant us the peace that passeth understanding. Let us see thy world as you intended us to. And please, let the soul of Richard Kline rest in thy kingdom. Amen."

ଓଃ ଓଃ ଓଃ

The ringing of the phone jarred their conversation to a close. Louise answered it. After she said hello and listened for a moment, she handed the phone to John.

"Hello, Dow?"

"Yes, what's going on?"

"I'm at Richard's house. I turned on his computer, and it's giving me an unformatted disk message when I try to access the hard drive. It appears that everything has been erased."

"Great. That's wonderful news. I'll be right over."

"Why is that great?"

"No time to explain, I'll be there in just a couple of minutes. Don't touch that machine again!"

John replaced the phone and returned to the chair where he had been seated. "Louise, Dow seems to think that is great news. I can't even begin to imagine why he is so excited. He is on his way."

"Why would that be good news that the computer had been erased? I would think that would be terrible news—if you were trying to find information."

"Sometimes, information which has been deleted can be retrieved. But the off chance that this could happen hardly seems to be a reason for excitement. But remember, Dow does not see the world in the same way as us."

ଓଃ ଓଃ ଓଃ

Dow reached into the drawer by his computer and pulled out his notebook disk case. He checked to see what disks were there and after making a brief survey, opened a drawer and retrieved a handful of disks from a specially constructed and locked disk case. He zipped the notebook shut and ran out of the door without bothering to lock it.

ଓଃ ଓଃ ଓଃ

"John, isn't that Ira coming up the walk?"

"Why, yes it is. He certainly made good time."

They got up, walked to the door, and Louise opened it. Dow came in with a large smile. "John, that's just wonderful news. I have been working on that damned disk, excuse me, Louise, and am getting nowhere fast. It appears to be a holocryptic code where the key is used only once. If that is the case, we need to have that key to understand it. Without the key, it is doubtful we could ever crack it."

"Okay, so you are not having much success on your end. Why are you so excited?"

"John, the vast majority of people do not understand how computers save information. I am excited, because I know of at least seven ways of salvaging information from a disk that has been given a new format."

"But once the disk is reformatted, isn't all the information lost?"

"Yes and no. If you did nothing beyond the normal activities, the information would be lost. However, if the disk has not been rewritten with new information, the old information should still be there. The problem lies not in finding the information, for the information has not been physically removed. Instead, the index of where that information was located was lost. If we can re-institute this index, we can find the information. Even without the index, we can still dump the information stored there. Remember, all information on a hard drive is stored as a series of magnetic spots. There is nothing in the format or delete command which resets these. They are still in place. With a little luck, we can replace the old format and retrieve the information. As a matter of fact, I am going to do that now. I'll call you if I have any luck. Louise, where is the computer?"

She escorted him upstairs and he closed the door behind him. He walked over to the machine, placed his diskette notebook on the desk, and unzipped it. He laid out his tools as carefully as a surgeon in preparation for surgery. He arranged them in the order in which he knew he would need them. He selected the first disk and slipped it into the drive. He reached for the switch and turned the computer on.

Chapter 14

Electricity filled the air. Tension blasted from sidewall to sidewall and from the curtained stage to the control rooms of the studio in the rear. Soon, the time for the weekly broadcast of the most important religious broadcasters in the world would be here.

The audience was nearing a frenzied level as they sat in eager anticipation of the appearance of The Hammer. Large digital clocks located seemingly everywhere counted down the seconds until he would make his appearance. There was a clock on every wall; on some there were two. Whatever direction the great man happened to glance, the exact time would be available. It wasn't so much that timing was important; it was absolutely paramount to the ministry. The clocks clearly said: 11:44:50.

In the small, elegantly printed programs that had been distributed to the people on their way to their seats, it said that the announcer would enter the stage at precisely 11:45:00.

The audience, three hundred of the chosen, noted the time and began to chant: 10 - 9 - 8 - 7- 6 - 5... As the curtain opened, Johnny Daniels entered from the left of the stage. He stood for a moment with his eyes pointing toward heaven, his hands outstretched, as if in supplication.

The silence of the audience was miraculous after the thunderous countdown as they, too, all turned their eyes toward the Almighty. After a moment, Johnny turned to the audience and shouted, "Who did you come to see today?"

"The Hammer of God."

Johnny looked over the group as if he had not seen them before. He shook his head slowly in agreement and screamed, "Oh yes, he is the Hammer." After a brief pause he continued, "What are you?"

"We are the anvils, the anvils of God."

"Why have you come?"
"To learn."
"To learn what?"
"The will of the Lord for his chosen people"
"Yea, verily." He paused for a moment and looked at the crowd. Then he continued, "And who knows the will of the Lord?"
"The Hammer of God."
"When you have learned the will of the Lord, what will you do?"
"We will cleanse ourselves."
"Cleanse yourselves of what?"
"Impure thoughts."
"Who will ask the Lord to help you?"
"The Hammer of God."

With each refrain the noise became louder. The audience was not aware of it, but within the confines of the acoustically-sound studio speakers were placed under each seat. On cue, these sweetened the audience's response by broadcasting carefully constructed recordings of previous audiences. Each speaker was omnidirectional and broadcast from a seemingly nonspecific source.

Each seat had been heavily insulated to prevent the person seated from knowing of the speaker's existence. Every show was taped and when the correct response—in the estimation of the producer and director—was registered, it too would be made part of the audience sweetener.

The crescendo of affirmation was reaching a fever pitch. The people sat with tears flowing and looks of rapture in their eyes. Johnny glanced at one of the clocks and the time read 11:57:30.

He spread his arms over the crowd as the Lord did over the masses at the Mount of Olives and waited for the crowd to calm down. The sweeteners became silent and Johnny closed his eyes, as if in prayer. His voice started as softly as a lover's whisper. "The time is nigh. The time has come for the realization of your hopes and dreams. It is time to greet the man who will lead you to the higher ground. Are you ready?"

The crowd shouted in unison, "We are ready."

"Are you ready for Him? Are you prepared to greet his servant on earth?"

"We are ready."

Casting his eyes on the ground, as if he were afraid to look up to see his arrival, he gathered himself for the final act. "Ladies and gentlemen, I present to you..." Time slowed to an impossibly slow pace. Johnny checked the clock again; it was important to time this just right. Satisfied, he continued, "The Hammer of God, His servant on earth, the Reverend Doctor Nehemiah Hamner!"

The digital clock now read 11:58:00. The thunderous applause threatened to raise the roof on the building. The sweeteners had been turned to maximum volume. The engineer watched the curtain to be certain he followed The Hammer's actions.

The purple curtain slowly parted in the middle exposing an inner curtain of frosty white. The mechanism opening the curtains rendered an effect which made them seem to be blown by a heavenly wind. This particular effect had cost over $10,000 and functioned admirably well. The heavy purple curtains began a graceful opening. Then the purest white gauze curtains appeared to stretch out to the audience to nearly engulf them. A mighty organ, which had been completely absent from the proceedings, suddenly burst into the first chords of The Hammer's hymn. The audience stood as one and began to sing.

> "A mighty fortress is our God
> A bulwark never failing
> Our helper He amid the flood
> of mortal ills prevailing..."

There was a brief flash of stroboscopic light as he walked through the curtains. A lapel mic clipped to a perfect tie coordinated with his crisp, white shirt and dark suit. Primed for his presentation, he began to sing.

> "For still our ancient foe
> Doth seek to work us woe

> His craft and power are great
> And armed with cruel hate
> On Earth is not his equal."

His voice has been described as being as loud as the cry of thunder in the mountains or as gentle as the rippling of a stream that passes beneath a low bridge in the spring. Now it echoed as the sound of mighty armies victorious in their charge: a bulwark never failing. Every word took on nuances of deeper meaning when it came from the Hammer of God.

His thoughts, mostly of the common variety, were amplified by his delivery until they resonated throughout the room. The hymn ended and he stood facing the audience with his arms outstretched as if he were praying for divine guidance. While the audience stared in rapturous silence, the seconds ticked by. The Hammer checked the clocks. 12:01:30. Still he waited, working to maximize the tension essential to his communication style—and to wait until the commercially produced introduction the television audience was seeing had ended.

Finally, when the digital clock read: 12:02:58, he spoke.

> Friends and servants of the Lord, I have traveled about in this great world of the Lord's creation and have visited with people everywhere. Everywhere there has been beauty and wonder to behold. I have been to the mountains of Tibet, where in every direction the hand of God is revealed in its glory. I have been to the depths of the Kalahari Desert. Here too, I saw the hand of God. But friends and servants, everywhere I have seen him, too. You know of whom I am speaking: the evil messenger traveling about spreading lies and deceit.
>
> You've seen him and his handiwork in your daily lives. For people, verily, he is everywhere. His minions are many. At times they seem to outnumber the stars in the sky or the grains of sand in the desert. Still, we will seek out this evil, this abomination, this bad seed, and crush it together. His end will be sure as he is crushed between the Hammer of God and his anvils.

Reverend Hamner stopped for a moment and waited for the applause to die. He searched for anyone not locked in rapt attention. He found none. The people in the audience were spellbound. They stared at him as if he were Moses, bringing the Ten Commandments down the mountain. Affirmed by their response, he began again.

> His methods are attractive, but his message is evil. Listen for him. You will see him in your newspapers. He is the one who is behind the headlines laughing at the latest travesty against God's children. He is the one who believes that all men can be laid low by the sins of their children who have never been taught the Lord's way.
>
> Oh, the Devil likes to deal with children. They are not wise enough to perceive his devious methods. They are easy pickings for his basket of souls. We must help them. We must show them the way—the way of the Lord!"

Thunderous applause greet him and he acknowledges it with a pause. Just before the applause would have begun to diminish, he begins again:

> Watch for him on your television. He is the one who is poisoning the youth of the nation with his litany of race hatred and jingoistic, humanistic, chauvinistic, pluralistic, paternalistic, and anachronistic abhorrence of all mankind. He tries to make us forget that we are all servants of the Lord. The lies he spreads are nothing more than viperous vituperation.

The Hammer waits a moment for his followers at home and in the audience to comprehend his words, knowing full well that what he has just said is important only in the rhythm. Some of the words he has just used are unknown to the anvils. He looks over the crowd carefully choosing one person in each row to make eye contact with. They stare back with a look of awe in their faces as he continues:

> We are a people together. We are the Lord's people. We are one, all servants of the Lord. We will conquer the

hatred. We will live to see a world where the color of your skin does not matter. We welcome all of our brothers and sisters of color. We know of their needs, and these needs for identity can be met within the tent of the Lord. You do not have to act like us. You have your own rich heritage to extol—but you must believe as one of us.

The Lord's tent is a massive tent. It has rooms for all of God's children. This tent is large enough for all people to come and join the master of all masters. We have room for the Hispanic, we have room for the Asian. We have room for all to sup at the table of the Lord's.

If you are a person of color, we love you, and need you to join with us. Together, we can fight against the outrages that society aims at you. For every African-American in jail, there is one white man walking free. A white man who, with his cowardly laws and rules, has forced the proud traditions of Africa into an affront against society. We recognize your needs and we salute them. We know we are a white society, which is so fearful that we condemn all people who are different. Here at the Lord's tent, we celebrate the differences between people. For in diversity is strength. The very act of being different is not an effrontery to the Lord, but a compliment.

Now, the devil has said that you are a people with lax moral values; we know better. The devil has said that you have no ethics and that physical sensations are the focus of your minds. More lies! Come and join with me, I can take you to the higher ground, a place above the injustices that the world has directed toward you. It is a place where all men are free and rich, a place where all people believe in the same Lord. Take my hand and walk to the higher ground, the ground of the Lord's.

He waits on his natural break for the applause; he is not disappointed. The applause is deafening. Satisfied, he changes his voice from the thunder to the gently flowing brook and sweetly says:

Ladies of the Lord. My sisters, have you suffered enough at the hands of evil men? Those servants of the devil who approach you as if you were a whore on the street. Have you seen the devil at work in these poor brothers? Do you know the names of their gods? These evil men worship the gods of lust, lasciviousness, lechery, and uncontrollable deviant sexual urges. They see you as only an object for sexual exploitation, rather than the handmaidens of the Lord who serve in His house.

Ladies, I have seen your pain and I recognize its worth. It is a pain brought on by the sins of the men who follow the Evil One.

But ladies, all men are evil and their only hope of redemption is through the Lord and his servants. Come, you evil men, and feel the wrath of the Hammer of God. I will smite the sin from you. I will break down the walls that keep you from being the Lord's. I will smite the evildoer where he stands and seek him where he hides in cowardice. I am the Hammer and I do His will. I will hasten the devil's departure to the regions of Hell where the Lord has sent him. I will help you to see the wisdom of the Lord.

Hola, senors y senoras y senoritas.

He went on and on detailing the same message to the Hispanics, as he had to the African-Americans. His message went on until he had greeted almost all peoples in their languages. When the digital clocks read 12:14:45, the organ began again, singing for his people with the golden tones of the blessed.

> "And though this world with devils filled
> Should threaten to undo us
> We will not fear for God has willed his truth
> To triumph through us!
>
> The prince of darkness grim
> We tremble not for him
> His rage we can endure

For Lo! His doom is sure
One little word shall fell him."

The Hammer bent to one knee, stretched out his hands to the audience and raised his eyes to heaven, keeping one on the clock. At 12:17:50 he rose to his feet and walked toward the crowd. His peripheral vision caught his cue that the commercial was over. He swallowed deeply and began anew.

ೂ ೂ ೂ

At the back of the audience a man carefully took notes on all that the Hammer said. He was a gifted stenographer who could not only copy the words, but had time to list both the intonations and methods of delivery. He wrote quickly and surely. He seemed as though he were one of the followers, but in reality he was one of the manipulators, a manipulator so skilled his presence would never be detected. His task was to take down the message word for word for later analysis. Though the broadcast was also videotaped, this man's observations were more important. For he could discern the nuances of the message, which held the key to effective communication. The semantics of the Hammer's speech were important to the Center, and their delivery even more so.

When he was through for the day, he returned to his hotel room and compared his notes to the prepared script, making certain that every idea which was proposed had been dealt with specifically and rapturously. He then took his portable computer to codify the information gleaned from his day's work. Once the information had been altered for use by the computer, he dialed a special phone number and fed the information into the master computers in Virginia. From there the information would be processed and improved until, by next week, a new script would be prepared for the Hammer of God.

For the Hammer was an instrument. He was a vessel carrying the message of the Center for American Heritage. As an actor on one of its many public stages, his performance was reviewed every time he spoke.

At the first sign of weakness, this weakness would be

dealt with severely. If the Hammer failed to do the job to Center standards, there were three others already being groomed, who now had the prominence and stature the Center needed to continue the process. The Center could not and would not tolerate incompetence or weakness, nor would they accept mediocrity. They demanded the best and received it. The consequences were dire and intimidating.

Reverend Hamner knew this and kept to script remarkably well. He understood that the same people who had created him could also destroy him. It had happened before.

Though he tried to not think about Reverend Jersey Land, his presence shadowed him on stage. Jersey, his predecessor, had soared to the heights only to be brought down by scandal and innuendo. A minister brought so low he could not even become a street preacher without the populace threatening him for speaking the words of the Lord. Jersey had decided he was bigger than the Center. He had been wrong. His story served as an "inspiration" to all who carried the Center's banner. They would never tolerate independent thinking by one of their servants. If you tried, you were destroyed. With the Center, there was no middle ground. And because the Hammer liked his position, he had no intention of being destroyed.

CHALLENGE

Chapter 15

Even for late February, signs of spring were everywhere in Virginia. Many people abandoned their winter coats and were wearing light jackets or sweaters in bright, sunny colors. The drab, colorless winter months were giving way to the increased light of spring. Even a small change like the absence of hats, scarves and mittens had a warming effect on people as they hustled from one building to another. It seemed such a simple thing, getting dressed without covering every inch of your exposed skin. Just having the warmth of the sun on the now exposed skin had a remarkable psychological effect on people. Smiles replaced frowns and good feelings among people were obvious.

Even the trees, dormant since their leaves were plucked by the stiff autumn breezes, were beginning to show signs of activity. One did not even have to look closely to see the buds on the branches. Here and there a leaf made a premature appearance, adding a little green, presaging the coming festival of spring. In the near South, spring came early and lasted a suitably long time. The locals understood that spring here is the most glorious time of the year. A time of great expectations, expectations for the coming growing season. It was a time, not of reflection, but anticipation. The promise of warm, fragrant nights where the blossoms' bouquet would color the world, and the wonderful feeling of the soft grass as it reached between your toes when you discarded your shoes and socks for a romp. The faith that the world would renew itself was replaced by the certain knowledge gained from watching it happen.

The entire area was in the earliest stages of becoming a paradise of blooming flowers and comfortable temperatures. Though these halcyon days would be forgotten when the stifling heat and humidity of the summer arrived, for now, they were in control.

ଔ ଔ ଔ

Darren Meyers left his car in his reserved spot and walked across the compound toward the computer center. The structures comprising the Center for American Heritage were clearly defined. High fences stood as sentinels to ward off the unwanted intruder. The appearance of the twelve-foot high chain link fence with razor wire on top gave the compound the look of a top-secret military base.

The constantly-manned guard shack reinforced this feeling. Anyone attempting to enter the compound without proper identification would be treated in a firm manner. If the intruders were foolish enough to persist, they were arrested and charged with trespassing. In fact, everything about the compound radiated an air of unapproachable officialdom. The signs on the fence, although not stating this was a government institution, were made by the same company using the same color scheme and typeface. At a simple glance, it could be assumed that the compound was owned by the government, rather than the other way around.

All of the buildings with their carefully manicured grounds were made possible by the computer center. Within its granite walls, was the greatest conglomeration of digital technology ever established.

The Center for American Heritage owed its existence to the peculiar passions of one man: Richard C. Hunter. Hunter's family had been a moderately connected publisher of advertising catalogs, when the broadcast industry was in its infancy. By being in the right place at the right time with the right connections, they had managed to become an American institution. Their publication of the listings for the coming week soon became an American necessity. This generated a great deal of wealth. Wealth in America could be turned into political power, if its holders were willing to do what was necessary for its accumulation. The Hunter family was certainly willing. The irony was that they promoted self-serving materials through the medium and, contrarily, tried to politically impose a form of newly-minted puritanism through this same medium.

With the necessity of working removed from this family, they directed much of their considerable fortune in other ways. Instead of helping our society and people, like the great philanthropists of the gilded age, they decided that it was their task to lead America away from the dangers of wanton lust—the kind that was actively promoted by their publication behind the scenes—and into a new age where religion and government would become partners instead of separate entities. To these ends the Center for American Heritage was established. Technically, it began as a think tank, a place where like-minded scholars could meet and prepare position papers and scholarly journals. But this methodology turned out to be far too slow. Instead, they expanded from their base of television and insinuated themselves into the mass media of the country until they virtually controlled what people saw, heard or read. Their existence was kept a strict secret. Few people knew of their dealings. Those who had some idea, were bought or threatened into submission.

Occasionally, there were rumors but these were dealt with in a timely manner, so the Center continued unfettered in its operations. There were twenty-one directors of The Center for American Heritage. With nearly limitless money and a self-righteous attitude, tempered by a brazen willingness to break the law if it suited their purposes, they became the de facto arbiter of American culture.

Within the walls of the computer center, every type of computer was represented from a lowly PC to several supercomputers. All of these machines processed their information under the direction of Darren Meyers. Darren was nearly forty-five years old and had worked for the company for twenty-three years, virtually all of his adult life. Darren entered the building and after saying good morning to the receptionist, moved to his office. He sat at his desk, turned on his terminal, pressed a few keys and brought up the SS report on the latest Hammer of God show.

The Syntax and Semantics report was a brainchild of someone in another division. Darren did not have the slightest idea who had conceived of the things or precisely how they worked. He knew that a considerable span of the company's activities revolved around the reading of these documents. His only responsibility was to personally remove them from the computer and deliver them to his superior, Jonathan Green.

In the Center, although he was in charge of the computers, he was not privy to the use of the information he routinely retrieved, stored and reported. He understood his function very well and was satisfied in doing his job.

He thought about the SS Reports. Even though it was not of his generation, the letters SS had a negative connotation. He privately wished they had been given another name. He had been told, briefly, that these reports were not designed to be negative, and he should not look at them in this light. Instead, they were designed to help the people who were spreading the Center's message do a better job. Though they were not designed to be negative, he knew they had on occasion been used in suspect ways.

Every morning a series of reports came through the computer center; they were dutifully passed on to the analysis section. Darren did not know exactly what they did with the reports. Their purpose was hidden within the serpentine organization of the company. He was only privy to those areas which were of a direct concern to him.

At times, when he allowed himself to think of them, he could generalize their nature. He remembered the SS reports on Reverend Land. These showed deviations from the normal range. He could tell because the report came back, much like a medical report, with areas of too much strength and too little clearly noted. The too strong categories were marked with a "+" and the too little denoted with a "-". Those areas determined to be acceptable were marked with an " *".

On Reverend Land's reports, the deviations began as just an occasional aside to the audience and ended when his SS report showed him out of the normal range on nearly all of the fifty different measurements encoded into the form. Their deviations were measured and reported with computer accuracy to the fourth digit past the decimal point.

These particular reports would have been worth many millions of dollars to potential advertising clients and politicians, because they represented such advanced degrees of specific knowledge in an area known publicly more for assumptions and relative truths. These were exacting measurements of the most complex creatures on earth: men and women.

The semantics project detailed the words which had a more universal meaning than others. These they stressed in the scripts which were prepared for their people who were in the public eye. These included the superstars of the airwaves, Reverend Hamner, Thomas J. McCarthy, Drew Cabot, Craig Thomas, and others, who the American audience assumed were unbiased news people. In reality, their messages were dictated and honed down to the letter for regurgitation. Even the minions of the recently popular Talk Radio were employees of the Center—not only the extreme right wing personalities, but also those on the left. By controlling the entire spectrum, they enabled the message to be controlled to the extent that the Center required. Their employees were dedicated to the furtherance of the message. If not, they were dealt with severely. If they did not follow their function properly, the Center attacked them until there was nothing left of either their professional or personal lives. They knew this and were more than willing to promote the Center's messages. The Center would not and did not accept anything less than absolutely the best. The moment you strayed from that standard, your career was over.

With Reverend Land, it had only been a matter of weeks of negative SS reports before the pictures of the good Reverend with several prostitutes made a nationwide appearance. The next week the news magazines were filled with the confessions of call girls nationwide. There were also reports circulated of child molestation, and worse. The fact these were obvious plants had been dismissed by the lap dogs of the Center, the news media and the so-called free press of the United States.

The once-powerful press had been brought into total submission. Instead of being the guardians of our society envisioned by the founding fathers, they had become pitiful toothless dogs who begged for an occasional scrap of meat to be satisfied. One more celebrity scandal to keep the people distracted from what was actually happening. One more missing white, blonde girl in Aruba. A storm to divert attention from the news they should be covering. Relatively unimportant stories that prohibited Americans from dealing with ideas and the consequences of those ideas. Anything to keep the people from concentrating on the Center and what its minions were actually doing to the land of the free.

Reporters, who at one time lived by a code to report the truth, were now co-opted in the easiest way possible: money. The truth is that they enjoyed their access to the Administration and Congress. The parties, the dinners at fancy restaurants, the golfing trips to St. Andrew's in Scotland, the houses on the beach and the all-expenses-paid vacations at the haunts of the rich and shameless all served to keep their voices muted in criticism and alarmingly raised at the prospect of malfeasance from any quarter.

Instead of being important members/contributors of the society, the people of the press had abdicated that control to the company. Now, they are like the junk yard dog who has lived past his point of usefulness. Certainly, the signs still were posted: BEWARE OF DOG. But the truth was that this dog was aged, blind, and without the will to confront anyone about anything.

Now, with the passing of years, even those who understood that the press was supposed to be an adversary to hurtful government policiest, seemed silent. By extreme measures those who understood were relegated to the fringes or our society. No one of any perceived credibility opposed the Center's policies successfully. Money was the root of their power and its reach could be insidiously subtle and pervasive. As they established themselves in the media, the government, and the judiciary, there was little anyone could do to oppose them. People too busy trying to survive had little time to do the research necessary for comprehension and had simply given up hope. When the Center controlled the absolute parameters and limits of the debate, there was little anyone could do to confront them.

When Jersey Land tried to show the world what they were doing, he was defrocked within the span of thirty-six hours. He had still not regained enough respect to be treated as anything other than a pariah. Whenever notice was conveniently posted as to his new location in the very same news media, he had to move on. The press regularly incensed the people's anger against this man, one who had nothing but their freedom from the slavery of ideas as a motive.

These matters were not listed among those Darren had the right to consider; his function was to keep the computers working and working efficiently. His task was to make sure the computers functioned better tomorrow than they did today and that the next day would yield even more accurate information.

He never thought about quitting. Everything he wanted in life was either his or easily achievable. He had married well and was now a rich man, in addition to being a brilliant one. His skills at tying together the disparate abilities of the computers were not unrecognized. He was now in charge of the computers and their programmers.

The programmers were an interesting group. Within the structure of the company, there were nearly thirty of the most talented programmers in the country. Here, the lore of the systems was not lost. Everything they did worked, and worked very well. None of the false starts and crashes which occur in the computers of this country were tolerated. No, they were efficient, dedicated and devoted to the goals of the company. These were posted over each work station.

>To protect the liberty of all men and women.
>
>To facilitate the human rights of all races.
>
>To provide reason where possible,
>
>explanations where not.
>
>To inculcate the beliefs of the founders.
>
>To keep the Center's existence secret.

Working for the Center was the only job Darren had ever had; it was the only job he would ever need. No one quit the company to move to another industry.

Occasionally, a few had moved directly into government service in the Executive Branch. But there was little difference in their jobs, for what the Center wanted was reflected in the many and varied policies of the current administration. When they lost an election, as was slated they would in the next cycle, these people would return to the Center or one of its many subsidiaries and no one would be the wiser. But, in general, once employed by the Center you were there for life. Quitting was simply not an option.

There were several reasons for this. The first was that the Center treated their employees very, very well. Darren realized that there was no way he could ever hope to match his package of salary and benefits in the outside world. The second reason was a little darker. You could not quit the Center without suffering the consequences. These consequences he understood could be severe. There would be a complete destruction of all credit status, news reports of illicit activities, and if they chose, a whispering campaign which would foster hatred and resentment among your friends and family.

No. The Center had Darren's absolute loyalty. It was a sacred trust he did not take lightly. He never thought about the consequences of quitting; in truth, he never even considered quitting. He was satisfied.

When he was recruited out of college, the representative told him that if he were chosen to work for them, he would never need another job. If at some future point, he wanted to quit, they explained, there would be consequences. The fact that they never stated how severe these consequences were was not a topic of consideration in Darren's life.

When he first heard the proposal, he thought they must be involved in organized crime. After the third interview, the people who talked to him laughed off his question but did allow the stipulation in his contract that if he suspected they were engaged in gangster-like activities, he would be free to quit and report to the authorities. They were even nice enough to list the types of activities they considered to be "gangster-like."

Of course, to his knowledge, they had never engaged in prostitution or gambling or drug-related activities. In truth, they had not—at least not exactly. The prostitutes for Reverend Land had been arranged, but the Center did not benefit from their activities—at least not directly.

If there was a benefit, it was not one which could be measured on the usual sort of balance sheet. X amount of dollars in and X amount of dollars out. No, the Center did not work that way. They did not have to. They were a highly-funded organization whose purpose was only known to a few people. And Darren was not one of them.

He stared at the report and carefully collated the pages, noting the numbers printed in the upper right hand corner. Taking the sheaf of papers, he placed them in the special notebook that would be personally delivered to his superior. Finished with the notebook, he started to leave his office for the short walk to Mr. Green's office when his assistant, Joyce Keller, came in with a look of consternation on her face. "What's the matter, Joyce?"

"I don't know. We had a system shutdown a few minutes ago. The computer reports someone is trying to infiltrate the master computer."

"Probably just a hacker who found a node by chance."

"Maybe so. Still, I don't like it; they managed to penetrate three levels before we caught him."

"Three levels! That is serious. Do you have any other information?"

"No, not really. It does seem as though the intrusion was from Michigan through the university net. Beyond that, I can't say. Do you want me to set a trace on that ISP?"

"Yes, but don't do anything until I get back. I guess we can assume if he made it through three levels of security, they will be back. Do you need any help?"

"No, I can handle it. I'll just load the Oracle program and set the ISP to the one he used. That should do it."

"The Oracle—Oh yeah, that's that one we wrote about three years ago. Well, go ahead. I will be back within forty minutes. If there is a further attempted incursion, call my cell."

With a thoughtful look on his face, he collected the papers and left the office. 'Someone trying to break in here? Whatever for? We don't have anything of value. Most curious.'

Chapter 16

"The reports are great, as usual. Was there anything else we need to talk about, Darren?"

"Jonathan, I don't know if I should tell you this—basically, because I'm not sure of its meaning. Well, anyway, someone tried to break through the security systems on the master computer."

"When did this happen?"

"A few minutes ago."

"They didn't get in, did they?" he asked with lines of alarm creased of his forehead.

"No, they were stopped at the fourth level. The thing is, they should have been stopped long before that point."

"Do you figure it's a hacker?"

"No! At least, I don't think so. They were too good to be amateurs or kids. No, this is a some sort of pro. An amateur would have been discovered and stopped much sooner. This person knew what they were doing. If they made it through the third level on the first try.... Well, I have some concerns about the next time."

"What have you done to stop them?"

"Joyce put one of our security tracers on it. You remember giving your approval for the writing of the Oracle program?" The older man nodded his head slowly. He wasn't sure if he had approved it or not, but if Darren said he did, he could accept that.

"That's the one we are using. If he tries it again, we should be able to pinpoint a location and report it to the FBI. Unlawful entry of computers is against federal law. So far, we only know he attempted to log on from somewhere in Michigan through the University Server System. That is not a lot to go on. There are literally tens of thousand of users on that system.

"We normally don't keep that program in memory

because it takes up too much computer space for the off-chance that someone might try to break in. If he tries it again, we will be able to access his system. It will be a surprise. Let me assure you, we have the best security in the world on our systems. I can't even conceive of someone seriously breaching that line of defense."

"Well, Darren, keep me informed. By the way, I had something come up in the computer area the other day. I almost called you, but I figured the problem was handled. Now, what I am going to tell you is not to leave this room, is this understood?"

"Certainly." Darren felt a cold thrill as his superior was obviously ready to confide a company secret to him. It had been his experience that such confidences inevitably led to increased responsibilities and the accouterments that accompanied it.

Jonathan Green leaned forward until his elbows were causing indentations in the leather top of the antique mahogany desk. His eyebrows narrowed and he spoke in a near whisper. "I think you will find it hard to believe, but we have an enemy. Someone would like to expose our activities to the world—not that we are doing anything wrong," he added hastily. "I have heard their allegations, and I can't believe them. If they were true, I don't think I would work for an institution whose purposes strayed so far from own.

"Still, there is at least one man who for one reason or another opposes us. I guess it all comes down to freedom. Or at least the illusion of freedom. People in this country have always had limited freedom, although some would prefer to think they have more. The truth is, all of our actions are dictated by the society we live in. We don't have a choice. If people really examined how little freedom they have, they would probably riot. The public remains blissfully ignorant about the reality of their situation. But every once in a while, we run into a person who believes he is entitled to more. I can't speak to his needs. I suppose such areas are best left to his own psychiatrist. Still, the failure to accept the limits of our freedom is a social abomination and leads to all sorts of discord, a development we oppose at every turn. Well, to return to the subject.

"Someone or some group opposes us. Surprisingly we have very little knowledge of these activities. In short, we don't know much about them, although they seem to have been gathering intelligence about us. We have been trying to analyze the nature of this enemy, but without much success. Prior to six months ago, he or they were chasing ghosts and shadows. Then, Jersey Land—do you remember him?—"

"Yes."

"Well, one of these people ran into Jersey when he was sober, a rare condition these days, and he divulged some of what he knew about us. It wasn't much. There aren't many people who have comprehensive knowledge of our important activities. Still, it seemed to have been enough to begin a snow-ball reaction. These adversaries appear to be intelligent and resourceful.

"It seems they kept their information on us in computers. The other day, after one of the most dangerous of them—how shall I put it?—ceased to be a problem, one of our agents cleaned out his computer files. I almost called and asked you about it but the man said he knew what to do. I only mention this because this represents a potential threat. My man said he reformatted the hard drive. He assured me that this would eliminate the problem. Will it?"

Darren sat back in the comfortable chair and self-consciously ran his fingers through his wavy brown hair. Looking pensive he replied, "It should. Under most normal circumstances, it definitely would. However, there are better methods than reformatting for removing data."

"What do you mean, 'It should'?"

"Well, when you reformat a computer's disk drive, you don't actually remove the information. Now, this gets a little complicated; do you mind?"

"No, fire away."

"When you save information to the disk, the information is saved as a series of magnetic spots. The information is saved to the disk in mass, but there is another piece of information generated by the computer. This is the location of the information you saved. This piece of information, which essentially contains the address of the data, is saved in something called the file allocation table or FAT. It consists of cylinder number, track numbers, and byte numbers. When you reformat, you don't erase the information, you erase the index in the FAT.

"Now, if someone could get to the computer before more information was saved into the locations freed by the reformatting, it is possible that they could re-institute the FAT and find the information."

"Could just anyone do this?"

"No, it would have to be a person who was fairly aware of the capabilities of the machine. Still, it is not that difficult There are some good commercially available programs which do this."

"If I told you we have a special program which erases files, would that ease the chance of the data being reclaimed?"

"It depends on how it works. The only way to do this for sure is to replace all of the information that was in the computer with other information. Even if they can't re-institute the format, it is theoretically possible to dump the data for examination. This would take a long time, because the data on a core dump contains all of the control characters the computer uses for reference purposes in addition to the data. How did the program work that you used?"

"I haven't the foggiest. Is it all right if I have a copy sent to you? I would appreciate it if you could look at it and give me a report. It has been preying on my mind lately."

"I'm certainly willing to do that. Just send over the program and let me look at it. You don't think our two problems are related, do you?"

"I don't like coincidences. In all probability they are not. It seems to me that our 'problem,' who ceased to be a problem, was also from Michigan. Circumstantial evidence is not the most reliable indicator and can lead to incorrect conclusions. Still, there is the possibility they might be somehow connected. If that is the case, I'm going to need your help."

"You know my staff and I will do whatever we can."

"Darren, there is a slight problem. This is a very private exercise, and I am telling you that you will have to do it alone."

"Can't I even have Joyce Parker? I mean, she is working on it now."

"Joyce Parker? Oh yes, I remember her. She's been with us for a long time, hasn't she?"

"Nearly twelve years. She is absolutely reliable and discreet. Besides, since she already knows of the problem, we don't want to make her too curious by not including her."

"I suppose that would be all right. You'll have to take responsibility for her actions. Is that understood?"

"Yes. Well, I'll let you know what we find out, and I will look at your program as soon as I get it. Was there anything else?"

"No, that about covers it. I will get the program to you as soon as I can. See you tomorrow."

଼ ଼ ଼

Darren left Jonathan's office and headed across the compound to the computer center. His mind was filled with the thoughts of a conspiracy against the Center. 'Why would anyone want to oppose us? Our operations make it possible for this country to function. Without us, there would nothing but chaos. At least we can lend a little order. These people must be insane.'

He passed through the doors, went to his office and buzzed for Joyce. In a moment she appeared, looking amazingly happy for early in the morning. "Darren, we haven't had another try at the computer. I did load in Oracle; that should do it. Why did you want to see me?"

"The problem doesn't appear to be isolated. Another division is aware of it. I have asked Mr. Green to allow you to work with me on the analysis. This exercise must be absolutely discreet. Is that understood?"

"Certainly. If we have another attempt to break in, what do you want me to do?"

"Oracle has a feedback option. I want you to use this to try to wrest control of their machine. If we can establish control from this end, call me. I want to see what is going on."

"Will do."

ଔ ଔ ଔ

Thomas Lanninga reached for the wine bottle and took a long pull. The bottle felt cool in his hand as he set it back on the park's grass. The wine did not have a warming effect, but only seemed to calm the feeling of desperation which haunted his mind these days.

The barrage of thoughts was overwhelming. When the wine lost its effect, these thoughts closed in on him. They were far too clear and rational in nature and upset him greatly. They drew a sharp profile of what he had become: a drunkard, a derelict, a curse on society.

He had possessed so much. Now, it only amounted to a loss, a loss without the decency to give something back. No, there was absolutely nothing gained by his actions. This necessary retreat into the solitude of the bottle seemed to be, at least, an answer.

In a corner of his mind that he visited infrequently now, Thomas knew it wasn't the right answer. But at this point, it was one feeble answer, a way to quiet the devils that stalked him, a means of fighting the inevitable guilt and shame they had piled upon him.

He did not remember purchasing the bottle. In fact, he could not remember ever purchasing one. The bottles appeared each day, as if by magic. In the morning, wherever he was, he would find one at hand. Other times, he stumbled upon them while walking down the street. In one subconscious part of his mind, the small remnant that remained the Reverend Jersey Land, he knew where they came from. But in the cloudy, but conscious portions that dictated his actions, he had no idea.

In a feat of less-than rational thinking, he assumed they were his by some divine right, a reward from the Lord for his many years of faithful service, a token to muffle the awful pain of having failed.

When the bottles first appeared, he gave them away. When his money ran down, he sold them. Now, he regarded them as the wandering Israelites must have received the manna from heaven: a gift, if not exactly from the Lord, to be treasured and used to sustain life—a life which at this point was devoid of meaning.

Still, he was not dead. He was alive. As long as his heart pumped, there was hope. A vague vision of a large wooden chest opening and biting insects, flooding out and stinging him, entered his mind. He raised the bottle to his lips and drank deeply. He set it down again. That thought was beat down, only to be replaced by another: what was the chest? He couldn't remember. He knew it had some significance, but these days insignificance was far more relevant.

He reached for the bottle and swallowed as great a volume as his throat would take at once. Drinking lead inevitably to intoxication, his means to erase the past—no, it was the present he wanted to black out. He did not know what city streets these were. It could have been L.A., Chicago, Atlanta. Where he was didn't seem to matter. His brain, once sharp and responsive, had deteriorated into the nothingness of alcoholism. This soulful mind that once contemplated the meaning of life and humanity's purpose on earth was now only concerned with drinking enough to forget.

He supposed he could find out where he was, somehow. But then again, it didn't matter, for the ground was cold and hard wherever he happened to be.

The bottle made a clink as he placed it down on the grass and it tipped over. Some child had thrown a stone from the park's path into the grass. That stone pushed the bottle into a spill. The wine gurgled into the grass. By the time he realized his life's blood was draining away, it was too late to do anything. He turned over and pulled his coat up to his chin and closed his eyes. He had drunk enough. Today, the devils would be kept down—at least for a while.

Deep in the recesses of his mind he thought he heard an angel singing. He couldn't formulate the words, but the melody was familiar. In his drunken stupor he listened for the voice again, clear and cold as the bell tower of the Lord calling his believers.

The Eighth Street Church organist was calling the parishioners through the carillon. This morning, he chose the simplest hymn: *He Leadeth Me*. Nothing grandiose or pretentious, it was a simple song of salvation.

The words began to form in his mind, as he strained to listen once more. Those words brought tears to his eyes as a child. Those words guided his life until he turned his back on the Lord and took up the mantle of man. They were simple words of faith, struggle, and renewal:

"He leadeth me, O blessed thought!
O words with heavenly comfort fraught!
Whate'er I do, Where'er I be
Still, 'tis his hand that leadeth me.
He leadeth me, He leadeth me,
By his own hand he leadeth me
His faithful follower I would be,
For by his hand he leadeth me."

The vision passed almost unnoticed. Still, a seed was planted, a seed that would spring to life and grow to maturity. The fruit would be the renewed belief that Tommy Lanniga was indeed a servant of the Lord. Somehow, as he was undergoing his trials, he had lost this information.

The only outward sign of this implantation was the tear that, forming in the corner of his bloodshot eye, dribbled down his cheek and finally lay spent in the grass, a transitory diamond in the morning sun.

The carillon began again and the Reverend Jersey Land remembered the words with conviction.

"Lord, I would clasp Thy hand in mine,
Nor ever murmur, nor repine;
Content, whatever lot I see
Since, 'tis my God that leadeth me."

Chapter 17

Dow came down the stairs with a broad smile and said, "Seems the person who reformatted the drive didn't do it quite well enough. I've managed to re-institute the format and am going to get some disks to retrieve the information."

"You can save it?"

"Yes, I have the stuff in the car. I'll be right back. John, I think we might have the means of finding out what is going on. Everything he wrote is still there. It is complete, all of his notes, his correspondence. It is wonderful that people do not really understand computers. If they made even a little effort to find out, it would make my job much more difficult. It seems such a simple thing. I guess it is kind of the way our society's going, that pattern of dismissing the correct way of doing things in favor of the easier one."

Dow returned in a moment with a plastic disk containing a CDR. He passed by John and Louise without speaking and went up the stairway. After a minute or so he returned and said, "Okay, I've got it set. Louise, this is going to take a little time; I hope you don't mind?"

"Ira, take as long as you need."

"Dow, do I need to be here? I should be heading back to the office."

"No, it's going to take a while to duplicate the files. This is a long boring job. Maybe it's the reason that so few people bother. If they only knew the transitory nature of data in a computer, they certainly would take the time to back up more frequently. See you later. After I have finished, I am going to take this stuff back to my house and put it in my computer. That will take me most of the night. Listen, I'll call you in the morning. What time do you figure to be in?"

"Sometime after nine. I don't believe I have anything earlier than that scheduled. I'll expect your call. And Dow, thank you for your help. I really want to know what happened. It's important to me—to all of us really," he added as he looked sympathetically at Louise.

ଔ ଔ ଔ

"Chancellor, Dow called. He asked you to call him back."
"Will you ring him for me, please?"
John removed his coat and placed it in the closet behind the door and moved to his desk. He would be glad when he no longer had to bother with the coat. It always seemed to be an obstruction. Whenever he went anywhere he had to think about what he was going to do with his coat. It was one more consideration in a world too full of things to worry about.
He had just been seated when the intercom light came on and Martha said, "Here he is."
  John picked up the phone. "Dow, what did you find out?"
"It is better than we hoped. There is some startling information on the disk. If I hadn't known Rich so well, I'd think it was the work of a crackpot. But Richard was never anyone's fool."
"What exactly are we talking about?"
"Details, amazing details about some sort of secret organization called the Center for American Heritage."
"Center for American Heritage? Never heard of it. Sounds innocuous enough. What do they have to with anything?"
"Everything. They are the ones. You remember the name, Jersey Land?"
"Vague recollection. Why?"
"They ruined him. Richard has extensive notes of an interview he did with him. Seems he was told what to say and when he didn't do it anymore, they went after him. As nearly as I can tell, they function as an intermediary between the government and the people. They receive no funding from anyone as near as Richard could tell. For years they were content to make suggestions and provide information. It seems in the last few years they have become emboldened. I have it all here. I can bring it over, if you'd like."

"That would be fine. When can you be here?"

"Ten minutes at the most. I'm already on my way out the door."

"See you then."

Chancellor Goslin checked his schedule to determine if he had any meetings scheduled. He did not. Sometimes, it seemed his life was one meeting after another, each a little more monotonous than the one before. Meetings were the ideal place for the pontificators to vent their passion on ultimately meaningless committee decisions.

When he first assumed the job of Chancellor, he studiously prepared for every meeting and took each of them seriously. Now, he had learned to "posture" the sincerity necessary and listen with a bemusement which did little to ease his boredom. All in all, they were still a big part of his job. He knew this and understood his obligations. On occasion he wished they would just send him a memo to let him know what they had decided. But then, that would be abdicating his responsibility, and he had no intention of ever doing that. So, although with reluctance, he attended every meeting he was scheduled to attend.

ଔ ଔ ଔ

Dow collected the papers and left his home for the school. The February sun was just over the horizon and already the icicles on the roof of the house were beginning to melt and drip into small puddles below the eaves. The constant dripping this time of year added a somewhat festive background sound which helped to ease the transition. The sun had risen clear and bright, and his eyes took a moment to adjust. He had been up late last night reading through the material. It was fascinating, even a bit shocking. When he finally calmed himself down with the help of a couple of over-the-counter sleep inducers, just enough to take the edge off, it was nearly 3:00. He carefully set his alarm so he could talk to John in the morning.

As he walked out of the door, still barely awake but full of power and knowledge to share, the man hit him. It was a sudden, sharp blow to his head with something very hard. He saw two pairs of wing-tipped shoes and carefully pressed wool slacks, fitted carefully to touch the top of the shoes in front and extend down the heel in the rear, as he sank into unconsciousness.

Leaving him lying in a pool of blood, they moved into the house and proceeded to take every disk they could find, as well as Dow's computer. They carried it out to the van and placed the material next to the computer they had retrieved from the late Dr. Richard Kline's house earlier. The old lady had not stirred, and the confiscation took place without a hitch.

They rushed to Dr. Jones's house but were dissuaded by his late night hours. They slept a couple of hours in the car before greeting him in the morning.

Using a set of keys one of the men removed from the glove compartment of their car, they moved toward Dow's vehicle. After a few tries, the lock gave and they checked to be certain there were no computer disks or other information-processing paraphernalia. Satisfied, they locked the car, returned to their vehicle and sped away. They didn't give a second glance to the prone professor on the porch. They had done this many times before and knew it would be some time before the man would wake up, if at all. This last possibility never entered their thoughts; if it had, it would have been ignored.

Like good soldiers, they never considered the fate of the enemy. Once you start down the path of consideration for those who oppose you, you can get lost and may never find your way out again.

ଔ ଔ ଔ

Chancellor Goslin took his morning paper and laid it on the desk. He used to read the paper from Detroit but, of late, decided he liked the Chicago paper better. He needed the news in the morning. He had tried the networks' morning shows on television and found them too simplified and cliched for consideration. Experimenting with the other happy talk clones, he began to see remarkable similarities. They shared the same guests, and their news stories were always almost the same, sharing both pictures and text.

Even more curious was the fact that the stories were often broadcast at almost precisely the same moment with little variation in either time or content. The coincidence went way beyond being remarkable, straying into the eerie and bizarre.

He found they all followed the same format and shared more than just their stories in common. The ubiquitous anchor people could have been exchanged with their counterparts on any of the others and it would not have made even the slightest iota of difference. The format was the same: five minutes of news read by a good-looking man or woman, entertaining weatherman, and then after the requisite commercials, a few minutes of interviews with either news generators or news reporters. After this sad swipe at credibility, they often had some actor promoting their latest movie or venture.

The sycophantic anchor people were enough to make him ill as they fawned and genuflected to their guests. On those rare occasions, when they tried to do hard news, they reduced the time spent on the story to such a ridiculously small amount that literally no useful information could be gleaned.

He tried to read more information into what the guests were saying but failed miserably. It was his experience in life that ideas, and even more so problems, require the juxtaposition of more than one viewpoint and careful analysis, as well as substantial time, to yield understanding, let alone set a course for short- and long-term solutions. It just reflected our society and the tenuous nature of information. That which required thought seemed to be discarded in favor of that which required no thought. It was too difficult to think of solving poverty; it was much easier to talk of the latest movie or sports event. Sadly, in the United States at the beginning of the twenty-first century, he wondered if we had turned into a society which can only deal with the physical, eschewing the intellectual.

He would have read the local paper in the morning, but the Mason paper was an afternoon edition. He skimmed the

Chicago paper looking for articles of interest. It was odd, some days he found almost the entire paper interesting. On other days, he found little of interest.

On this particular day, he was through with the first section and had tossed it down onto the pile of advertising circulars. Bending forward to grab the second, he saw a small blurb about Reverend Jersey Land being arrested in Hyde Park on the south side of the city near the University of Chicago.

If it had been anyone else, there never would have been any mention in the paper. As he read the brief article, he thought about this, and something suddenly clicked in his mind. 'Jersey Land was the name that Dow mentioned just a minute ago. What in the world was going on here?'

He gave the article a closer examination. After determining that there was no more information to be gained, he tossed it down again and reflected on what he had read. His mind was filled with many more questions than answers as he went through the motions of reading the rest of the paper.

He turned to the next section and began his inspection of each page. Years ago, he decided that was the problem with television and radio news: you had to listen to everything. In a newspaper, you only read those stories which interest you.

Somehow, having all of the news that you wouldn't take the time to read forced upon you seemed a terrible effrontery. What gave them the right to choose what you would learn about? Why did they have a hand in your decision as to what to ignore? Did anyone elect them? Does anyone even supervise their activities? Sometimes he found their reporting to be so unfair and biased that his brain screamed out against the travesty.

Frequently, some politician would carp against the liberal or the conservative press when, in fact, that was not the problem. The problem was that the people who were putting out the news seemed to have another agenda. He instinctively knew this to be true, but did not fully understand what it was.

Questions of perception haunted him daily because he suspected he knew the answers, and his suspicions were very unsettling. It was as if the American people had ignored their duties as citizens. The void in thinking had been filled by a mindless recitation of meaningless, innocuous information. Little of that information could be classified as either news reporting or news making, for these activities contributed nothing to the conscious understanding of the public.

Now, the American people could be led as if there were a leash connected to the collar of servitude worn conspicuously and proudly about their necks. A collar they could remove, but would never think of doing so. A collar showing their allegiance to the presumed majority. A collar which also had the effect of deigning them as non-entities in a world of non-descript manipulators.

Finished with the paper, he placed it in the recycling and checked his watch. It was fully thirty minutes after the time when Dow said he would be here. A dram of worry crept into his consciousness. 'What had happened to him?' He pressed the intercom button and asked, "Martha, did you hear from Dow?"

"Not a word. I thought he was coming right over?"

"That was the plan. Listen, I tried calling his house but there was no answer. I think I'll drive over and see what's happening. I'm a little concerned. It is not like him to miss an appointment, especially one that he made."

Climbing into his still-warm car, John headed to the house that Dow had inhabited for nearly twenty years. The street was not busy, particularly at this time of the day. It was nearly 10:00 A.M. Most residents are where they are supposed to be for either work or school. The fact that Dr. Jones' street was a cul-de-sac minimized traffic even further.

When John finally turned his car off in front of Dow's, he had not passed another car or seen any evidence of people moving about.

As he rounded the car and stepped on the curb, he saw what appeared to be a crumpled blanket on the porch of Dow's house. As he moved closer, he suddenly realized it was Dow.

He ran up the steps and placed his fingers on the carotid artery to be certain he was alive. Thank God, there was a pulse! Rushing inside, he found the phone and dialed 9-1-1. He was so intensely focused on Dow's condition and the urgent need to get medical help on the way that he didn't even notice that the house was in a state of disarray.

After giving the requisite information to the operator, he moved to the porch and took off his coat to cover his friend and help keep the morning chill away.

The ambulance rounded the corner in a matter of anxious moments. They carefully placed a board under Dr. Jones' back and strapped him in tightly. They were certain to use a neck brace for they had no way of knowing the extent of his injuries. John followed the ambulance to the hospital and parked in the visitor's lot. He carefully locked his car and rushed into the emergency room.

For the second time in the span of forty-eight hours he was back at the hospital's ER department. This did not sit well with him. He tried to think about the last time he had been here, and was unable.

There was a definite motion swirling about his campus. Something was happening. Although he did not yet know the nature of the threat, he was certain that it existed. The proof was that one of his best friends was dead and would be buried in the morning. Another colleague and friend had just been admitted to the hospital in a very serious condition. John had never been more frightened in either his personal or academic life.

Chapter 18

Chancellor Goslin sat pensively in the waiting room of the hospital for a few minutes before realizing he had not called either Martha or his wife about Dow's condition. It simply had not occurred to him. After finding Dow on the porch in a pool of blood, his mind tumbled out of control.

He was by nature a studious man who found himself suddenly thrust into an unfamiliar world. This world, where actions occurred so quickly and with such frightening results was not one of his choosing. He preferred the academic environment where changes were implemented methodically and then only after careful consideration.

He felt as though everything was moving too damned fast. As hard as he tried, he was having a difficult time adjusting his mind to this new and different standard. All of his life he had judged things by looking back into his training.

Now, he had nothing with which to compare the incidents of the last few days, no reservoir of experience from which to draw. He was wandering a dusty, unfamiliar road without markings. His travel surely had purpose—to arrive at the "answer." But when he came upon the answer, would he even recognize it, and then what?

These jarring episodes left him clinging psychologically to the arms of the waiting room chair to ground his emotions and take stock of his responsibilities. After relaying the news of Dow's condition, he returned and picked up a week-old news magazine. He distracted himself by looking through a periodical for something of interest, but failed to find anything of substance, just more fluff pieces on various celebrities. The thought that we had degenerated into a nation of watchers rather than participants entered his mind. Unable to focus on that, he dismissed it as being irrelevant right now and closed his eyes.

Oddly, in the midst of ER waiting room commotion, sleep

found him. The next thing he remembered was his arm being gently shaken by his wife Diane. "C'mon honey, it's time to wake up."

"What? Where? Huh? Oh, Diane, how is Dow?" he asked groggily as he pulled himself back to consciousness.

"The doctors aren't sure. He's in a coma. They've called in an expert. It's too early to tell if he'll recover. They don't think he's in any immediate danger, but the prognosis is uncertain..."

Her tears started to fall. John stood up and held her close. Through the muffled emotions he heard her say, "John, what is going on here?"

He embraced her tightly, attempting to impart some of his presumed strength and whispered, "I don't know. But I'm going to find out."

Out of the corner of his eye he saw Detective Johnson arrive and motion for John to join him. He hugged his wife for a minute more and then helped her to the same chair that had given him strange comfort.

After the frenzied rush to the hospital a weakness took hold of her, as she slipped into the seat and fumbled in her purse for tissue. Reluctant to leave, John said, "Diane, I'm sorry. I need to talk to the police. I'll be back in just a moment. Are you going to be all right?"

"Just give me a couple of minutes. It's just that I feel we've been invaded. I'm frightened. What if you're next?"

"I won't be," he said without conviction, for that possibility had already entered his mind. He gave her arm a squeeze and walked across the waiting room.

"Chancellor Goslin, good to see you again," Detective Johnson said as he extended his hand. John shook his hand solemnly. "Yes. I only wish the circumstances were better. Dr. Jones is in a coma, and they are not certain of his recovery. What have you found out about this incident?"

"Nothing. No one saw anything. No one heard anything. It's as if it didn't happen. There is, however, one piece of information that you are not aware of. Richard Kline's house was burglarized last night and a computer was stolen."

"Was Louise hurt?" Anger flashed in his eyes.

"No, she wasn't even aware that anything had happened until this morning. She went to close the door on the upstairs room this morning and noticed the computer was gone. She called us immediately. We responded and are checking the house for signs of forced entry or fingerprints. I am not optimistic. It seems like the same type of entry that occurred at the Administration Building. As a matter of fact, it is so much like the other incident it is eerie. If your watchman had not been assaulted, we would have never known that someone had been there. Are you people at the college involved in some sort of activity that I should know about?" he asked with a look of concern in his eyes.

"You've accepted Mr. Kelly's story?"

"No doubt about it. We have an affidavit from the emergency room physician, indicating someone forced him to breathe noxious fumes, probably ether."

"I hope Mr. Kelly is going to recover. In answer to your question, no, I do not believe we are involved in anything of a nefarious nature. Now, two of my friends are either dead or nearly dead. I want to know the reason why. How can a respected man be assaulted at his own house at 9:00 in the morning and not even have one witness? Why would he be assaulted anyway?"

"Chancellor, I'd like to give you an answer, but I don't have one. We're sparing no resources in the investigation of these incidents. I'd like to plan a time when we can talk."

"That might be beneficial. Can you call me at my office? I'll check my schedule."

"Certainly. By the way, how did you happen to go there?"

"I didn't just happen to go there. Dow called my office earlier and said he would be arriving in about ten minutes. When that time stretched to more than half an hour I naturally became concerned. After calling his house but getting no answer, I decided to drive over to see what the problem was. I can't explain it, I just had a feeling that something was wrong. Dow is very responsible. The fact that he missed an appointment he himself made led me to believe that something was amiss. When I arrived, I found him on the porch."

"Did you call it in immediately?"

"As soon as I realized Dow was down. The door to his house was open, and I dialed the emergency operator after checking him over. I waited outside until the ambulance arrived. I followed them here and have been here ever since."

"Well, that about ties it up for now. I'll call you later to set up an appointment."

"Understood, although I am not sure I can give you any more information. As far as I know, the only time I'll be busy will be tomorrow for the funeral. After that I believe my schedule is relatively open. Normal university activities have shut down."

"Of course, the funeral—I'll call after lunch."

The men shook hands again and separated, John to comfort his wife and Detective Johnson to complete the paperwork. John sat next to Diane and put his arm around her shoulder and tried to calm both her and the rampant thoughts plaguing his mind.

John considered that they had taken the computer from Richard's house and had also taken the computer from Dow's. With the information about the Center for American Heritage contained on both machines, what did that leave them? Not much. A vague reference to some group and their activities and an equally obscure reference to a former television preacher. Just not enough to go on. His mind strained for understanding. It was all beyond his grasp.

A nondescript nurse in white interrupted his thoughts as she came over to inform him that Dr. Jones was being sent to surgery within the hour. "They believe there may be an occlusion forming. They have to try to relieve the pressure to ward off the risk of brain damage." The words were nearly meaningless. All that mattered was that, in addition to his grave condition, Dow would now have to undergo surgery.

John felt strength ebbing from his body. Slumping deeper into his chair, he closed his eyes. 'None of this was necessary. Why are we caught in this whirlwind of illegal activities? It just didn't make sense.' Everything he had ever believed was suddenly hurled into question.

'Why would anyone be concerned with what a few old dusty university professors were doing? What was going on that required such actions, apparently by this previously unknown group? How can we set things right so that no more people get hurt?' The questions came and left without answers, leaving him numb in their wake.

ೞ   ೞ   ೞ

Jonathan Green reported to his superiors: the computer that had been reformatted might not have been erased as well as they would have liked. His superior, Judge Patrick Conley, noted this information and called an internal number that only a few who worked for the company knew. He made his report succinctly and clearly. Almost before he hung up the phone, the problem had been addressed. The action did not require even a momentary hesitation. The path was clear and the fact that the Center had people who specialized in such things made it even easier.

The order was given to confiscate the machines in question and to destroy them. At this moment, both computers were lying at the bottom of Lake Michigan. The agents had taken their car to a nearby public fishing pier and in a matter of minutes the computers were unceremoniously dumped through the remnants of winter ice and into the deep water. No one would ever read the information on these machines again. There would be no more incursions by computer or other methods.

When the agents reported it had been necessary to assault Dr. Jones, it was dismissed as no more important than if they had hit a dog driving into work that day.

Certainly, something to be avoided, but hardly noteworthy. Just in case, it was decided that the professor's condition would be monitored in the event further action was warranted.

ೞ   ೞ   ೞ

Darren Myers waited for another attempt to break into the computer. It never came. He was disappointed, as he was prepared and confident that he could pinpoint the location. Joyce monitored the computer while he was at his meeting with Jonathan Green. When he returned, he relieved her so she could take a break. Nothing happened. While he was waiting, a courier brought the reformat program from Mr. Green. He examined it carefully. It was a standard program using the DOS command. This was the program that did not replace the data but merely removed the index from the file allocation tables. He made a note of it and returned to his office to call his superior.

After dialing and waiting just a moment he was connected. "Jonathan, I don't think that program would work very well."

"Why not?"

"It is not much different from the standard DOS reformat program. Again, it doesn't erase the information. It just eliminates the directory of where the information is stored. There is another command which is essentially an UNFORMAT program that can restore the lost information."

"If this ever comes up again, is there something we can do?"

"Absolutely. We can just buy an off-the-shelf cleaning program. With people wanting their privacy, there are a bunch of them available. All probably as good as we could do—and a lot cheaper."

"When you order the program, get a network license as well. Without disclosing too much, I can say the immediate problem has been taken care of. You shouldn't be bothered again."

Darren knew better than to ask how he knew that. And the fact of the matter was that he had expected another try at the computer and it had not happened. Sometimes, he felt as though he were just a small cog in a complex machine whose purpose he did not even begin to comprehend.

Though it would have seemed a natural area for investigation, he never bothered doing so. The Center provided him with a good job. Their purpose was to be helpful to the people. He did not see any reason for causing problems. Still, deep in the recesses of his mind there were questions—questions pointing to activities Darren suspected may not be in their charter. Still, he suppressed these feelings and continued doing his job.

☙ ☙ ☙

Jonathan Green smiled to himself as he hung up the phone. No, there would be no further problems. He continued to work on the paper he had been drawn away from by Darren's call. It was another in a series of standards and practices papers his office had written.

This particular piece would be delivered to the television networks. It would have the areas delineated that were not acceptable for commercial advertising. The paper itself was nearly forty pages of single-spaced type. Not that it had been written at one time. No, this document had been under development for decades.

When application was made for the first licenses, the Center decided that they would have a say in the information that was broadcast. At that time it was a relatively simple matter to instruct the new owners of these stations about the nature of the information standards, both content and presentation, to be distributed in this country. Since they had established themselves as a beneficial entity, the precedent had been set for them to continue.

While reviewing the document, the thought was with him that it was his task to make certain that the Center's focus and message remained in the forefront of the American people. It was a complicated paper which stated clearly and explicitly which types of advertising would not be allowed. The substance of the report was in two sections: that which would be prohibited and that which was acceptable. He was nearly finished updating the smaller of the two and would move on to the kind of advertising that would be allowed.

He knew his job was important and he had to follow confidential internal Center guidelines which gave him the direction he needed. At this time they were very concerned with making certain no minority group would be offended by anything on television. There were many aspects to this document. Some had to do with minority relations, some with stereotyping, such as which stereotypes would be allowed, which had served their usefulness and had to be discarded. The examples of discarded stereotypes were legion.

Everywhere a person looked, their vestiges remained. Italians ate spaghetti. Poles danced the polka. Asians ran dry-cleaning stores. Black men sat on the corner drinking. Black women had babies in their arms. White women looked as if they dropped off the cover of a beauty magazine. White men wore suits to work. Black kids played basketball. White kids played the piano. On and on, one after another the cliches and stereotypes wove their way innocuously through American society. The Center had been the perpetrator of many.

Jonathan knew that there was a division whose sole function was to invent new stereotypes. The methods of creation were easier now than they had been. They had nearly 200 years of history to help them. Now, it was just a question of honing what was already there. They simply took public perceptions and reinforced them. It was a subtle task, but in the end it was very effective.

If the only commercials allowed for minority viewing featured stereotypes, then those stereotypes would be reinforced until the people themselves internalized them. Even though, in the end, these stereotypical presentations were no more accurate than blind guesses, they had the effect of becoming credible and real.

Everyone wanted to be part of a group; it gave people an identity, a feeling of belonging even when stereotypes were negative. The Center, by emphasizing these traits, managed to perpetuate such feelings. The reasons for doing so were darker and more sinister, but Jonathan Green was not aware of these. The rationale and justifications had been forged up the ladder. He had no need to be privy to underlying explanations and strategies.

It was Jonathan's job to make certain his superior's goals were implemented and guidelines were followed. He was very good at his job, and the messages he created would be clear and reflect the mindset of his employer.

Chapter 19

Janna pulled the down comforter over her head in an attempt to block the morning sun's rays from her eyes. Although she'd been awake for a while, she had not bothered getting out of bed. She was enjoying her time in that pleasant world between the evening's slumber and the morning's wakefulness.

It felt so good to cuddle under the warm comforter that she saw no need to get going. She knew it must be getting warm outside because she could hear the sound of the snow melting off the roof. On this Friday morning she was fascinated, as she always was, by the sound of the ice breaking up on the lake.

When it begins to warm in the north, the ice break-up is a physical sensation, as well as a seasonal one. Lying in bed, she heard the ice cracking. In the cold and stillness of the deep forest, the sounds echoed like rifle shots.

Although these sounds were infrequent, the very act of listening for them helped her to clear her mind. She kept thinking about the incident at school. There just had to be something she was missing. Too often for comfort, her thoughts were drawn to the lecture hall.

She attempted to remember every detail of that day—the clothes she wore, what she had for breakfast, turning on the tape recorder, the professor's demeanor—in short, anything that could have remote bearing on the event. She saw and felt the texture of the day in her mind, the nuances of each picture frame before and after that horrible happening. It was like her subconscious was telling her there was something more, something she had missed. But whenever she got close, it danced darkly off into the distance. 'What was it?'

She just didn't know. She just kept replaying the incident in her mind, attempting to discover some small piece of information she had overlooked or repressed. Reluctantly, she pulled the covers back and felt the rush of cold air as it rushed to quell the warmth. She shivered and reached for the heavy robe on a chair near her bed.

Generally speaking, bedrooms of the North are not treated with the same deference as other rooms in the house. It is like the human body: when our bodies get cold, our blood supply shuts down the extremities and concentrates on keeping the head and chest warm. In the house, bedrooms are treated as extremities and nearly neglected by the heater in favor of the main living rooms. She remembered some mornings seeing her breath as she got out of bed.

She snugged the terry cloth robe up tightly and headed to the kitchen, her feet moving in an odd shuffle Northerners use to keep their feet from being on the floor too long. It is about the same motion that people from the South use on hot sand.

As she left her room, the smell of freshly baked cinnamon rolls assaulted her nostrils and she began to salivate. Her mother was up early. The aroma of fresh rolls baking was enticing, and she instinctively associated it with her mother.

She sat at the table and looked across the lake. Here and there, water birds landed near the shore. There were ducks of all varieties, Canada Geese, and although she couldn't see them, she could hear the loons. Farther off a couple of forlorn fishing shanties bravely battled the spring thaw—their roof lines taking on a decided angle as one side sunk a little deeper into the ice.

She thought about them for a moment and remembered that some people just let the little houses sink in the water and then retrieve them with their boats when the waterway is clear. Her mother poured her a cup of coffee and placed the pan of rolls within easy reach.

Janna smiled and said, "Thank you. It's the one thing I really miss about home. It is silly, but in the dorm we have to walk downstairs to eat. Nothing seems to have the smell of good food cooking. It all seems so packaged for lack of a better term."

"Well, you eat as many as you would like. I didn't mean to wake you. I know your father and you were arguing all night about what that tape means. I figured you both could use the rest."

"We weren't arguing, Mother. We were discussing. I thought we did a pretty good job of keeping the noise down. How did you hear us?"

"Mothers have their ways. Oh, Janna, I am so glad you are home. I've missed you terribly. It's lonely without you."

Janna reached her hand across the table and gently pressed her mother's hand. She smiled softly and resumed eating. After a moment she asked, "Where's Daddy?"

"He walked to the corner to get a newspaper. He should be back in a minute. Can I get you another cup of coffee?"

"No, I'm fine."

Janus Joseph entered the house at that moment and immediately headed for the kitchen and those rolls. "Janus, you get out there and take those boots off; look what you're doing to my floor."

He smiled and headed to the door with roll in hand. He removed his boots and still chewing heartily, got a cup, filled it with coffee and sat down. "Morning, Janna, did you sleep well last night?"

"Fine. It is an amazing transition from the noise of the dorm to the stillness and quiet of the lake. It took me a little while to go to sleep, probably because of the lack of noise. It looks to be a beautiful day outside. Is it warm?"

"Mid-forties, I'd guess. The snow is starting to melt pretty well. Did you hear the ice?"

Janna nodded and continued eating. Her father was studying the paper. After a moment he hesitantly said, "Do you know a Dr. Ira Jones?"

"Dow? Yes. Why?"

"He was assaulted at his house yesterday. He's in the hospital and in critical condition."

"What! He's my computer teacher. I really like him. Let me see the paper."

Janus handed it to her. She read the article repeatedly, searching for information. When there was no more to be gleaned from the meager account, she handed the paper to her father with a look of intent concentration in her eyes.

After a moment she said, "You know, Daddy, that kind of plays into your theory about some sort of conspiracy. Dr.

Jones is the campus computer expert. If any of this has to do with computers, he would be the logical one to have had a hand in it. Now, he has been assaulted."

Janus looked away from his daughter and stared over the water. After an awkward moment he said, "Janna, have you ever tried listening to your tape over the headphones?"

"No, why?"

"Maybe the isolation that comes from the completeness of dedicated sound would help. I've been thinking about what you said about missing something. The mind is a funny thing. Sometimes, we can remember things that happened a long time ago as if they happened yesterday. Other times, those things which are closest to us are lost. It is like having a word on the tip of your tongue. The more you want to remember it, the further it gets from you. Maybe you are too close to the problem. Or, perhaps you are not close enough.

"There are two ways to solve the reluctant memory experience. The first is by going on to a completely different activity, the second is by immersing yourself in the area where you know the answer will be found. We have been up here for a while now, and the answer has not come to you. Perhaps, it is time to try the other method."

"Maybe you're right. I'll try it right after I eat."

The bright sun shining on the vestiges of the white snow created an overload of light. Janna averted her eyes from the window and concentrated on her coffee.

03 03 03

Kara Morrisy reported for her usual shift at the hospital. She was a supervising nurse in the Critical Care Unit. She had just checked the charts of her patients and determined that the other personnel were present when the phone rang. "Hello, CCU. Kara Morrisy speaking."

"Kara, this is Kira."

"How ya' doing, Twin?"

"Pretty well. Listen, Sis, do you have a patient named Dr. Ira Jones there?"

"Yeah, he's here. What did he do that the local news

people are interested?"

"Nothing much. I just want you to keep me informed of his condition. Or rather, any change in his condition. My sources tell me that he is comatose."

"That's right. I guess—I can give you a call."

"'Preciate it. Listen, I don't want you to get in trouble, are you sure it's okay?"

"Shouldn't be a problem. I don't know what I can do beyond that. I'm not about to sneak you in."

"Understood. Just let me know. I'll see you at Mom's later. Bye."

മ   മ   മ

Janna walked to the stereo and plugged in the headphones. Since the tape was still in the machine, she rewound it. Listening intently as the familiar words rang out, the earphones brought the experience to her with much greater clarity. She reached for the volume dial and tentatively turned it up. The sound was deafening, but she ignored the speaker and concentrated on the background noise.

She listened closely. Even the many times of repeatedly listening to the tape had not acquainted her with the activities taking place in the room at the same. She was amazed by the prevalent sounds of shuffling feet, pens clicking in and out, student movements. Then she heard the words. She never would have heard them without the earphones. But with them blasting the sound out, she heard the malevolent voice saying, "C'mon old man. Do it!"

That was all. A simple message speaking volumes. Someone knew he was going to do it, and they were anticipating the action which had surprised everyone else. "C'mon old man. Do it!" The tape ended and she reached for the rewind button waiting anxiously for the tape to find its beginning. It seemed imperative to listen again. She listened and the words were there a second time. Suddenly, the memory flooded back to her.

She had been nearly late for the lecture and had taken a seat in the back. An older man in a suit was sitting next to an empty seat. He didn't look much like a student, and she had to excuse herself as she shuffled by. He had a notebook, but was not taking notes in the traditional sense. Instead it seemed to be some sort of form he was completing. He was writing in shorthand. She remembered thinking that if she knew shorthand, she could dispense with the tape recorder.

She took the earphones off. With her face ashen and sullen she said, "Dad, I think you ought to listen to this."

He crossed the room to the stereo and adjusted the headphones as he placed them in position. Janna left the volume dial alone and watched as her father listened to the tape. After a moment or so, he rewound it and listened again. He removed the headphones and looked at her and said, "Did you hear that?"

"The man saying to 'do it'?"

"Yes, I did. I remember the man now." She went on to explain the circumstances of her arrival. He listened to her and when she finished he said, "You know we should tell someone about this, don't you?"

"I suppose. But who are we going to tell?"

"Probably the police. But I'm not sure of the procedure. I think we should take it to the campus security and see what they say to do with it. It's about 10:00 and we can be there in a little over two hours. Do you want to go?"

"Yes, I think it would be best."

ଓ   ଓ   ଓ

John and Diane Goslin went to their car after the funeral reception and drove home without speaking. There really was nothing to say. At this point of their lives, they knew the inevitable was coming. Richard had been a friend for years. It was very painful to part with him on such terms.

Actually, if they had considered it, it was hard to part with friends on any terms. The service was moving, and Reverend Taylor did a remarkable job of conducting the ceremony with dignity and hope. The problem was, the day had been dedicated to an activity no one would have elected. It was forced upon them all, as death always is. But this death was personally violent, unthinkable, unforeseen! And now, the unwelcome activity was over.

This still left the better part of the day to deal with—the emptiness and desolation of the funeral closed in on them. It all seemed so pointless. 'Why did Richard do it? What could have possibly been in his mind at that moment?'

John knew that everyone has stared inside of themselves and found that bit of blackness we cannot seem to eradicate. Still, most of us manage to live with it. It is a part of our being. If we cannot handle the frustrations of daily living, the area can become so large as to overcome us. But there are signs. Nothing can happen without at some level our knowing the nature of the problem.

John thought about the stages of life as he drove down the narrow street. When first married, there are many other weddings to attend. When your friends start having children, there are showers and parties. The action tames down until you begin the circuit of high school graduations. Then the friends' children get married, and on and on. The last group, ritual function that your friends and you will ever do together is the funeral circuit.

When John was younger, they followed the wedding ceremonies so often that they could anticipate the words the minister would say. Now, at the beginning of the dance of death, they were just beginning to learn the tune. A tune they would know all too well before they took their place at the dais to pass from this earth.

It is a time of consideration, a time when most of us question beliefs with a quiet hope that springs eternal, even in the trail of a lifetime of doubt and brittle faith. An existential "maybe" hovers around the finality of death. Perhaps there may indeed be an escape, a way to keep on living in some other form, an unseen path into an unknown future.

Hope can cloud our vision, but faith has a way of making that hope seem palpable and real. It is a presumed reality for a future where we will greet friends and family on the other side. Human consciousness has always harbored the belief that there has to be something more to life than this vale of tears we tread each day, this strange compilation of wildly opposite experiences of, and responses to, life.

They arrived at their house and Diane went in. With a heavy sense of loss and moist creases around his eyes, John returned to the office. He had set up an appointment with the detective, and he decided to disclose everything he knew of the situation. It is one thing to play with a puzzle, quite another when the puzzle turns out to be dangerous and deadly.

Even in his present state of paranoia, he failed to notice the other car mimicking his own car's movements. Oblivious to the other vehicle, he parked his car and walked slowly inside. He felt as though the world had fallen upon his shoulders. It was a feeling of dread and utter discomfort, a weight pressing down, attempting to force him into the ground.

Martha arrived before him and was on the phone when he walked in. He stepped quietly around her desk, removed his coat and sat. Stupefied was the best word that he could think of to describe his position. He sat there while his mind did mental gymnastics around the events of the three days since the precipitous incident had happened. 'Only three days!' It certainly seemed like he had been living this nightmare for much longer.

The intercom on the phone buzzed and he picked up the receiver. "John, Dow is doing a little better. He is still in a coma, but his vital signs are stable, and the doctors seem to have some optimism. They anticipate it could be another forty-eight hours until there is any change. In that time, things could get better."

"Thank you for that news, Martha. I certainly hope things improve. We could all use a dose of good news. You can take the rest of the day off. I have an appointment with Detective Johnson in a few minutes, then I'm going home. Thanks for coming back. You know how much I appreciate your help."

"That's okay, I'll wait until the detective gets here before I leave. Is there anything else you need?"

"Nothing comes to mind."

Chapter 20

Janus pulled the car into a fifteen-minute parking place, and they walked to the campus security office. Lately, the more he was with his daughter, the more he realized how much she had matured in the last five months. It wasn't so much a physical change, for she had always been a beautiful, capable girl.

No, the change was in attitude. She had nearly completed that final step from being a child to an adult. He marveled at the fact that it seemed like only a few years ago when she sat on his lap and begged him to read a story, "just one more time."

It is a wonderfully difficult time for parents to realize that their children are almost grown and soon, they will no longer need the kind of advice and guidance they have always offered. It is an age-old process of growth in the human species. Babies are helpless and need their parents to live. As a child grows, the need for the parent diminishes. Janus had considered the final step, when roles are reversed and parents need the children for various forms of support, completing the cycle. He knew that at some point they would need Janna to help them, and just the thought of it felt odd. Still, until now he had not given much thought to the stage of the parents' adult relationship with grown children. That mystery was beginning to unfold before his eyes. It suddenly seemed like a gift.

ଔ ଔ ଔ

Janna had only seen the sign to the campus security office, but she never had a reason for entering the offices. They were located in the back of the Administration Building with the only access being from the rear facing the grove.

The campus police force consisted of a group of five: two

male officers and three female. Their primary function was to serve as a liaison between campus activities, student activities and the local police. Anything of a criminal nature was handled initially by the campus security but almost invariably was turned over to the community police for investigation and prosecution.

This was true because they had less statutory authority than the regular police. Though they had limited authority, it was usually enough. When Professor Kline took his own life on Tuesday, they secured the area and arranged for the students to be interviewed by the police.

The department was run by Jim Davis, a retired police officer who enjoyed his job. The mostly part-time staff looked up to him, as most people did—he was 6'10". Big Jim enjoyed this transitional phase between his career as a Sergeant of Detectives in Chicago and what would soon be his retirement. He didn't need the money; if he hadn't enjoyed the job, he never would have taken it. But he did enjoy keeping a hand in law enforcement, as well as the opportunity to interact with young people.

He first heard of the job when he was spending time at his summer home near South Haven. He purchased the property when he was in his thirties. He and his wife had made many improvements over the years until it had become more than a summer cottage; it was now a home.

After leaving the large urban police force, they moved there permanently. He casually wrote a letter of inquiry to the university and it snowballed from there. The chancellor wrote back and asked him to come in for a talk. The two hit it off, and Big Jim was named head of campus security.

It was a way for he and his wife to spend the days between when he had completed his minimum time in Chicago and the point when full retirement would take effect. They enjoyed the security and friendliness of the small university town of Mason and intended to stay in the area.

After a lifetime of dealing with the hardened criminal element, it was refreshing to deal with people whose main offenses consisted of getting a little too drunk or partying a little too boisterously. Even in this modern day, there was not a lot of drug activity on campus. The students here were too smart to indulge in such destructive behavior.

Although there were many reasons, the lack of proximity to a large city likely helped. In any case, he enjoyed the fact that there was so little sinister activity. Certainly, there was the occasional report of pot-smoking. Big Jim investigated these personally.

When he found evidence, he made sure it would never happen again. He dealt with each case severely, and if, in his opinion, the parents had to be notified, he did so without remorse. In his opinion, it was a lot better to have a kid mad at him than in trouble with the law. There usually was no repeat offense. If there was, he turned the case over to the police without hesitation. Everyone is allowed one mistake; two is one too many.

In his seven years of campus work, he had only turned nine cases over to the local police. Even with his taking the liberty of giving chances, Harmson University was a model for other universities to emulate. That was the way Big Jim liked it.

Big Jim leaned back in his chair and watched the sunshine splash on the Oak Grove. Here and there groups of students passed each other with only a nod of their heads to acknowledge each other's presence. It was the tentative nod of those who are unsure of themselves, but pretending not to be. The campus had been remarkably quiet since last Tuesday. Jim figured it would be Sunday before the activity began to pick up again. Many of the students decided to go home for the long unplanned weekend. The main reason was that when the students no longer had class to occupy their attentions, they began to spend money, and most were probably broke. He leaned back in the chair and closed one eye.

Janus walked to the door and read the legend that said, "KNOCK THEN ENTER." In the outer office was an empty desk and chair. As they passed the threshold of the outer office, Big Jim rose to greet them. He moved quickly out of his office and down the hallway, casually flicking out a massive hand to turn on the lights.

"Can I help you?"

"Yes, I am Janus Joseph. My daughter Janna is a student at the university. She was in Dr. Kline's class."

"Terrible thing. I am sorry, Miss. What can I do for you?"

"Janna taped the lecture. We have discovered that someone in the audience knew what was going to happen."

Big Jim shook his head to help clear the cobwebs away and said, "What did you say?"

"I said, we have evidence that someone in the audience knew what was going to happen."

"Did you bring the tape with you?"

"Yes, I have it right here."

"May I see it?"

Janus handed the tape to him and watched the large man rummage in a closet for a tape player. After several minutes he found one and slipped the tape into the machine. Before he could push the play button, Janus said, "You can only hear it by turning the tape extremely loud and listening with earphones."

"Is that so? Well, I don't think I have any. Do you mind if I just listen? However, it would be helpful if you could point out the place where you think you hear this person."

"I didn't say, 'I think I hear.' I said 'I hear.'" There was frustration in Janus' tone. The large man did not seem to be very competent, and Janus did not want to waste his time. "Well, anyway, go ahead; I will point it out to you."

The tape hissed as Big Jim turned the volume up as high as it would go. When the point where the man was mumbling under his breath neared, Janus raised his finger in the air; when the words were played, he pointed at the machine. Big Jim listened intently. Janus, because he knew they were there, could hear the words quite clearly. He did not harbor much hope that the security officer would. He was wrong.

Big Jim, who had spent a good deal of his professional life listening to wiretaps in Chicago, could hear the words much more clearly than Janus. It was a certain ability to shut the world out and concentrate on the murky sound. A way to look beyond the reflective surface of the water and penetrate to the depths.

He pressed the stop button and went to the desk and sat. 'What should he do with this tape?' It was a problem. The university had already been dragged through the mud on this case. Any further complication was sure to have negative effects for all involved. He thought about it for a moment.

"Mr. Joseph, I can hear what you described perfectly well. The question is: What do we do with it?"

"We should turn it over to the authorities."

"Sure, that's easy enough. But I can't turn this over without authorization. I suppose you could, but why don't we see if that authorization can be found? I'd like us to work together on this if possible."

"Sounds okay. Whom do you think you should call?"

"Most of the staff are gone for the weekend. I thought I saw Chancellor Goslin's car. I'll give him a call. If we need authorization, he's certainly capable of giving it."

He picked up the phone and pressed the key for the operator. The campus operator answered immediately, and he asked to be put through to the Chancellor's office. Martha picked up the phone and listened to the campus chief's explanation that there had been a development in the case. She placed him on hold and pressed the intercom button. John answered, "Yes, Martha, I thought you were leaving."

"I will as soon as the detective gets here. You trying to get rid of me?" she said with just a hint of coquettishness in her voice.

"Of course not. I just wanted you to have some time, too. Well, anyway, what can I help you with?"

"I have Jim Davis on the phone. He's with a parent who brought in a tape made last Tuesday in Dr. Kline's philosophy class. He seems to think it's important enough for you to be briefed as soon as possible. You'll want to speak to him, won't you?"

"Yes, no...wait. I have a better idea, Why don't you have them come over to my office now? I'd like to hear the tape. Detective Johnson should be here in a matter of moments. I'm sure it will be of interest to him also."

Passage from the basement to the first floor was made by a connecting hallway and stairs. Janus observed that the building was old. It had been some time since the methods used for its construction were in vogue. He didn't know the exact age, but it appeared to have been built around the turn of the century. The rough mortar and the general age of the bricks, coupled with the obvious discrepancies in the size of the bricks gave an indication of that era. Now, bricks are manufactured to exact specifications; they used to be made to a more general standard. Today, the differences between them had been reduced to less than 1/16 of an inch. Before the turn of the century a variation as great as 1/4 of an inch was tolerated.

When they arrived at the office, they were immediately ushered in by Martha and shown to chairs around a large conference table. Janna took a seat next to her father and Big Jim sat across the table from them. Jim Davis plugged in the tape player and rewound the tape.

"Mr. Joseph says that it is much clearer if you use headphones to listen. I don't have any. But I can say that I have listened to a lot of wiretaps, and you become quite adept at listening to the conversations which occur in the background. You do this out of necessity. It is very rare that your primary source of information speaks clearly enough for you to hear. Well, that's another subject. Anyway, what he says he heard, I can verify with absolute certainty."

He pressed the play button and the noise of the tape filled the room. Jim kept his finger near the pause button, and when the tape came near the place where the incriminating words were located, he stopped it. The sudden silence was shocking as the area which had been filled with sound was suddenly as still as a mausoleum, "This is the portion we are referring to. It helps to try to let the louder voices pass you by and listen only for the background. It is like a magician's trick. If you spend your time watching what he wants you to watch instead of what he doesn't want you to see, you will never understand the trick. The same here; if you spend your time listening to the speaker, you will forget what you are trying to hear."

He pushed the button and the tape resumed. The words became more clear on every pass through the machine. It was like the spots on motion pictures that tell the projectionist to be ready to change reels. Once you know they are there, you see them every time. If you don't know they are there, you don't notice them.

John closed his eyes and tried to calm himself. It had been very difficult to listen to his friend's last words. Still, at the point where the officer said they would be, the words were there. This certainly shed a new light on the event. It was a suicide that had been coerced. A coerced suicide is simply murder.

Silence filled the room. John felt he should say something, but was not sure what to say. 'What could he tell these people?' If he had information to share, it would be one thing. He did not. He was simply stunned.

The seconds ticked off before he cleared his throat and said, "Detective Johnson of the Mason Police will be arriving in a few moments. I would like you to wait and play him the tape. I don't know what to do other than that. In this staid old institution we have had one apparent murder and an attempt at another. It is probably beyond the time to bring in the authorities, but better late than never.

"I just hope that we can make amends with the police and they can help us out of this dilemma. I will try to explain everything that I know when he gets here. Right now, why don't we take a break and wait for him? I can ask Mrs. White if she can find some refreshments. It shouldn't be long."

They left the room, each needing a moment to process this new revelation alone. Martha scurried about the room, as if she had hungry relatives from out of town arrive unexpectedly. Soon, she was able to satisfy everyone's physical needs, although they all knew there were emotional layers of need no one seemed able to address. They returned to the table. John said, "Martha, when Detective Johnson gets here, I want you to sit in on the conversation. I think there might be some information you are not aware of. Before he arrives, however, would you mind calling the hospital and checking on Dow?"

After a moment she poked her head into the room and looked sadly at Chancellor Goslin. "There has been no change."

"Thank you." He turned his attention to the young lady and said, "So, Janna, you're a freshman here. How do you like it so far?"

"Very much. It's a little different from what I thought it

would be. I guess I was expecting the students to be a little more, how shall I say it, studious."

"That is to be expected, Janna. College, in many ways, is a microcosm of society. We have all of the elements and disparate personalities that make up our society represented. Some are serious and dedicated, some are not. You might be surprised to find out that some of the best students are those whom you would think would not be. It has always been that way. Don't you agree, Mr. Joseph?"

"Yes. The amount of time a person spends in studying is not necessarily indicative of anything. I remember..."

His words were interrupted by the arrival of the detective. Martha ushered him in and together they joined the group, taking the two empty chairs at the other end of the conference table. John shook hands with the man and introduced everyone, except Big Jim.

Detective Johnson greeted him warmly and said, "Well, I wasn't expecting a big group like this. What is the occasion?"

"Janna recorded the last lecture of Doctor Kline. On the tape she has discovered that someone in the audience not only knew what was going to happen, but was actively urging Dr. Kline to kill himself."

"Really," he said dubiously. "Can I hear the tape?"

The rumble and hiss of the recorder filled the room once again. One more illusion was snuffed out with the clarity of the truth.

Chapter 21

The studio on the east side of Washington, D.C. was buzzing with excitement as the scheduled broadcast neared. Though the show was aired every Sunday morning, as the time grew closer for the ON THE AIR light to come on, the tension on the set seemed to increase proportionally.

What began with normal activity burgeoned until it took on the appearance of opening night in the theater. People with looks of determination in their eyes made their way from one location to another doing their best to ignore any distractions.

Technicians scurried about, headsets clamped in place and microphones perched near their mouths trailing cords behind them like sinuous vipers. Here and there a cameraman cleaned the lens of a huge camera, taking care to wipe the lens with special paper and finishing the job by using compressed air to remove any remnant of dust. Having finished the cleaning, some checked the casters to be certain the large machines would roll effortlessly without a hint of rumble.

The director's sheet was attached to a clipboard mounted on the camera dolly within easy view, with the timing sequences written in red letters. By the end of the show the sheets would be rewritten at the director's discretion. All variations would be noted with the large green felt-tip pen dangling from a string attached to the clipboards. Camera angles were listed on the sheet across from the times and duration of each shot. The three camera operators knew their jobs well. Each of them checked their phones to be certain the director could give necessary instructions to the cameras.

In the studio, the noise was more like a murmur than the actual sound of voices. Everyone talked in hushed tones, as if their words could be picked up and inadvertently broadcast to a waiting nation, creating a potential faux pas of immense proportions.

Changing the camera's perspective often enough to keep

people interested was one of the many duties of the director. This challenge was accepted and met with a vigorous response. The process of transferring information from one person to another by talking is a difficult task to keep engaging. On television, it is much easier to direct a segment in which there is visible activity, rather than just people talking.

"Talking heads" have been the bane of directors since the inception of television. It is one of the realities of the trade that information not amenable to presentation by either action or illustration tends to bore the audience. The problem is exacerbated by the fact that the information being presented was valuable, and because of its nebulous nature, was most efficiently delivered by someone simply announcing it.

But Americans need to be entertained. Failure to entertain often translates as failure to communicate effectively. It is one of the paradoxes which TV presents to the director. The fantastic potential of the medium to impart knowledge and wisdom are constantly filtered by the perceived need of the viewers for entertainment.

Through the years, researchers have concentrated on making this type of presentation stimulating. It had always been assumed that the public needed the information TV could provide, so any effort whose purpose was to educate and inform should be enhanced as much as possible. This assumption presupposed this was the way for information to be delivered. Much of the research centered on camera angles and the frequency of changing camera views in order to keep the interest level high.

Here on the set of *Perspectives on Washington*, the latest research was taken very seriously. For that reason the director was the best in the industry.

This show was one of the many showcases of the Center for America Heritage. Its success hinged on the staff qualifications and performance matching those exacting standards. Everyone on the set knew their jobs. They also knew that their professional reputations depended on the unmatched quality of programming they could generate. Only four of these people knew in detail by what criteria their success was measured.

While numbers of viewers was one of the criteria, it certainly was not the most important. The Center was much more interested in the demographics of who was watching rather than the raw numbers generated by such a primitive measure. The Center had done extensive research to determine the make-up of their audiences. If they could entice the people they wanted, the raw numbers were secondary.

In our society positive public opinion can be achieved in a number of ways. The most notable way is to have a groundswell of public opposition or support for a certain activity or concept. The opposition to the Viet Nam War was one of these groundswells that the Center, though they tried their best, could not defeat.

Eventually, they saw the direction public opinion was moving and manuevered themselves behind the groundswell in order to direct it to more positive ends. They managed, in this way, to prevent Gene McCarthy from assuming the mantle of the Democratic Party at the Chicago Convention. They managed to make George McGovern, a quiet scholarly man, seem like a dolt, thereby effectively limiting his candidacy. This process continued into a new century with the "swift-boating" of a presidential candidate and incessant personal attacks—attacks routinely made out of whole cloth in the bowels of the Center on anyone who would try to derail the subjugation of the electorate dictated by their agenda.

The late sixties' demise of the Center's plans had precipitated the first and only resignation of a Director. But in the end, it made them stronger, because they learned that they too could face limits in their power. In the last thirty-five years by recognizing these boundaries, they effectively undermined, subverted and stretched them to the point where they were now practically meaningless and hopelessly theoretical.

Prior to this breakthrough in the cultivation of power, the Center attempted to confront groundswells in public opinion. Now, they moved to direct, influence, manipulate and often compound them, once detected. Their detection methods had been sharpened until they could ascertain movement to or from a position before most people were even aware of the disagreement. They had perfected their control of information to a point where people believed primarily just what the Center wanted them to believe.

They could dictate the thought patterns of the majority of the American public and did so without conscience. People behaved in a manner prescribed by the leaders of the Center. Nothing, at this point in American history, was beyond their sphere of influence. By defining the message in content and presentation, they were able to promote a war of choice against a largely irrelevant Arab leader, a man so pitifully self-indulgent as to write romance novels while subjugating his people. Having decided that a war would be good for America, the Center promoted it endlessly until it became a foregone conclusion, in spite of the active opposition of millions of people.

Once the war commenced, the information, and more importantly, the pictures were tightly controlled. The national media was given a script, a plan for bamboozling the public into supporting a war that was not needed against an enemy that was not a threat.

By convincing people who regularly persuade others, they were able to cause more change with less effort than any previous methodology. Opinion leaders are those people who make a special effort to keep informed on the subjects in the public's consciousness. These few people tune into the discussion shows, such as *Perspectives* and by being informed, spread the information among their groups.

The identification of such people was one of the keys to the success of the Center's policies. With the statistical methodologies they had developed, they could identify "opinion leaders," or OLs for short, with nearly unerring accuracy. They had polished the process to the point where no contact was even necessary. They could find them by doing a brief background check and computer run.

The Center determined this process by categorizing the information gleaned from thousands of interviews. Though crude at first, they distilled the raw information until just the essence remained. By a simple glance at a data sheet they could discriminate between the people who were buffoons and those who were genuinely looked to for information.

A list of nearly 1,000,000 OLs was housed in the Center

computers. These individuals were targeted by the Center for use as OLs to distribute their message, so they could not be identified as being directly manipulative. The Center was more interested in control than movement and so concentrated on the indirect method.

The staff of *Perspectives on Washington* consisted of the elite of the Washington news establishment. Although different guests were present every week, the moderators remained the same: Craig Thomas, noted liberal commentator, and Drew Cabot, right-wing writer.

The fact that these two men agreed on almost every issue was never forthcoming in their broadcast. They were chosen primarily for their folksy way of communicating, as well as a certain intangible ability to be perceived as kind and wise through the eye of the camera.

The format of the show was simple: the guest was asked questions by both men. Questions were slanted toward one position or the other. If either of the two interviewers had trouble phrasing their questions, properly worded questions were provided to them through ear pieces. After the questions were asked, the guest would respond and a discussion would follow. It was a simple format, daunting in its complexity.

In the world of television the simple becomes difficult because of its very simplicity. The explanation for this oxymoron is that simplicity spells boredom, and that would never do.

The message from this show was too important for the Center for American Heritage to have less than the best possible people involved, each of them giving the Center's message in the best possible light, while never revealing the source of their wisdom.

Every idea presented on the show was also reinforced in the various other media, at almost the same moment. Their allegiance, whether they were aware of it or not, was to the Center. The Center took great pains to present their positions as being the most reasonable of potential solutions. By the cumulative effect of introducing an idea in one medium, discussing it in another, and embellishig it in many others, they were able to shape the national agenda. And even more importantly, they were able to control the contours and leanings of public dialogue about the agenda. Any idea seen as dangerous to the Center's position was either never discussed or openly ridiculed.

ରେ ରେ ରେ

The four men responsible for the show sat in the conference room with the doors shut tightly. Each of them was aware of the importance of the others. Craig and Drew sat back and listened as directives were spelled out by the Center's man, Harold Hunter.

"Art, last week's show was not exactly what we specified."

Arthur Comstock, the director, felt a small tug of fear at the base of his spine and his sphincter tightened noticeably. He sat up in his chair and looked at the older man and asked defensively, "What was wrong?"

"Actually, several things. I want to go over them one at a time so there will be no more mistakes. Does everyone understand?" He glanced at the three other men who were seated at the table and their eyes were fixed on him. "To begin with, the cameras seemed sluggish. According to our latest research, camera angles must be subtly changed every fifteen seconds with a variation of no more than a second and a half. Full camera switches must be made within forty-two seconds with a deviation of no more than two seconds. You know that as well as I do.

"Still, upon examination of last week's show we found that both of these timing sequences were off by at least three seconds on several occasions. Once the gap stretched to nearly ten seconds. This is just plain unacceptable. Keep a closer eye on it, will you?"

Although the comment had been phrased as a question, it was not; it was a directive. Art swallowed hard and silently cursed the operator of camera number 2 and planned to chew him out again for coming into work tired and sluggish. He didn't give a rat's ass if the cameraman's son had been up sick all night and his wife and he had ended up taking the boy to the hospital at three o'clock in the morning. The fact the man sat by his son's bed and comforted the boy through a bad night of appendicitis could not be seen as relevant.

He simply could not afford to have such thoughts cloud his judgement. If the cameraman was too tired to work, he could have called in and one of the replacements could have been used. The man should be willing to give up the day's pay in favor of doing the job right.

The Center was not interested in excuses, only results. With his eyes examining the grain of the wood on the table he replied, "Certainly, I didn't realize the variation was that great. It will be corrected."

"I knew it would be. Now, you two. What in the world are you guys doing out there? Last week, on three separate occasions you left the script and made spontaneous, non-scripted observations that we consider to be dangerous. I don't want to spell it out for you again, but I will. You are here to present ideas in a certain way. If you cannot do this, you will be replaced with someone who can. I only know of ten to fifteen replacements for each of you. You are simply not that important. Don't start believing your press clippings. You can be replaced or destroyed at my discretion. Do you understand?"

"I'm not sure. What observations were in error?"

Harold Hunter looked at him with a cruel grin and said, "Let me remind you of a few things. Drew, do you remember when you said—just a minute, I have it right here." The older man shuffled some papers, looked at Drew Cabot and read, "I don't see why you just don't get together on this budget. You seem to be so close in principle."

"I said that?"

"Absolutely. I have the transcript right here. If you want me to get the tape..."

"That won't be necessary. I believe you."

"Do you understand the danger inherent in that situation?"

"I know we are supposed to avoid examining the concepts and concentrate instead on the differences. I am sort of confused beyond that point."

"Let me spell it out for you both. It is not in the country's best interest to have people concentrate on their similarities. Instead, we need people to emphasize their differences. If people were aware of the things they have in common, it could lead to social disintegration. At this point our society exists on many levels. If people discovered the fact that we all live in pretty much the same way, do you think they would be satisfied? No, if people understood their own exploitation, it would mean an end to our society as we know it.

"We at the Center are primarily interested in the well-being of the country. Individuals and their problems are basically meaningless to us. We concentrate on broad issues for the country. We decide which issues are to be discussed and even more importantly..."—he paused for effect, taking the opportunity to remove his glasses and place them on the table— "...what the basis of that discussion will be. Can you imagine what would happen if the people who have been laid off from their jobs in the last year, realized that we have advocated such things so that the prices of products for a majority of the people can be lowered? By lowering these prices we are able to keep people working at a barely living wage. If they understood how to stop these activities, do you think that would be desirable? Do you two want to work for five bucks an hour?

"How could you afford your new Lexus if people understood we are actively undercutting the worker in order to raise the salaries of management and protect the investments of our people? Gentlemen, make no mistake about it, we are here to further the American system. If people realized that painful measures are sometimes necessary, do you think we could stop them from destroying the very fabric of our society?

"What would happen if they realized that we are doing this to further the separation between lower classes and the upper echelons of society? How happy do you think they would be? This separation is absolutely necessary for the American system to continue in a world market. Our theoretical sociologists have concluded this adjustment period will extend for no more than ten years. After that point, with American resources pretty much intact while the rest of the world's will be depleted, we will again be strengthened and dominant. Do you realize what would happen if people realized that by the use of computers and computer-controlled manufacturing and design that we could end the system of capitalism forever? How do you think they would react if we told them that scarcity, that parent of capitalism, is nearly irrelevant?

"Gentlemen, trust me. We know what we are doing, and we have the best interests of the country foremost in our consideration. We see the matter as a long-term problem. Short-term answers are not desirable, for they have no eye to the future. If any of these concepts I have just described gained popularity, the world as we know it would disintegrate into chaos. There would be riots, and the farmers would protest."

"Are all of those things that bad?"

"Glad you asked that, Craig. Yes and no. The yes part is that we could be moving our society toward a utopia. Still, it all depends on perspective. I know you would like to read and travel for a living, as I would.

"If all people were like us, the problem I just presented would not exist. The problem is a lot of these people would not have anything to occupy their time except for a fascination with affairs of the flesh. So, our society could end with the stink of booze or the destitution of thought brought on by engaging in mindless physical stimuli such as drugs and sex. We could degenerate to the level of slaves to our own desires and then easily be conquered and destroyed. This must be avoided at all costs for the American System must continue. Are there any more questions on this point?" He paused briefly studying the three men for any signs of disagreement.

Finding none, he proceeded. "The third issue I want to bring up deals with the treatment of female guests. On last week's show, Craig actually made an effort to escape the welcoming hug for our female guest. This is unacceptable. If we are to succeed with our message, you must continue to treat all women as potential sexual conquests. This is absolutely essential. When the opportunity for touching in any way arises, take full advantage of the situation. While the guest is talking, try smiling in your most lecherous way. I don't believe we have time for a discussion of this point, especially considering we have talked about it many times before. Still, the basic point must be raised: it is in the American people's best interest to keep sexual differences in the forefront of current thought. We have had the campaign for equality in place for nearly fifty years, and our methodology is sound. We actively promote a few women on the national agenda, while limiting the majority to their traditional roles as low-paid housekeepers or part-time workers. Your cooperation is needed, and I want to see a little lasciviousness over the airwaves. Initially, both of you were chosen on the basis of gender appeal. Use those abilities as often as possible."

The men split up and went their separate ways. The two "stars" returned for makeup application, while the director and the Center's Mr. Hunter went to the control booth where they had a better view of the broadcast. Art sat in his chair, picked up his headphones and slipped them into place. He quickly checked with each camera operator and stressed the importance of responding to both the sheet and his direction.

The stars returned from the dressing room and took their places. Art cued the music, the floor manager flipped the ON THE AIR light. The set became deathly quiet. The floor manager watched the clock and listened in his earphones to the director counting down the seconds, 3 - 2 - 1. He pointed to Craig and the show began.

There were no further mistakes and everyone was satisfied for the moment. During the following week there would be similar meetings, and those issues would be discussed again. It was a constant battle to keep the show promoting the Center's wishes. A battle won every broadcast.

Chapter 22

After the tape ended, Big Jim pressed the stop button and silence returned. Everyone sat quietly as the seconds ticked by. It seemed that no one wanted to break the pall of silence. People were both shocked and disappointed. It seemed that everyone wanted to keep their thoughts to themselves as they considered the implications of the tape.

Those who had heard it before were amazed at the clarity with which they now heard the damning words. Now, they could hear the admonitions to "Do it" as clearly as they could hear the professor's voice on the tape. Janna thought she may have been hearing the words on a subconscious level. If that were the case it would explain her fascination with the tape.

As if the bullet had only in that irrevocable moment penetrated Professor Kline's skull at the sinister bidding of someone or something else, each individual in the conference room sat stunned.

Finally, almost by default, Detective Johnson said, "Well, I think I'd better hear everything that anyone knows about this affair." Disconsolation showed in his voice as he was attempted to maintain his self-control. He was thinking, 'Why hadn't they come to him in the first place? It would have saved so much time and needless suffering. Have these people been watching too much television or reading detective novels and taking them too seriously? This was not a plot by a frustrated writer—this was real. One man had been killed and another lay in a coma with his chances for survival questionable. It would have been so much better if they had told the truth from the outset. Now the trail could be cold.'

He removed a notebook from his jacket pocket and waited for someone to begin. Each of the parties looked to the Chancellor, as he rose from his seat and began to outline everything he knew about the week's events.

His delivery was crisp and professional. It was as if he

were addressing a cadre of potential donors. When he told about finding the disk in Richard's safety deposit box, he reached into his pocket and retrieved the original. He gave his accounting as clearly and succinctly as he could.

Detective Johnson interrupted him only to clarify a point. He carefully wrote down the particulars and satisfied himself with the knowledge that the truth was being told. Some matters, such as this, never have the advantage of being exposed to scrutiny.

He took the disk from the table and placed it in his pocket. He was not sure that he would be able to do anything with it that had not already been done. The ironic truth was that when the police had a problem involving computers, they were likely to call on Dr. Ira Jones.

Still, the State Police did have a crime lab near here and maybe they could do something. It was at least a longshot worth his effort. The rest of those in attendance sat quietly and listened, each of them finding something interesting and frightening in the Chancellor's report. Janus appreciated his logical assumption being seconded by the facts, although he still wondered at the implications.

Janna found herself marveling at her father's prescience. Big Jim was utterly fascinated by the tale of intrigue and violence. Most of his professional work involved less subterfuge and the more direct violence of muggings and armed robbery. The surreptitious nature of these activities interested him. Martha had heard some of this before but even she was surprised by some of the information. Though the information was new to her, she displayed little emotion. Finally, John took his seat.

The detective completed writing in his notebook and then closed his eyes for just a moment to gather his thoughts. When he spoke it was without conviction. "Some additional information has been uncovered. You may not be aware, but when an individual decides to end their own life, the law requires an autopsy, even if all the *facts* of a case point to a simple suicide. According to the report I received on Dr. Kline, his system showed evidence of high levels of the psychotropic drug, Amvec. The coroner's explanation indicates that the presence of this much of the drug would make a person despondent or potentially suicidal. It far exceeded normally prescribed doses. The effect on the body is the exact opposite of an anti-depressant. At these levels it creates what is known as 'suicidal ideation'—in other words, extreme depression."

"Are you sure?" the chancellor asked incredulously.

"No mistake. Was anyone aware of his use of this drug?"

"Not that I am aware of..." John Goslin let his voice drop before proceeding. "Can I at least ask Louise about this?"

"Please do. The more information we have, Chancellor, the better chance we will have of unraveling the ugly snare of knots in this case."

The detective looked at their stunned expressions and continued, "I'm not sure how to proceed. If I were the visiting detective at an insane asylum, I wouldn't expect to hear a more amazing story. Still, I am not, so I'll take your word for what I have just heard and what appears to be unfolding here. I seem to have little choice as the facts bear out the explanations. But have you all considered the ramifications of what you've proposed?"

One glance at the faces of the people around the conference table told him that they, indeed, understood the implications. Furthermore, they probably saw some things he had not yet comprehended. He said, "Let me get this straight. Dr. Jones called you and told you that the information he recovered pointed to some secret organization. Is that right?"

"Yes, it is. He gave us a name: The Center for American Heritage. He also told me of the Reverend Jersey Land having a certain knowledge about their operations, which he shared with Richard."

"Okay, I've got that. Now, the computer where the information had been saved was stolen. Is there any possibility that Dr. Jones would have transferred this information to another location?"

"I suppose that is quite possible. My computer knowledge is not all that great. I do remember Dow encouraging me to keep my important documents—donor contacts, staffing budgets, and other university documents—in more than one location. I tried it for a while, but I found it too time-consuming. Now, I just print a hard copy and Martha files it. I do know he is a positive nut for duplication."

"Chancellor, if he were to keep copies, where do you suppose they would be?"

"We could check DORA."

"Who's she?"

"It's not a she. It's his personal computer in his office."

"Who can you get to do it?"

"Detective, do you really think we should have more people involved? I'm not sure. I don't want to jeopardize any more staff, students, or anyone for that matter."

"Perhaps you're right. Is there anyone here who could try?" He looked around the room. Janna quietly raised her hand while brushing her hair back from her eyes. The detective looked at her wistfully. "Do you think you can get somewhere?"

"I don't know. But I certainly can try. I have some experience with computers." Her father smiled. Some experience! He liked the quiet confidence his daughter exhibited. It verified his feelings about her impending adulthood. She had been fascinated by computers since the first time he brought one home from school for the summer. She took to the machines the way his ducks took to their daily handouts. By the time she was a junior in high school, she knew more than her teachers and was an accomplished programmer, as well as an operator.

"Well, in the absence of anyone else giving it a try, I can't see any harm. Is that okay, Chancellor?"

"Fine with me. I am not sure what kind of security he placed on the machine, but I don't see any harm in her trying. I can accompany her over to the Com-Math Duplex. Mr. Joseph, could you go with us?"

"Certainly, I don't think I'll let her out of my sight for the foreseeable future. This whole situation is bizarre and obviously dangerous."

"Well, that's one piece to work on. Does anyone else have any other ideas?"

"What about Jersey Land?"

"What about him, Chancellor?"

"I just saw that he has been arrested in Chicago."

"Where did you see that?" the detective asked.

"It was in the Chicago paper."

Big Jim suddenly sat up straight at the mention of Chicago, his old stomping grounds, and asked, "Chancellor, do you remember where the paper said they are holding him?"

"No, I don't remember. I am not even sure that it was listed. I think I threw the paper in the garbage. Martha, did anyone dump the trash?"

"I don't think so. Most of the janitorial staff has been off for these three days. I placed a call about the fact that the floors hadn't been vacuumed this morning, and no one answered."

"You think I should go look, Jim?"

"I guess. I still have some friends on the force. If we can find a location, I'll make some calls. Maybe we can try a bit of rehabilitation and see if he can provide us some of the information that he gave to Dr. Kline."

John left his chair, walked through the connecting door to his office and retrieved the paper from the trash can. After spreading it out on his desk, he began to search for the article. When he found it, he was amazed he had seen it at all. It was just a small piece on the corner of one of the back pages. He scanned it to determine if he had been correct, smoothed the paper and returned to the conference table.

He took a few seconds to read the article in depth. Finding the location, he announced to Big Jim, "It says he's being held, pending arraignment, at the Hyde Park Station."

"That's good. I have a friend there. Tom, what do you think we should do?"

The detective folded his hands in front of him and thought for several moments before answering. "The only clues to this affair seem to be somewhere else. The information may or may not be in Dr. Jones' computer. If it is there, we may or may not be able to access it. The only other clue seems to be this Reverend Land. It wouldn't hurt to at least talk to the man. Jim, do you think you need official intervention on this?"

"Tom, I'd rather not. If we make it formal, it may cause problems. The procedure with drunks is for them to pay a fine and be released. If they can't pay the fine they are either sent to Cook County Jail or released, depending on conditions."

"Released? How long do we have?"

"It usually takes a day or so for a place to open up on the court's docket. I suppose we have until tomorrow morning."

"Are you free to drive there today?"

"Yeah, I can go. It's just, what do we do with him once we find him?"

"I don't know. Depending on his condition, I suppose I could lock him up downtown. I don't know what good that would do. Anyone else have any suggestions?"

"I could bring him to the lake with us. We have a spare room. Karen will be dismayed, but if we can be of any help..."

ଔ ଔ ଔ

The watcher took another pull on his coffee and averted his eyes from the door to the Administration building. His peripheral vision made him aware the group was leaving the building. He had been listening through the bug placed in the chancellor's office that first night. In fact, some of the conversation did not come through clearly. He wasn't aware there were six people in the room. The tall man in uniform walked to the cluster of police cars and climbed into the nearest one. The two older men and the girl walked down the sidewalk, while the local detective went to his unmarked car and drove off.

The Chancellor's group was moving faster than he expected. They turned the corner before he managed to get the car started. He dialed the phone as he drove and reported the group was dispersing. Another car would pick up the campus officer. From the general direction that the detective drove and his attitude in the conference, he could tell that he was heading for the station.

While he talked, he did not consider it important to report the campus security officer was going to pick up Jersey Land. He knew the Center had destroyed that man, as surely as if they had killed him.

"Just a minute," he said into the phone as he stepped on

the gas. Now that their backs were to him, he kept his eyes pinned on his quarry.

The red and blue police flashers in his rear view mirror shocked him. This couldn't be happening. He watched as the impossibly large campus security man exited the tiny car and moved toward him. He reached for his wallet and license and waited, while keeping his eyes focused on the people moving toward the Com-Math Duplex.

ଔ ଔ ଔ

Out of the corner of his eye Big Jim had seen the car start and do a U-turn. The revelations of the previous hour had set his mind on edge, so his perceptions were sharpened. All of the talk about conspiracy and real evidence of attacks put him on alert.

When the car turned the corner with a single occupant talking on the phone, he flipped the lights on and patched through to the local police. He asked to be connected with Detective Johnson and waited a moment for the detective to respond. Tom said, "What's up?"

"I have a car stopped on DeKorne Street. He appeared to be following the Chancellor and the Josephs. What do you want me to do with him?"

"Delay him for a minute. I'm just a couple of streets over. I'll join you."

ଔ ଔ ଔ

The watcher did not turn off the car. There was no sense in invoking needless activity on the part of the campus officer. Still, if the local became too inquisitive, he was poised to leave. He had the sure and certain knowledge he could operate with impunity because he worked for the Center.

There was nothing that could be done at a local level which could not be undone with a simple call to a designated number he had committed to memory. The large man walked toward him with intent and said, "Get out of the car, please."

This was the time of decision. If he got out of the vehicle, he would be helpless. Here in the car, he could drive to safety. He tried to delay a decision. Smiling congenially he said, "What's the matter, Officer? I don't believe that I was doing anything wrong."

"Just get out of the car." Big Jim left off the please this time. His face was rigid as he waited for the man to respond.

"I'm sure there has been some sort of mix up."

"No mix up. Get out of the car!"

The watcher pretended to be getting out of the car, slipped the gear shift into the drive position and jammed the accelerator. The tires squealed. The man turned his gaze to the front. Too late! The detective's car was burning rubber and closing fast. The man tried to pull another U-turn but was hit in the rear door and the car came to a screeching hault. The crash threw his head into the steering wheel and knocked him unconscious. The phone fell to the floor and his partner on the other end kept repeating, "I can't find him. Where did he go?" Big Jim rushed to the car, opened the door and looked inside.

ଓଃ ଓଃ ଓଃ

Tom had seen what was happening as he rounded the corner. He noticed the exhaust coming from the stopped car and assumed that the man might try to make a run for it. He had eased his car in front of the watcher's. He walked around the passenger's side of the car. When the man reached his decision to try to run for freedom, his car traveled less than five feet.

Chapter 23

The man did not regain consciousness and continued to bleed profusely during the short ambulance drive from the campus to the hospital. The EMT attendant donned rubber gloves and administered first aid. He sat at the head of the stretcher holding a bandage on the man's head.

Detective Johnson was seated in the back. He decided to accompany the suspect in the ambulance for two reasons—the first being that he very much wanted to talk to the man, and the second was more practical; his car was wrecked.

He called the station and a tow truck was on the way for his car. He stared at the man in the expensive suit whose face was bloody from the nose bleed and a large gash on his head. He seemed to be of an indeterminate age, somewhere between young and old. His hair was cropped neatly. Even in his disheveled and unconscious condition, it was still neat. His shoes were high-end, as was his watch. He was almost the exact opposite of a street criminal. He was a person who would not appear to be out of place anywhere.

As he watched the Emergency Medical Technician exchange the soiled bandage for a fresh one, he thought of what a sad commentary on the state of the world it was when an individual could not even help a stranger without being concerned for their own safety. In the helping professions, latex gloves were now required when dealing with bodily fluids. Teachers kept them in their desks, police officers had them in their cars, and every corner of the medical community was touched by the omnipresent latex.

When they arrived, the two EMTs removed the stretcher from the truck, the wheels clicking smoothly into position. On the short ride through the electronic doors, the man began to stir. His eyes flickered for a moment and soon closed again. The emergency room doctor did a quick scan of his pupils and finding nothing amiss, went on to the next patient whose injuries were deemed potentially more life-threatening. He returned several minutes later and walked to where Detective Johnson was seated. "I don't think it's anything serious. I think we should schedule an X-ray and keep him overnight for observation. Is that all right?"

"I guess. When can he be released?"

"Assuming nothing is wrong, in the morning."

After the doctor walked away, a nurse returned with the necessary paperwork, requiring Detective Johnson's signature. The watcher was then wheeled into a private room. Shortly after his arrival, while the man was being seen by the doctor, Tom called the station and arranged for an officer to guard the room.

He traveled with the orderly as he wheeled the man up to his room. Tom saw the officer and motioned for him to follow. He held the door as the orderly wheeled the watcher in, aligned the gurney with the bed, and pressed the brake home. He helped the orderly transfer him to the crisp white sheets of the hospital bed. He then joined the officer in the hall. The watcher was left alone in the darkened room contemplating his next actions.

Big Jim had followed in the campus security car and met Tom in the hallway. "Is he going to be all right?"

"The doctor says there doesn't appear to be a concussion. I guess the question is, what do we do with him? I can arrest him for resisting arrest, but beyond that there isn't a whole lot to go on."

"Who is he anyway?"

"Frank Smith of Alexandria, Virginia. There was no other information in his wallet."

"Where did Chancellor Goslin say this center was located?"

"Let me check my notes." He removed his notebook and shuffled through the pages. "Let me see, ah...here it is. No city listed, just Virginia."

"Do you think he could be one of them?"

"I don't know who else he could be. I have some pointed questions to ask him when he wakes up. You still going to Chicago?"

"Yeah, I'll leave in a while. I should be on my way by

3:30. With a little luck, I can be there before the night shift checks in. I don't think this will take long. I should be back by 11:00. I'll check in with you."

"Good Luck. Hope the traffic isn't too bad."

Suspecting that the name Frank Smith could be an alias, Detective Johnson decided to have a technician take the man's fingerprints. He walked down the hall to make the arrangements.

ଓ ଓ ଓ

The crash caused Janna's group to turn around in surprise. The sudden sound of the collision and the lights of the campus cruiser added an air of danger, particularly in the wake of the heavy meeting they had just left. The three stopped for only a moment, as there was very little to see. "What do you suppose that's all about?" Chancellor Goslin asked.

"I'm not sure. Perhaps somebody didn't want a ticket." Not knowing that the inicident was intimately linked to their own activities, the three forged ahead to the task at hand.

"I'm curious about the computer. Janna, do you think you can do something with it?"

"I don't know. Dow Jones is something of a legend when it comes to computer security. If he doesn't want us messing about, I'm pretty sure there will be little to be accomplished."

They arrived at the complex and entered. Though classes had been canceled, the building remained open for those students who wanted to use either the computers or the math labs. They walked down the corridor to Dow's office. John fumbled in his pocket and after a moment located the master key. He carefully inserted it and opened the door into the darkened room.

From a cursory glance he could tell DORA had been left on and a shimmer of hope gleamed in the darkness. If Dow left the machine on, perhaps he had been sending data to it.

There was a screen saver showing, so he moved the mouse to bring back the normal screen. Janna moved past him and sat at the desk. She noted that there appeared to be some sort of communication program loaded, and a message was printed on the screen:

Text file transfer complete

Exit (Y/N)

At this point she had a problem. If she exited the communication software, where would the computer's progam take her? Based on experience she believed there were two possibilities: one of these would be for the computer to defer to a simple DOS level where she might be able to find some information; the other would be that the computer might go back to a shell program that would display a menu. Even with a cursory glance she could tell that it was not using the omnipresent Windows Operating System.

Because Dr. Jones had designed his own operating system, Internet Browser and utilities, she was not overly optimistic. "I'm not sure what I can do with this, but I'll do my best."

ଔ ଔ ଔ

Kara Morrisy, Kira Morris' twin sister, dialed the phone. After several rings a groggy voice answered. "H'lo—do you know what time it is?"

"Listen, Sis, I am not your bloody alarm clock."

"Kara, what's up?"

"Dr. Jones is out of the coma. I just checked him a minute ago and he gave me a wolf whistle."

"Men! Well, anyway thanks. What time is it? Oh it's a little after 11:00. I hate these bloody early morning news shows. I mean I have to be in the studio by 5:00 A.M. I'm on my way. I really want to talk to him. Who needs sleep anyway? Thanks again."

ଔ ଔ ଔ

The trip from Mason to Chicago left little in the way of thrills for Jim. He had completed this journey so many times that he could do it on auto-pilot. He went by his home after leaving the hospital and changed clothes. It would be better not to show up in uniform. He checked his wallet to make sure he had at least two hundred dollars. A little short, he stopped by an ATM on his way out of town. He wanted to be certain that he could make bail.

As the miles peeled off, his mind focused on the Center for American Heritage. It was like a magnet that pulled him back again and again. 'What an idea. Some sort of organization that was so powerful, it could influence—even dictate—public opinion, personal choices and activities.' His thoughts drifted in an out of a circle of fear and hatred. 'Who do they think they are to tell us what to think?' A righteous anger burned inside him and promised not to be extinguished easily.

೮೩ ೮೩ ೮೩

"Frank Smith" had been awake for several hours. He checked his watch; it was nearly 10:30. He had a desperate need to go to the bathroom, but he held it until he could make up his mind what to do next. Finally, after agonizing minutes, the pain got to him, and he took a tentative step from the bed. His head felt like it was about to burst. He felt dizzy and his legs seemed to be made of rubber. He strengthened his resolve and walked cautiously to the bathroom. He didn't turn on the light, but found the stool by touch.

He stumbled back to the bed when the door popped open and the lights came on. A pretty nurse entered his room accompanied by the guard. "How are you feeling?" He did not answer.

"C'mon fella, I heard you get up to relieve yourself. I know you're awake. How are you feeling?" Frank didn't say a word; he just stared at her.

"Well, let me take your pulse and blood pressure. Then, I'll leave you alone." She went about her business calmly and professionally. She turned to the guard and said, "This is a good night; the patient down the hall who had been in a coma for days, came out of it a little while ago. Now this one appears to be awake as well."

Frank cleared his throat and croaked. "What patient down the hall?"

Startled at his sudden verbal interest, she answered, "I can't tell you that, but he had been in coma. He appears to be better now. He just whistled at me."

Frank gave no outward sign that he was either pleased or dismayed by the news, but the reality was the news had hit him like a slap. He felt fairly certain he knew the comitose patient to be Dr. Dow Jones. He knew what he must do. "Can you help me up? I have to use the bathroom again."

"Do you want me to get a bed pan?"

"No! Listen, I can walk with a little help."

Kara Morrisy leaned over to help him up, as she reached her hand toward his arm. His other arm swung around and grasped her by the throat. The officer instantly released the strap on his gun and started to pull it out. "If you pull on that gun, even a little, I will kill her." The guard cautiously let his hand drift away from the weapon and rest at his side. "Remove your belt and place it on the bed with two fingers."

When the officer hesitated, Frank squeezed a little harder, causing Kara to gasp for air. "Do it now!" He detached the buckle and carried the belt with two fingers over to the bed and lowered it gently.

Frank reached for the belt while maintaining his grip on Kara's throat. He removed the gun from the holster and pushed the nurse at the same moment. As she stumbled to the officer, he reached out to help her.

"Where do you think you are going, Mr. Smith?" the officer asked stonily.

"Get into the bathroom, both of you."

"No."

"Then I guess I'll have to kill you here. He released the safety on the gun and drew it to firing position. As his finger began to press the trigger, they staggered to the bathroom. Frank reached for the handcuffs which were in a pouch on the back of the belt. He removed them and said, "All right, on your knees on either side of the john." They complied. He took the handcuffs and handed them to the officer. "Snap this on your right wrist and pass it behind the toilet." After this operation was completed, he ordered, "Nurse, snap that to your left wrist."

He examined them and determined that the cuffs were indeed fastened. He then hit the cop on the head with the butt of the gun. The nurse gasped as the guard slumped over. He grabbed a towel from the rack and gagged Kara. He turned off the light, closed the door and headed out of the room for the nurse's station.

At this time of the evening the lights were subdued in the hallway and he saw no one in either direction. He moved behind the desk and checked the circular chart rack for Dr. Jones' room number. The chart was not in the rack. Momentary fear welled up inside of him and he began to panic. He regained control of his emotions and looked at the desk. The chart was where Kara had left it.

He examined the chart and easily found the room number. Walking quickly down the hall he found the room and stepped inside. Dow was sitting up in bed with the lights on, when the man stepped inside.

"Can I help you? —Wait, you are one of them. Help!"

The man moved quickly to the bed. Jerking the pillow from behind Dr. Jones' back, he pushed the gun firmly into its softness. "I'm sorry about this, Dr. Jones, I really have no choice in the matter." As the muscles in his exposed arms tightened to squeeze the trigger, Big Jim leapt from the bathroom doorway with a quickness that belied his size. He swung his fist decisively and hit the target with full force.

Frank Smith felt the impact just before the lights went out.

Big Jim rubbed his knuckles and said, "Ouch, man this guy has a hard head! Are you hurt, Dr. Jones?"

"No, I'm fine. Listen, I am pretty sure he was one of the men who attacked me."

Big Jim removed his belt and carefully tied the unconscious man into a chair. "Just lucky I stopped by. I wasn't even lookin' to drop in on you. I just wanted to see if Detective Johnson was around. His wife said that she thought he was at the hospital. When I walked in, the nurse recognized me from the university and told me that you were awake. I thought I would drop in and—well, it was a lucky thing."

Both men were breathing shallowly at the realization of what had just nearly transpired.

Chapter 24

Kira Morris looked good. Of course, it was her job to look good. It was not much short of a job requirement. In this modern age of telecommunications it was no longer necessary to be intelligent—if it ever had been. Still, there was no place in the focused eye of the camera for anyone who was less than physically attractive. Those who were "normal" looking were sometimes reported on, but they were not those who did the reporting.

She did a cursory glance in the mirror before she left her car. Mirrors were among her favorite haunts; she frequented them often.

In the sleepy old town of Mason, having an assault of a prominent member of the faculty of Harmson was big news. Though she had fulfilled the Chancellor's wishes by calling his office to verify the connection, she still felt there was more going on than she was being told. It was a stroke of luck that her sister was the nurse in charge of the unit where Dr. Jones was being treated.

With her inside information, she would beat the newspaper and the other stations by interviewing the formerly comatose professor. Life was good.

Since it was long after visiting hours, she entered through the emergency room entrance. Her cameraman, Scott, had been less than enthusiastic about accompanying her. However, orders were orders. Trailing her like a dog on a leash, he carried the heavy camera and battery pack. The night clerk recognized her immediately and with an eager-to-please smile asked, "Can I help you, Ms. Morris?"

"Can you tell me how to get to CCU?"

"Certainly, but visiting hours are over. Why do you need to go there?"

Kira flashed her best insider expression. "I need to see my sister about something."

"Why do you need the cameraman?"

"I don't. He was out on another story with me, and I didn't want to leave him in the car. Besides, we can't very well leave this expensive equipment unguarded."

The night clerk seemed satisfied and said, "Follow the yellow line on the floor to the West elevators and go to the third floor. The unit is to the right. By the way, I like your news show. I never miss it."

"Thank you very much," she said breathing a sigh of relief. These officious little people are near death on hundreds of stories. People whose obligations lie with their employers and common sense. If they do their job properly, it is very difficult to gather and report the news. Luckily, most of them succumb to the star quality of a TV reporter. Where would our society be without the benefit of the local television news?

As they moved down the yellow line, Scott hummed *Follow the yellow brick road*. Kira failed to see the joke and purposefully pushed on. Pressing the button for the elevator, she paced back and forth waiting for the machine to respond. Patience was not one of her stronger personality traits.

Even though the short ride from the ground floor to the third floor was accomplished quickly, she stood before the door rocking from foot to foot waiting for the door to open. When it did, she ran down the hall to the right. She was expecting the hallway to be darkened and essentially empty. She was wrong.

Instead of the subdued atmosphere she expected, she gazed through the double doors at a scene of near madness. Police were everywhere. The lights were fully lit. Here and there groups of people were gathered. Crime scene technicians moved about doing their jobs.

She turned to Scott and said, "Get this, will you? We can edit it later. Something is sure going on. We may as well try to get whatever we can." She burst through the double doors with the camera light shining on her back and charged down the hallway.

Detective Tom Johnson saw her coming and excused himself from the small group he had been talking with. He walked toward her with his hands out as if he were warding off the devil. "Turn that camera off, please."

With microphone in hand, she walked toward him and said, "Why? What is going on here?"

"Turn the camera off, and maybe we can talk. I have no wish to have this televised."

"What about the public's right to know?"

"Turn the camera off, or I will have you removed."

With a small gesture behind her back, the light faded and the cameraman relaxed and lowered the camera from his shoulder. He kept his finger on the trigger which caused the camera to record.

"Look, you with the camera. I have been to the movies, too. I can see the recording light is still on. Turn it off, or leave!"

Scott did not wait for further instructions but removed his finger from the button. Detective Johnson asked, "Why don't you put the lens cover on it? That way there can be no mistake."

He complied. Kira turned, handed him the microphone, and walked up to the detective. "Off the record, what is going on?"

He looked at her and measured his responsibility to the department and to the others involved in their search and said, "We had an incident involving a nurse and an officer who was guarding a patient."

"What happened?"

"The patient, who was being held for questioning, decided to leave. He assaulted the nurse and the officer and forced his way out of his room."

At this moment, Kara walked out of Frank Smith's room rubbing her wrist where the cuff had recently been removed. She looked scared and her throat was mottled from the man's hand. When she saw her sister, she ran and hugged her.

"Kira, it was awful. I thought I was going to die." Kira returned her hug and held her tightly. Kara's tears began to flow as she sobbed softly into her sister's shoulder.

ଔ ଔ ଔ

Though it was still late February, the windows on both sides of the car were slightly open. The smell emanating from the back seat was enough to drive the Josephs to this extreme action. Reverend Jersey Land smelled badly—a noxious mixture of stale urine, vomit and spent alcohol. It was all they could do to contain their disgust.

His clothing was a shambles. His shoes didn't match, and it appeared as if he had never had clean socks. His overcoat was stained in every conceivable place. His teeth were yellowed and his hair unkempt. A beard, rather whiskers, sprouted from his face. His glasses were dirty and bent. A piece of black electrical tape held one bow to the frame. He appeared the perfect picture of an alcoholic derelict.

They had just returned from the Chancellor's house. The computer, DORA, was too well protected for Janna. The frustration of the afternoon's activity was eased by a marvelous supper and good conversation with Chancellor and Mrs. Goslin.

Before they left the lab, Big Jim Davis agreed to drop off Reverend Land at the Chancellor's house after recovering him from Chicago. While waiting for that anticipated rendezvous, they played a game of Bridge to pass the time. Bridge can be fun, especially when the combatants are near the same level. If one party is better than the other, it can be boring. Finding the proper partner is difficult, but Janna and her father won as often as they lost and that made the game interesting. The rest of the group enjoyed watching their unique relationship profiled in the game as much as the game itself. Given the circumstances, it was a comforting distraction for all of them.

It was nearly 10:30 before Big Jim returned with the man who had become such a mystery. They said hurried goodbyes and laughed nervously about meeting again for another Bridge competition.

Reverend Land was not cooperative, nor was he uncooperative. He was simply unaware of his condition. Big Jim came in and tried to prepare them for the smell. "I've got your Reverend in the car. Let me tell you, he stinks. It is sad to see a man in such a condition. Well, I guess if you can't do anything with him, I can bring him back. Just let me know."

They left immediately. It was a long drive back to the lake as the sound of the tires on the pavement screamed down the deserted highway.

They made the trip in near record time. With no other traffic Janus decided to push his speed a little higher than usual. It was a good feeling to see the lights of their home glowing in the night darkness. After they parked the car, Karen greeted them at the door and walked into the garage to help her husband bring in the Reverend Mr. Land.

The Reverend was still out of it. He was at the point where he didn't care where he was, as long as someone let him sleep. They placed him on the bed, and Janus bent over to remove his shoes. The stench was incredible. It was with great relief that he closed the door and left him to sleep.

It had been a long time since Tommy Lanninga had been in a proper bed, He literally felt as if he were sinking into what he'd always imagined a cloud would feel. The cleanliness of the room wrapped itself around him while he slept and helped with the healing process. He was a long way from being a whole man. Still, between the awakening of religious fervor and the pristine environment, there was a chance he might recover.

ೞ ೞ ೞ

"So, what are you going to do with him?" Big Jim asked.

"I don't know. I have to find a doctor to release him. After that, I'm taking him to jail. We have something significant to charge him with now: attempted murder, assaulting an officer, just for starters. I don't want him out of a cell. Ms. Morrisy was pretty shook up. She said that she saw a look in his eyes which she hopes to never see again. She said 'It appeared to make no difference to him whether we lived or died. It was as if we were bugs on a window pane and he was about to use a fly swatter.'"

"Did you get an answer back on the prints?"

"Not that I know of. I had the tech forward them to the FBI. But that usually takes nearly a day for an answer. It is a lot better than it used to be, still less than we would like."

Detective Johnson walked to the emergency room. The attending physician accompanied him and did a cursory examination of the manacled patient. He grunted several times and finally turned to the detective and said, "It appears there is nothing amiss. You can take him to the cell, providing you keep an eye on him. If there is any change in his condition—vomiting, or such—let us know."

Detective Johnson nodded to the one of the officers and he jerked the man to his feet and pushed him down the hallway. "Well, Jim, I'll keep you informed. I think I'll have one of my officers park in front of the Chancellor's house. I don't like the fact that this man was following him. You watch yourself, too. I'm not sure what we have stirred up. But I don't like it much. This man has all the markings of a professional killer. It's the cold eyes. He looks at you, but does not see a person, only an obstacle to overcome. When I was in the service, I saw that look, that absence of conscience in soldiers who had been too long on the line. It is as if the soul shuts down and any action is sanctioned without conscience. It is the constant battle between the innate humanity of an individual and the obligation to pursue a function. In this man's case, I believe his function is to protect something. What that is? We don't know."

଒ ଒ ଒

Diane Goslin kissed her husband good night and rolled over on her side. They had taken the time to put the dishes in the dishwasher and set the rest to soak. Now, at the end of a trying day, it was time for sleep. "They seem like nice people."

"Who?" he replied sleepily.

"Janna and Janus Joseph. I liked them a lot. I always felt I would have liked to have a daughter. And if I had, I would have liked her to be like Janna. Quiet, but not demure. Intelligent, but not flashy. Mr. and Mrs. Joseph should be proud."

"I agree. I like him too. It is sad; we pay too little attention to the public school teachers in this country, yet they are the backbone of our educational system. The way he described their life sounds idyllic. I mean, nothing more important to think about than reading books and feeding the ducks. Sometimes, I wish we could think about retirement. I still enjoy the job, but it does not leave enough time for us."

They were saying their good nights when the phone rang. He reached over to the night stand and picked it up. "Hello."

"Sorry to disturb you, Chancellor. This is Jim Davis. I am at the hospital and we just had an incident down here. Did anyone inform you that Dr. Jones was out of his coma?"

"No, that's great news. What else happened?"

"You remember me telling you about that man we caught following you this afternoon?"

"Yes, what about him?"

"Seems he did not like being held at the hospital and tried to kill Dr. Jones."

"Good God! Is Dow okay?"

"Luckily, I stopped by to say hello. I went to see Detective Johnson. I'd been on the road for a long time and I was using the bathroom in Dr. Jones' room, when the man walked in. I was able to dissuade him from any further violence," he said with a chuckle.

"What are they going to with the man?"

"Detective Kelly says he is going to charge him with two counts of assault, one count of assaulting an officer and attempted murder. Should be more than a few years before he sees the outside again."

"Are you still at the hospital?"

"Yes. Is there something I can do?"

"Could you tell Dow that I will be in first thing in the morning. Tell him we were worried about him and that we are relieved and grateful that he is recovering."

CB   CB   CB

Fred Wesson dialed the phone number he had memorized years ago and waited a moment before it was answered. "This is Mr. Wesson, on vacation up in Michigan. Can I speak to the Judge?"

"Describe your problem."

"Mr. Smith has been arrested and is being held at the

local hospital. From what I could tell, some sort of campus cop stopped his vehicle. He tried to get away but failed to notice that another car had blocked his way. He crashed into the car. I called the hospital and his condition is fine, but for some reason they would not let me talk to him. I just wanted to inform you of these developments."

"Thank you, Mr. Wesson. Leave me your number. I will get back to you before morning on corrected procedures. Understand?"

"Absolutely. My number is area code..."

Chapter 25

Janus returned from his morning walk. The day had dawned gloriously. The hoarfrost decorated every weed and tree with skills that even the greatest painter could merely envy.

The morning sun glinted through the weeds, illuminating them as if a distilled essence of the purest light had been internalized. Absent any wind, occasionally a bird swooped from tree to tree. In the distance, he could hear the sound of a squirrel jumping between trees. In the stillness of the morning, the trees crinkled as though made of delicate glass.

Karen busied herself in the kitchen and had breakfast waiting. They ate in silence. There was too much going on to exchange small talk. Janus was in a quandary about what to do, or even what to say. He shared most of their experiences with his wife. Still, there were some things he held back. He did not mention the fact that the professor who had been assaulted, was involved in the same activity as Janna and he. It was better not to worry her on a chance that something might happen. Thoughts crashed into his mind which twenty-four hours ago would have been dismissed as delusions. Suddenly, these delusions were taking on more than a patina of reality—they were sure and solid.

He had no way of knowing what occurred at the hospital. Still, the fact that the police were involved in the situation was enough to cause him concern. The entire story, which unfolded in the Chancellor's office yesterday afternoon, had changed him. The change was not at all welcome. Sometimes, it is better to be ignorant, he thought, particularly when facts are less than fulfilling. With the knowledge he now possessed, he did not feel more enlightened. It was as if he'd just caught the magician at the magic store buying tricks. But they were sinister tricks with real daggers and ominous consequences.

It was nearly 10:00 A.M. and neither Janna nor the Reverend had stirred. "After breakfast would it be possible for you to run to town?" Janus asked Karen.

"What for?" she asked.

"We're going to need some supplies for our guest. From the smell of him, I think we better start from scratch. Can you go to the discount store and get a few essentials?"

"Yeah, that's probably a good idea. What size?"

"Karen, I'm not sure. I do know that he's quite a large man. I would guess forty-four trousers with a thirty-three inseam. Oh, and can you get an extra large shirt and sweater, too? Also get some size thirteen shoes. If they are too big, we'll replace them later. Oh, and can you see if they have some sort of coat available? I'm afraid all of mine are far too small. Be sure to pick up toiletry items as well: a shaver, shaving cream, toothbrush, toothpaste, and lots of aspirin. He's going to have the worst headache of his life."

"It should take me about an hour. Is there anything else?"

"No, I'm just going to read the paper and have another cup of coffee. I would go myself but you know—"

She certainly did know. She wasn't about to stay in this house with that derelict around. The thought of her and Janna being alone with an unknown stranger in the house was not appealing. No, going to town had to be done. Janus said that it was important, and that was enough for her.

෪ ෪ ෪

The drive to the hospital was enjoyable. This place, which had caused John so much consternation in the past week, was suddenly heralding beacon-quality good news. Dow was going to be all right—cause for celebration!

The thought that Dow could shed some light on the current situation was almost forgotten in the euphoria of knowing that his friend would recover. The drive from his house to the hospital took little time. He walked through the front doors of the hospital with a lightness in his step that had been absent for some time.

From his many visits, John knew which room Dow had been assigned, so he walked jauntily past the attendant to the elevators and pressed the up button. Even the pitiful music in the elevator sounded like the New York Philharmonic on this particular day. Seeing symbols instead of words for the buttons on the elevator did not offend him as much as usual. Today was a good day. His smile was infectious as he exited the elevator and headed for his friend's room.

The evening's excitement on the medical unit had passed and everything returned to normal. The critical care nurses still whispered in the break room about the activity, but as far as the public was concerned, nothing had happened. The attending nurse recognized him and said, "Good morning, Chancellor. Did you want to see Dr. Jones?"

"Yes, I do. How is he doing?"

"Well, in a word he has been wearing out that call button wanting to know when you would arrive. I guess the best thing is for you to go and see him and decide for yourself." She got up from behind the desk and walked with pride toward his room.

This unit was not always able to save a life. The specter of death regularly hung over the third floor. When their efforts were rewarded by patient recovery, it felt good. Success was a balm to soothe the wounds of those all-too-frequent times when their best care was found wanting.

Dow was sitting in bed and eating breakfast. Eggs, sausage, and toast were heaped on his plate. A carafe of coffee was within easy reach and a large glass of juice completed the repast.

Over the last forty-eight hours he had not been able to take in solid food and was fed intravenously. This caused him to appear more gaunt than usual, a trick John would not have believed possible.

When he entered the room, Dow quickly set down his fork and held out his hand. John took it and then, in very uncharacteristic fashion, hugged his friend. John was never one to go in for outward shows of emotion. However, on this occasion it seemed to be the thing to do.

"Ira, I am so glad that you are going to be okay."

"I know, John. It just seems so strange to be in the hospital when I haven't even been sick. I don't think I would like to repeat the situation."

"How are you feeling?"

"I have a headache."

They both laughed. There was still a great deal of tension in the room. The idea that he could walk away from the boatman on the river Styx twice in a matter of days with nothing more than a headache was absurd. "No, I mean it, Dow. How are you?"

Dow did not answer right away, but considered his response. "I don't know. Everything appears to be the same—except me. Something is changed. I can't tell you what it is, because I have not lived with the change long enough to understand it." His eyes drifted to the window; he was silent for a moment. "Well, anyway, tell me everything that's been happening."

John brought one of the hospital chairs near the bed and began to carefully unfold events. It took him a full twenty minutes to bring him up to date on the various developments. When he told how he reached his decision to ask the police for help, Dow agreed completely. When he told of the Joseph's girl trying to access DORA, Dow laughed. "I'm not sure I could break into DORA. Did you know that I transferred the entire text file from Richard's computer to DORA?"

"No, but I had my suspicions. What in the hell are we dealing with here? I don't think I have ever been this scared. I'm starting to see threats in every shadow."

Dow again considered his answer. "I don't know. I didn't get a chance to read too much of the data. But what I saw was shocking and disturbing. The shocking part is that such a malevolent organization could exist in a country predicated on individual freedom. How can the limits of our freedom be dictated by an organization that answers to no one? The other thing, the disturbing part, is that they appear to be so ingrained in complex aspects of our culture that I have very few ideas on how to combat them."

"Well, that can wait for a while. Has your doctor talked with you about when you might be released?"

"He said that it might be possible to leave on Sunday morning. He wants to observe me, at least for the day. I guess there is a chance that I could spontaneously drop back into a coma. He says that it is unlikely and exceedingly rare, but he doesn't want to take any chances. Just in case, I want you to know that I built a failsafe into DORA."

"Failsafe? What do you mean?"

"If something happens to me, I want you to be able to access the information. My desk drawer, the third one down on the right side, has a false bottom. It is only the depth of a disk. You couldn't tell it was there unless I told you. Remove everything from that drawer and get a screwdriver. Force the screwdriver down along the back side and it should pop open. Inside there is a disk. It will supersede all commands to disable the computer. It will be as if I turned it on myself. I would write down the passwords and codes, but this is more secure. There are seven levels of access to the computer. The diskette will take you to all but the last one. The last one would not be of any use to anyone but an extremely adept low-level programmer. I don't want the information contained in the seventh level around after me. There are too many programs that could be used for less than noble activities. Do you understand?"

"Certainly. I don't believe that anything will happen to you though, Dow. I am so glad you are back."

03   03   03

"I have the report on Frank Smith's prints from the bureau."

"Let me see it, Sergeant."

Tom Johnson took the report and read that Frank Smith's fingerprints were not on file with the FBI. It didn't surprise him. He expected as much. Still, proper procedure had been followed. He handed the report back to the sergeant and continued to fill out the charge forms. He had done three of them so far and expected to do another three before he was finished, when the phone rang.

"Detective Johnson?"

"Yes, this is Johnson. What can I do for you?"

"This is Kevin Thomas from the Justice Department in Washington."

"Mr. Thomas, what can I do for you?"

"I want all charges against a man identified as Frank Smith dropped."

"No."

"I'm sorry, what did you say?"

"No way. This man attacked two people and tried to kill another. And there is strong suspicion he attacked a third, which we are still investigating. There is no way I will ever let him walk." There was an ominous silence on the line. After a minute of dead air, the man said, "I'm sorry that you feel this way. I was hoping I could get some cooperation from your office. It will be hard on you, if you don't release him."

"Are you threatening me?"

"Absolutely not. I am trying to explain the way of the world to you. Well, I can see that our conversation isn't going anywhere, so good morning."

When the receiver clicked in his ear, Tom got up and walked to the water fountain. Suddenly, his mouth was very dry. He returned and sat in his chair. He was having a hard time believing that someone was not playing a joke on him. There was no way he could release an accused felon with so much irrefutable evidence for conviction.

To begin with, he simply did not have that kind of power. A complaint had not been signed by the offended parties, but he had no doubt they would be willing to do so. He could not simply release him because some suit in Washington wanted it done. He shook his head at the stupidity of the situation and picked up the phone to dial his chief.

While he had the phone to his ear and was reaching for the buttons, the phone rang.

"Detective Johnson, this is Chief Weller. Can you come into my office?"

"Certainly, Chief. I was just picking up the phone to call you."

"I know," he said and hung up.

ଔ ଔ ଔ

Deep in the recesses of the person who had once been Tommy Lanniga, child of God, something was stirring. Like a cleansing rain, the crisp sheets, clean smell of the room, and kindness of these people had been seeping into his consciousness as he slept. In his condition, although his body was calling for more of the drug, he almost imagined that he had crossed over. For nothing—at least that he remembered of this earth—could approach the purity he felt in that clean white bed.

Through the windows, the golden light played off the trees of silver, refracting into a rainbow of colors. Everywhere his eyes settled the world was silver and gold.

He lay contemplating what to do next. He reached around his body for the bottle that was always there. He could not find one. He tried to sit up, but the pain drove him down. He searched the room in vain and closed his eyes. Sleep took him and he rested for a while.

Within minutes, he woke again. This time his nose tried convincing him that he was in heaven. The aroma of bacon and eggs mingled with coffee permeated the air. It smelled wonderful.

ೞ ೞ ೞ

"These look just fine. Do you think we should let him sleep longer?"

"Janus, I think we should let him sleep as long as he possibly can. Isn't sleep the cure for most ills?"

"I suppose. It's just that I want to begin the process of healing as soon as possible."

"But aren't we doing it already? I mean the sleep is a way of replacing the spent charge. We want him to come back from whatever hell he was in. To make that journey, he needs sleep."

ೞ ೞ ೞ

Getting out of bed was proving to be more difficult than Jersey Land remembered. It was as if the bed were sucking him down. When he finally managed to swing his legs over the edge, they met the floor with a thud. Smelling that wretched odor he had come to live with, he wrinkled his nose in disgust. In a monumental effort he lifted himself from the bed. He stood, at first bent and broken. Then in a modest show of rebirth he stood up straight. It felt good.

He opened the door to a new world. Two people sat at the table. He did not know who they were, nor did he care.

"Good morning, Reverend Land. How are you?"

"Please, just call me Tom. It has been quite a while since I deserved to have the title Reverend linked to my name. Who are you?"

"I am Janus Joseph. This is my wife Karen. We brought you to our home last night."

"Why?"

"That can wait. Which would you prefer: a bath or a shower?"

"Bath, and then a shower. I can't even remember the last time I took one. That seems like the thing to do."

Karen lifted the packages from the floor and started fussing through them. Unwrapping a complete change of clothes, including the bath items, she handed them to him. "There is a fresh towel in the linen closet."

He stumbled into the bathroom with the towel and other items in hand. He closed the door and turned on the warm water, water which might help to reclaim him from the garbage-heap of society.

Chapter 26

The shower and shave did wonders. Although Jersey Land had abused his body for the past year and a half, he was still a handsome man. Removal of the grime and stubble revealed pleasant features and sharpened his image. His hair was still long and unkempt, but a haircut would alleviate this problem. He entered the bathroom a broken man and returned, at least in appearance, on the road to recovery.

He took a place at the table and closed his eyes to pray. His prayer was the prayer of all supplicants. He asked for forgiveness for his past transgressions. He begged the Father for one more chance to walk in the ways of the Lord.

As he prayed, the doubts crept in as they had so many times before—doubts that he could ever again be worthy of speaking for goodness, for he had been exalted and then despised. Now, he only wanted to find himself. He had not really prayed for more than a year, but it seemed to erupt quietly and naturally inside him. He concentrated his mind to ask the Father for guidance along the road that wound before him. A serpentine slash cut into the mountains where he could not see what lay before him—a rocky path that would be dangerous and unpredictable with many obstacles to overcome.

That small spark struck by the carillon still burned. But the fire of belief was not yet kindled. He knew the road ahead would be hard, but he could now see that the "easy" way had not proven to be so.

That first bite of food was wonderful. He began to eat in earnest and soon cleaned his plate. Unfortunately, his stomach was unprepared for the assault of even healthy food, and he was sick. After half an hour of severe cramps and nausea, he managed to make it from the bathroom into the bedroom where he fell asleep again.

"Poor man," Karen said.

"I wish there was something we could do to help him."

"Did you want to call Dr. Fakar?"

"That might be a good idea, Karen. Maybe the doctor can prescribe medication to help ease his way back. I'll call his office. They should still be there. Do you think we can get him in this morning?"

"It could be. But what are we going to find out?"

Her question hung in the air unanswered. Going to the cupboard, she returned with a pair of tongs and a large garbage bag and headed into the bathroom.

"Where are you going with those?"

"I am going to remove his clothes. I don't believe that washing these rags would do any good. The clothes we got him are a fresh start."

"Good idea. The smell was starting to get to me."

When Karen walked outside with the clothes, Janna came out of her room. She started to head to the bathroom, but her father stopped her. He pulled out a spray bottle of disinfectant and preceded her into the room. He sprayed and wiped all surfaces at least twice, some three times. Satisfied, he emerged and said, "Just wait a moment for the smell to clear. How are you doing?"

"Pretty good. I'm still awfully sleepy. How is our guest?"

"He got up, took a shower and tried to eat breakfast, but couldn't hold it down. He is resting again. There, I think the bathroom is all right now."

He called the doctor's office and was told to have the man there in about thirty minutes. The doctor had some time left at the end of the morning, and he did not work in the afternoon on a Saturday. Hanging up the phone, Janus awakened the Reverend and told him they would need to leave shortly. He then grabbed his coat and a small bag of cracked corn and bread crumbs for his ducks and geese. He walked out in the morning sun to attend to his chosen duties.

ଔ ଔ ଔ

"Look Detective Johnson, I'm getting my orders from on high. I'm afraid we'll have to release the man."

"Why, Chief Weller? I mean we have him. He attacked and nearly killed a prominent member of the faculty at

Harmson. He attacked an officer and a nurse, took the officer's gun and attempted to kill the man he attacked earlier. I just can't see any reason..."

"I guess there are two ways to look at this. You are right in what you say. But the professor is going to recover, and the nurse and officer are not hurt permanently. The only damage that I can see is that he crashed into your patrol car. That cost will be taken care of."

"By whom?"

The Chief smiled. "Well, it doesn't really matter what you think. He is due to be released this morning; there isn't much that you can do about it."

"Does the prosecutor concur?"

"Not that it is any of your business, but he is well aware of the situation. Why don't you take the rest of the day off and forget it? Just chalk it up to experience."

Tom stared at him for a moment before getting up to leave. He offered no goodbye or any other communication. Beyond angry, he had crossed over the border to that strange land of human emotion: seething hatred.

Here, action is not only desired; it is required. What could he do? He was happy with his career, at least he had been until a few moments ago. He had no desire to leave the Mason Police Force. So there was very little he could do, at least officially. Still, action would be taken; of that he was certain. He returned to his office grim and determined.

ଔ ଔ ଔ

Kira Morris straightened her hair for the fifth time that morning in the rear view mirror.

She had spent the evening comforting her sister. Kara was really shaken-up. It is a mind-numbing experience to be gripped by hands of violence and then to brush that close to death. Kira had even crawled into bed with her last night, as they had in the old days when one of them was scared. It was while she offered her shoulder to her crying sister that she decided on her next course of action.

It was easy to wake up before Kara, though she surprised herself by sleeping so late. It was nearly 9:00 when she showered. Before leaving she looked at her sleeping sister and felt a kind of sisterly love she had not felt in years. There was very little chance that Kara would wake up before she got back. The attending physician examined her after the assault and prescribed sleeping pills for her to take at home.

It was in Kira's mind to enter the hospital and interview Dr. Jones. Without considering whether this was a moral thing to do, she dressed that morning in one of her sister's spare uniforms and quietly took Kara's employee identification from her purse. It only took her a few moments to fix her hair the way her sister wore it.

Although they had become less and less alike as they grew older, they were still remarkably similar in appearance, even when they didn't try. Now, she did her best to take on the persona of her sister. The mannerisms she knew as well as her own naturally fell into place.

Her plan was simple. Using her sister's key card, she would enter the hospital by the employees' entrance, go to the third floor, interview Dr. Jones, and be gone before anyone even knew she was there.

Looking in the rear view mirror was unsettling—it was her sister that stared back. She sometimes forgot she had a twin; their lives had taken such different courses. Looking at herself dressed as a nurse, she felt a twinge of regret.

She left Kara's car in the lot and walked confidently up the walkway. She slipped her key card in the slot and heard the electronic lock activate. She entered the door. There was no one around as she moved to the elevators.

She exited and searched for the numbers on the rooms. She was after 314S. The even-numbered rooms were on the right. Down the hallway, a doorway opened and a heavy set nurse backed out with a medication tray trailing behind her. She seemed shocked to see Kira and greeted her warmly, "Kara, I sure didn't expect to see you today. How are you?"

Kira cleared her throat and pretended that she couldn't speak, but gave the high sign to show that she was doing fine. Mercifully, she saw room 314S ahead and waved goodbye. She entered the door without knocking and was surprised when a deep voice asked. "What can I do for you, Nurse? I ate my breakfast and the other nurse just gave me my morning pills."

"Dr. Jones, can you keep a secret?"

He smiled and answered boyishly, "Depends on what it is."

"My name is Kira Morris. I am a reporter for *I Witness News* in town."

"You are not. I don't know what kind of game you are playing, but you were the first person that I saw after I woke up yesterday—and a beautiful sight it was," he added with a grin.

Kira looked at him incredulously for a moment and then remembered her own deception. "No, that wasn't me. That was my sister Kara. We're identical twins."

"Really, well I suppose that makes sense. Still, if you don't want anyone to know, I won't tell. What can I do for you?" His expression sobered.

"I've been interested in the activities over at Harmson University, and you seem to be the focal point, at least one of them. What exactly is going on?"

"I'm not sure I am at liberty to discuss that."

"People have a right to know. I am the voice of the people, and I want to be able to keep them informed."

"I don't disagree with you. But people might get hurt if I start talking. I don't want that to happen. If there were another way, I'd use it. But there isn't."

"I guess I see your point. If you can't talk about that, can you at least tell me how you are doing? Are you feeling well?"

"I don't seem to have a lot of ill effects except for an exceptional headache which sometimes diminishes, but never goes away. I am looking forward to going home tomorrow."

"What were the men—?"

Her question was interrupted by the buzzing of the telephone. Dow reached over and picked it up.

"Hello, Dr. Jones. This is Detective Johnson. I felt I should call you and tell you that Frank Smith, the man I believe assaulted you, is being released this morning."

"Why?"

"I can't discuss that other than to say, it is against my

wishes. But then again, I don't seem to have a lot of say in the matter."

"Detective, I have a guest from the TV news in the room, so I am not free to speak. Can I call you back?"

"Certainly, I just wanted you to know that I did not support this action. In fact, I tried to prevent his release, but was unable. You say you have a member of the press in the room? Who?"

"She says her name is Kira Morris. I don't watch television, but from her appearance, I may have to start."

Kira smiled. She was not unmoved by an unsolicited compliment. There was a long silence on the phone as Tom thought about his options. What could he do to shed some light on this action?

Officially, he could do nothing, but maybe someone else could. One of the things he could do would be to tell the news media of the man's release, without his name being mentioned. If anyone asked, he would deny it. Hell, they couldn't prove he talked to her by the phone record. The phone record would show that he called the hospital. Finally, after the silence strayed beyond awkward he said, "Dr. Jones, can you put Ms. Morris on the phone?"

Dow lowered the phone and said, "Ms. Morris, Detective Johnson would like a word with you."

Surprised, she picked up the offered phone. "Yes?"

"Ms. Morris, you know my feelings about the press, but I feel compelled to give you a story. I want no mention of my name—ever. Can you promise me this?"

"Yes, your rights are protected under the constitution, and I am not able to be compelled to reveal my source. I believe in this. I assure you I will never tell anyone who told me."

"You know, it's funny, but I believe you. All right, here's the scoop. The man who assaulted your sister, the officer, and probably Dr. Jones, is being released from the county jail this morning. All charges have been dropped."

"Who authorized the release?"

"I don't know that, but I received a call from Kevin Thomas of the Justice Department in Washington asking me to release him. When I refused, someone went over my head. He appears to be a likely suspect. If you want to film the release, be at the south door of the county jail at 11:00 this morning. That is the time when prisoners are released."

"Is there anything else you can tell me?"

"No."

"Thank you very much."

"Ms. Morris, if there was any other way, I would have taken it. No offense, but television news makes me ill," he said as he hung up the phone.

Kira heard the click and pressed the button to end the connection from her end. She quickly dialed the number of Scott, her camera man, and luckily found him at home. "Scott, I need you to bring the equipment and pick me up at my sister's house in twenty-five minutes. Can you do it?"

"Sure, I guess. But what's the big rush?"

"Trust me, this will be worth your while, as opposed to that wild goose chase last night. I think this will be very interesting. I'll fill you in when you pick me up."

Without even saying good-bye she hung up the phone and started to leave. "Dr. Jones, when you feel you can talk about what happened, would you call me at this number?" Her tone was sincere and serious as she handed him her business card.

"Do you mean I can't call you unless I have some information?"

She smiled coyly and said, "Depends on what you have in mind. I might be interested."

"Then I'll call for sure."

She left the room and hurried out of the hospital. She had to be ready to be on camera in twenty-five minutes as Kira Morris, not Kara Morrisy. She started the car and headed for her sister's.

ଔ ଔ ଔ

The waiting room was nearly empty and they were the last remaining group of people. Janna stayed at home while Karen and Janus struggled mightily to get Reverend Land first into the car and then into the office. After about ten minutes the Medical Technologist asked them to bring him to a small room where blood and urine samples were taken. They made it back to their seats and waited another fifteen minutes.

Finally, the nurse said they could go in. With Karen on one side and Janus on the other, they led the man into the small examining room.

He was awake, but very ill. He needed them to stop the car twice on the ten-mile drive from the lake to the doctor's office. Still, he was not uncooperative. Somewhere inside of him he knew these people meant him no harm and, in fact, were here to help him.

He sat on the table, moving from side to side to keep his balance. After several awkward minutes, Dr. Ahmed Fakar entered the room. He greeted Janus warmly and said, "What seems to be the problem?"

"This is Reverend Jersey Land. He will be staying with us for a while, but he is not feeling well. For the last year or so, he has been in an inebriated state. We are trying to help him."

"Well, let me have a look."

The examination took less than five minutes. Aftermaking a note on the chart, he asked to see them both in the hallway.

"This man is very sick; he may even be dying. I can't tell for sure without running a series of tests. His urine and blood tests both indicate there might be some major problems. I can prescribe medication to alleviate the nausea and help him combat the need for alcohol. But that's about it."

"Thank you, Doctor. Let's see what your medicine can do for him. If he needs treatment later, are you available?"

"Certainly."

The ride back to the cottage was interrupted by a stop at the pharmacy, where Karen had the prescriptions filled. Reverend Land slept in the back seat.

As the moving vehicle flashed framed scenes of late winter, the most poignant image was what Janus saw in the rearview mirror. It gave Janus pause to see the wreck of a man in their back seat. The nobility that seemed to grace his face earlier had fled. Instead, a tentative skeleton remained. Not sturdy. Not upright. A man, for all intents and purposes, beaten to a pulp by society. Yet, the grace Janus saw that morning gave him hope. Maybe, just maybe, time and rest would prove an elixir. There might be a chance to ease the pain he had caused in his own and others' lives.

Chapter 27

Kira took the microphone from Scott Kramer and walked toward the rear entrance of the jail. It had been built in the late sixties in one of the rougher areas of town. Today the streets were not busy, as they were during the week. There was an occasional passer-by but, in general, it was a desolate morning in this sector.

She checked her watch: 10:53. In seven minutes, Frank Smith would be released. "Are you ready? How do I look?" she asked. Scott gave a thumbs up and nodded.

"This is Kira Morris, *I Witness News,* reporting. I am standing outside of the Axton County Jail, here in Mason. In a few minutes, sources tell us, a travesty of justice will be committed. A man, identified only as Frank Smith with an unknown address, will be released from jail without being charged. He was being held while officers completed investigations. Sources tell us that there is sufficient evidence to bring Smith to trial. There are eyewitness accounts. He was properly Mirandized, and all procedures have been followed. The alleged crimes include: assaulting two civilians last night at Memorial Hospital, taking an officer's gun, and attempted murder of another patient. There is also some indication that he may have been involved in the near-fatal beating of Professor Ira Jones last Thursday.

"Why is this man being released? That is the question that we hope to have answered this Saturday morning."

She lowered her microphone almost imperceptibly, and Scott placed the camera into a standby position. The gesture would be unnoticed on the television screen, but it was enough to let her camera man know she was finished for now.

The morning air was light with just a touch of warmth. She paced back and forth collecting her thoughts. She excelled in this arena. In the intervening years since leaving college with a degree in broadcasting, she had honed her skills. What she said became secondary to the way that she said it. Physical gestures were key. Although not consciously aware of it, she played her body as if it were an instrument. Being fully present helped her to focus those energies.

On this Saturday morning, she had a great desire to express her contempt for the unjustified release of this felon. She projected what she thought would occur into a series of potentialities and plotted her reactions. She thought about how she would be perceived. If she were too shrill, she could not elicit the kind of response she wanted. If she appeared too timid, no one would pay attention to her. She was a professional at her job, and the correct attitude would be displayed.

Mr. Wesson waited in the parking lot until the appointed hour. He left his car to walk to the door of the county lockup to wait for Mr. Smith. Rounding a van, he noticed the female reporter. A curse escaped his lips, but he continued walking. That was all they needed—some bimbo with a microphone and camera. Comparatively speaking, they had encountered more trouble on this particular exercise than they usually did in a month of Sundays. There was something about this situation that told him it was getting out of hand. At each turn, agents and others were neglecting to do what the Center expected. Such miscalculations and failure to adjust to new circumstances were unusual. Normally, such small inconveniences as they had experienced would be just that: inconvenient. No, these incidents were being blown out of proportion, and Mr. Wesson saw potential consequences at every corner.

Obviously, the woman with the camera crew was a symptom of this. But only a symptom. Things started going badly long before this. No, it was hard for him to pinpoint the exact point where things began to deteriorate. He supposed it was when it was decided to have the old fart kill himself. It would have been simpler, cleaner, just to kill him.

The professor was getting too close for some time and needed to be taken care of. But someone in Virginia decided that it must not appear as if anyone else was involved.

The fabrications the Center created were top notch. Any normal person would react in the same way when faced with "evidence" of child sexual molestation and drug abuse—complete with spurious pictures and testimonials. The psychotropic medication, Amvec, had been introduced to darken the man's mood. He recalled how easy it had been. Since the local pharmacy that the professor used for his blood pressure was part of a national chain, they simply injected one of the Center's pharmacists as a fill-in. From there, it was a cinch to substitute the drug for the professor's prescribed medicine.

But the old man crossed them up by spewing that philosophical mumbo-jumbo in a lecture. And instead of committing the act in private, choosing instead to do it in front of his students. This had not been part of the plan. And in his view, it was all a massive mistake on the part of the Center's staff.

He sat in on the class and it was his voice that had been recorded. He'd been following the professor for over a week, waiting for that moment when he would follow the Center's directive. His had been the voice on the phone giving the ultimatum. He said that if it was not done by 3:00, the story would be on the evening news.

He sat in the university hall and listened to the lecture. The professor did not break one of the tenets of the agreement, but he certainly bent them severely. The Center decided to honor their commitment. As the hour neared, he could tell the man was going to do it. In his anxiety and paranoia about what Kline might say, he had been actively urging him on.

If his voice had not been recorded, the incident might have already been forgotten. But it had. As he walked through the parked cars toward the designated location where he would meet Mr. Smith, he never considered that he might have been one of the major causes of the dilemma—in the person of the female reporter who faced them now. He assumed the problem had been with his superiors, or with the old man, or anyone else. He was perfectly willing to blame others for his own indiscretions. The truth was that he had brought attention to bear on the Center's activities. The reporter's involvement could be traced directly to his lack of discipline. He knew but did not choose to acknowledge it.

The reporter didn't notice him, as he lurked among the cars out of sight. One of the predominant rules of his job as an operative was to try to blend into the background as much as possible. He saw the doors open and Frank stepped out.

The reporter moved toward him. "Sir, excuse me. Kira Morris, *I Witness News*. Do you have any idea why the charges against you have been dropped?"

"No comment."

"Is it true that you know someone in a position of authority who interceded for you?"

He glared at her with venom dripping from his eyes. He cursed her under his breath and said, "I'm sorry Ms. Morris, I cannot answer your questions."

Frank saw Mr. Wesson and headed across the alley at a quick pace. Kira attempted to follow him, but Scott was having a little trouble moving and keeping the camera in focus. In reality, her quest was not to catch him. She had already learned as much as she could or would from him. Her object, rather, was to show him running away. She turned to the camera and said, "As you can see, the man identified as Frank Smith has 'no comment' on the situation.

"This case raises many questions, questions this reporter will pursue to the best of my ability. The people of Mason and the State of Michigan have a right to know why a violent assailant, confirmed by ample evidence and eye witnesses, is being released with all charges being dropped. It appears that our justice system is being tampered with and compromised. We'll keep you updated with our on-going investigation." She repeated her gesture of lowering the microphone and Scott turned off the camera.

"Good job, Kira. I think that'll broadcast real well. I don't believe he was aware of it, but I think we caught his curse with your mic. It always makes the subject appear so evil when we can bleep out obvious curses, especially when they are directed against you. I'll check it out when we get back and let you know. By the way, that dress makes you appear almost virginal in front of the camera. The contrast between his dark suit and your light appearance should be effective."

"Good, I think we are going to have to contact Chief Weller and the Prosecutor. I'll make the calls when we get back. Who's the director tonight?"

"Sheryl—the intern."

"Good, we won't have to explain too much. Someone

with a lot of clout is involved in this, and I suspect they could prevent our story from being broadcast. We'll see if they can get away with nearly killing my sister."

෫ ෫ ෫

The medication did wonders. Reverend Land was beginning to feel human again. The doctor recommended a bland diet, clear broth and mild bread. He was particularly cautioned to stay away from food that's hard to digest, such as fats. In retrospect, the bacon and eggs were probably the worst thing he could have tried to eat. So with a new charge, Karen busied herself in the kitchen for a good part of the afternoon preparing homemade chicken stock. The smell from the pot permeated the house and added a wholesome air. Reverend Land rested when he first returned from the doctor's. Now, he was up and walking around.

"Sir, if you have a pair of gloves and a hat, I would like to go for a walk along the beach. The coat is very warm, but for some reason I'm still chilled to the bone."

"Certainly. Would you like some company?"

"Not yet, I need to be alone for a while. I still feel very queasy and my head is killing me."

"I understand. Listen, if you go down by the beach the ducks and geese will gather around. There is a box of feed just outside of the door. I'll get you a bag. If you would like, that is?"

"That would be...nice." He said the word like he had almost forgotten its meaning.

Janus grabbed a bag from the kitchen drawer and handed it to him. The sun was edging toward the horizon, as orange tendrils of light spread through the woods illuminating the trees in random fashion. The effect was of a patchwork quilt created from nature's own fabrics. Here a sparse oak, still hanging onto the vestiges of last year's growth of leaves. Over there a full-grown white pine stretching its massive trunk to the sky with just an umbrella of needles to provide it with nourishment. All interconnected by patches of snow.

When Reverend Land left the porch holding onto the bag, the ducks and geese began to swarm at the water's edge.

There was a tumultuous noise of feathers flapping, ducks quacking, geese honking, and the water being disturbed. The contrast between the stillness of the late afternoon and the frenzied activity at the shore was amazing. He quickened his pace, arrived by the water, dipped his hand in the bag and spread the corn and bread crumbs out as evenly as he could. Their obvious enthusiasm over the meal encouraged him, so he dipped and spread a little faster. A smile erupted on his face and he began to chuckle to himself. After running out of food, he went back to the house and knocked on the door. "Would it be all right if I had some more food for the ducks?" He had the innocent, first-time look of an eight-year-old boy.

Janus smiled and said, "Take as much as you like. Are you enjoying feeding them?"

"Yes, it gives one a feeling of accomplishment and well-being. Thank you for suggesting it. After filling his bag he returned to the beach. When he'd left there was still food floating in the water or resting on the bottom. Now, the water was as clear, as if it had just bubbled out of the springs that supplied the lake. He reached into the bag and filled his hand about half-full with food. Instead of just scattering it about, he tried to give it to the smaller ones who might have not been getting as much in the feeding frenzy of the larger birds.

Long dormant, nearly forgotten thoughts burst into his conscious mind. He considered the feeding of the ducks in terms of one's faith and the spreading of the gospel. He tried to force these thoughts down, but they sprang back even stronger. From the degradation of his sickness was being born a new man—a man of conviction who would not compromise. He would do the Lord's bidding again.

From the depths of his despair a new life dedicated to the Word was beginning to stir. A life which had been abandoned and defiled was suddenly moving with determined force through a canal of rebirth. The compelling force was a faith growing stronger every minute. That faith was tempered by fires of the hell he had been living. He knew his faith would have to be more solid than the walls the Center had built to hide themselves. If his strength continued to come back, perhaps he could be the "hammer" to help break down those walls and expose their activities to the light of truth.

ଔ ଔ ଔ

On the second ring Janus answered the phone.

"Hello, Mr. Joseph. This is John Goslin, how is everything up there?"

Janus filled him in on all of the particulars. He seemed pleased that Reverend Land was showing progress. "I think it was a combination of conditions. One of these was that he had begun the change before we arrived. In time, I believe he might have made moves toward recovery and wholeness himself. I don't know what drove him to do what he did. But there will be time to discuss that later. Right now, I want him to do the best job he can of becoming well."

Chancellor Goslin told him all that had happened in Mason. It took several minutes to convey the actions of the man identified as "Frank Smith." Janus became visibly agitated. The more he heard, very real concerns for the safety of his family crowded his mind.

"I talked with Dr. Jones this morning, and he feels well on the way to recovery. He is due to be released tomorrow morning. I'd like to meet with the people involved. Would it be possible to have the meeting at your cottage? I believe it is far enough away from town to prevent..." He let the thought die on his tongue.

Janus answered right away, "Yes, certainly, I think that would be wise. What time should we expect everyone?"

"Let's shoot for noon. It is about a two-hour drive up there. Since Dow is not scheduled to be released until 8:00, I want him to go to his computer and get any information that he can. We need to fill in as many blanks as possible before deciding what to do."

"Okay, we'll see you then. Is there anything else I should know?"

"Can you get the *I Witness News* show in your area?"

"I believe it is on the cable. Why?"

"It seems our Mr. Smith, who caused the trouble at the hospital last night, has been released from custody without being charged. I must say that I am not surprised at that turn of events, but Detective Johnson was mighty upset. Well, to make a long story short, a reporter by the name of Kira Morris was at the jail when the man was released. I don't know who tipped her off, but I have my suspicions. Her report at 6:00 should make for interesting viewing."

৪ ৪ ৪

The intern director was not used to dealing with the stars of the show. Normally, on Saturday night she only had to deal with the substitute anchor people. The stars required a certain deferential treatment. Kira was no different.

When she and Scott prepared the report, they only listed it as an interview about the Harmson situation which would run 1:54 seconds.

Sheryl noted it on her time sheet and did not think to preview it. If she had asked to see it beforehand, she stood the risk of offending the "star." When that happened, she knew intern directors were dispensible.

Even when the story ran, she thought it was a good one. The man's curse had been bleeped by the most annoying sound that Scott could find. It had the effect of making the man appear to be some sort of amoral monster. She thought no more about it until later.

Before the news was over, the phone lines were lit. The secretary answered nearly every one of them with a simple, "Thank you for your concern. We will pass it along." There was one call that she did not answer. When the caller identified himself as the owner's representative, she passed it on to the station manager who was at home. The result of that call was that the station would not have any more reports of that nature concerning this much maligned individual.

But the damage had been done. A spark was smoldering in the tinder of public opinion. A television station in Detroit picked up the report because it looked interesting. Harmson University was a nationally known institution, so other stations replayed the tape. Each station that played the tape received the obligatory call from the Center and promised to drop the story. Still, the damage had already been done.

Chapter 28

"I have a copy of the tape from the local station's *I Witness News* show if you would like to see it, Jonathan."

"I suppose I should. I'll be right over, Judge Conley." Jonathan Green did not like being called at home, but it was one of the responsibilities of his position, and he understood the urgency of dealing with potential problems. If they didn't deal with them as small problems, they would not diminish. In fact, they would fester until becoming all-consuming. Through experience, both men knew the way to deal with matters of this nature was quickly with very little room for equivocation.

Without saying a word to his wife, other than to state he was needed at work, he left the house near the Center and drove the half-mile with his mind full of questions, questions focused on what the Judge had decided to do. 'How could he be of service?'

His function as liaison officer for the stations was sure to be used. It probably would not even be necessary to get ugly. His first thought was to remind the stations of their responsibility for reporting accurate, non-political news. This story, while it was true, could be discredited by the very nature of the people involved. The man identified as Frank Smith would be removed from the area this evening and would never be seen in that region again.

Since there was no possibility of re-apprehending him, the charges would remain 'dropped'—no matter how much public outcry there was over the case.

Jonathan assumed they ran Smith's prints through the FBI and found nothing. It was not that his prints weren't there, for they were. He had been an FBI agent, and being fingerprinted is required of all employees. Some years ago, Darren Meyers used access codes given to the Center by a high government official to place a resident computer program in the FBI's fingerprint identification software. It tagged all of the fingerprints of the Center's listed operations staff.

When the computer found a match, the program would over-ride the positive match and replace with an "ITEM NOT FOUND" message. The program itself was a fancy bit of high tech sleight of hand, which worked to ensure that the Center's people could never be identified.

He removed his identification card from his wallet and showed it to one of the two guards at the gate. He examined it carefully with a flashlight, while the other moved to the passenger side of the car, removed the safety strap from his gun and stood with his hand hovering ominously.

After being waved through, he parked the car in his designated space and walked through the compound. The night air, although still chilly, was warming as trees swayed gently in the evening breeze. The building housing both his office and the Judge's was lighted from the outside, but on this Saturday night, the only inside light came from the office of Judge Conley.

Jonathan knocked softly and entered without waiting for a response.

"Sit, Jonathan."

Jonathan looked around the room. The only difference in the room from his daily conferences was that the doors on one of the massive bookcases was opened, leaving a combination television/video player clearly visible. As he sat in the chair in front of the Judge's desk, the room darkened and the screen burst to life.

An attractive lady introduced the story. He watched as a man he barely recognized exited the building. He heard the curse that was bleeped out and saw that Mr. Smith joined Mr. Wesson. As the two men hastened away without saying anything to the reporter, he saw the problem.

Why the curse? Why slither away in a cloud of guilt? It all further complicated the situation. Instead of the Center being cast in its rightful role as white knight and protector of freedom, it had the opposite effect. He shook his head when the report concluded, "I'm afraid he didn't handle that well."

"Agreed. Where do we go from here?"

"Well, since this was not picked up nationally—it wasn't, was it?" The Judge shook his head no. Jonathan continued, "I can only assume our policies were sound and they functioned in the way they were intended. I don't know, but my gut feeling is that this incident will dry up like a mud puddle after a storm. For a while everyone might see it, but eventually, without follow-up information, it will dissipate."

"I suppose you are correct. Still, the problem is: can we limit any further revelations?"

Though he had not sent the men to do the job, he was aware of what was going on and felt somewhat responsible for at least sympathizing with his boss. It was a hard job to always insure the Center's directives were carried out. Now, some female reporter had successfully identified one of the operatives and plastered his picture all over the television with accusations that could prove very damaging—if they were ever proven. At this point, that was the extent of what they had to deal with. Making sure that such accusations were unfounded and unsupported was the critical task before them.

Instead of occurring as an isolated incident, this particular nuisance had grown out of proportion to its relative importance. It was turning into a disaster of almost unprecedented proportions. Such a crisis had not threatened the Center for more than fifteen years. The reason this reporter was successful was that the incident occurred on a Saturday morning, when most of the regular staff at the television station was absent. If the regular staff had been present, the story would have been screened and bumped before it was broadcast. The reporting did not fit into the recommended format and guidelines. The rules on political coverage would have served nicely in this instance.

Although by using the systems in place they had succeeded in keeping the tape from being broadcast on a national level, it had been picked up by enough local stations to cause a problem, a problem that Jonathan correctly assumed was falling into his lap. The Judge did not want sympathy, he wanted answers. How can we stop this? This incident was very minor. Its severity was being exaggerated by the Judge's assumptions. It was an aberration the report was broadcast in the first place; pure, blind luck it had been picked up by other stations. The story crossed the invisible boundary and lay in the area of speculation, something normally not broadcast. Still, it was probably better to deal with it in the recommended manner rather than ignoring it and assuming it would go away. Jonathan agreed with the Judge's reasoning.

ଔ ଔ ଔ

Janus switched off the television when the report was finished and shook his head. "She did a good job. Just the right play of emotion and fact."

Reverend Land changed his position on the couch in an uneasy way and said, "I know that man."

"Really? How?"

"Did I tell you those people manipulated me after the initial revelations?"

"No, you haven't told us anything. We assumed you would when you felt able."

"Thank you for that. Everything is still spinning in my mind, but I am starting to make sense of it again. On my television show, I offended the power brokers by calling all people to follow God's word, regardless of their background.

"It seems such a simple thing, but that was not the message they wanted to convey. Their message was more subtle; they were after people's attitudes. No, they were not after conversions or trying to save anyone's soul. Religion, or Christianity for that matter, were always somewhere in the background. They saw the show as a means to control folks. They wanted to influence and shape attitudes.

"As nearly as I can tell their major emphasis is on fragmenting the people. They are interested in reinforcing cultural differences and racial hatred, although their message on the surface is the opposite. I don't know the reasoning behind this, but I guess that is open to speculation. It is my feeling that they need to divide the American people inorder to maintain their control over them. They will use any means to drive divisive wedges.

"Cultural identification on government forms is a Center idea. So is teaching children in a language other than English.

They claim publicly that they are trying to deal with 'new muliti-cultural realities,' but this is not the case. What they are trying to do is keep people from actually thinking about what they read or hear or see.

"So, instead of being an instrument of God's freedom, I was an enslaver of the worst kind. I guess I knew it all along. But I was a poor farm boy from Iowa with dreams of saving the world from the disaster it has become.

"When I left divinity school, I had a fire that would not be quenched. I took a job as a minister in a church that had been through three ministers in the previous year. No one the Classis sent was right. Some were too tall, some too short. Some spoke too long. Some preached well, but not long enough. Since I was just out of school and needed a job, I was sent.

"It was just a small church in a backwater town in Iowa. But to me it was the challenge for which I had spent my life preparing. I preached to as few as fifteen people in those early days. But I never let the size of the congregation gathered diminish my message. When people left, they were happy and full of the Lord's love. I developed a reputation for giving a joyful message.

"I could sing some, and that brought more people into the church. My church started to grow. I worked hard, harder than I ever had. When you are 'marketing' the word of God, you have a good, solid, worthy product to sell. But nothing will sell itself. I was a good salesman.

"Soon a local UHF TV station—remember those?" Janus nodded. Janna looked confused, but Reverend Land went on, "Well, they came and offered to pay the church money to broadcast our service. I convinced the Consistory of the wisdom of such a venture. By this time I was becoming enamored of my abilities to present the gospel. Soon, a station in another community started broadcasting our services. The offerings which came in, unsolicited at first, from the television audience gave us enough money to expand our services to the community and to pay other stations to broadcast them. Perhaps that was the step I never should have taken.

"It wasn't too long after that when a man, from what I later learned was The Center for American Heritage, approached me with a proposal to put my show on nationwide. I accepted their terms, which seemed to be the same as mine. I later learned they were not. But when I first started, everyone was happy."

"So, how do you know that man?"

"He was one of the SS observers."

"What is an SS Observer?"

"I don't know the entire scope of their operations, but I do know that anyone who is on their payroll as a spokesperson—no, I will not speak in their foul doublespeak—spokesman, has his performance graded daily by an observer. They are skilled social observers. Their comments deal with everything from the audience reaction to the message and the form of presentation to the content. They also search for deviations from the recommended messages. At the beginning I didn't grasp how much control they would want over the content of my message. To me, it was nothing less than the Gospel. To them, it was a self-serving medium with another agenda entirely."

"So, what does the SS stand for?" Janus asked.

"Syntax and Semantics."

"Oh, I see," he said—but he did not see at all. It was an area about which he knew little. What he did know could not be placed into a methodology that would be useful to understanding such manipulation.

Janna's interest was piqued though, and she chimed in, "So when did the trouble start?"

"About three years after I first broadcast nationally. I had done a show about the Scriptural text in which Paul wrote about love and the sanctity of marriage. Evidently, this offended the Center. I was summarily called in and warned about such deviations in the future.

"Now, this made me mad. When you are a minister, you assume that you are trying to do the work of the Lord. These people were saying their message took precedence over what I perceived the message of the Bible to be. This was a conflict without resolution, for I knew that I would do His work, whether I did it on a street corner or in a cathedral.

"One week I became ill and had to be hospitalized. They

sent me to a hospital in Virginia, near their compound, I suppose. I've gone over it a thousand times in my mind, and I suspect I was poisoned. I don't know this, have no way of proving it. But it is the only conceivable way they could have come up with the pictures..."

Reverend Land's voice broke and he began to cry. Tears filled his eyes as he explained how he only wanted to do what he perceived as the Lord's work. When he reached the segment of his story which concerned the photographs, he lost control of his emotions and had to stop. "I'm sorry, folks—Can you give me a few minutes? It still bothers me to talk about it. But I do want to tell you the circumstances that led to my condition."

He excused himself and walked into the bathroom. Janna turned to her father and said, "He seems to be so sincere and cooperative. Can these people be so cruel?"

"Janna, I know you don't like it when I say that you are still young, but in my years of living I am still surprised when I see the way we treat each other. It is a crime. While I am not a particularly religious man, I understand those who have a great passion for their beliefs. That does not offend me, but I am much more deeply offended by those who show by their actions that they believe in nothing."

Having regained some composure, Reverend Land walked from the bathroom to the chair and sat again. "Again, I am sorry. While I was drugged, they must have arranged to take some photographs. There were a variety of pictures of me in sexual situations with women, men, and even children. Each set of photographs was more lewd than the next. I was not even aware these had been taken. I was sick and sleeping through these activities. I didn't think about the visit to the Center's hospital having a sinister connotation until later. When I attempted to exert what I perceived as God's will, they showed me the pictures. I understand why they did this.

"I demonstrated to them that my task was to preach. If I could do it from the lofty electronic cathedral, fine. If that were to be taken from me, I would still preach. I would preach on the street corners if I had to. They needed to control me. Their pictures worked for a while. The photographs haunted me night and day. To think that I could be used and degraded in such a manner horrified me. It belittled me as a minister, but it also maligned my faith. But what could I do? I couldn't quit. They made it clear that if I resigned, the pictures would be released immediately. So, I tried to do what they wanted me to and remain faithful to the Gospel. I tried very hard. But with little success.

"Their beliefs became an anathema to me. When I tried to forget what they threatened, they reminded me. Finally, in order to find sleep at night, I took to having a glass of wine. But the pressures were building. I was constantly torn between doing the work of God and the work of men. So instead of a glass, it turned into three glasses, then four, then a bottle, and so on.

"Finally, I could take no more, and I rebelled. In retrospect, that was not a smart thing to do. But I did it anyway. The pictures were in the evening newspapers. I was kicked off the pulpit and out into the street. Everything I had worked for was gone. I was left wandering the streets, nothing less than a pariah. Then when the pain became overwhelming, I crawled into the bottle.

"They made it easy and must have had someone watching me. Every morning when I woke, there was another bottle nearby. I drank and could remain drunk until I no longer had any other life—only the destructive habits of a drunk."

Chapter 29

John Goslin turned off the alarm in a rush. The morning patter of the disc jockey jarred him awake. Though the station was classical, any interruption to his sleep was unappreciated. If he had been fully awake, the man would probably have been perceived as talking in the hushed tones typical of those stations. In his present semi-awake state, the announcer seemed to be shouting.

The sun had risen and the light through the windows forced his eyes open. He gazed on the new day and said to his wife sleepily, "One more day before February is history. Good."

She mumbled something equally meaningless in response and turned over to get a little more sleep. Since John would be leaving in about an hour to pick up Dow and head up North, she had the entire morning to herself. She looked forward to a morning with time for any activity she chose. Whether it was simply reading the newspapers or watching an old movie, she relished the solitude.

John had asked her the day before if she wanted to ride to the Josephs' cottage; she declined. Her answer came so quickly that it surprised her. She enjoyed these intermittent times when she could do what she wanted. They were rare enough in the normal daily routine. The emotionally draining events of this particular week were anything but routine. Right now, when it came to choosing between riding for four hours in the car or having a quiet and recuperative morning, the choice made itself.

She lay there quietly after the alarm sounded. Her eyes were closed, but inside she turned life over and over again to look at it all. There was a twinge of guilt about her decision. She knew that the problem with driving there today was that it related to his job—and she was tired of his work. It would be just one more function in a long line of obligations. Once more, she would have to act the part of the fawning wife-creature. And she'd grown weary of the role. Sometimes, she just wanted him to retire. They had certainly earned the right to relax a little.

When this horrible, inexplicable thing with Richard happened, it affected her deeply. She knew that both of them were struggling emotionally and psychologically to cope with the death and all its unexpected consequences. She wanted more than ever to just be done with it.

She looked forward to wintering in the South, taking long walks on the beach, and watching the weather reports about the terrible weather at home. Still, John would hear not hear of it, at least not yet. They discussed it many times. The bottom line was that he still enjoyed going to work in the morning to that academic world that had always been his own. He even enjoyed the social receptions, the fund-raising and parties. Someday, he would change his mind. She wondered if the devastating events involving his friends and colleagues at the university would influence him.

No, her own frame of mind was brittle today. It would be better for both of them for her to stay home. She'd worry for him here.

In the states along the Canadian border, the passing of February will not bring bad feelings from any but the most devoted snow lovers. It is one of the two true winter months. Usually, the snow will come and stay somewhere near the end of December and disappear near the middle of March. January and February seem decidedly dedicated to winter storms and sub-zero temperatures. Often in these months, the thermometer will be below the freezing point for weeks at a time.

On occasion, massive snow storms clog everything for days. Here in the North, these storms are treated as more of an inconvenience than the life-threatening disaster a dusting of a few inches of snow might herald elsewhere in the country.

With the sun streaming on his face and the prospect of an interesting day facing him, John convinced himself to face the cold floor of the bedroom and eased out of bed. Rising in the morning was one of the aspects of getting older he had trouble with. He had a growing awareness that when his body had been in the same position for a significant amount of time, it became difficult to move. It required prior thought and a great deal of effort. He stood up and reached for his robe. He felt as though he were standing perfectly straight, when in reality he was bent like an old gnarled tree. He found the robe which he'd left draped over a chair the night before and moved slowly into the kitchen to brew some coffee.

While the coffee was heating and filtering its aroma through the house, he showered and dressed. His morning gloom had passed, and he was excited and interested in the day beckoning him. All of the people involved in this strange case were going to be in the same room to make plans to combat them. The only surprise was that Dow insisted Kira Morris be invited. So, the group would be complete. He made a mental note of who all would be there:

1. Himself
2. Detective Johnson
3. Big Jim Davis
4. Kira Morris
5. Dow Jones
6. Reverend Jersey Land
7. Janus Joseph
8. Janna Joseph
9. Karen Joseph

As he listed each name he thought of the strengths and weaknesses they brought to the group. Since it was his natural position to be in authority, he assumed he would facilitate. This was a daunting task, for he had no idea what they should do. Maybe some of the others had ideas to share. He would certainly listen to any and all suggestions, since this confrontation planning was completely alien to him.

The coffee hit the spot, and he was soon ready to leave for the hospital. He pulled the car into the circular drive and was surprised to see Dow waiting in a wheel chair just inside of the glass doors with Kara Morrisy behind him. When Dow recognized his car he attempted to stand, but a firm hand from the nurse put him down in the wheelchair. The doors of the hospital slid noiselessly open, and he rejoined the world.

ଔ ଔ ଔ

Big Jim drove from his cottage and parked in front of the apartment building Tom Johnson called home. There was no wait, as Tom was ready to go. He came out to the car with a crudely written map in hand. They only exchanged greetings before Big Jim wheeled the four-wheel drive truck back onto the road and headed out. Jim owned two vehicles. After driving to Chicago, he had spent enough time in the car, so he drove his truck this time. He greeted the detective, "Do you think those two guys are still following people?"

"Don't know for sure, Jim. Do you want to circle by the hospital and make sure they aren't followed?"

"Tom, I think we should. I mean it won't take us that much longer, and I would feel better about it."

"Okay, let's do it."

Big Jim turned the four-wheel drive around and headed for the hospital. They did not want a recurrence of the previous day's activities and were going to be very careful.

ଔ ଔ ଔ

Dow asked, "You remember that we are going to pick up Kira, don't you?"

"No problem. Where does she live?"

Dow gave him the address and proceeded to offer directions. In all of the time that John had known Dow he had never seen him act giddy. He showered in the morning, and what little hair he had left had been neatly combed. He looked like one of the freshman boys waiting in the lounge area of a dorm for his date. The only thing missing were the pimples.

Kira met them in the driveway where she had been busy wielding a shovel. She had knocked what remained of the snow banks down with an apparent fervent hope that the sun would melt the rest of the stupid snow. Not fond of snow, she only tolerated it because of her job. She had been sending resumes to stations in the South, but so far had not had an offer. She knew people who said they loved to cross-country ski and snowmobile, but she had a hard time believing they were serious about it. How could they love something so cold?

John drove the Cadillac easily. The automatic temperature control sensed the water in the radiator was warm enough to send to the heater core, diverting it so the fan came on and warmed the car. Only six blocks away, they reached the COM/MATH Duplex quickly. Dow led the way into his particular kingdom. After opening the door Dow literally ran to DORA and turned the computer on. He entered a string of characters and was in. The first thing he did was to duplicate the files on a CD-ROM. Then he proceeded to print out the information contained in them. He eschewed the dot printer and sent the output to the laser printer in the lab.

He calculated that the information would comprise about 100 pages without the control characters which had been in the encrypted file. The laser printer was capable of printing twelve pages per minute so they had about a ten-minute wait for the printer to complete its run.

He took Kira on an impromptu tour of the facility. John sat in the lab feeling very much as if his presence was being ignored. He was glad of this and did not mind taking the time to collect his thoughts.

When the printer finally stopped spitting out paper, Dow collected the pages and they left to continue their journey.

ଔ ଔ ଔ

Reverend Land rose before everyone else and was back to feeding the ducks again. He had been doing this at every opportunity. He seemed to become stronger every day. His mood was even improving, although it was obvious that he still was in a great deal of pain. The 300 count aspirin bottle they purchased for his use was nearly half empty. He had been taking them as if they were candy.

Still, he looked peaceful standing on the shore by the clear water. The ice had receded until it was 20 feet out from the shore. Here and there a duck sat on the ice too shy to come and get the food. Janus watched as Reverend Land tossed an occasional handful that way.

Suddenly, Janus detected the sound of singing coming through the windows. He strained to hear. Faintly, as if it were far away, he heard the words:

> " . . . how sweet the sound,
> That saved a wretch like me.
> I once was lost, but now am found,
> Was blind, but now I see.
> T'was grace that taught my heart to fear
> and Grace my fears relieved.
> How precious did that grace appear
> The hour I first believed."

The voice was clear and calming, as smooth as the wind on the water with the passion of conviction. He opened the window a crack to let the music in. With his face to the lake Reverend finished the song. Janus had tears in his eyes. It had a power and majesty Janus never imagined possible. He closed his eyes, overcome with emotion.

Reverend Land was indeed getting better. The message of atonement from a life bereft of the good things of living to a world where all cares cease to have meaning was an elixir the world could use.

Janna walked out of the bedroom and said, "Who was singing? It was wonderful!"

"Reverend Land. Look at him feeding his flock. You know, seeing him improve daily makes a difference in how I perceive the man. When we brought him here, I thought he was as slimy an eel as I had ever seen. Now, I feel—I want to say pity, but that is not the right word. Rather, there is a dignity in him I would have never believed possible. His growth lends credence to his message. I believe he could convince many people of the need for a change in their lives."

"So, Dad, when is everybody coming?"

"Should be here in a couple of hours. That reminds me. I have to help your mother with the sandwiches and stuff. You can't have people over on Sunday at noon without at least feeding them something. We planned on barbecues and chips. I am looking forward to this afternoon. What do you think we should do?"

"I'm not sure. I feel strongly that they must be stopped. But at what risk? I mean whoever confronts them will have to deal with the venom they can spew, venom whose potency cannot be easily dismissed. Remember, they convinced Dr. Kline that it would be better to kill himself than deal with them."

Janus looked down at the floor for a moment. His thoughts ventured far away and into the depths of what they could have possibly said to Dr. Kline. Hearing the story that Reverend Land told did not make him approach the problem with a clear mind. Finally, he said, "You're right. Whoever goes after them must be beyond the point where he or she can be hurt. Someone who is not dependent upon a job or in need of a career. I suppose it would be better if one of us were very wealthy. But we are not. I want to think about this for while. That is a good observation."

Reverend Land finished his chore and walked slowly from the beach to the house. His white hair was blowing softly in the gentle breeze. His face expressed, more than anything else, great calm. His peacefulness was exhibited in the easy way he moved and his small smile, telling of many secret thoughts. He entered the house and said, "It is a beautiful morning. Is it Sunday?"

"Yes, it is. Why?"

"I was wondering if there was a church near?"

"Down the road there is a small Lutheran Church we usually attend. We are too busy today, but you could go. Would you like me to take you?"

"If it isn't any trouble. I appreciate your help more than I can express. But I would like to attend. What time is their service?"

"The service starts at 10:30. If we leave right now, you will be on time."

"Can I go, please?"

Reverend Land got into the passenger's seat and sat quietly. Janus explained that he had to help Karen prepare for the visitors but would be glad to drop them off.

Janna, who volunteered to go with him, sat in the back. The drive was less than a mile. The church was high on a hill overlooking the lake. Janus left the two in the parking lot and promised to pick them up in about an hour.

Reverend Land led the way, as Janna followed. They took the bulletin from the usher and sat near the front. Reverend Land sat with tears welling in his eyes. His face seemed somehow purified and glowing in the morning sun, as it passed through the windows in the front of the church.

The view through the windows was inspiring. It offered a panorama of the lake and the hills beyond. The blotches of white contrasted with the evergreens with just a hint of spring resting on the forest.

Reverend Land lifted a Bible from the book rest located on the back of the pew in front of them and studied it. Janna looked around to see if she knew anyone; she did. The organ began to play and the hour passed quickly.

~ ~ ~

Big Jim wheeled the four-wheel drive behind the Cadillac and followed them to Kira's apartment and then the college. As he watched the Chancellor drive, he knew they were unseen. It wasn't all that surprising as the pick-up was much higher than the Cadillac. From the rear-view mirror John would have seen nothing more than the bumper of the large vehicle.

They waited in the truck while they were in the building. After less than half an hour, the three left. Big Jim did not start out right away but waited for something to happen. He wanted to make certain that no one was following.

Suddenly, it was there. A car that had been parked a block down the street pulled out and in a few seconds passed them. At the wheel was the man known as Mr. Wesson.

Jim started the truck and circled the block in the opposite direction. Chancellor Goslin had stopped at a light. The car the others saw was two cars behind him. As they turned the corner, Big Jim wheeled the truck between the front of the Wesson car and the vehicle ahead of it. Both men got out. Big

Jim walked up to the door of the watcher's car and said, "Listen, I don't want you following anyone. This is my last warning. If I ever see you again, I will hurt you. I may be old, but you can plan on it."

The man started to protest, but Jim walked back to the truck. Detective Johnson joined him in a moment with the stems of the two tires from the passenger side. As they slid into the seats they could see the car begin to list. When the light changed and the man tried to go, he realized he had two flat tires and pulled to the side.

෴ ෴ ෴

After several minutes, the highway loomed before the Cadillac as they headed north. The rest of the journey was uneventful as they drove through the patchwork of white and green nature had provided. Kira and Dow sat very close together; John thought he even saw them holding hands. He smiled. It would be wonderful if his friend could finally meet a lady. Though Dow had his computers, John thought a man needed more. Someone to tell his problems to, someone to listen to his thoughts. Every person needs this—Dow was no different.

When Dow first noticed his interest in Kira, he realized how much he had been missing. The chance for this happiness served to make him anxious. For the first time in years he actually cared about his appearance.

෴ ෴ ෴

They followed the car all the way to the Josephs' place and pulled into the driveway just after them. The first thing the group did after greeting each other was to express their surprise that they had been followed. Together they walked down to the cottage. Janus rushed to greet them.

Tom Johnson said, "Good morning, Mr. Joseph. This is a beautiful place you have here."

CHALLENGE

Chapter 30

Karen brewed a large pot of coffee and arranged the table with cups, paper plates, and the condiments. The group soon moved indoors to get warm. Janus excused himself after seating everyone, extricated his car from behind the other two vehicles and drove to the church.

ೞ   ೞ   ೞ

"I am a little nervous about meeting these people. I mean, one of these men brought me here, right?" Reverend Land asked.
"Do you remember that?"
"Not clearly. I know I was in one place and suddenly I was in another. It is not a giant leap of logic to assume that someone brought me here. I know it wasn't you, so I can only assume it is one of these men."
"Big Jim Davis brought you from the jail in Chicago. He used to be a police officer there."
"I guess I don't have to ask you which one is Big Jim," he said with a smile. "He'll be the big one. Right?"

As the group entered the cottage, Janus played host, introducing everyone to Reverend Land. Big Jim's thoughts at this moment could best be described as incredulous. He stared at the man with the white hair and small smile and said, "Mr. Joseph, you are indeed a miracle worker." He offered his hand to Reverend Land. "I am pleased to meet you, Sir."
Reverend Land looked at him thoughtfully and responded modestly, "I am pleased to meet you—although I understand we have already met. I can't remember it, but I would like to offer you my thanks for bringing me here." The tears began again, so he excused himself, went into the bathroom and closed the door.

Tom looked at Big Jim and quietly commented, "I find it hard to believe. This does not seem to be the wretched waste of humanity you described to me."

Big Jim nodded in agreement. "You're right. But you should have seen him two days ago. Mr. Joseph, whatever you are doing, you should go into the business of detoxification and get rich."

"We did very little. There was a spark in the man that needed time to grow and become a fire for living. All we did was allow him the time. The local doctor helped a little, and good food helped a little. But, more than anything else it was self-directed."

"Do you think he could have done it without you?" Tom asked.

"I don't know enough to even offer an opinion. I have a feeling, not supported by evidence, that he might have. It was as if we weren't even here. He needed a safe respite from the life he had been living. I believe that he might have found his way back in time. Did you know that the Center was feeding him booze every day?"

"Really, now that is interesting. How do you know that?" Kira asked.

"He told us of his fall from grace and the reasons behind it. I don't want to discuss it. If he thinks it is important, he'll tell us about it."

"I have read the documents and it is true," chimed in Dr. Jones. "They destroyed him, as surely as if they had taken a gun and shot him."

Chancellor Goslin moved from the back of the group and said, "I think we ought to eat, so we can get down to business. Thank you again, Mr. and Mrs. Joseph, for having us."

As soon as he finished his announcement, Mr. Joseph suggested where people should sit. Reverend Land returned and took his designated seat. Just as everyone was about to begin eating, he interrupted the group with a casual clearing of his voice and said, "I would like to offer grace, if it is all right?"

When no one objected, he spread his hands over the table, lifted his eyes to heaven, and prayed.

ఎ ఎ ఎ

"So, Janna what kind of computer do you have?" Dow asked.

"It's a PC. I built it myself. It is not the latest and greatest, but it's a decent machine. I know it is probably not up to your standards, but I like it."

"What sort of Internet connection?"

"DSL."

"That's good. I think they may have identified the University Net. If I go in now, it will be from a different address. We might want to do that in a while."

Big Jim helped himself to his fourth sandwich and was filling his coffee cup for the third time when he said, "I suppose we are here for a purpose. Why don't we get on with it?"

Chancellor Goslin agreed and suggested, "Let's get the food out of the way and begin." With everyone helping, the dishes were soon cleared and everything removed, except the coffee cups. Chancellor Goslin stood up looked at the group. After they quieted down, he said, "Dow, can you give us a brief overview of what we are up against?"

"Certainly, I'd be glad to." Dow stood at his seat, reached for the sheaf of papers he had placed on an end table behind him and spread them on the large table that seemed to anchor this unusual group together. He took a few minutes to look them over and then he began. "The Center for American Heritage is the most powerful organization in the country. They have made inroads into everything we identify with the American experience.

"In the past they used a variety of methods to control the flow of information. As this country became more sophisticated, it was necessary for them to become more adept at handling information. While this is important, it is not the most important piece of information.

"No, the Center for American Heritage owes its existence to the dedication and money of the Hunter family. Its founding purpose was much different that what it has become. Originally, it was set in place to help get the conservative agenda considered. Now, it has grown in strength until they are capable of determining not only the agenda, but the parameters of the discussion. They owe allegiance to no one and will not compromise their message. They are vindictive, protected, and extremely dangerous to deal with.

"Everything about the Center is a well-guarded secret. Very few of the people who work there know the full extent of the company's involvement in the daily life of ordinary citizens in the United States. One man, Grant Larson—the current Executive Director—knows the full complicity of the company in modern American life. His path to the top was straight. A graduate of an ivy league law school, he was recruited to the Center right out of law school. He has never worked for anyone else and he never will. He is the director, the most powerful man in the United States."

Dow paused a moment to let this sink in. "Let me repeat that: Mr. Grant Larson, a man whose name you have never heard, is the most powerful man in the United States. Now we are getting into an area way beyond the ken of the political scientist. You were taught when you were a child that the President is the holder of that title. That is incorrect. The President serves at the discretion of Mr. Larson.

"His power is astounding. He can have the president impeached, if it suits him. Witness the problems of our previous president. In truth it was a simple dalliance, not something that met the standards of high crimes and misdemeanors. Yet, he was impeached and his legacy damaged. The potent venom was so well placed that it enabled the Center to dictate the next president. Do you honestly believe anyone would vote for that hollow puppet of big pharma and big oil without some ready hands and deep pockets?

"He can make or break any individual or organization in this country. The Center learned early in its existence that information was the key to power, and the Center simply has amassed and has access to more information than anyone on earth. If they wanted to, they could tell any person in this country all of the indiscretions they had committed from the time they took a piece of candy at the corner store, to the time they fudged figures on their income taxes. If the information they have in their files on an individual is not sufficient, they can invent new, irrefutable 'information' nearly instantaneously. I believe Reverend Land can testify to their ability to do this. Is that not correct, Reverend Land?"

"It most certainly is—but how do you know?"

"The information is contained in the files that Dr. Kline put together. I won't embarrass you by specifying its nature, other than to say the records are clear: this information was fabricated to malign and destroy the Reverend."

"You have proof of this?"

"Proof is a hard word. These documents contain a record of sort, but it is not explicit. Although it does not mention you by name, the reference and the trail of data tampering is undeniable."

The expression on Jersey's face was a curious mix of vindication, rage and hope.

"Let me continue. The company is divided into eight divisions, each with a director reporting solely to Mr. Larson. The directors know of the existence of the others, but they have little, if any, interaction. Their orders come directly from the desk of Grant Larson. The divisions are: news, sports, religion, politics, minority involvement, publishing, television, and motion pictures. Every division is broken down into arenas of activity, each with separate controllers. The news division is structured into three areas: Print Journalism, Television Journalism, and Radio Journalism. The managers of these report only to their director. He, in turn, reports to Mr. Larson.

"The sports division's structure reveals another three arenas of activity: Professional, Collegiate, and Amateur Sports. Their special area of interest is to make sure that the latest dictates of the company are carried out in their area of responsibility. These could be as simple as making sure that the political correctness issue is followed by the teams, or as complex as choosing the correct player for stardom."

"But, Dow, why is this bad?"

"Kira, the problem is this: they want to control. They don't care about the relative validity of a one position or another. They are above the fray. Now, they support a non-sexist stand. If it suited their purposes, they would do the opposite. In fact, I have found evidence that they are actively involved in both sides of some—in effect, controlling the entire agenda. Whichever way public opinion sways, you can rest assured that the public has been led there, as surely as if they had been led by a ring through their nose. Do you understand?"

"I guess I need to hear more to begin to put my head around this monster."

"Even the subject of religion is divided into four areas: Protestant, Catholic, Jewish, and Other. Their purpose is to make sure that religious organizations do not oppose the Center's wishes. The *Hammer of God* show is one of the company's main weapons in the Protestant area."

Reverend Land interrupted and said, "Reverend Hamner is a good man. Remember, they control what he says and does. I am pretty sure that he ended in their employ the same way that I did. Don't be too quick to judge their instruments, because they may be victims, as well as victimizers."

Dow sat down and said, "I am sorry, I am getting a little tired of standing. Listen. The key to understanding the Center is in grasping its political nature. Nothing happens in this country without political ramifications. The Center has elected every president since they have been in existence. Every congressman is subject to scrutiny by the organization; every governmental organization has the Center watching them. The FBI and CIA are supervised by the Center, and if they err, corrective measures are taken without regard for the costs to individual or family lives. Nearly every mainstream issue and the focus of major events in the United States are the result of either the Center's actions, or lack of action.

"No book can be published and nationally promoted without the blessing of the company. No national television show can be syndicated without their tacit approval. No major producer can find the means, short of taking the money out of his own pocket, to make a movie opposed to the Center's agenda. If he does manage the production, national distributors will not handle it, or reviews will be 'arranged' to ultimately control public opinion.

"Even advertisements must follow Center guidelines. Nothing that happens in the public arena is beyond their ability to influence and, in most cases, control..."

Dow continued his overview for the next thirty minutes, providing more information, punctuating each case with examples. It was a mind-numbing experience to sit and listen to your beliefs exploding like bubbles blown on the wind, while sunlight danced on the carpet of the Josephs' home.

When he finished, he put his papers back in order and waited for the questions. There were none. Everyone was too shocked to even ask. It all seemed so logical. Every time they turned on a television and one talk show host or another was discussing some subject, the same subject was being broached in a variety of ways and media. It just made too much sense not to have a central clearing house for such information. It seemed the country had become conditioned by the manipulations of the Center to not find this odd. Now, with the facts being exposed, everything was becoming clear. It was like a mousetrap slamming shut.

The little facts that niggled at you and caused you discomfort, were suddenly explained, and the explanation ran true. Everyone knew this and sat back in their chairs pensively.

Challenge

Chapter 31

Seconds turned to minutes as the group sat in deep, uneasy concentration. The silence in the room became pervasive. Each considered the ramifications of what they had just heard. So many things were explained. How could they not have seen this before? Everything was clear. The explanations given to them in childhood suddenly were first discounted and then abandoned. There was a sense of being cheated out of a meaningful perspective. Dow had no negative feelings about lifting the veil obstructing their vision. It was necessary.

John finally broke the silence. "I suppose it was inevitable."

"What do you mean, Chancellor Goslin?"

"Mr. Joseph, Jim, we are old enough to have a perspective on this issue. I meant to say that it was inevitable that someone is controlling the way we think about things. Historically, the United States has seemed to have been manipulated more than it has not. Several of the wars we have been involved in prove this point undeniably: Korea, Viet Nam, the Middle East come to mind. If public opinion had been believed, or if there were a reason to ask the public about such ventures, most of them would have been forgotten. Still, there is the possibility in many cases that we would not have become involved without some external influence.

"I guess the most disturbing thing is we always assumed that this manipulation was internal. The government seemed like the likely suspect. And since the officials are elected, we could change them, at least in theory. The reality is that this is not true. The laws have been molded to make it nearly impossible for an incumbent to be defeated. But sometimes it happens. I guess that when one of these incumbents is defeated, if we looked closely enough, we could probably find The Center for American Heritage's influence. So, we are left with a group in charge we know nothing about. A group without allegiance to anyone, except themselves. More importantly, a force not accountable to anyone, anything or even to clear values that have been freely chosen.

"Now, we find out these same people are actively controlling the content, flow and presentation of information to an extent that public opinion about important, vital issues is tailored to their design. As absurd as it may be, the reality is that our own thoughts and feelings about the world are being shaped. What gives them the right? No wonder Dr. Kline was driven to this extreme choice. All of this flies in the face of what the intellectual life is about, what our lives at the university are about in the teaching of young minds." The chancellor looked exasperated.

"Nothing gives them the right. But that does not mean they will give up their insidious power and position easily or willingly," Dow observed.

"I know. I think I can see it more now than I could this morning. It frightens me. I am not sure there is anything that we can do. I mean we are too few to actively counteract them. Their position as an historically empowered group, with apparently inexhaustible resources, almost precludes our ability to intervene. What are we to do?"

"The coma I was in was a weird experience. I mean I was not awake, but I was not asleep. I had a lot of time to think, and I may have the makings of an answer."

"Please, Dow, continue. In this dark tunnel, I think we'd all appreciate seeing a light," Detective Johnson said with sincerity.

"They have one area of weakness we can exploit. They have sold their souls to the computer. Although they think they are in charge of the world, I may just be able to control their computers."

"To what end?"

"John, everything they are doing hinges on manipulation of information through computer technology. That is the danger that our society faces now. Even these people with their apparent honed knowledge and skill fail to understand that when you abdicate personal responsibility for technology, that technology can be corrupted. I guess you could call me the great corruptor."

A smile stole onto his face and his eyes danced around the group brightly. "Listen, there are two ways we can approach the problem. The first is by taking absolute control of their systems and forcing public disclosure. The second would be to slip into the machine and place information into their files."

"Dow, do you mean we could either force them out in the open or cause them to do things to hurt themselves?" Kira asked.

"I think we could do a great deal of damage with the first option, but they might be able to wrest control back and undo the harm. It would hurt them, but I believe they could recover. They must be in a position of weakness before we attempt that method. It isn't just enough to cause public exposure. From my reading of the material, they can shape, and in most cases, control the public's opinion about nearly any subject.

"Suppose we caused them send out a press release which detailed their position historically and politically. Do you think anyone would believe the releases were accurate? I don't. I don't even believe it would be published because no second source for the information could be found. No, they must have their presence exposed in a more subtle way. We must force them into doing things they would not normally do. If we can get them moving to arrest rumors and busy answering questions, they may screw up. We can be prepared in case the opportunity presents itself, but I think we should try the more subtle approach first. I think we can cause them to make mistakes. The best way I can think of for this to happen is for us to help them," he said with a sardonic smile.

Kira looked confused and self-consciously brushed her hair back from her face, "What could you do? I mean, can you give us some examples?"

"Sure, how would you like to be the guest reporter on *Perspectives on Washington?*"

"You could do that?"

"I believe I could. And you, Reverend Land, how would you like to go and sit in the front row at the *Hammer of God* show?"

"Preposterous, I know the way things work. It's not possible. The audiences for these shows are picked months in advance and carefully screened. There is no way that anyone could infiltrate that group."

"I'm sorry, but I think you are wrong. Remember when I said they had a weakness in the computer area? I believe that Kira can be the guest reporter and I believe you could confront the Hammer on national television. If we decide to do something, I believe these two options would be valuable. They use current-controlling software in their machines. Even though the programs they run are exotic and subtle, the means to run them is pedestrian. There are ways of controlling the controlling software. I know how to do this. I guess you could ask why would we want to?

"I can tell you that even though their presence is pervasive in our society, they become vulnerable when they leave the background and shadows and come into the light."

Kira and Reverend Land were fantasizing about what they would say under such conditions. Finally, Reverend Land spoke up. "Dr. Jones, do you mean that you could provide the evidence you have of the harm they've done to me and the methodology involved, and I could expose these documents and their methods on television?"

"Yes, I believe I could. What would you say?"

"I will have to think about it. It is not an easy question. I assume that once we use a method like this, it will be lost to us? Probably, at least for a while. Perhaps we could bring it back again, but I don't know this. I think it is safe to say that if we go public we are only going to have a limited number of one-shot deals."

"So what do you want to do?" Chancellor Goslin looked over the group and waited. Janna fidgeted in her seat and finally tentatively raised her hand "My father and I were talking about the possibility of retribution from confronting them. Have any of you thought about that?"

A look of gloom passed from person to person. They, whether they chose to acknowledge it or not, had all thought of that contingency. Janus spoke up, "I believe if any of us are to confront them openly, we should be in a position that is unassailable. We cannot let someone vulnerable take them on.

Their position could be exploited. Take Detective Johnson. I assume if they wanted to they could implicate him in some sort of scandal which would end his career. Kira might be terminated if she tried to oppose them. Of course, there is the possibility that you could be honored for exposing them." Janus continued, "Chancellor, the university could be made to suffer. I guess I am in a position that at least has possibilities. I mean after all, the house is paid for. I have a state pension that cannot be taken away, and I don't participate in any public activities they could exploit. Oddly enough, I believe Janna is in a similar position. Students have few property rights or civic responsibilities. Besides, even without their intervention, our society tends to dismiss the young's behavior.

"Beyond that, I don't see a lot of people in this room who could be used. I mean, Chancellor, you aren't about to retire from the University are you?" Mr. Joseph asked.

"No, I suppose not. Diane has been hinting that she would like me to. But no, I have not given enough thought to the matter. We do need to remember, however, that the Center has demonstrated that it is not above violence. Any one of us, any one at all for that matter, who dares to undermine their efforts or expose their tactics, could fall victim to violent backlash."

Reverend Land cleared his throat and said, "I don't think they could hurt me anymore than they already have. They have maligned me, taken everything from me and left me with nothing. When you don't have much, it becomes easier to risk it. I mean what are they going to do to me that they have not already done? I am no longer afraid of their most vicious threats."

A silence permeated the room. They had three people who were willing to try, when suddenly a deep voice from the back of the room boomed out. "I'll do what I can. I have pretty much retired and my pension is secured. I think the University could probably overlook any negative stories that might come out about me. Isn't that so, Chancellor?"

"I believe we could. Listen, I don't want to make a snap decision here. Dow, why don't you see if you can get into the computer at a level where you can gain us an advantage? I think that's the first order of business. It may not be necessary to sacrifice anything for these people. Maybe we can't do anything, and the best thing to do would be to just let it go. I mean, they have been around this long without someone being able to expose their activities. What make us think that we are going to succeed where so many others have failed? Who do we think we are?" John's honest expression of doubt and reality was linked to the sting of his friend's death. He knew now more than anyone that Richard's investigation of the Center was the cause of his death.

"Excuse me, Chancellor. Janna, can you show me to your computer? I would have brought my laptop, but I didn't think it necessary. What I'm going to do is not that difficult. Besides, each computer has an identifiable code in the operating system. Since I use the same system on DORA, I thought it best to not raise any more suspicion."

"Sure. Do you mind if I watch?"

"No, it might be a lesson in and of itself. Just so the whole day isn't wasted," Dow added with a grin as he went for his briefcase. Janna led the way to the small room in the back of the cottage she had established as an office. She sat in the comfortable chair in front of the machine, pressed the surge protector's switch and waited. Dow took a disk case from the briefcase, loosened the velcro straps and placed it on the desk. There was room for twelve disks in the cloth carrying case. He only had it half full, but he knew what all of the programs were and exactly how they might be useful to them.

ଔ   ଔ   ଔ

The phone buzzed and Darren got up from the couch to answer it.

"Darren, this is Joyce at the Center. It seems we have someone trying to invade the system."

"Did you run the Oracle program?"

"Yes, I did. We had it set up to search for incoming incursions from the university net. This intrusion is from a different ISP. It's a DSL line somewhere in area code 517."

"517? Where in the hell is that?"

"The eastern part of Michigan except for Detroit. Do you want me to re-calibrate the Oracle Program?"

"Yes, I want to know who is trying to get in here. Listen, I'm coming down there now. Can you tell how the invader is doing?"

"Yes, I can. They are doing very well. They have circumvented the top three levels. There are only two more levels before we will lose them."

"How long did he take on level three?"

"Just a second, I will check." He listened as the keys clicked in the background. After a moment she came back on the line and said, "Three minutes, thirty-two seconds."

"Wow, that's fast. How long has he been in the system?"

"I have that right here. Ten minutes and fourteen seconds as of right now."

"Can you disconnect him?"

"No, I don't think I can. What do you want me to do?"

"Keep an eye on it. I will be there as soon as possible."

ෂ ෂ ෂ

"Janna, are you paying attention?"

"Yes, what is going on?"

"We are in their system. I have encountered three levels of resistance and overcome them. I am now at work on the fourth. It looks like I should be through in another thirty seconds. Wait..."

The screen cleared and a new message appeared in the center of the screen:

THIS AREA RESERVED FOR LEVEL 5 PERSONNEL
PLEASE INPUT THE CURRENT PASSWORD.

Dow typed some commands which did not show on the screen. Janna asked, "Why can't I see what you are typing?"

"The characters are not listed on this screen. I assume somewhere in Virginia someone is watching us break into their system. I want to do this fast. I have seen this kind of security setup before. It is marketed by California Securecom. I have beaten it before.... I am almost through this layer now. Once we get below level five there will be no way for them to stop us. From our lower level incursion we can erase any trace that we were ever here—should drive them buggy trying to find us."

                     os   os   os

When the phone rang on the desk, Joyce Parker reached over to pick it up without averting her eyes from the screen. "Yes?"
"This is Darren, has he gotten any deeper?"
"I thought you were coming in?"
"I'm in my car, almost there. Again, has he gotten any further?"
"Bad news, Boss; he is through level four and attacking level five. I can see what he is doing, but it doesn't make any sense to me. It is all in Hex. I suppose I could have it printed out and I could interpret it in time. Do you want me to?"
"Sure, why not! Listen, I will be there in less than three minutes. Try to think of something that can stall him. Did you re-calibrate the Oracle?"
"I have it running. It has been working for about a minute and a half. No results so far."

                    os   os   os

"We are in!" Dow said triumphantly. He sat back in the chair with a broad sense of victory across his face. After a triumphant moment, he reached into his disk case and pulled out another disk. With a few deft keystrokes he caused the machine to access the disk and loaded a program into the computer. While he was waiting for the disk to finish loading the program, he made a couple of notes. They were nothing but hexadecimal numbers. Janna recognized them, but could not read them without a calculator and a chart.
After the disk light went off, Dow called the communication program's file transfer menu up and he typed a string of instructions and pressed the return key. Then he giggled.

◌ ◌ ◌

Darren ran into the room without taking off his coat and went straight to the computer. Joyce saw him coming, but she also saw that the Oracle program had completed its run and she pressed the key to display the information. The screen cleared. The computer looked like it had been turned off, when the cursor started going back and forth across the screen. Each pass through it left a little trail of yellow in the middle. The trail seemed to be getting bigger and it had taken on the appearance of the edge of a ball. Soon the screen featured nearly a third of a large yellow ball. "What in the hell is that?"

"You got me, Darren. On the next pass the yellow trail was broken in two pieces in the middle. It continued on. Suddenly there were two eyes facing them in the middle of the yellow ball. A sinking feeling entered both people as the rest of the stupid smiling face manifested itself on the screen. After the mouth had been formed a simple message appeared in large letters at the bottom of the screen:

Have a Nice Day!

Chapter 32

"Why are you laughing?" Janna asked.

"They set up a program that I assume was trying to pinpoint our position and phone number. I just gave it something to report."

"What?"

"It is just a stupid smiling face. One of my students wrote it about five years ago. It takes almost forever to complete as it creates the image one line of resolution at a time with a counting loop to make it go very very slowly even on the fastest machines. It was an exercise in using machine language, array processing. I was so impressed I kept it. It just seemed to be so absurd. It is a fairly large program and the idea of spending so much time in its creation was funny.

"I was laughing because whoever is on the other end of this line was anticipating something very different. I can see them huddled around the computer expecting to outsmart the infidels and having the smiling face start to appear. They must have stared at it for several minutes before realizing what it was. I have a feeling that they did not appreciate the sentiment.

"Well, do you want to rejoin the others. I have established my path into their systems and can use it whenever I want. I believe that the break we'd hoped for has been delivered!"

They left the room and headed back to the others. Though they had not been gone long, the group was starting to break up. Returning to the table, everyone resumed their previous positions. After the coffee cups were filled and the general talk died down, Dow announced, "With Janna's help, I've accomplished what I wanted. I now have an absolute link into their systems. Something patently illegal, but considering the circumstances, totally justifiable. From this inroad, I can eavesdrop on anything they are doing, as long as it is computerized. With my inroad, I can place information into their system, or I can cause them to release information they normally would not. I don't know what everybody wants to do. It is my recommendation that I spend some time watching and learning. If I can trace general patterns of usage, then I can effectively counteract them when the time comes."

Chancellor Goslin rose from his seat and said, "Does anyone else have recommendations?"

"Dr. Jones, does this mean that you can intercept orders and change them?"

"Detective Johnson, I can intercept the orders if they have been given by computer. If they choose to use some other means of communication, I cannot."

"Won't they know you are there?"

"No, I am good at what I do. I have erased all records of any incursion. I believe they know I have been there..." He glanced at Janna and smiled. She returned it. "...but they'll never find me again, Tom."

Reverend Land rose from his seat with a concerned look in his eyes and said, "Are you sure? These people can be ruthless."

Dow responded to the look with a serious tone in his voice, "Thank you for your concern, but there is no way they could find out when I am there and when I am not, short of scrapping the system and starting over. Even with my knowledge and experience, I don't think I could find anyone who entered the system the way I did. It is in the nature of the machines and the way they are set up. I just used what they have given me. Every system has the capacity for expansion built in. I just expanded it to include one more terminal. The only thing different I did was to not include my terminal in the system reporting files. In essence, I will be there for any and all messages and will have access to all levels, but I will be invisible."

"Dow, are you saying that you would like some time to look around and get a feel for their operations?"

"Yes, John, I think that would be wise. After all, we all knew that definitive answers would not be found when we came up here today. I guess the question we wanted to answer was whether or not we could do something about the clearly subversive and destructive activities of the Center—and finally, to decide if and how we wanted to proceed. I can report to you that something can be done. The choice of doing it or not is up to all of us together. Even at this point, I think we should delay the decision for a couple of weeks. We just don't have enough information. I, for one, am not comfortable entering into some sort of irreversible action without knowing the facts or the ramifications of our actions. A planned delay will give me time to see what can be done. I'll use the time to place certain programs which could help us complete our task, if we elect to do so. If we decide not to, the programs will not compromise their system."

"Does anyone have any objections to meeting again in two weeks? We don't have to meet here, we could meet in the board room at the college, or over at my house. I am sure Diane would not mind."

"Chancellor, I don't have a problem with people coming here. I think the main advantage of this location is that they don't know who I am, and from what I just heard, they were not able to follow you here," he said with a grin and a wink to Tom and Jim.

"Thank you very much, Mr. Joseph. If no one objects, why don't we agree to meet here in two weeks and determine our next steps?" As he looked around the room and saw no objections, the meeting drew to a close. There was a sense of accomplishment for each of those gathered. There was also a sense of identifiable fear about the risks they were taking and the hope that their actions would be as transparent as Dow indicated. The last thing any of them wanted was further violence by the Center or its operatives.

The rest of the day passed quickly. Soon the sun was inching down toward the horizon, as most of them headed back to Mason. The group met for over three hours after Dow gained entry into the Center's computers discussing just about everything, but all conversations returned to the situation at hand.

Reverend Land was going to stay with the Joseph's for a while longer, and everyone else had jobs to go back to. Janna had her work at school to catch up on. Big Jim was still in charge of campus security and Kira had to do the news. Chancellor Goslin promised to arrange for another professor to lighten up Dow's work load so he could concentrate on the job at hand.

ଔ ଔ ଔ

The image remained on the screen, as an insult might linger in the air. Joyce brought a chair and sat by Darren. The detailed face reminded them their system had been compromised and that someone had intentionally invaded their sacrosanct code of operations.

"What do you want to do, Darren?"

"I don't know. Get that smiling son-of-a-bitch off the screen. It is distracting." Joyce reached for the key to clear the screen. As soon as she touched the enter key, the image was gone. The system returned to normal. "Do you think we should report this?"

"Report what? That we think someone broke into the system and we failed to stop them? Or perhaps that someone played a computer trick on us?"

"You don't have to be rude."

"I know, I'm sorry. It's just that—I don't know what to do. If we report the system has been compromised, we end up looking incompetent. If we don't report it, we stand the chance of the intruder finding information we don't want him to find. It is a quandary."

"Can we catch him and shut him down?"

"Perhaps. It will depend on how deeply he went into the system. From the looks of the Hex Code you printed out, I think it can safely be assumed he went in deep. I suppose we can try. We probably have a little time to search. I will have to report this in a few days. But for now, let's keep looking."

ଔ ଔ ଔ

Detective Johnson climbed into the truck on the passenger's side with a look of concern on his face. Big Jim noticed this and asked, "What's bothering you, Tom?"

"Jim, somehow we are going to have to keep more than an eye on these people. I don't know what this so-called Center has in mind. But I do know that the law is nothing more than an inconvenience to them. Given their evident history of subterfuge and meeting out their own brand of 'justice,' all of the innocent people here today are vulnerable targets. Do you have any suggestions?"

"Considering what happened when you arrested Mr. Smith, I gather the department will not be a lot of help. Is there something else you can do?"

"You're right. Officially, I suppose there is not much I can do. I can, however, arrange for some quiet surveillance. I suppose, if there were money for such a thing, some of the officers I would trust with my own life might want to moonlight. I could approve that."

"I'll talk to Chancellor Goslin tonight. I can get back to you. It's possible the University could come up with some discretionary funds. I was thinking of asking some of my old colleagues from the force if they would like to spend a few weeks in beautiful Mason, Michigan."

"That might even be better. If you do, can you let me know who they are so we can coordinate efforts to maximize protection?"

"Sure. Listen, I'll call you tonight and let you know what is going on."

The rest of the drive went quickly as each man was alone with his thoughts. There was a sense of anticipation and anxiety for the confrontations that were sure to come.

ය ය ය

Time slipped into a familiar pattern of work and school. Kira and Dow continued to see each other and were growing closer by the day. He was so different from anyone she had ever known that each encounter became a new adventure. He helped her to slow down enough to see the world she had been missing.

He was so different from her. His was a world she had never dreamed existed. To live for ideas and thoughts was alien to her. She tried it and found a depth and freedom that somehow felt like home. They spent their time working on the computer and talking about the nature of public perceptions. Though she had spent most of her career in molding public opinion, she never understood her critical hinge-like function. It was a revelation to her that she herself could be more than an image. By finding the reality of her situation, she became very conscious of what she was doing and how it had consequences for the public. Subsequently, her reporting improved because she reflected on the meaning and implications of everything she said. She still had to cover the usual fluff pieces and superficial reporting typical of the medium, but she also began to consider seriously her thread's place in the fabric of public perceptions.

Kira had spent her life trying to be beautiful and, as she now understood, vacuous. Dow's presence gained her access to avenues of intelligent dialogue about important issues she had only given cursory nods to in the past. She became much more interested in computers and their phenomenol reach. She even bought a high-powered laptop for her home. She also developed an interest in the hardware aspects of the news. Prior to this time she'd had little interest in the technological aspects of the news business. Now, she found herself in the control booth at every opportunity finding out how things were done. She even brought Dow there on a number of occasions to sit while she did the news. He seemed to have a tremendous interest in the transparent technology behind the presentation of the news.

She learned all that she could because it seemed to be something that Dow liked to talk about. In addition to the grave matters they were both researching regarding the Center, Kira wanted to nurture the intense bonds that she sensed were growing between them. The days sped by.

Dow was spending long hours with his own complex pieces of the equation the group had discussed. She knew his eyes were tired and he was getting very little sleep, but he was unrelenting about getting to the bottom of the American Heritage operations they all knew were subversive to the Constitiution and dangerous to the public. Still, between the hard work, they found time for shared meals and even the occasional overnight. She felt as if she were truly happy for the first time in her life. There was not only a compelling sense of meaning and purpose. There was a depth of love for another human being she had never before wanted, let alone dared to risk.

ଔ ଔ ଔ

Janna concentrated as much as she could on her studying. It is hard to come to a strange school from a small town. There are so many distractions that tempt the student. She had an almost constant stream of young men calling her to go for coffee, or to the movies, or some such thing. She managed to put them off. She did not feel comfortable spending her freedom in such a way. There would be time for such activities, and besides, her roommate probably dated enough for both of them. Sylvia's grades suffered, but she was having a good time. If she had not been so bright, she probably would be failing.

Sitting in the darkened room, just before retiring, they regularly had long discussions about nearly everything. The end result would almost always be an agreement to disagree. They got along fine, because more often than not Sylvia was out, leaving Janna the run of the place. It was an element of solitude she appreciated.

Still, she persevered. Although her grades were excellent, she hadn't much time to dwell on the activities of the previous week. Things returned to normal, almost. Everything except her. The weight of those very real events had changed her. It seemed that the world itself had changed. The knowledge she possessed of the Center's activities alerted her to the fact there were forces at play in the world she never recognized. And now that she had been made aware of them, she saw evidence at almost every juncture.

She thought about the fact that her father had identified the Center without being aware of its existence. She likened it to the astronomers who discovered planets by calculating the differences in orbits of other celestial objects. To her it was a monumental feat of logic. Her admiration for her father grew tremendously.

☙ ☙ ☙

Reverend Land continued his recovery. He began each day by walking to the crossroads with Janus. They developed a good friendship as hours melted into pools of stimulating conversation about the vexing cultural, political and spiritual dilemmas of our time. Janus relished this more than he would have believed possible. Though he and Karen had been happily married for 43 years, she did not enjoy these mental gymnastics. Reverend Land improved daily and soon ventured on long walks by himself.

One day Janus asked, "Where are you off to this afternoon?"

"Oh, I have been visiting with Pastor Ericksson at the Lutheran Church. We are having an interesting time. Usually, we just have coffee and spend a little time in prayer. It has been a long time since I felt clean enough to ask forgiveness, and he is helping me find my way again. You and your wife have been most gracious, but there are things to discuss that can only be discussed with another minister. Pastor Ericksson is a good man. I hope you are not offended by my leaving?"

"No, not at all. In fact, I think it's wonderful."

"He has asked me to offer the sermon on Sunday. I am still thinking about it. Perhaps I will. If I do, it would be nice if you and your wife would come?"

"If you decide to offer the sermon, we will be there. By the way, I think that you are recovering nicely. Must be all of the fresh air."

"That—and good friends."

One afternoon, Reverend Land brought a ministerial robe back to the Joseph cottage with him. Janus assumed that he would be preaching in two days. He never saw him make a note or study the scripture. Instead he would go for long walks in the woods or sit on one of the lawn chairs by the beach. Janus could tell he was deep in thought.

When Sunday morning arrived, they went to church. Janus watched as Reverend Land left the car and headed to the back of the church. He was greeted warmly at the door by

Reverend Ericksson. He clasped him on the back and ushered him into his office.

As the service commenced Janus heard Reverend Land's rich voice ring out in the hymns and anticipated the moment when he could see the fallen minister try to make the final climb from his pit of despair.

Reverend Ericksson introduced him as simply a guest minister who was vacationing in the area. Janus took great pride in his friend as he stepped to the pulpit and began.

> Welcome to the House of the Lord. Some of you may know me, many of you do not. Who I am is not important, for I am a servant of the Lord. I have come this day to offer the simple message of salvation that the Lord gave to us in the form of his only Son.
>
> All of us have sinned. We spend our days doing our best to forget that we are children of the Lord. We harbor thoughts we would not want to share with others. We do things we are not proud of. Sometimes the darkness enters our souls, and we forget that we are servants of the Lord who can walk in his holy light.
>
> Even with our constant denial of the truth of our faith, there is hope. The hope that springs forth like the flowers in the spring, the marvelous world of wonders that the Lord has given us. A world which can meet all people's needs.
>
> I have come to offer the hope that is a light unto a darkened soul, the light of the Lord. The light that will illuminate the darkest reaches of your soul. The light that shines to blot out the abominations of the world.
>
> We are simple people: men and women, boys and girls, yet all made in the image of the Lord. We are his servants. We have been put on this earth to do his work. There is no other calling transcending his calling. We can go to work or school each and every day and forget for a time that we are the chosen of the Lord. Though we forget, He does not. He watches us and knows our inner thoughts. When the cares of the world reign supreme, He can make them vanish with a simple word. We have only to ask for his help and it will be given.

Instead of asking, we spend our lives trying to correct the deficiencies of others—while ignoring our own. The Lord is the light unto our feet, yet we constantly deny the light. We believe in the Lord only when it is convenient. When it becomes awkward we retreat into the nothingness of the world....

For nearly thirty minutes Reverend Land preached. He started out tentatively, yet with each passing moment the fire of his message became more apparent. The congregation was transfixed by the older man with the white hair. His simple message of hope and faith was taking root, and the people responded.

The light from behind the pulpit framed him as his image seemed to grow. The people who were there that day would talk for weeks about the sermon they had heard. Though the words were simple, the message was eloquent. It had an impact.

When he finally reached the benediction and said, "May the Lord watch between me and thee while we are absent one from another," the congregation was enraptured.

After he sat the people of the congregation whispered among themselves. The collection plate was passed around and people gave. People gave much more than normally and were glad to do it. The light of the Lord had been given to them, and they left the church with their spirits uplifted and their minds believing in the wonders of the world. Reverend Land's eyes were filled with joy and humble gratitude.

Chapter 33

"Joyce, is everything backed up?"

"It will be in just a moment." She reached down, removed the cartridge and replaced it with another. "One more to go. Wait a second. What do you intend to do?"

"I'm going to shut down and restart everything from the backups. It should eliminate the intruder. If we take out whatever inroads he made, he should be gone. How long?"

"Got it, now! Ready for system shutdown."

Darren flipped the master switch and the room became quiet. Frighteningly quiet. He checked his watch. He wanted to wait a full five minutes before trying to re-institute system. Sometimes the charge of electricity which re-energized the microprocessors found an outlet and continued on its circuit far longer than the manufacturer said was possible. If he waited that length of time it would eliminate any possibility of something being left in the system.

"Joyce, I'm going to pull the switch now. Watch the monitor for me, will you?"

"Got it. Go ahead."

He pulled the master switch to the side and the computers in the room began their memory checks. The prompt arrived on the screen and disappeared again as the Center's software was loaded. After a full two minutes of loading, the familiar logo was displayed in the middle of the screen. "OK, Darren, we have it."

"Good. Prepare to insert the backup tapes on my command."

"Ready."

"Put tape #1 in, please."

He watched the monitor as the information that had been in the system before the intruder was reloaded. When a computer receives a new file, it will replace the existing file with the new file of the same name. Darren knew ways to circumvent this procedure, but he wanted the files replaced. It was his hope that whatever the intruder had done would be erased by the loading of the old files. After about fifteen minutes of watching he saw the DOS message instructing him to put in the next tape and he asked her to do so.

There were ten half-inch cassettes to load; each of them took several minutes. The data transfer rate was the best available in the industry, but it still took time. After nearly an hour they finished backing up the system.

"Well, I hope that did it. Do you know any other tests we can perform to see if he is still there?"

"I want to do a directory by directory search of all files added today. Use the file reader called "Display". Display was a program Darren had written that would list the contents of any file he chose. Sometimes what it displayed made no sense to anyone not schooled in the particular assembler language for the machine, but it would list all information.

They started their task with heavy hearts. There were more than 10,000 different directories to search. With a bit of luck they might be done by morning. For some reason, it never occurred to them to close the connection to their Internet server—a mistake that would have immense ramifications. But their network could not be shut-down. That would effectively end their ability to control information.

଒ ଒ ଒

"Kira, I love you. I never knew how much I was missing. I can't imagine life without you. Will you marry me?"

She was taken aback. The question had been asked much sooner than she would have believed possible. What did she want to do? Her entire life had been built on assumptions. Now, these very assumptions were being questioned. She had assumed that in time she would move to a larger market. From the larger market, she hoped she could attract the attention of one of the networks. Now, she was being asked to alter her dream so dramatically. She could hardly believe it when she said, "Yes." It seemed like the most right decision she had ever made in her life.

He embraced her. Happiness had found them. Less than a month after meeting, they had fallen deeply in love. Dow was nearly 48 and Kira was 29, or at least that's what she told everyone. She was actually 34, but in her business being too old is a detriment to a career. So, she was 29, and had been for some time.

"Kira, I have something to discuss. I hope it doesn't change your opinion of me."

She stiffened and sat back. "What is it? I can't imagine anything changing my love for you."

"Well, the truth of the matter is that I'm quite wealthy."

That was totally unexpected. She assumed he made decent money as a professor, but she had never noticed anything about him that spoke of wealth. "Sure you are," she said with a laugh.

"No, really, I am. Although, I think it's one of the best guarded secrets around. No one knows, except you now. A number of my programs are licensed to big corporations; they pay hefty fees for their use. I'm also paid for doing security checks. And I'm compensated quite well by the university."

"So, Dow, how rich are you?"

"Very."

"C'mon, I mean are you a J. Paul Getty or something?"

"No, but I guess I could easily be called a millionaire."

Her heart went to her throat. She had accepted him as he was. Now, this unassuming, soft-spoken academic was telling her he had resources she'd not imagined. She put her arms around him, hugging him tightly. "This won't change a thing, I promise." And she meant it. Kira had been so captivated by this complex, loving man, his wealth really was irrelevant. But it made her smile to think he'd worried about it.

೮ೃ ೮ೃ ೮ೃ

"Got that mangy son-of-a-bitch! Caught him hanging around the system files. Come here, Joyce. You want to see him leave?"

"Love to."

As Darren pressed a few keys, a DOS message came on the screen:

Delete File/ HARINGGHOTI.RUD Y/N

Without thinking he pressed the Y key and watched his troubles disappear before his eyes. It was 7:00 P.M. on Tuesday night. The last twenty-four hours had been a non-stop marathon of checking files, reading code, and pressing the search for this intruder. Now they had expunged him.

"Let's go out for a drink! I'm buying."

"I'll get my coat," Joyce answered.

ଓ ଓ ଓ

The planned two weeks seemed to race into history. It was Sunday morning and time to head north. Dow and Kira drove up in her new car. John drove the Cadillac and the two police officers made the drive north in the Detective's Chevy. All arrived at the appointed hour and prepared for the conference.

Chancellor Goslin spoke the first few formal words. "Welcome back everyone. I trust you had an uneventful two weeks. That's what we hoped for, isn't it. I know Dr. Jones has spent a tremendous amount of time and energy in behind-the-scenes analysis. We're all really anxious to hear what you've uncovered, Dow. Would you mind briefing the group about what you have found?"

"Not at all, John. You're right. I have spent the last two weeks in a wonderland of subterfuge and misdirection. I have learned the way The Center's organization works inside and out. I can tell you that Mr. Smith is now stationed in California. Mr. Wesson is still in Mason but has strict orders to wait for our next move. There has been a lot of chatter on the line between Mr. Wesson and a Jonathan Green. They are having a hard time accepting we are not running about chasing our tails. They know about the surveillance efforts to protect us and are waiting.

"Darren Meyers and his assistant, Joyce Parker, with the highest level clearance in the Center's IT security, believe that I have been removed from the system. I let them search every file until late Monday afternoon. I loaded in something they could find, and they responded just as I anticipated.

"I was having such a good time watching *them* actually chase their tails that I felt sorry for them. So, I set up a red herring for them to find. They believe they have succeeded. I guess they are not as erudite as we assumed. I named the file—" Dow reached for a piece of paper and with a red marker wrote the word:

HARINGGHOTI.RUD

John Goslin read the string of syllables HARINGGHOTI RUD aloud and started giggling. When he regained his composure he said, "That's the George Bernard Shaw thing, isn't it?"

"Yes, it sure is," Dow said with a glint in his eye.

"I'm sorry, I don't get it. Why are you two laughing?"

"Detective Johnson, George Bernard Shaw once became so frustrated with spelling in English that he made up this word, GHOTI. That word is fish."

"How?"

Chancellor Goslin got out of his seat and actually felt like a teacher again, as he borrowed the marker and paper from Dow. "It goes like this. The GH is from enough," as he wrote with a flourish the word *enough*. "The O is from the word *women*, and the TI is from the word *nation*. When you put them together, you have the word *fish*."

"Exactly. And when you think that *rud* is a word that means red, I named my file herringfish.red. But they bought it anyway. I was just trying to have a little fun. I had another file in place if they didn't bite on the first. But they did.

"They stopped looking for me. They believe their systems are intact and unaffected by my presence. They are dead wrong. I've put in place a variety of software that can have results from annoying to devastating. I can implement the programs from anywhere, simply using a portable computer.

"With Kira's help, I've arranged for the delivery of automated camera equipment to the sets of both *Perspective on Washington* and *The Hammer of God* shows. These have already been implemented and were used on today's show. I sent their directors and technicians on a training session last week. They are even very excited about the technology.

"After studying the way they do things and the lack of checks they have on their systems, I've come to the conclusion that they are definitely vulnerable. We can take action to erode their power—if we choose to."

"Dow, tell us about the methods you would use to attack them."

"John, I believe they are most vulnerable when they leave their cocoon in Virginia. Two of the television shows they absolutely control have already been mentioned. I believe we can cause them the most trouble, at least publicly, through these two major network programs, which are watched by million of viewers. The main reason for this is that both of them go over the airwaves live. If we were to interrupt a taped show, they could destroy the tape, and we would be no further ahead.

"If Reverend Land is ready for a confrontation, I can have him placed in the front row of *The Hammer of God*. The cameras and microphones will be under my control."

"I suppose I am ready. I want to make them suffer. Not physically, for I wish ill to no man. But I want their organization exposed and displayed for the world to see. I am ready to do His work again."

"Good, I thought you would say that. Now, I want to wait for two weeks. I will start the machinations necessary for you to be in the front row. Will anyone else go with him?"

"Dr. Jones, I'd like to go," Janna said.

Her father answered, "I'll go with my daughter and my friend, Reverend Land." Janus noticed that Big Jim had his finger raised and he recognized him.

"Count me in. Someone has to go along to keep an eye on things, in case they get rough. I seem to be the most likely in this group. I would like to go along, if you will have me?"

Reverend Land acknowledged him, "I will be glad to have you three along. I think that is about the extent of what I want my entourage to consist of—just the four of us. It should be an interesting experience."

"Listen, people, you have to hear Reverend Land speak. It is wonderful. He has had them eating out of his hand at the local church and I believe he is ready. We have talked long and discussed much in this time. I believe the time has come for action, and he is capable of it, believe me." Janus said with conviction.

"Well, that is half of what I term our assault. The other half will come as a complete surprise to at least some of you. Kira and I are to be married. She has also agreed to get out of the news business. With a bang, I might add. She will be the guest journalist on the *Perspective on Washington* show. Now, I need someone to go with her to keep an eye on her. John, I am counting on you. Tom, do you think you can travel to Arlington as security?"

"Sure! Why not? I don't know what I can do, but it should be an amazing challenge."

Chancellor Goslin looked pensive and said, "Sounds like an interesting time. I have never been in the audience of one of these shows."

"John, they don't have an audience. You are going as her father, and Tom, you will be acting the part of her husband. But don't get any big ideas—I have spoken for her," he added with a boyish glint. "So, there we have it. In two weeks we will send out two delegations. The first will go to California to participate in *The Hammer of God* television show. Three people will accompany Reverend Land. Janna, her father, and Big Jim. You be careful in California, Jim. They might recruit you to play basketball or something. The second delegation to D.C. will consist of Kira, Chancellor Goslin, and Tom Johnson for security."

He reached down and retrieved his briefcase. I've tried to anticipate your responses and have prepared travel packets for each of you." He drew the manilla envelopes out of his briefcase and handed them to each person. As they were opening them, he said, "Ive included everything I could think of for your journey. In each packet is an airline ticket, pre-paid hotel registration, pre-paid rental car scheduled to be at the airport when you arrive and $1,000 in expense money. Can anyone think of anything at all I've overlooked."

As if on cue, everyone protested about the cost of the packets. Dow answered them, "Listen, I can afford it. And, after all, you are the ones who are traveling into danger, not me. I will be in my basement, safe and sound. By the way, John, you should see the equipment I purchased with Kira's help. I will have to have you down there. It is amazing. I will be ready to begin practicing being a director with the new remote cameras installed at the studios. My only question is, what am I going to do with all of that stuff when our job is finished? I suppose I could give it to the college," he said with another knowing glint in his eye.

Janus got up and poured himself a cup of coffee and said, "Dr, Jones, have you anticipated what will happen after we disrupt these shows?"

"In the immediate aftermath, we'll have off-duty security in place for your 'fast get-aways'! Beyond that, your guess is as good as mine. I believe they may try to do something stupid. I have taken care of most contingencies and will be monitoring. I'm sure it will be necessary for us to to meet the week following these planned incursions. We can gauge their reactions and make recommendations at that time. Between now and then, if we could all be considering possible follow-up scenarios, particularly with the media, that would help us prepare for that next phase. The level of success we experience will, no doubt, dictate those subsequent steps."

Chapter 34

The trip from the Gerald R. Ford International Airport seemed like a dream to Kira. When they arrived in Washington, the rental car was waiting at the airport. The flight was direct and short. She was nervous, but her anxiety was eased by the two men who accompanied her. John Goslin looked so distinguished in his three piece wool suit, and Tom, with his athletic, physical strength, gave her comfort.

Tom drove, while she sat in front and Chancellor Goslin sat in the back. At the hotel there was a fruit basket waiting from the *POW Show*—she learned that was how the Center staff abbreviated their references to the program.

They enjoyed the historic decor of the hotel and had a nice dinner that evening in the room. Kira called the show's producer when they arrived, as her invitation requested, and thought no more of it. The night passed without incident.

John knocked on the adjoining door to the suite and Kira let him in. "Good morning, Chancellor. Did you sleep well?"

"I suppose. Are you ready?" Tension lined the natural furrows of his face.

"I guess— Dow and I outlined some questions for me to ask and a statement to use if he judges the time to be right. I am not sure what the reaction will be. It promises to be challenging. We are not breaking any laws or anything, but I'm not accustomed to this kind of clandestine activity. Even as a reporter, this tops the charts. I know I'm going to feel like one of those neophyte political actors at the Academy Awards Ceremony, pushing a dissenting viewpoint. I hope that I can transcend this, but it will be difficult."

"I see what you mean. How can you propose something so preposterous as the Center without looking like a fool? I don't know the answer. I suppose you must remain calm in your delivery and dogmatic in your search for answers."

"That is what I intend to try. I don't want to dilute the

information we have by accusing too much. I would rather concentrate on a small area where we can illustrate their influence. If we can gain this small victory, the larger victories may be possible. Dow's view is that we must not try to think in such a way as to only expect immediate capitulation from them. Instead, we must prove a small point, demonstrating how irrefutable the existence and the illicit activities of the Center really are. From that small point we can move on to broader issues for consideration, such as the extent of the Center's infiltration in the media, corporate and governmental institutions. However, I will pay attention to what is going on, and Dow will be talking to me through the earpiece. If the opportunity is there, we can do more. We went through the procedure last Sunday, and it worked very well. It's just that so much seems to be riding on the outcome of our efforts here. I know my presence needs to be compelling, so my energies are going into concentration on the goal. It really is a matter of keeping our 'eyes on the prize'—more than anything I've ever done in my life, in fact."

"I'm going to go check on Tom; he should be out of the shower. Are we supposed to drive, or will they send a car?"

"According to my contact from the call last night, a car will be sent. The hotel will call for us when it arrives. As we planned, I think it would be best if one of you brought the rental car. I'll feel more secure knowing we have a means to leave, if we should have to make a quick exit. Their car will be here in about forty minutes."

"Kira, Dow is very special to me. He is like the son I never had. His happiness is of great importance. I don't want anything to happen to you. Be careful."

She moved closer to the old man and gave him a hug. Of late, she had been seeing people in completely different ways. Now, she recognized that there was nothing more important than being happy with the people around her. In the past month, she had developed a depth of friendship with this unlikely band. "I will be. Besides, Detective Johnson will be there. He seems to be very thorough and vigilant."

"Agreed, he is a good man. Well, let me know when it is time to go. Though I am used to getting up early, 5:30 A.M. — well, my gears aren't turning yet."

☙ ☙ ☙

Harold Hunter adjusted his glasses one more time as he looked at the folder he'd been sent on Kira Morris. It just seemed so odd to have a local reporter—from Michigan, of all places—as a guest on the show. He checked it out when the first advisement of guests arrived a week ago. It was absolutely legitimate. He sent three different e-mails asking for confirmation from the Center. Each came back with the same answer. He almost called, but he had strict orders to use the computerized mail system, whenever possible. The language of the last e-mail convinced him of the legitimacy of the reporter. He also knew he could be replaced if he pushed too hard.

He was very happy with the new computerized camera system. His team first used it two weeks ago, and its application was smooth and flawless. Everything moved as it was supposed to. He felt as if he had been given a reprieve. He didn't enjoy haranguing Arthur Comstock about the length of camera shots. Now, with the new system in place, he no longer had to do this. The cameras had a setting controlled by the central computer, which would limit them to the latest figures.

Now, the cameras could not stay focused on an individual past the time when research dictated maximum impact on the audience. They set off a discreet signal when the time got close, and the perspectives were automatically shuffled.

It had been a heady time for him and Arthur, learning how the equipment worked, but now that they were in place he was happy with them. He and Arthur were required to attend a special three-day training. They came away able to program the technology in such a way that the cameras helped to make measurable improvements in the show. And, that couldn't hurt their own semi-annual evaluations.

He left his office to attend the pre-show meeting with Arthur, Drew and Craig. The hallway seemed almost deserted this morning, but it was still early. When he entered the room, the men were all in their customary places. He said, "Look, fellows, I don't have anything negative to report. According to our study, last week's show was the best we've produced. Camera times and angles were nearly perfect. The only variations were in hundredths of a second—I will gladly accept these. I do have one announcement. In the Center's judgement the show was taking on too much of a capitol bent, so they decided to have a guest journalist from a local television station. Our guest this week is Ms. Kira Morris." He opened the folder and removed the 8 X 10 glossy picture of Kira and handed it to Arthur. "As you can see, she is a beautiful woman. And astute too, if I can believe the bio I have been sent on her. She is likely to be nervous, so if you gentlemen can turn on the charm a little, it would be appreciated."

Drew Cabot took the picture from the director's hands and whistled. "Wow, she is quite a looker. I think I could be very friendly to her." Harold smiled. He liked it when his people reacted as they were supposed to. He decided he didn't have to encourage them to be lecherous with Ms. Morris; he could just let nature take over. He continued, "I've called the hotel. She should be here in a few minutes. Arthur, can you brief her on the procedures and give her the list of questions I have prepared?"

"Be glad to."

"Well, good luck and good show!"

Kira was escorted from the front door to the makeup room. Sitting in the make-up chair, she felt at home. It was such an intrinsic part of her life that it was almost akin to her morning shower. The act of allowing someone to groom you for the camera was pedestrian, common, and oddly relaxing. It helped her to concentrate on the task ahead. When she was nearly finished, a man came through the doorway unannounced. "Ms. Morris, I am Arthur Comstock, the director. I understand that you have done quite a bit of local television. I am here to assure that this is no different. I have put a list of questions on the teleprompter. I have a copy for you here. Please, don't allow yourself to vary the questions from the script. The guests have been briefed on the questions to be asked, and we don't want to have an incident. About the only place there is room for variation is if there is a discussion involving your particular locality. If that is the case, you are welcome to ask questions or make comments concerning your local area. Any questions?"

"No, I think you've about covered it. How long before you call places?"

"Ten minutes, are you ready?"

"I will be. I'm a little nervous, but I appreciate the opportunity to appear on your prestigious show," she said with a laugh. Kira also wanted to come off as naively grateful.

"As well you should be, Dear. If you do a good job here, the sky is the limit for your career. Many important people will be watching this show today. I hope things go well for you. You seem to be a lovely girl."

"Are you sure you are okay, Kira?" Tom asked after the director left.

"I'll be fine. Did you see the way he looked at me? I haven't felt like a piece of meat for a long time. Maybe that's the strategy. They are not openly rude, just subtley offensive. As if by not being openly obnoxious, they can make themselves less reprehensible."

"Could be. Listen, I will be right here. John drove the car, so we don't have to depend on their transportation. Dow's airline tickets say the flight is scheduled to leave at 11:25 from Dulles. If everything goes well, we should just make it. See you after the show. Good luck!"

Knowing he had to be careful and alert, Tom went to find a vantage point for the show.

One of the director's assistants knocked and said, "Ms. Morris, Mr. Comstock has called for places. Are you ready?"

She did not answer but opened the door and walked into the hallway. The tan suit she had chosen was resplendent against her brown skin. She followed the young man to the set, where he ushered her to a guest chair.

Craig Thomas leaned over and said, "You are Ms. Kira Morris, I believe. I am Craig Thomas, pleased to meet you."

"Mr. Thomas, as if I wouldn't know who you are! I have watched you on television and have read your column for years. An honor to meet you, Sir."

"Are you trying to make me feel old? Because you certainly have succeeded."

Kira blushed and said, "Not at all. I am pleased to meet someone of your stature and credentials."

"Don't butter him up. You know how those damned liberals are," Drew said with a smile. "Drew Cabot, Ms. Morris. I also am pleased to meet you. Are you ready for this?"

"I suppose. It is scary though."

"Just follow our lead, we have done this lots of times. It will get easier after the first few minutes. If you want to listen and watch for a while, we can cover for you. No need to answer now, but if you don't pop up with the questions right away, we'll simply carry the dialogue."

"That's very kind of you." She couldn't help thinking how patronizing they were, as they planned to control her every comment in the same way they controlled countless other guests each week. The truth was there was no dialogue, no honest consideration of the topic, of any topic. The totally scripted presentation left no room for analysis or thoughtful clarification of issues, no matter how important that process would be to the public.

The cameras looked very strange without people attending them. They moved on motorized wheels which could manuever only within the area of the track. The track was not really a track; that was just a term left over from the early days of movie-making. Instead, these cameras sat in a shallow box. The sides were three inches high and the box was lined with a seamless material. Imbedded within this material were sensors which fed back the exact location of the camera to the controlling computer. The cameras moved quickly and without a hint of jerkiness.

Kira watched as they were checked out. She knew that in the basement of Dow's house nearly a thousand miles away, he stood poised to take control of the cameras from the local computer.

The large digital clock on the rear wall read 10:28:30, when the assistant director announced firmly, "Everyone, the show will begin in one minute. Last chance, are your earpieces functioning?"

He watched the three as, one by one, they answered the director's call by raising a finger out of camera view. The cameras were positioned, and it was show time.

The guest turned out to be an Assistant Secretary for the Department of Housing and Urban Development. Kira stuck to the script and was the last to ask one of the inane questions she had been given. The answer was pat and almost unintelligibly couched in "Washingtonese." The first portion of the show moved quickly. When they went to break, Kira heard Dow speaking through her earpiece. "Honey, are you ready?"

She nodded. The guest left and the three of them were preparing to discuss the news. The two men were at ease, joking about where they were going for dinner after the show. The assistant director returned, did the countdown and pointed at Drew.

With a confident grin the host slid the oily words into the national airwaves: "Welcome back, we'd like to turn our undivided attention to Ms. Morris, a local reporter from Michigan. Ms. Morris, from your perspective does this whole world of Washington seem to be an overwhelming place?"

"Mr. Cabot, it most certainly is. I have heard there is an organization called the Center for American Heritage that controls most of what goes on in this capitol city and, in fact, reaches into American citizen's lives in countless ways unknown to the public. Can you tell me about the activities of this Center?"

In the booth Arthur Comstock turned to Harold Hunter and said, "What the fuck did she just say?"

"Oh, my God! What is going on here?"

"I am sorry Ms. Morris, could you repeat the question?" The words were barely out of his lips when the voice in his earpiece screamed, "No, you stupid son-of-a-bitch. Don't ask her that!"

Kira smiled and said, "I am sorry. Let me clarify one specific issue. This show, *Perspectives on Washington,* is owned and operated by the Center for American Heritage, and you are on its payroll. Do you think this is in the public interest?"

"You can't prove that!"

"I'm afraid I can. I know more about this show than either of you. Did you know that Mr. Hunter receives his orders directly from the Center?"

Dow watched the view from the three cameras. Hearing the reaction in the control room, he pressed switches to swing camera #3 and an audio taping mechanism that way. He spoke into the microphone attached to his headphones and said, "Kira, this is going better than I expected. Go for the speech."

Dow moved a few controls as Kira had taught him to do and the screen split in two. One camera was focused on Kira and the other was observing the scene in the control booth.

"Arthur, get that fucking camera off her. Go to commercial, do something!"

"Don't you think I'm trying? My controls are locked. I can't get control of anything. What do you want me to do?"

"Hello audience, My name is Kira Morris. I am here to tell the truth. This show, which is followed faithfully by millions of viewers like you and me nationally, is a sham. Each and every guest appearing here is screened and approved by an organization you have never heard of. There is no freedom of speech exercised in this studio. What we hear each week is canned text written with the express purpose of shaping our opinions and our votes on the important matters that ultimately govern our lives.

The Center for American Heritage was established by the Hunter Family. They used their fortune to promote an extreme right-wing agenda. They own and operate the national networks and have infiltrated the media in every arena. As a news journalist, I can confirm that *Perspectives on Washington* is a prime example of how far the tentacles of their reach has gone to usurping the freedoms upon which our country was founded. At this moment, as repugnant as it is for me to report to you, the subversive and illegal operations of this Center for American Heritage are beginning to unravel. It will take months, and possibly years, to expose the extent to which they have destructively tampered with the public trust."

Arthur was beyond panic. He was running through the control room shouting at everyone. "Get that bitch off the stage. She is exposing too much, everything!" He did not see that the camera had been moved to a position where it now pointed at the control room. The light which indicated the camera was active would have been on, but Dow instructed the computer to leave it off. He continued his raving. "I want that cunt removed from the stage before she reveals any more. Harold, is there something you can do? You are always so good at telling us what to do. I mean, who we can have as guests, what we have to ask them. Come on, you son-of-a-bitch, I want some fuckin' answers."

The scene was bizarre as Kira outlined in broad strokes the frightening agenda and its dark implementation by the Center for American Heritage. The camera never blinked in its observation of Arthur Comstock and Harold Hunter, as they confirmed Ms. Morris' statements by their behavior.

Tom Johnson stood to the side and watched the scene. At one point, the two pale-faced show hosts got out of their seats, moved toward Kira and tried to interrupt. He removed his gun from his shoulder holster and stepped into view. He called out, "You two, let the lady be!" The gun was not pointed at anything but the floor, but they got the message and sat down. He was glad his bluff had worked—under the circumstances, he was not prepared to do more.

For ten minutes Kira gracefully delivered a thoughtful, damning indictment and concluded: "There is ample evidence that the Center and its operatives have repeatedly resorted to violence against innocent people to accomplish their ends. I personally know of one death and multiple assaults. It is clear through their influence in the White House and over hand-selected judges in the courts, as well as many members of Congress beholden to the Center, which resourced their elections: they are the most powerful men in the United States.

"This is only the first of many revelations of corruption. It will take courage and determination on your part—all of us, as citizens of this country—to honestly examine the evidence and carefully ensure that real justice is rendered to the guilty and those who have been victimized by the clandestine activities of the Center for American Heritage. I want to appeal to each and every one of you to remain alert, vigilant and open-minded as the truth unfolds over coming weeks. This may well represent the greatest challenge to our internal strength that our nation has ever faced."

Those in the studio stood, stationary and stunned. Millions of people in the their family rooms sat, confused but awakened, sober witnesses to an historic moment in televised journalism. Finally, the cameras went still. Dow switched off his connection with the equipment when the show went off-air at the scheduled time, quietly whispering into the mic, "How I do love you, Kira." Tom moved quickly to her side. He gently took her trembling arm and led her out the back to the waiting car.

Silence fell on the set of the last show of *Perspectives on Washington*.

Chapter 35

The phone rang and Jonathan Green put down his Sunday paper to answer it.

"Jonathan, you had better get to the Center—now!"

"Why? What's happened, Judge?"

"The worst possible scenario. Someone has managed to expose our operation on national television, and that boob of a director, Arthur Comstock, confirmed everything the bitch said." The words blurted out of his mouth rapidly, fearfully.

"Hold on a second, Judge. I don't know what you are talking about. Now, slowly, what has happened?"

"*Perspectives on Washington.* Did you watch it?"

"No, I hardly ever do. What happened?"

"Somehow, a female reporter was invited to be a guest on the show. I don't know how it happened, but the bottom line is she profiled the Center and made multiple allegations of illegal activities over live television. Who knows what she can document, but she was credible! That wasn't the worst of it. The broadcast went split-screen. While one camera focused on the gutsy broad, the nobody reporter telling the story, another zoomed in on Harold Hunter and Arthur Comstock, with audio feed, as they went nuts in the control room. They were exceedingly profane and managed to confirm everything the bitch said. It was catastrophic. We have a crisis of unprecedented proportions.

"Grant Larson has called all department heads and their assistants to a meeting. Get here as soon as possible! I don't know what we are going to do, but we'd better do something pretty damn quick!"

෴ ෴ ෴

Tom and Kira came running out the service entrance of the studio. Tom jammed his gun back in his holster in time to grab the back door of the rented car. They tumbled in and slammed the door, "Go! Go like hell!" Tom said.

John smiled. "Guess I don't have to ask how it went, do I?"

"No, everything was perfect. Dow managed to control the whole situation from Michigan. It actually went better than expected. Kira, I don't think you could see this, but the director and the Center's man were shouting about you and how you were exposing everything. There is no way they could claim innocence; in fact, their unfiltered reactions revealed the beasts they are. Are you okay?"

"I think so. I just can't stop shaking. I think I'll be fine when I get home."

CS   CS   CS

Janna led the way down the aisle, followed by her father, Reverend Land, and finally Big Jim Davis. The pleasant usher gave them a finely embossed program. She sat in the fourth seat off the aisle, her father next to her, then Reverend Land, and Jim in the aisle seat where he could stretch his long legs. Their trip to Los Angeles was without incident. Janna was excited about going to the set of a real television show. She checked her watch, although with all of the clocks on the set it seemed unnecessary. Her watch read 11:30. By comparing the digital clocks on the wall she calculated the difference in time between Michigan and California. Three hours seems like such a long time. It was 8:30:33; the show would begin with Johnny Daniel's warm-up in fifteen minutes. She closed her eyes, sat back in her chair and waited.

Reverend Land was deep in prayer with grave thoughts about what he should say, and whether or not he should even say it. In a way, The Hammer did the work of the Lord, although his message was not the one people needed to hear. Looking around, he saw those who were happy to be here, delighted they had been chosen to be part of the audience for the most popular religious show ever on national television. Their faith-filled anticipation cast a sharp spotlight on his quandary.

He checked the wireless microphone on his lapel and felt

for the sending unit on his belt. Dow had assured him his voice would be heard. He closed his eyes again, deep in thought.

Big Jim was looking for exits and checking for security personnel. He assumed there was going to be trouble, and he would not permit anything to happen to his people. He was older, but in remarkably good shape. And his physical presence could not be ignored.

The rental car was parked around in back. He could see there was a back door, up a small flight of stairs, and to the right. At least that was where he saw the exit sign. He leaned over and whispered to Reverend Land, "I'm going to check to make sure where that stairway leads. Be right back."

When he started to mount the stairs an usher rushed up and said. "I'm sorry, brother, where are you going?"

"I have to use the restroom. Is there one down that hallway?" he asked, pointing through the doorway.

"Yes, there is. But you will have to be quick about it. The show will start in less than 10 minutes. After it begins, you won't be permitted back into the theater."

"Won't take near that long. Thanks."

ꞈ ꞈ ꞈ

Grant Larson turned off the large monitor in the conference room and said, "OK, gentlemen. Any ideas?"

The men looked down at the table, or at the wall, anywhere to avert their eyes from what they had just seen. This was an unmitigated disaster. Whoever had orchestrated that television show did it to inflict the most possible damage.

"Larson, do we know who was controlling the cameras?"

"No, we don't, Judge. We know it was someone from outside the studio. Somehow they got into the computer system and ran the whole thing by remote control."

"Did we stop the woman?"

"No, she got away in a waiting car. We do know her identity. An agent has been dispatched to her residence."

"C'mon, Gentlemen, I need answers. We have one more television program to be aired this morning. In thirty minutes *The Hammer* show will be broadcast live from California. Do we know that the same thing is not going to happen? Look at that table all you want to; we are in deep trouble here and I need answers! What are we going to do? Mr. Larson, is it possible to talk to the director of *Perspectives on Washington*?"

"Judge, I suppose it is. Let me call and put him on the line." He checked the number in a small notebook and dialed. He placed the phone in the cradle while pressing the switch to put it on speaker. The rings resounded in the room. On the third it was answered. "Harold Hunter, may I help you?"

"Harold, this is Mr. Larson. Can you put the director on the phone?"

After a moment Arthur Comstock said, "Yes, what can I do for you, Mr. Larson?"

"Answer our questions," he said with restraint.

"All right, I'll try."

Mr. Larson held his hand toward the Judge, "Go ahead, ask away."

"Mr. Comstock, are you sure that someone in the studio was not running the cameras?"

"Absolutely. There was a barely audible voice talking to Ms. Morris from the first break on. I tried everything. Nothing worked. How bad did it look?"

An ominous silence hung in the room. Arthur could hear it and swallowed deeply. "Is there something else that I can help you with?"

"How recently did you get that computerized camera system?"

"Oh, it's brand new. It came in about three weeks ago. Harold and I attended the training. We were the only people there, except for the crew from some religious show."

"What religious show?" demanded Grant.

"*The Hammer of God*, why?"

"Mr. Comstock, you are fired!"

He reached over, pressed the button to disconnect the line and sputtered, "Shit!"

☙ ☙ ☙

Dow pressed the keys necessary to connect him with the *The Hammer Show* and established control over the equipment. A thin smile stole over his face as his fingers moved along the keys. This one would be a little more difficult. He could not be in communication with the Reverend, so he would have to follow his lead. He tested his control by minute increments, confirmed it was in place, sat back and waited for the show to begin. He did it in such a way that no one suspected that he had taken control. Their controls would appear to work normally, but once he pressed the button, his commands would be met first.

※ ※ ※

After the audience concluded the countdown, Johnny Daniels stepped from behind the curtains to thunderous applause. The noise in the studio was tumultuous. After several minutes of unbridled cheering, he stood with his eyes focused on heaven and his hands held out as if he were blessing the crowd. The noise ceased almost immediately, and the audience joined him in prayer.

Even when he began his warm-up routine the audience was already enraptured. His interactions further elevated the excitement to a fever pitch. As he introduced The Hammer, the thunderous organ began the opening chords to *A Mighty Fortress*. The enthusiasm in the room was incredible. Janna looked around and saw the people nearly swoon at the sight of The Hammer as he emerged from the curtain. People were on their feet singing as loudly as they could.

When the On-Air light went out, Johnny invited everyone to sit down. They complied. Janna stared at the Reverend Doctor Nehemiah Hamner and marveled that he never looked at the audience, except when he was singing. Janna assumed this pattern would follow through to his sermon. The light flashed on again, and The Hammer was back on the air.

※ ※ ※

"What's the name of our man on that show? Quick!"
"Richard Francis," someone shouted.
"What's his number? Oh, never mind—I can find it." He looked in his book again and dialed the phone.

While he wait for an answer to the ringing, he said, "Judge, will you tune in that—that stupid show on the monitor. I want to see this for myself."

"Hello, this is Richard Francis. How can I help you?"

"Mr. Francis, this is Mr. Grant Larson at the Center. We have reason to suspect that something unplanned, something bad, may happen on your show. Is everything there okay?"

"Yes. The show just began. By the way, thank you for the camera system. It works wonderfully. I was surprised to receive it, but I appreciated the note of explanation you sent."

Those words and the knot of fear forming in his chest confirmed what Grant Larson most dreaded. He had sent no note. He knew nothing about the cameras on this or any other televised show. He felt as though he were drowning. He said sarcastically, "You're welcome. Glad to be of service. Listen, can you check with your director and make sure that everything is really okay?"

"Sure, glad to. Hang on—"

Control room sounds of a television studio filled the room, and the receiver. The director shouting instructions to the board operators. Commercials being readied for playback. All was as it should be. A glance at the monitor showed that The Hammer was well into his message. He was a forceful speaker, and anyone would marvel at his ability to present the message so clearly. Suddenly, deep, resonant tones of singing came over the television. The voice was oddly familiar. As Grant Larson listened to the words of *Amazing Grace* he recognized it. "Oh, my God! That's Jersey Land!" he shouted.

ଔ ଔ ଔ

Without fanfare Reverend Land stood up, pressed the switch on his belt and began to sing. Softly at first, but gaining strength as the words took hold of him. He turned to face the audience and his voice suddenly boomed out over the speakers. The reaction from Michigan had been nearly instantaneous. When he heard the speakers come on, he relaxed his voice a little. The audience turned away from The Hammer and sat captivated by the tall man with white hair and his simple song of redemption.

Big Jim got out of his seat and stood off to the side. An usher moved toward Reverend Land, but Big Jim stopped him with a look and by opening his coat and revealing his gun. The camera on the stage suddenly swivelled and faced the audience. Jim noticed and motioned for the Reverend to face the camera. He did so without missing a note.

The audience did not recognize the tall man yet, but they were mesmerized by his voice.

The director was having a fit, running from console to console yelling instructions. Nothing worked. Ashen in face Richard Francis came back to the phone admitting, "We have a problem here. The show seems to be running itself! What do you want me to do?"

"Nothing. Don't make it worse than it already is," Grant said and hung up the phone.

He turned back to the group and sat down. "Gentlemen, I don't know what to tell him. If we repeat another scene like the fiasco in *Perspectives on Washington*, it will just make the situation worse. I suggest we all return to our offices and start removing incriminating materials. It's over. By morning, the news media will be storming this place. I'm sure they will have search warrants, court orders, whatever. This will be the biggest news story of the decade, if not the century. Go! Go destroy whatever you can. I want nothing left by morning."

ଔ ଔ ଔ

Reverend Land finished his song and walked up the stairs to the stage. He moved with a quiet confidence that belied his anxiety. Once on the stage he turned, faced the congregation and began, "Some of you know me. Some may have forgotten. My name is Thomas Lanninga. I used to preach on this show as the Reverend Jersey Land." A gasp went through the audience from coast to coast.

"Listen to my story and believe what I tell you. It is a tale of woe, a story of personal misjudgement, corporate lies, the vengeance of liars, and finally, forgiveness and redemption. Job himself might appreciate this story.

"I made the mistake of believing some people whose interests were not my interests, and definitely not the Lord's.

There is an organization called the Center for American Heritage. There are some evil men at its helm, and they, in fact, are the power behind this show. They dictate the message. When I saw the conflict between the Word of God and the message they wanted me to deliver, I protested and was intentionally, methodically destroyed at their hands. I was not the first whose life and career were maliciously targeted. There were others before and since my demise. And if they are not recognized now, we will not be the last. Their goals are to manipulate all of us, to influence our decisions, our culture, our politics, and to eradicate the freedoms which were once the pillars of our democracy.

"But just as Christ, the Son of God, rose from the depths of the grave to overcome, I come to set my story—and what is dangerously becoming our history—right. These people who use the Word, the very words of God himself, for their evil ends must be stopped. I am nothing. Like each of us, I can say: I am only a servant of the Lord. But I have been given one of the most critical messages to all of us, the sons and daughters of our loving God. We must repent our evil ways and walk in the light of the Lord. America, fall down on your knees and beg his forgiveness. We can no longer be complacent. We can no longer be complicit. The cross we are now being asked to carry is courage to face the truth, to face a subversive enemy which has dared to desecrate our intelligence, our faith, and our democracy with lies."

ೃ ೃ ೃ

Dow felt an inner swell of pride as he moved switches to control the cameras. The Reverend continued his message of atonement, as cameras followed his every move. He appeared to gain strength from the response of the audience. His message became more potent, more compelling. Reverend Hamner disappeared behind the curtain to stay out of his way.

Dow carefully fingered the equipment and knew in his heart that what he was watching was the rebirth of a minister of the people, no longer the invented Reverend Jersey Land, but the Reverend Thomas Lanninga, whose love and gifts had always been ordained by his congregations.

Chapter 36

When the show finished, the audience rushed the stage. Not one person had a look of anything but admiration for the Reverend. When Big Jim motioned for Janna and her father to come, they left their seats and stood behind him on the stairway. "Janus, will you go get our Reverend. I think we should get out of here. I'll stay in case someone tries to...."

Janus rushed to comply. Approaching the minister he said, "You did it! It came across wonderfully. Jim wants us to leave now, and I think we should. Can you come with me?"

Reverend Lanninga turned and looked at his friend. His face had taken on a glow of deep gratitude and peace missing since Janus had known him. There was a strength in his voice, "Certainly, by all means—let's get out of here."

The three walked down the hall with Jim trailing behind. They exited the studio at the rear entrance. They entered the waiting car and headed for the airport. No one said a thing. All involved were concentrating on their own thoughts. It had been a powerful and wonder invoking half-hour.

The majesty of the simple message had not been lost on them. Reverend Lanninga sat in the back seat and thanked the Lord for the strength to do His will. Big Jim eased the car onto the entry ramp for the freeway and pressed the accelerator for the home stretch.

ઝ ઝ ઝ

Dow relinquished control over the studio in California by breaking the connection. He felt a warm swell of excitement inside himself. It had worked! It had really worked. Often plans do not unfold in reality as designers might like. But this had really worked. Machines are easy to control. Their actions can be utterly predictable. The human species is not.

In the weeks of preparation, he'd considered many negative scenarios in his mind and tried to prepare for them. Still, that element of doubt remained. Now, those doubts vanished like the wisp of smoke from a campfire on a windy day.

He turned to the monitoring computer connected deep within the Center's systems. Observing increased activity on the computers in the Center, he tried to determine what they were doing. When he began to see a flood of "Delete File" messages, he understood. He managed to lock up the controlling computer. Anyone who was knowledgable would have been able to break his temporary hold, but apparently no one was there to do that.

His fingers moved over the keyboard and established the link that could not be broken. He reached into his pocket for a notebook and wrote the names of the programs he placed within the system. He typed the word : RELEASE.

To every news organization in the country the following FAX was sent:

Center for American Heritage

Founded: 1952

Central Headquarters: Alexandria, VA

Subsidiary Offices: Los Angeles, Atlanta, Boston, Houston, Chicago, Miami, New York, Las Vegas

Current Director: Grant Larson

Chief Financial Officer: Tobias James

Traceable Financial Assets: Excess of $263 billion

    (Questionable accounting practices)

Additional Assets offshore

    (No record with the U. S. Internal Revenue Service)

Archives and current files of the Center for American Heritage document:

· verifiable financial links to three recent U.S. presidents

- routine and significant communications with four of five current FCC Commissioners and seven FCC chairmen over the past three decades
- major campaign financing ties to dozens of congressional representatives
- disguised ownership of four national television and cable news networks, hundreds of major radio stations, and expanding incursions into wireless and satellite technologies
- significant holdings in professional sports organizations
- dominant sponsorship of multiple conservative religious networks
- sanctioned backdoor computer access to FBI, CIA and Pentagon files

The press release went on for four pages outlining many of the Center's subversive operations, which Dow had uncovered while examining the contents of their tightly secured databases. The information he highlighted would be sufficient for even the most lethargic reporter to find a story—and even the most reticent news station to be forced to broadcast. It included: offshore bank account numbers traceable to judges and elected leaders; complicity through political voting patterns; media conglomerates screening news coverage by agenda; corporate power brokers in the defense industry, pharmaceuticals, energy and other private sector arenas dictating policy. The broad brush strokes of incrimination could not be dwarfed by the standard hype of the Center's lofty self-stated goals.

The details of specific logs and email chains were even more sinister: ordered surveillance of Dr. Richard Kline's research into the Center's programs, detailed instructions to agents regarding "elimination of the professor at any cost," vile drug-tampering with the intended loss of Kline's life, vilification of Jersey Land through staged child pornography, documented violence against Dr. Ira Jones and countless others, even ties to a new breed of organized crime. All were cast under the public spotlight with stunning clarity.

The press release, with its damning evidence, was sent instantaneously, not only across the United States but internationally to agencies like the BBC World. Hundreds of news organizations listed in the master files of the Center for American Heritage had been used for years, absent their logo, to manipulate policy, shape culture, distort truth and lie to the country's citizens. Those same avenues were now being used to expose their own criminal and immoral activities.

ೞ ೞ ೞ

Inside the White House there was a hesitant knock on the door of the oval office.

"Mr. President, I'm afraid—I'm afraid we have terrible news."

"Of what nature?"

The Chief of Staff spoke, at first with lifeless words. As minutes melted into hours the voices of the two men rose and fell in waves of denial, desperation and rage. The realization that their scheme and complicity in the Center's operations was being exposed was mind-numbing, shocking, impossible to absorb.

When the phone buzzed softly, the Chief of Staff picked it up. "I need to speak to the president."

"Certainly, Mr. Larson. It's Grant."

"Very well."

"Listen, we are in deep trouble here. As far as I know the entire history of the Center is being disclosed as we speak. Even select files are being dispersed world-wide. You should know that your name comes up prominently. It is probably time for you to think about the transition after your departure. Your family—think of your family now."

Finally alone behind those heavy doors that had served as such a symbol of prestige and power, the president gazed out the window on the incongruent spring scene, his face ashen, his life empty of promise. Although the warm air was pleasant, an icy chill ran through his veins. For a moment he envied Richard Kline, the man he'd never met, the man who had courage in his pursuit of the truth, but lost his life in the fray. For a moment he wished he could trade the professor for his own life. Perhaps he would have done it better justice.

ଔ ଔ ଔ

Tom pulled the car up to the terminal and checked his watch: just 20 minutes before departure. He turned the ignition off and walked around to retrieve their suitcases from the trunk.

The three left the car behind parked in the NO PARKING -TOW AWAY ZONE and moved quickly through the terminal. No one stopped them or questioned their passing. Tom took the keys and dropped them at the rental office. "The car is out front. I don't have time to move it; could you have someone do it for me?" With the keys he placed a $100 bill. The clerk brightened and said, "Absolutely, Sir. What kind of car is it?"

Reaching the airline's lounge area in time to hear the boarding call for their flight, they checked their luggage and moved through the jetway to the plane.

ଔ ଔ ଔ

If the car had entered the Los Angeles freeway system at almost any other hour, there could have been delays. But early on a Sunday morning, the traffic moved remarkably well. Jim checked his watch and discovered that it had been only fifteen minutes since the end of the television show. He turned on the radio to hear reports about Kira's disclosures and confirmations inundating the media from all over the country. They all laughed out loud at their unlikely coup and broke into a rousing chorus of "*A Mighty Fortress is Our God.*"

News organizations were trying to find Kira anywhere and everywhere. The Associated Press had stationed reporters outside her apartment to wait for her return. Seeing the unbelievable level of activity and the numbers of photographers, Mr. Wesson quietly slipped away.

ꜟ ꜟ ꜟ

Dow checked his notebook again. He entered more commands. The files on individuals were his next target. He'd found them while perusing the system and had inserted a program in those sectors.

He now pressed the correct combination to begin the program's execution. It was deceitfully simple, hardly more than a few kilobytes of code, but it would freeze the computers of the Center absolutely. They could not delete the information, nor could they change it. They could physically destroy the system, but the pertinent files were backed up on the Harmson University mainframe under Dow's protection.

Dow sat back and laughed quietly to himself. "Teach them to mess with us." He reached across the control boards, pulled the master switch and silence reigned once more. The computer flashed the shut-down prompt and Dow switched it off. He listened as the disk slowed and stopped. Outside he was greeted by a beautiful Sunday afternoon. The temperature was expected to hit fifty today. Turning his face to the sun, he felt its welcome rays caress him softly.

The recently-purchased cell phone whirred in his pocket. Seeing the number, Dow immediately answered, "Kira, where are you?"

"In the air yet. We should be landing in about thirty minutes. Will you still try to meet us?"

"Yes, I've done what I needed to do. I'll leave in a few minutes and will be waiting. Oh, and by the way—Hell of a good job!"

"You think?" she asked coquettishly.

"You know I do. Are you—? Is everyone all right?"

"Tired, but fine. You want to talk to the chancellor?"

"Kira, I can't wait to know you are safely here with me. But, yes. Please put John on."

"Chancellor, Dow wants to speak to you." She pushed the tiny phone toward him. John looked at the miniature instrument festooned with symbols his aging eyes strained to decipher. Taking the phone gingerly, he held it to his ear. "Dow?"

"John, it worked. Everything worked."

"Did it? Even the press release?"

"Yes, just sent it moments ago. I also froze their computers. It's going to be a long haul to untangle the web of deceit they've been meticulously building for decades. But it's a beginning, John—let's hope the beginning of the Center's end."

"Dow, you have done an amazing job. How can we ever thank you! We'll see you in an hour or so."

The plane continued rocking against the early spring clouds. The seatbelt sign had been illuminated since take-off. This turbulence was no match for what he and the others had undergone in the intervening weeks since Richard's death. Looking at the young woman sitting next to him and Mr. Joseph, he settled deeper into the seat and took stock of it all.

His friend and colleague's career had been spent around academic matters, the substance of ideas, and the future of students like Janna. In his last year, in his final days, Richard's determined research took him to a dangerous edge where the best human ideals collided with prejudice and its sinister subjugation of both democratic dialogue and values. For the first time in these many weeks, the chancellor felt there was some justice and meaning in the events that had shaken so many in seen and unseen ways. Yes, he thought that Richard could finally rest in peace. His sacrifice would not be forgotten. This unlikely crew of educators, administrators, law enforcers, minister, journalist, and student who picked up his frightening trail would have pleased his friend.

John remembered the words of the philosopher Edmund Burke on a discreet plaque in Richard's office: "The only thing necessary for the triumph of evil is for good (people) to do nothing."

John smiled as he closed his eyes.

Challenge

About the Author

Bob Hoffman is a husband, father, teacher and writer living in Muskegon, Michigan. During the last sixteen years, Bob has written numerous books. He believes that a successful writer is most often someone who has lived enough to put their thoughts in perspective. Bob has served on the advisory committees of many entities concerning the process of writing. His joy is in both writing and showing others how to capture their thoughts on paper. Bob has been married for thirty-three years to Yvonne and is the father of two sons: Lee, a twenty-one-year-old student at Michigan State University, and Chris, an eighteen-year-old senior in high school in Norton Shores. Bob has written in many genres, including the techno-thriller, short stories, stories for young adults, children's stories, science fiction, literary fiction, non-fiction, philosophy and poetry.

Serving as co-author, Bob's most recent publication is *Silent Screams of a Survivor: A Polish-American Boy's Holocaust.* (Acorn Publishing, 2004)